Blood on Their Hands

He never gets off the couch—except to stock up on snacks. He loves TV more than anything—including his wife. That's just part of *The Trouble with Harry* by **Stefanie Matteson**—and it's enough to drive even the most understanding woman to distraction . . . or worse . . .

In **Brendan DuBois**'s *Her Last Gift*, a young widow plots to get revenge on the owner of the high-tech company where her husband worked himself—literally—to death . . .

When two exotic dancers end up dead in steamy south Florida, tennis-playing P.I. Rory Calhoun finds himself in the middle of a mystery that's sizzling, seductive—and *very* surprising. Find out how he solves it in **Jeremiah Healy**'s *The Lady from Yesterday* . . .

In **Rhys Bowen**'s *Doppelganger*, a young Jewish man walks to the edge of a cliff—and makes a last, desperate attempt to save himself from the Nazis . . .

When her husband has an affair with her best friend, a troubled woman finally admits how much she loves him. And in **Tom Savage**'s *One of Us*, you'll discover just how far—and how low—she'll go to get him back . . .

Continued . . .

Praise for

Blood On Their Hands

"[S]omething worth a nibble on almost every plate that passes."
—*Kirkus Reviews*

"A diverting addition to your summer reading list . . . an entertaining hodge-podge of homicide."
—*RT Bookclub*

"Genre fiction is keeping alive the short story collection as evidenced by [this anthology] featuring some of the most established as well as the newest mystery authors."
—*Sun-Sentinel*

"The stories about ordinary men and women who do shocking things are interesting studies of human nature, intriguing, puzzling and suspenseful."
—*Daily Oklahoman*

BLOOD ON THEIR HANDS

Edited by Lawrence Block

BERKLEY PRIME CRIME, NEW YORK

If you purchased this book without a cover, you should be aware that this book is stolen property. It was reported as "unsold and destroyed" to the publisher, and neither the author nor the publisher has received any payment for this "stripped book."

This is a work of fiction. Names, characters, places, and incidents either are the product of the author's imagination or are used fictitiously, and any resemblance to actual persons, living or dead, business establishments, events, or locales is entirely coincidental.

BLOOD ON THEIR HANDS

A Berkley Prime Crime book / published by arrangement with the author

PRINTING HISTORY
Berkley Prime Crime hardcover edition / July 2003
Berkley Prime Crime mass-market edition / September 2004

Copyright © 2003 by Mystery Writers of America.
Cover design by George Long.
Interior text design by Kristin del Rosario.

All rights reserved.
This book, or parts thereof, may not be reproduced in any form without permission. The scanning, uploading, and distribution of this book via the Internet or via any other means without the permission of the publisher is illegal and punishable by law. Please purchase only authorized electronic editions, and do not participate in or encourage electronic piracy of copyrighted materials. Your support of the author's rights is appreciated. For information address: The Berkley Publishing Group, a division of Penguin Group (USA) Inc., 375 Hudson Street, New York, New York 10014.

Visit our website at www.penguin.com

ISBN: 0-425-19924-X

Berkley Prime Crime books are published by The Berkley Publishing Group, a division of Penguin Group (USA) Inc., 375 Hudson Street, New York, New York 10014.
The name BERKLEY PRIME CRIME and the BERKLEY PRIME CRIME design are trademarks belonging to Penguin Group (USA) Inc.

PRINTED IN THE UNITED STATES OF AMERICA

10 9 8 7 6 5 4 3 2 1

"Introduction," copyright © 2003 by Lawrence Block
"Her Last Gift," copyright © 2003 by Brendan DuBois
"JoJo's Gold," copyright © 2003 by Noreen Ayres
"Black Heart and Cabin Girl," copyright © 2003 by Shelley Costa
"One of Us," copyright © 2003 by Tom Savage
"A Trail of Mirrors," copyright © 2003 by Tracy Knight
"Along for the Ride," copyright © 2003 by Aileen Schumacher
"Red Meat," copyright © 2003 by Elaine Viets
"The Maids," copyright © 2003 by G. Miki Hayden
"Guardian Angel," copyright © 2003 by Elaine Togneri
"The Day of the 31st," copyright © 2003 by Henry Slesar
"Another Night to Remember," copyright © 2003 by William E. Chambers
"The Trouble with Harry," copyright © 2003 by Stefanie Matteson
"Any Old Mother," copyright © 2003 by Charlotte Hinger
"Guile Is Where It Goes," copyright © 2003 by Dan Crawford
"Doppelganger," copyright © 2003 by Rhys Bowen
"Bloody Victims," copyright © 2003 by Mat Coward
"Safety First," copyright © 2003 by Marcia Talley
"No Man's Land," copyright © 2003 by Elizabeth Foxwell
"The Lady from Yesterday," copyright © 2003 by Jeremiah Healy

Contents

Introduction ix
Lawrence Block

Her Last Gift 1
Brendan DuBois

JoJo's Gold 23
Noreen Ayres

Black Heart and Cabin Girl 35
Shelley Costa

One of Us 59
Tom Savage

A Trail of Mirrors 71
Tracy Knight

Along for the Ride 91
Aileen Schumacher

Red Meat 103
Elaine Viets

The Maids 119
G. Miki Hayden

Guardian Angel 137
Elaine Togneri

The Day of the 31st 155
Henry Slesar

Another Night to Remember 181
William E. Chambers

The Trouble with Harry 195
Stefanie Matteson

Any Old Mother 213
Charlotte Hinger

Guile Is Where It Goes 229
Dan Crawford

Doppelganger 241
Rhys Bowen

Bloody Victims 253
Mat Coward

Safety First 269
Marcia Talley

No Man's Land 281
Elizabeth Foxwell

The Lady from Yesterday 299
Jeremiah Healy

INTRODUCTION

It All Started with Poe

Lawrence Block

IF you want to blame someone, try Edgar Allan Poe. He's the guy who started it. Or did he? Maybe this would be a good place to mention Mauritz Christopher Hansen. A Norwegian writer, born 1794, died 1842. In 1827 he published "Novellen" ("The Short Story"), an armchair detective mystery concerning a case of murder and revenge. So he got there first, well ahead of Poe's "The Murders in the Rue Morgue," but he wrote in Norwegian, with the result that nobody ever heard of him. Well, nobody outside of Norway. Matter of fact, you wouldn't have heard of him either, if your Norwegian friend Nils Nordberg hadn't told you about him. Memo: E-mail Nils, suggest he translate Hansen for *Ellery Queen's Mystery Magazine*. Either "Novellen" or his short novel, *Mordet paa Maskinbygger Roolfsen* ("The Murder of Engineer Roolfsen").

Still, what did Hansen start? If a tree falls in a forest, and only Norwegians can hear it, it's not exactly the shot heard round the world, is it? Poe started it, but who cares? I mean, how many lame introductions have already trotted out poor old Poe? Think of something else, will you?

* * *

IT'S a rare pleasure to introduce *Blood on Their Hands*, the latest collection of stories by members of Mystery Writers of America. MWA, as its name implies, is an organization of American mystery writers who . . .

DUH. *Who write American mysteries, and they hammer them out one inspired word at a time, even as you are attempting to pound out this introduction. Do you really want to bore everybody with the history of the organization, explaining how a handful of hacks and drunks banded together, adopted the motto "Crime Does Not Pay. Enough!" And, when they weren't busy hacking and drinking, got on with the serious business of giving one another awards. You can fill space this way, but do you want to?*

It's a fine organization, MWA, and virtually every crime writer of distinction is proud to be a member of it. But everybody knows that, so why waste their time telling them?

Start over.

The stories you are about to read . . .

. . . ARE *guaranteed to cure cancer, ensure world peace, and solve once and for all the problem of global warming. They're excellent stories, as it happens, but what can you say about them that will make them more of a treat than they already are?*

IT'S my great pleasure . . .

YEAH, *I can tell. You know something? You've done too many introductions, my friend, and you're getting worse at it, and you were never that good in the first place. You always used to start out by decrying the whole idea of an introduction, urging readers* *to get on with it and read the stories themselves, and now you seem determined to prove how dopey an introduction can be by mumbling and stammering and generally behaving like an idiot. You promised them an intro. Write it, will you? Just spit it out!*

IT all started with Poe.

GREAT, *just brilliant. "It all started with Poe." And here's where it stops.*

Her Last Gift

Brendan DuBois

In the darkness of her car, Laura Tyson sat in the stillness, holding the 9mm Smith & Wesson in her right hand. In the past two months she had become quite familiar with the heavy piece of weaponry, visiting her brother twice a week at the police station, where he allowed her to use the shooting range in the basement. Her brother Jake was a detective and the first time she had told him she had bought a pistol, he had said—only half-jokingly, she was sure: "You don't plan on shooting anybody soon, do you?" She had smiled at her younger brother and said, "Of course not." So over the weeks he had demonstrated the pistol's safety, how to load the magazine, how to clear a jam in the action, and how to hold it correctly while firing. And each time when she left, he had looked at her with his pale blue eyes and said, "You doing okay?" She had always lied, saying, "Yes. I'm doing the best I can."

She shifted the pistol from one hand to the other, looked up the driveway on the hill where the lights marked the home of Hank Zamett, where she planned to go in a few minutes. She remembered what her brother had said, about shooting anybody soon, and she sighed. Aloud she said softly, "I guess it depends on what your definition of soon is, Jake."

She placed the pistol down on her lap, again marveling at how heavy a small object could be. Not only the weight of the metal and plastic and lead in the cartridges, but just the heaviness of the potential, she thought. Each little cartridge had the potential of changing everything, of wounding someone severely, of taking away somebody's life and livelihood. Among the many things the pistol represented, it was a thieving instrument, able to take so much away with the single pull of the trigger.

Laura rubbed her rough hands together, suddenly flinched at a memory of Jess, kissing her fingers, gently moving the rough skin against his face, laughing: "My dear one," he sometimes said. "I thought artists were such delicate creatures. You have hands that could smooth down a plank." She had laughed and had never taken offense, since it was true. Her hands were always rough and chapped, from working at the potter's wheel in her tiny studio, playing with the clay, manipulating it and firing it and working with it, day after day. But she had never minded what he had said about her hands. Jess had always said that they had a perfect marriage: he had the brains, she had the brawn, and with that, they would have a long and happy life together.

She wiped at the tears forming in her eyes. Jess had been dead for more than two months now, taken away by the man up on the hill, and she wondered how that thief would react when he came face to face with the thieving tool now in her lap.

The pistol was then moved, from her lap to her open purse. She closed the leather purse and stepped out of the car, slinging it over her shoulder, and she started walking, up to the lights.

THEY should have never been attracted to one another, never mind becoming husband and wife. She was tall and angular, with long legs and a skinny chest, and he was short and squat, built like a fireplug. Her politics leaned left, his leaned right. She was nearly a vegetarian, while he loved to eat meat at least once a day. They had met at—of all places romantic and loving—the local library book sale, when both of their hands had reached for an old paperback of H. P. Lovecraft short stories. That had led into a discussion of Lovecraft and his works and Arkham and Miskatonic University, and that had been followed up by a lunch, dinner, and a movie, and a year later, a small wedding ceremony in the Congregational Church in town.

She had a very small business making pottery, barely enough to keep her off food stamps, and he modestly said that he was a genius. Which was true. Jess knew computers, knew the Internet, and knew how to rig up little bits of technology that dazzled her, but she could hardly even keep up with him as he discussed fiber optics, webcams, sound files, infrared transmissions, and the like. Once he had rigged up a tiny camera at their door which was linked to the doorbell, so if somebody rang the doorbell, it would interrupt whatever program was being run on Jess's computer and would show a photograph of who was at the door. She had been amazed at the pure uselessness of the idea. Why not just walk over and see who was there? Why had he done such a thing? And her husband had laughed and said, "Because I can, that's why."

And she had gotten him back as well, making intricate little bits of pottery, statues or bowls, giving them to him over time, and once he had asked, why do you keep giving me gifts? She had laughed in return, saying, "Because I can, that's why."

Jess worked as a consultant, which meant long weeks away at corporations across the country, followed by equally fun weeks at home, when he didn't have to work and they could go canoeing and stargazing at night and rent old movies and not move from their tiny house for days on end.

Things were fine, were wonderful, until he had met up with the man with the big house. Named Hank Zamett.

UP the driveway she walked, the leather bag hanging off her arm, it gently bumping into her side as she went up to the large house. She thought she could make out the heavy shape of the pistol as it bumped against her. God, the damn thing was heavy, and she sure hoped it wouldn't break the other object she had in her purse. She looked up at the house, recalled when it was first built last year. The previous house on this lot had been an old Victorian, owned by a lawyer from town who had served two terms in the U.S. Senate during the latter part of the nineteenth century. The house hadn't been particularly historical or noteworthy, which was why there was no protection in place when Hank Zamett bought it and had it razed to the ground. The stained glass windows in the door, the walnut wainscoting, and the delicate spires on the roof, all torn up and smashed and crushed, and then, a bigger and more modern house had been built. A MacMansion, the locals had called it, for it was three times as large as its neighboring house. But Hank had money, Hank had the will, and what he wanted, he usually got.

She went up to the front door, rang the bell. She had been in the house exactly once before. This was going to be her second visit, and, she knew, was going to be her last.

* * *

It happened one cold October day, when the heat had gone out in her studio, and she had spent a long hour or two, trying to figure out why the heat wasn't making its way to the register. She was cold and her fingers and knees ached, and her back was throbbing, from having crawled around the basement, trying to trace the heating lines going out of the ancient oil furnace. The problem had been a malfunctioning thermostat. Ten minutes after replacing it, Jess had come home and had shown her a magazine, one of many hi-tech journals that littered his own office and workspace.

"See this guy here?" he had said, pointing out a photo in the magazine.

"Yeah?" she had replied, washing her hands yet again, hearing the *tick-tick-tick* as heat finally started crawling into her studio. The photo showed a beefy-looking guy, hair slicked back, wearing glasses and a satisfied smile on his face. He was in an office, sitting with self-assurance on the edge of his desk, and though there was snow visible outside, he was wearing a short-sleeve shirt, revealing a thick and muscular bicep.

"That's Hank Zamett. The guy that bought Senator Hudson's place. The guy that founded Zamett Systems. A real mover and shaker in the industry. He's quite impressive, Laura."

She looked at the photo again. "He doesn't look very impressive to me. He's wearing a summer shirt in winter, it looks like."

Jess just smiled. "He always dresses like that. He's a competitive weight lifter, triathlete, mountain climber. Likes to show off his biceps."

"Sounds like a nut," she had said.

"A very wealthy nut, and he wants me to come work for him."

Right then and there, she should have said no. Should have taken that magazine away and burned it, if she had been smart, if she had listened to what was going on in her mind. For she didn't like the hungry look of the guy, sitting on his desk like that, showing off his body like some great ape in some remote rain forest tribe, showing that he was king of the hill.

"That sounds nice," she had said, and a week later, it was too late. Jess was now working for the man with the hungry look.

SHE rang the doorbell at the front door, waited a few seconds, and then rang it again. The door opened up and Hank Zamett was there, wiping his face with a small hand towel. He was wearing gray sweatpants, a white tanktop shirt, and a suspicious look on his face. "Laura," he said. "Um, hi. Look, I really don't think we should be talking. Your lawyer and my lawyers might get upset."

Laura had expected this response, and said, "Oh, come on, Hank. Don't tell me you're afraid of lawyers, now, are you?"

That got him, made his eyes flash a bit. Hank always liked to say, in private and in public, that he wasn't afraid of a damn thing. She said, "All I want to do is talk. For five minutes. Give me five minutes and then I'll leave. All right?"

He shook his head. "Five minutes . . . that's okay, Laura, but it's not going to change my mind. You know how it is. Business is business."

She walked into the big house. "Sure," she said. "I know exactly how it is."

SO Jess had gone to work for Zamett Systems, and only after trying to ease Laura's mind. There would be a solid salary, great benefits, no more juggling expenses and tax issues with being a consultant. There would be no travel, so no more weeks alone in the house. The main facility was only ten minutes away, and he'd be home early enough for dinner, every day. Zamett Systems would give him all the support he needed, to really work on some great projects, and the money potential with the stock options was great. She had just said one thing, one thing only: "But I thought you liked working for yourself, Jess. I didn't think money mattered that much to you."

And he had said, "With money like this, hon, we can do a lot. Travel. Get a better house. A house with a studio that doesn't have a lousy heating system. Doesn't that sound great?"

Of course it did, and of course, Jess—sweet, genius, innocent Jess—had no idea what he had just agreed to do.

SHE followed Hank down a hallway, and she was pleased that he had brought her to his office. Two of the walls had floor-to-ceiling windows, overlooking a finely mowed lawn and some apple trees off in the distance. The office had bookshelves with books that looked unread, some cabinets with antiques, and a large lamp in the corner. He sat down in a big leather chair, in front of a desk that seemed to be the size of her studio. He wiped his face again and tossed the towel on the floor. "Okay, Laura," he said. "The clock is ticking. Five minutes."

She put the purse in her lap, said to him, "Hank, I brought you something. Something I've thought about for a while."

And with that, she reached into her purse.

THE first couple of weeks on the job, Jess would come home at 9 P.M. Or 10 P.M. Or 11 P.M. She soon adjusted to eating alone at home, and Jess would be full of apologies and excuses. He was adjusting to being an employee, and not a consultant. He had a steep learning curve if he expected to do well at Zamett Systems. Hank Zamett was expecting a lot from him. It all sounded reasonable and fair and perfectly understandable, but all Laura knew was that she missed those long afternoons, when he was back from some consulting gig and she didn't enter the studio, and they explored the hills and woods and lakes near their home.

A couple of times she had been a bit more aggressive, and had packed up a dinner and had gone to where Jess was working. The place, right from the start, had given her the creeps. Her own work area was dirty and crowded, with pictures and posters on the wall, dirt on the floor, a radio blasting classical tunes from the local NPR station, and overflowing wastebaskets. A mess to be sure, but her own mess. The cool and quiet and well-lit place that Jess was spending more and more of his time in looked to be like an asylum for both the equally gifted and disturbed.

Jess's own office was one in a series, down a long white corridor. She went through the open door and sat down in front of his desk, a metal thing that had a neat pile of papers, a clock, and a computer terminal with a huge screen, and three of her own little pottery creations, lined up on the edge of the desk. Light came in from overhead panels in the ceiling and there was a whiteboard on one side that covered nearly the entire wall. On the whiteboard, in different colored inks, were strings of numbers and symbols and acronyms that made her head ache to look at. Jess sat behind a computer terminal, face pudgy and red, and just as she unpacked a salad for herself and a steak sandwich for Jess, a burly man blew into the place like he owned it, which was true. She recognized Hank Zamett from the magazine photo, and he was dressed just like the photo: dress slacks, bright tie, short-sleeve shirt cut to show off his biceps.

"Jess, look, we've got to get a better handle on—"

"Excuse me, Hank, I'd like you to meet my wife, Laura."

He turned, like he was first noticing another human was in the office. "Oh," he said. "Hi."

"Hi," she said in return, and she noted the quick up-and-down look from his eyes, knew the look well. She had just been evaluated as a possible bed partner, and Hank Zamett had just dismissed that possibility in about a second or two. So what, she didn't think being overlooked by a creature like Hank Zamett meant anything, but she was surprised at how sour she felt. It was like she had failed at a contest she was sure she didn't want to be in.

Hank went over to Jess's side at the desk, and they started talking in a form of English she couldn't follow. She waited and waited, until the grumbling in her stomach grew too loud, and she slowly and silently ate her salad. Hank and Jess kept on talking. They kept on talking for quite some time, and then the two of them got up and went over to the whiteboard and both started scribbling in acronyms and symbols. She waited for a while longer, and then picked up her purse and empty salad bowl, and walked away.

HANK looked surprised at what she had pulled out of her purse. It was a small bowl, made by her own hands and with the help of a memory of dear old Jess, and she carefully placed it in the middle of the clean desk. It was brown with streaks of black, with what looked to be a piece of glass centered on one side.

He stared at it, like he expected it to start rotating or emitting sparks or some damn thing, and she said quietly, "See what that is? It's a decorative pot. I make a lot of these. I also made a fair number for Jess. I made it with my own hands. Something I worked with, something I pulled from the ground. Do you see the point? When I made that pot,

I did something that my ancestors and your ancestors did thousands of years ago. Stretching centuries behind me and centuries ahead of me, there have been and there will always be potters. Always."

His eyes seemed to darken. "Is there a point to this?"

"Yes, Hank," she said. "You think you're on top of your game. You think you're the very best. You think you've got the world by the tail, that everything is breaking your way, will continue to break your way. And what I'm telling you is that what you and your people do did not exist thirty years ago, and will not exist thirty years in the future. You're just a flicker of motion on the world's stage. Nothing else. Hank, you don't count."

Now his eyes really were dark. "Sorry Laura. I do count. I do count a lot. Wall Street and Silicon Valley and the trade press all agree, as do my employees. I don't care what you think about my time on the stage. And speaking of time, I think it's time for you to leave."

She shook her head. "No. Before I leave, I want you to make things right. For what Jess did for you."

He shook his head in reply. "Nope. Sorry. My lawyers said I was totally within my rights. And bringing some sort of crappy gift"—and he made a dismissive gesture to the pot with his hand—"isn't going to change my mind. Okay?"

She sighed. All right, then. "Okay. One more thing."

She went back to her purse, this time pulled out something that wasn't crafted by her hands, but by some unknown craftspeople in a Connecticut River Valley facility of Messrs. Smith and Wesson. She pointed it right at his meaty face.

"Do you think this might change your mind? Hank?"

And seeing the look on his face brought a strange emotion to her, an emotion familiar yet distant. And then she recognized what she was feeling, something that had not happened to her since Jess died: happiness.

BESIDES the increased hours at work, Laura noticed that Jess was starting to slip. Always a bit chunky, he was really starting to pack on the pounds, and it was easy to know why: their afternoon walks or bicycle rides had gone away, the meals eaten at home had mutated into vending machine snacks eaten at his desk at work, and a few times—instead of taking the several minutes necessary to come home—he would sprawl under his desk and sleep there. He was forgetful, he was snappish, and instead of spending long minutes admiring her pottery—especially the little gifts she brought to him at work—he would smile, say "nice," and then change the subject.

"Jess," she said once, as they were getting ready for bed. "You've got to start taking better care of yourself. It's not healthy."

Jess tried to reassure her. "Sweets, it's okay. Honest it is. We're trying to get through the beta test of a new product, something that will make the investors sit up and take notice. Just a few more weeks and it'll get better. Honest."

"You sure?" she asked.

"Positive. Look what we're doing . . ." he started, and then he went into a long discussion of miniature cameras and transmitters that could allow anyone with the aptitude of changing toilet paper, the ability to wire up one's bedroom, one's house, hell, one's car, to allow 24/7 surveillance or videography. Home security, web presence, the whole ball of wax available in one inexpensive package. He even gave her a demo with some gear in his computer bag that he had brought home, and she nodded in the right places and gave out the usual exclamations of interest and amazement, while she watched the minutes slip away.

Just when Jess went on about the possible military aspects of what he had been working on, she kissed him. "My smelly genius, it's way past your bedtime. Come along."

He grinned, like a puppy being praised for a particularly elaborate trick, and he put the gear away. So they went to bed and Jess fell asleep in a matter of moments, and all night long, it seemed, his legs and arms trembled, and he whispered to himself, like his mind was still back at work, not letting him loose, not giving him any respite at all.

HANK'S look of surprise quickly turned into anger. "Laura. Put that down. Right now."

"Nope."

"Laura, put the gun away. All right? Put it down and walk out the door, and I won't press any charges. We'll pretend this never happened."

Laura made a point of sighing quite loud. "You see, Hank, you're making a mistake. You think that what you're thinking is going to make a difference. You think I really care about any possible charges that might come my way."

"Threatening me with a weapon, that's very serious," Hank said, eyes flickering down to the pistol and up to her face.

"Maybe. Then again, maybe I'll just plead the distraught widow excuse, and I'll get off with a stern lecture. Are you willing to risk that?"

Hank looked again at the pistol, made a presentation of slumping his muscular shoulders. "Okay. You win, Laura. What do you want? Money? Part of the profits? A plaque with Jess's name out in front of the plant?"

She didn't let the weapon waver. "How stupid do you think I am, Hank?"

He didn't answer.

She said, "I've been selling my own handiwork for years,

and I know all the ins and outs of negotiations and deal making. Trust me, you haven't gone into serious negotiations until you've gone into some of these small country stores with old Yankee retailers. Do you think I'll believe for one moment that any kind of deal or agreement that we come to in this office, with a pistol pointing in your direction, that this deal would last out the evening? Of course it wouldn't. I'm not that stupid. It's too late for you to start offering me money, Hank, or a deal."

"What do you want, then?" he asked.

"Justice," she said.

"You came to the wrong place," he said.

She moved the pistol a few inches, brought her free hand up, and held the pistol in the approved firing stance. She pulled the trigger, drilling a hole in the plate glass window right behind his desk. Hank jerked and his face turned white, and when he looked back at her, she said, "Wrong answer, Hank. Care to try again?"

THE first time Laura went to Hank Zamett's house was the evening of a warm summer party, a party to celebrate the completion of a certain milestone in the development of a pretty tricky piece of software. Jess hadn't been feeling well all day, feverish and headachy, and she wanted to keep him home, but he insisted. "This is going to be important, sweets. Real important. Besides the employees and senior staff, there are going to be a number of important VCs in the crowd."

She tried to make a joke. "VCs? Viet Cong?"

But he didn't appreciate the humor. "No. Venture capitalists, hard-eyed guys with lots of money to invest and who are careful who gets it. A few years back, you could squeeze out whatever you wanted from VCs with a half-assed business plan and some high-end computer servers. Since the Nasdaq meltdown, that's changed. You need to show them real stuff that'll get real customers interested in spending money. Not a singing sock puppet."

At Hank's large home, it looked like something out of *The Great Gatsby,* with tents up in the backyard, caterers, and live music. She moved through the crowd, a fruit drink in her hand, not really wanting to talk to any of the other guests, all of whom were associated with Zamett Systems. She had enough talk about the company with Jess around; she didn't need any additional discussion tonight.

In the large backyard she found a spot near an old dead apple tree, its wide trunk offering some solitude. She stood there and sipped her drink and was startled for a moment: she could hear voices. She peered around the trunk, saw two men, dressed alike in tan chinos and bright polo shirts. Their faces weren't familiar, and as they talked, she realized that there were two of the fabled VCs, money guys who could make or break a company through the effort of writing a single check.

Laura could only catch snatches of the conversation, but what she did hear pleased her: the system that Jess had come up with, had designed and worked on, looked to be a potential hit. The VCs were impressed with the demonstration, and were ready to give Hank Zamett whatever he wanted. Good, she thought. Very good. Maybe that would lessen some of the pressure, lighten some of the load, and get Jess back to a normal life.

Then, the VCs voices got louder, and they laughed at what they were seeing. Laura looked around again, saw Hank leading a group of his folks—including Jess—out to the field. Hank had his shirt off and was juggling a football, up and down.

"Look there," one VC said. "Mister macho man struts his stuff."

A laugh. "Sure does look ridiculous, doesn't it?"

"That's his whole image, man. Macho hi-tech warrior. Keen mind and buff body. Not afraid of anything in the business world, not afraid of anything else as well."

"Is it true he challenged Ellison to a boxing match?"

The second VC guy laughed again. "Yep. Said something like sailing was one thing, but getting into a ring and pounding somebody else's head in was something else. Lucky for both of them, Ellison ignored him."

Out on the field, a scrimmage as such was going on, a touch football game it looked like, with guys and even some gals out there, running plays. Hank was the centerpiece, the quarterback, tossing the ball with accuracy to his workers downfield. She smiled at seeing the lumbering form of dear old Jess, being the good employee, trying to fit in with the team.

The first VC said, "How much practice did it take for him to make those plays?"

"Who knows? But that's Hank Zamett. Take away his macho guy image, and he's just another hi-tech geek looking to make a buck, one of thousands."

"Yeah, looking to make a buck with our help."

"Sure, but—"

And Laura didn't hear the rest of the conversation. The game was suddenly over. The people of Zamett Systems were clustered about a form on the ground, a man who wasn't moving, a man who looked like—

"Jess!" she screamed, dropping her drink, running up to the field, running up to where Jess's poor young heart had just given out.

THE sound of the shot caused her ears to ring, and she grinned at Hank. "Man, that sucker sure was loud. You see, every other time I've pulled the trigger, I've had ear protection. How are you doing?"

Hank's face was now the color of his tanktop T-shirt. "Laura . . ."

She looked on the carpeted floor, and then quickly bent down and picked up the spent cartridge. It was still warm. "There. I know how particular you can be about your surroundings. And sorry about the window and all that, but I had to get your attention. Do you see my point, Hank?"

A tiny nod. She waved the pistol at him. "I'm sorry, Hank. How about a word or two tossed my way? Okay?"

He said quickly, "I understand."

She tried a smile. "Oh, that's pretty good, Hank. But I don't think you do understand. I don't think you understand what it's like to be a widow at my age, to see her husband pour his life—his honest-to-God life—into a company, and to see him die for his efforts. For that's what happened, right? You worked and worked and worked poor Jess to death, and for what? This fancy house? This office? Your company?"

Hank said not a word. She shifted in her chair. "And what did you think I was going to do? Play the grieving widow and go away and hide? After what you did to him?"

He started speaking slowly, as if afraid the wrong phrase, the wrong syllable, would cause another shot to ring out. "Laura, I do understand. Honest. And no doubt I was too harsh and too business-like in settling Jess's affairs with the company. But we can go beyond that. Honest we can."

Laura said, "Oh, yes, before this night is over, we are certainly going beyond that."

And she fired again.

EARLIER in her life she had never quite understood the phrase "one day at a time," or "getting through it, hour by hour." Laura had never really had any tragedy or misfortune come by her way, and it had seemed like an incredibly complex joke, until that long weepy afternoon, the day after Jess's funeral, when she realized that This Was It. Never again would she hear his voice, never again would she feel his lips against the back of her neck, never again would she wake up in the middle of the night from a bad dream and be comforted by his gentle, slumbering presence next to her.

That's when she would sit on the couch and stare at the blank television screen, and the light green numbers on the VCR. Watching each minute flick by on the clock seemed to take hours, and it both fascinated and horrified her, that this deep grief, this dark mourning, could seem to take so long. Her days were interrupted by phone calls, by friends and family stopping by, and she would watch herself talk to these people, like she was standing just above and behind her body, quietly admiring how she could talk without breaking down in tears.

But the tears did come. A week after the funeral, an embarrassed-looking teenage boy, wearing a blue, ill-fitting security uniform, came by with a cardboard box with Jess's possessions. There weren't that many items in the box, and the young boy shoved a bunch of papers and receipts to sign—which she did, automatically—and after he left, she sat down, cross-legged on the floor, to go through them. There were some pens and pencils, a plastic lunch container, some of his own books, and at the bottom, tumbled and broken and shattered, were all the little bits of pottery she had given to him as gifts over the month.

That day, she had cried for a very long time.

"So," Laura said, looking at the corner of the office, where broken colored glass was now spread across the floor. "I guess I took out that lamp shade over there. It looked like a Tiffany. Am I right?"

Hank nodded, lips clenched tight, his hands now trembling on top of his desk. Laura went on. "Not a bad guess on my part. And I suppose I should have been a better guesser, back when you sent that poor kid over with Jess's stuff. Right? I mean, I should have guessed that hidden in all that paperwork that was sent over would be some release forms. Of course. Absolving you and the company of any guilt in Jess's death, making sure that any and all projects that Jess worked on, that Jess dreamed up and designed, all those projects belonged to you and the company. One hundred percent. That I wouldn't get a single penny. Tell me, Hank, is that the usual cost of doing business? Working your people to death? Cheating the widow of one of your brightest stars? Is that what you do, day in and day out?"

Hank cleared his throat, seemed to choke, and then cleared his throat again. "It was all legal. Strictly legal."

Laura steadied the pistol again in her hands. "Sure it was. But was it right, Hank? Was it?"

He didn't say anything.

HER own lawyer was a retired district court judge, Leo Cutler, specializing in wills and divorces, and he had no good news for her the day she saw him.

"I'm very sorry, Mrs. Cutler, but the forms you signed were all drawn up correctly. We may have a case that you signed these forms under mental duress, but it could be a very long and drawn-out affair. Zamett Systems has a high-powered legal team in their corner. They could bury you with years' worth of motions and countersuits."

She sat stiffly in the chair, hands folded in her lap. "Are you suggesting I drop it?"

The older man shook his head. "No, I'm just telling you that the chances of success are quite slim. I don't think we have a chance."

Laura stood up. "All right, then. I'll do it myself."

Leo look confused. "Do what?"

As she walked out the door, she said, "Make one more gift. For Jess."

SHE took a breath, stood up, and was pleased again to see the flash of fear in the man's eyes. She drew down the pistol to his chest and said, "This is it, Hank. I've already wasted two rounds on you, and I'm not going to waste anymore. Any last words?"

A whisper. "No."

"I'm sorry, I didn't hear you. What did you say?"

Tears were now forming in his eyes. "Please, Laura . . . don't."

"Don't do what?"

"Don't shoot me! Please!"

Laura said, "Go on, Hank. Now you're making an impression. Keep on begging. I like the sound of that."

Now the tears were going down his red cheeks. "Please don't shoot me! I beg you! Please! I don't want to get shot . . . please, for the love of God, Laura, please don't shoot me . . . I'll make it all up to you, honest to God I will . . ."

Laura leaned over the desk. "Like you did to my husband? Like that?"

He shook his head violently, weeping, snot now dribbling out of his nose. "That was wrong . . . I know it was . . . Laura, please, I beg you, please don't shoot me."

She said, "Give me one more round of begging, Hank. Tell me what a miserable son of a bitch you are. Tell me how you hurt people."

Hank nodded frantically. "That's right, that's right. I am a miserable son of a bitch. A weak bastard who hurts people, day in and day out. I swear to God I'm sorry. I won't do it again. I swear I won't. Laura, just . . . please don't shoot me . . . I don't want to die!"

Now she was really smiling, and even though the pistol was double-action, she thumbed back the hammer for emphasis. Hank started screeching. "You promised! You promised you wouldn't hurt me! You promised!"

"No, Hank," she said calmly. "I just asked you to give me one more round of begging. I didn't promise you a damn thing."

And she kept the pistol aimed center at his chest, as she pulled the trigger back, as fast as she could, the explosions sounding even louder in the office.

ALL things considered, the police were very polite, and only toward the end, when she had signed all the necessary paperwork for the bail bondsmen, did her younger brother Jake come in to see her. She got up from the interview chair and kissed him on the cheek, and he started talking and she said, "Jake, please, no lectures tonight. All right? I'm quite tired. I just want to go home."

He glared at her as he looked at some paperwork on a clipboard. "You're a lucky woman."

"So I've been told."

"Hank Zamett is still deciding on whether to press charges on you for assault, and the department is still deciding on whether to charge you with reckless discharge of a firearm."

She said innocently, "Is there a law against discharging blank cartridges?"

The glare continued. "That was dumb and out of line, Laura. Bad enough you had to fire off two real ones in his office. When you fired off those blanks, you damn near gave him a heart attack. Why? For Jess?"

"No," she said. "For me. Look, can I go?"

He turned to the door. "Sure. I'll drive you home."

"Thanks."

* * *

LATE at night, she sat before Jess's computer, her pottery-worn fingers tapping hesitantly at the keyboard, gently moving the mouse around, trying to get the files ready, the files she was getting ready to post and e-mail around the world. On one of the little graphics on the screen—icons, right?—she double-clicked on the mouse, and a miniature movie screen popped up on the computer. There, in full sound and color, was Hank Zamett, macho man who was afraid of nothing, whimpering and begging like a baby boy.

Fair enough. Came out nice. She did what she had to do, and in an instant, it was all sent out across the Internet. Very shortly, millions of people around the world could see Hank Zamett in action, a type of action that she was certain would drive him and his business into dust.

She sat back in Jess's chair, rubbed at the armrests, imagined she could almost make out his scent there. Oh, Jess, she thought. I do miss you so. She moved the chair about and then picked up a piece of pottery. Some hours ago it had been on Hank Zamett's desk, and only through some judicious moves on her part was she able to retrieve it and put it in her purse, before the cops arrived. She tilted the pot and looked inside, at the electronics gear that enabled this little piece of hers to act like a surveillance camera, a camera that had been in a perfect place to catch Hank in all his glory.

Laura brought the pot up to her lips, kissed it gently. "For you, love," she whispered. "One more gift for you."

JoJo's Gold

Noreen Ayres

"**All** you turkeys is just narrow-minded. You got no power o' vision," JoJo said. JoJo had this big idea he could find gold ore beneath the sand on the beach. I could not hold that against him. Every man must have his dream. But JoJo's dream turned him into the devil's own target.

I get ahead of myself. You have to understand how we *were* together, what a team the four of us made, how that makes what happened all the more a cause for grief.

Cindylee was of our company. Cindylee would listen to JoJo go on about the gold, then say, "You got the IQ of a watermelon, JayJay."

He would just eat it up. There she'd be, standing with the wind whipping her skirt, pasting her hair to her cheek. She'd be eating an apple and spitting out wrinkled peel she didn't like.

And Buddy, he'd be all casual laid out on his army blanket spread there on the sand, and he wouldn't even look over, just tell JoJo he was a sun-fried fool.

JoJo would pluck a bottle cap off the bottom of his metal

detector, toss it toward Cindylee, and wait for that cockeyed smile where her lips disappear but her eyes glow with sea-shine. Then off he'd go, waltzing with that widget he thought was his gold-finder but to us looked like a saucer on a broomstick.

Each of us, we had our talents. That's what made us stand alone or stand together, did not matter at all. Cindylee could find clothes by just snapping her fingers. People leave clothes on benches, window ledges, over tree limbs, as if they know Cindylee will be coming along when she is in the right need for something to wear.

Buddy now, I swear: Dollar bills sail through the air and into his hand like paper airplanes. Pay phones spit out quarters when he passes by. Folks with holes in their pockets and hay in their heads stroll along the edge of the sand in front of him, dropping coins in his path. That's Buddy.

Now me, I got a good eye for recyclables. Once I carried a chair which was right out there on Coast Highway where anybody could have grabbed it, carried it down to the thrift store and got a whole twenty bucks for it. I can spy a mess of bottles from a mile away. I scrounge for stuff left out for trash pickup that the city sure don't need.

And JoJo? He could stash more stuff in his beat-up golf bag than marbles in a gunny sack. He could turn a profit on wire coat hangers, old cans, and car keys. What he'd do, he'd sell them to an artist in Laguna, and this artist would make tinkling mobiles out of them to sell to the tourists as if they had never seen a thing so clever. If only JoJo hadn't gone and got greedy, we would all be back to those heavenly days.

It started when JoJo made off with a book on minerals last June. He used to lift books out of the library, see. Not a thief, no no. But if you don't have an address, you can't get a library card. So yes, JoJo would filch books, but the thing was, he always brought them back *in* when he was done. Then the library went and put in those electronic doodads that could spot a gnat's knuckle. The result of which was to make JoJo stop bringing books back. So you could say the library itself contributed to the crime. He could get them out all right, because he'd just open a back window and drop them to the ground, but throwing them back up was not a viable option, as the businessmen say.

Anyway, that book on minerals he did not return, and this is what he learned: Salt domes form around oil deposits. "What's in the ocean?" he says.

Fish and garbage, we say.

"In the *water,*" he says, like a chemist. *"Salt,"* he says. He figures if oil is attracted to salt, then there's a chance gold and other precious ores would be too. Figure out where the salt domes are under the sand, then tell the mining companies. The mining companies could dig it out, JoJo would collect a finder's fee, and we could all be in tall cotton.

I said, "I don't see no salt domes, JoJo."

"*Dunes* are domes, dummy," and JoJo liked the sound of that, and we all laughed. Dunes are domes, dummy. "It's here, boys," he'd say. Boys, even though there was Cindylee. "It's here," he said, "I just hafta find it."

"Always you just hafta find it, you numbskull," Buddy said, who never had more than a dishwashing job in the last thirty years, but what he did own was opinions.

It would go on like that, our bunch hunkered down at the spot we called The Place by the foot of the cliff near the Hotel Laguna. Movie stars used to stay at that hotel. It's got a tower, a red Spanish-tile roof, and a private stretch of white sand marked off by signs with hardly anybody on it. Every morning we'd meet up just the other side of that stretch, smoke a cigarette, and talk our talk, and then JoJo would haul out his detector from his golf bag and go out on his skinny legs till he was no bigger than a gull in our sight. We'd watch him swing that chunk of steel over the sand like a slow man sweeping a rug that already been swept. Then the rest of us would pool our pennies for half a six-pack to kick off the morning. We would split up then and meet back at The Place a couple hours later.

So this one day we were lounging around on some ratty towels the laundry boy from the hotel let us have, and here come JoJo walking his metal detector like a pup on a string. He had on a new pair of pants and redder-'n-hell suspenders but the same old lop-eared boots.

"So JoJo," Cindylee says while putting on her second sweater because it was a chill April. She's about forty—younger than us but not as good lookin'. "You among the wealthy yet?"

"Who says I can't find gold on the beach?" He holds out his wrist and shows us a thing gleaming.

Buddy gets up for a look. "Holy crackers," he says—Buddy's religious. "It's a Rolex or I'm a blind surgeon." It was a watch all right, but I can't tell a Rolex from a Rolaid, so I said the smart thing, which is *no*-thing.

JoJo commenced to tell how he come by it. "Down by those hang-over houses, is where I found it." He looks at Cindylee. "One of us could wear it once in a while," he says.

"You could put a poster up, offer a reward," Buddy says.

"Now why would I do that?"

"Get money on it without going to jail."

"Where they gonna call, One-Eight-Hundred-Sand?"

Buddy's face falls. "Oh, yeah."

I ask, "You find the fancy clothes too?"

JoJo's wavy hair had recent water on it. All along I'd figured he was sweet on Cindylee. He was sure looking sprite this morning, and his eyes were clear as the wink of a dime.

"Lady in a alley tossed 'em out a window," he says. "Seen me passing by, said, Now there's a fella'd look good in these. Whoosh, plop!, I get a new wardrobe."

"Right," Cindylee says, "and I am from Par-ee."

"Don't argue what the Lord provides," Buddy says, his face open to the wonder of it all.

"This female philanthropist toss out the Rolex too?" Cindylee said.

"I told you," JoJo says with a hurt look, "I found it on the beach."

And that was all he was going to say. He turned his face so that from the side he looked like a real mad cat.

We walked up the sidewalk to the bakery near the hotel and bought two chocolate-chip cookies.

Next day, no JoJo.

Day after that, no JoJo.

He wasn't at the Methodist church where they give out soup and sometimes even a room so you can take a nap. He wasn't on the bench at Forest Avenue. He wasn't at The Place, anytime we saw. At dusk, after the neckers went home, when we might find him scanning the rolled-around-in sand for pocket booty, he was nowhere to be seen.

The day after that, Buddy stopped a cop who was already stopped, really. The officer was out of his squad car, sitting on a wall near steps that go down a full story to the beach. Buddy said he guessed the cop was looking for bad guys out on the flat green sea. For Buddy to stop a cop was a brave thing to do, because Buddy is shy as a bill in the breeze. He got up the gumption to ask the police officer about JoJo. The cop knew who JoJo was, even down to his last name, which, if I didn't mention it, was Waverly, a fact I was not apprised of till the moment Buddy told me.

Well, among other rude things the cop said, this is how he answered Buddy: "Guess your pal took a midnight dip after one too many Thunderbirds."

Buddy says, "Whaddya mean?"

And the cop says, "He bobbed up yesterday near Three Arch Bay."

WE couldn't believe it, JoJo drowned.

Cindylee said no way would that man take a swim and forget to come up—he didn't like the water. No way would he be in it of his own free will. She wanted us to go talk to this cop herself. I said I'd as soon watch, thank you, from across the street.

But I tagged along, me behind Buddy, behind Cindylee. While she walked, she lifted the edge of her pink skirt to her nose and eyes, sniffling at the news about poor JoJo. Beneath her skirt were long green pants and beneath those ankles thin as net poles. Meanwhile, I'm thinking about JoJo's metal detector and that golf bag I could use because pardon me but my duffel's ripped.

We found the cop same place Buddy did, one hand and one foot on the low rock wall and his elbow propped on his thigh so his fist could hold his chins up. He wasn't facing the water this time, but looking down-beach, along the row of houses hanging over the sand, where JoJo found his watch. The three of us coming toward the fella that way, I'm surprised he didn't get shook up, but he barely glanced at us until Buddy spoke. "Officer," Buddy said, "these are my friends here, Cynthia Lee and Harley Boone. Harley wants to ask you something."

I gave Buddy a look to kill but found my voice.

"Uh, did JoJo Waverly have, like, a instrument for metal detection upon his whereabouts?"

Cindylee's eyes were asking what wave I washed in on.

The officer shook his head and looked us up and down, each one.

"Was there a golf bag, uh, recovered from the area of the

happening? It would be white with green flaps and green stitching."

"I don't believe so," he said, blue eyes reading me.

Cindylee was on him like a terrier on a mouse. She even moved up to his inner space if you know what I mean, and the man leaned so far away I thought he might tumble off the wall.

"You found him where exactly?" she demanded, a quiver in her voice. "In the water, out of the water, on the rocks, where?"

The cop stood up then and pointed southward. "Spread-eagled on the sand," he said, "crabs crawling on him."

I thought I saw satisfaction on his face. I could have shoved him over the wall.

It flashed on me about how it must have been there for JoJo, cold and alone on the sand, and I had to change my thoughts to a picture of JoJo when the gulls came walking up to look in his face and he thought he was in Tahiti. Maybe he *was* in Tahiti, if Heaven or Tahiti takes men who think doors left open are meant for them.

Then I remembered the gold watch on his wrist and asked the officer, "How about his, you know, clothes?"

"The victim's clothing is available for those who furnish him burial, but far as I know, there are no relatives of record," the Mr. Blue said. "You know of any relatives?" He looked at me in a way made me want to see what was on down the road.

"No, sir."

"Then I guess we're done here."

Buddy rolled his eyes at me.

We moved along. Back on the sidewalk, we passed by people eating. JoJo told us once that in Japan it's impolite to eat and walk at the same time. I don't know about that. I just wait for somebody to leave a half a sandwich on top of the trash and I don't care if he's walking, chewing, and smacking the top of his head at the same time when he does.

We slowed down at the Whaling Wall, which is where these big blue whales used to be painted on the side of a building by the hotel parking lot. The whales were smiling, headed out to sea. At first they used to head inland till somebody told the artist better and he did it over. Now they're gone the way all things go, painted over for good, voted down by a city council that is supposed to know a wiser way. That morning though, when the whales were still there, Buddy moved under the baby one, and we all leaned there soaking up a cloud-peep of sun, while the hotel parking lot attendant glared at us but kept his distance.

I said, "You notice that officer's skunned-up knuckles?"

"No ma'am. I didn't." Buddy calls me ma'am sometimes. He is getting stranger all the time. I think he needs Vitamin B.

"Did you notice that cop's *wrist*, what he had on it?" This from Cindylee. Her eyes were bright as boat lights. She unknotted her sweater-arms from around her neck and fought her fists through them as the wind came up from the beach. "You should pay attention. You too, Harley." She smelled like hotel soap pieces the Mexican boy sets out the back door. "JoJo's *gold*," she said. "Right there on his wrist."

"Gosh," Buddy said.

"Son-of-a," is all I could say.

"JoJo told me he saw somebody leave out those hang-over houses with stolen stuff in a trash bag, *twice*," she said. "I go, 'It's not you, is it, JoJo, taking that stuff?' He's like, 'I may be ugly but I'm not dumb.' "

"You never told us that. About JoJo," I said, "seeing somebody."

"Just 'cause I practically sit in your lap all day don't mean I have to tell you every blasted thing."

"What else he say?"

"He knew where the thief stashed the stuff. I'm all: 'You

stay away from that, JoJo. Don't be poking around now.' And he goes. . . . You know what he goes?" She was looking at Buddy, a big-eyed baby if babies had a fringe of hair below the ears and needed an afternoon shave. "He goes, 'It's an officer of the law, but don't you be tellin' nobody. An officer of the law who had found himself a way to finance his retirement.' Then he says, 'How'd you like to accomp'ny me to the City of Lights in the great state of Nevada, all the way in a limousine with your feet up on the seats and me pourin' champagne?' " Two tears rode down her cheeks like steam drips on a restaurant window. "JoJo's gold, that Roll of Decks come outta that cop's stash," she said.

"No way!" Buddy cried out.

"Don't be lookin' to a brass shield for justice, Buddy, nor *God* neither," she said.

My heart was throwin' horseshoes. "I'd sure like to get my hands on that metal detector," I said. "First off, maybe I'd use it to brain some certain body."

Cindylee tore away up to the sidewalk when the parking lot attendant came strolling our way. We followed.

In a little bit, she said, "I knew that cop in vocational school. He was a noodle then, and he's a noodle now. He made pipe bombs in his parents' garage."

Buddy and I tossed glances. It's hard to know sometimes. We walked on, and after a block we went on our separate routes.

After that, I didn't see Buddy or Cindylee for two whole days, and I figured they'd marched off for better pickin's, but I was lonely and sorry they'd just take off without a goodbye. It was harder getting along without splitting the spoils, you might say. I stopped in to a little Unity church for breakfast the third day. The woman there has extra bagels a lot of times. Then I went back to The Place. Lo and behold, Cindylee and Buddy were there. And Buddy had JoJo's golf bag. I said, "Where the heck you get that thing?"

"Asked for it," he said. "I spotted it in the officer's car the other day when he had the trunk open, and I just asked for it." Imagine. Buddy, the one who'd wet his pants before asking could he use the rest room. JoJo's metal detector was in the bag, he said, but it was broken. The plate thing was gone off the bottom, and it sure couldn't detect itself. Since then, Cindylee had been using the handle to turn over trash, so she wouldn't have to bend so much. Her cheeks were rosy and she had on a new dark sweater.

Buddy offered me the golf bag and I took it with genuine thanks. "But what are you going to use?" I asked.

"Holy crackers," he said, "what am I going to do with that clumsy thing when I'm sittin' in Tahiti?"

"It's Tahiti now, huh? And just how you going to go about that?"

"The world is full of bounty," he said, "and we are obliged to partake of it." He was wearing a pretty good bomber's jacket he found by the restaurant where all the waiters wear bow ties. I shook my head and looked at them both real close, but if there were tales to tell, the two of them had a bad case of laryngitis.

Buddy started acting really different after that day: smiling at Cindylee all the time, spitting out more words than crackers have crumbs. Once I came upon him and Cindy eating chocolate-chip cookies all by themselves. I was hurt but didn't let on. Cindylee had on red pants and men's socks with a diamond pattern that made her ankles look thicker. Maybe that gain was from all the cookies, I can't say.

Then last week I'm looking at the front page of the local paper through a news rack, and at first I couldn't be sure because of a split running down the middle of the plastic shield that was all yellowed from sun, but then I make out it's a picture of our Mr. Officer Blue. I put real money in the news stand slot and took out the paper. For good measure I took out a couple other copies, too, and left them on top for those less fortunate than I. It seems Mr. Blue had reached the end of his days upon the rocky shoals. That is to say, Mr. So-Sure-of-Himself was not as sure*footed* as he might have liked to be. He fell off the very same wall upon which he formerly gazed at pirates on the sea. That sorry man suffered a plenitude of head wounds. In a tidelet below, he was found face down.

The paper said he was last seen conversing with a woman in dark clothes and a beret. That was two weeks ago.

Myself I've only tried on one beret, the one I recently took ownership of. I don't know why people wear them. They seem like only half a hat to me. I keep meaning to give this one to Buddy for his cold noggin, but it's hardly any good because it only covers one ear at a time. It works okay to put my small stuff in if I have a rubber band to twist it off with. But I definitely should offer it back to Buddy. It was in the golf bag, down the bottom, when he gave the bag to me, so I guess he came upon it first. Maybe it's the one that woman wore who the paper said was talking to Mr. Blue before he took a Humpty-Dumpty fall off the wall, who knows? All I know is, it still has sand in it no matter how I beat it out, like someone used it for a bucket for booty, just like me.

Come to think of it, that beret just might look good on Cindylee. It's been a while since I seen those eyes a-glitter. Maybe I'll truck on down to The Place and see if Buddy and her are still stuck up or maybe, shoot, stuck together. Ye-siree.

Black Heart and Cabin Girl

Shelley Costa

Here *is how the story ends: he buys an ax. It's a Sears Craftsman ax and it feels right in his hands, smooth and heavy, and he has always been satisfied with his Craftsman table saw and belt sander. Affordable and reliable tools, that's what he's always liked.* Chopping yourself some wood? *the salesman asks, whose name pin says* JIMMY THIRTEEN YEARS OUTSTANDING SERVICE. Yes, chopping some wood, *he tells Jimmy, who smiles. As he signs the Visa charge slip, it strikes him that at some point a man starts to shape what he says to please. If he had started sometime before the final two days of his life, he wonders whether the story would end differently. Would he, for instance, be buying this ax? When he gets home, he stands the ax in the corner of the bedroom, then decides to move it to the basement because it seems cruel to alarm Diane, the woman he married four years ago after he drove Jo Verdyne forever from the lake. In a dark corner behind the furnace, he stands the ax against the cinder block foundation, next to the small wooden stool he had set there just yesterday to hold the straight razor that had once belonged to his father, who used to enjoy stropping it into a kind of fatal perfection. When he turns the blade* *softly against his hand, he marvels how, with the merest touch against his skin, a line of blood suddenly springs, and where that line begins is Black Heart, and where it ends is Cabin Girl.*

JO sat alone on the port side of the water taxi, where she'd be able to see up the north arm of Lake Temagami on her first trip back in sixteen years. Seal Rock, Devil Bay, Point of No Return—even Stone Maiden Cliff. Places where the wind would kick up suddenly and churn the water into threatening white caps, places where the steep rock discouraged casual climbers before they discovered the warm, breezy lookouts at the top, scented with mats of brown fallen pine needles. She knew the taxi would turn west and head across the wide channel by Bear Island, the Indian Reserve, before the landmarks from her childhood would come into view, but she liked the idea that Temagami had gone on without her all these years. Half her life had been spent elsewhere, after all. Despite what she thought when she was a barefoot eleven and learned to clean fish and run the skiff almost as well as old Will Stanley, the caretaker at the lodge. Despite what she thought when she was twelve and the Hackett boy kissed her one night on the main dock only she wasn't sure she liked it very much even though she told him she did.

The water taxi Doral, with an outboard the size of a doghouse, sputtered through the No Wake zone at the landing, then flew her through the gap where the lake opened up, veering around shoals in a path rippled by a light wind from the southwest. The lake water, in some places hundreds of feet down to boulders left behind by the last Ice Age, was blue and green and gray, all the colors of clean and cold. She was five hours north of Toronto—and twelve hours north of Baltimore, where she taught baby chemistry for nine months a year at Johns Hopkins and had a townhouse she called home for want of a better term. It was May twenty-ninth, and according to Ellroy, the driver, who had the words SKATEBOARDING IS tattooed on one chunky bicep and NOT A CRIME on the other, the ice had gone out late just two weeks ago. He smirked at her, like the information was sexy somehow, and turned back to his windshield.

Three years ago her grandfather Carl Verdyne had died and left her the lodge Wendaban—a grand old two-story log building with eighteen rooms and a wraparound porch—which had been in the Verdyne family since 1904. Jimmy Stewart had fished there. Carole Lombard had lounged there. It had hosted titans and famous runaways and wonderful, wealthy derelicts who were looking for good food, drink, and a bed in a wilderness setting for a week. Those were the days of the great passenger boats that glided up and down the lake in a kind of ephemeral elegance. The days of fish crematoria, where all the uneaten bass and pickerel and lake trout were heaped and burned, days when an abundance of all things created only festive kinds of problems there in the Canadian Northwoods. Jo only heard about those days. By the time she was growing up, the movie stars were gone and the fish were an event, middle-class families from upstate New York were the guests, and the only wealthy derelicts who still came were completely uncelebrated.

For the first year after her grandfather's death, she denied the place, let the employees go, and paid the taxes. For the second year, she howled silently at the pain of the inheritance, fretted about the former employees, and wondered just how much longer the one-hundred-year-old logs of Wendaban could stand without any human attention. There were a couple of faceless offers to buy, during this time, and it was only the possibility of letting Wendaban go out of the family forever that made Jo realize she could never do it. She was no lodgekeeper, but maybe the beautiful Wendaban was no longer a lodge. In the third year after her grandfather left her the property where she had spent the first thirteen summers of her life—until the accident—or what she called the accident, the thing she could never name without capsizing into her own doubts—she gave up and hired a Toronto lawyer with expertise in setting up nonprofit organizations, a couple of Wendaban's former employees, and twenty minutes ago, Ellroy the water taxi driver, who, according to his tattered business card, also provided firewood and laundry service: WE GET YOU THERE, THEN KEEP YOU WARM AND CLEAN.

SHE moved into her grandfather's old room on the first floor of the lodge because it got the morning sun, and she took the handle "Cabin Girl." *When we're all grown up,* Christine had said when they were twelve, *we'll have our own VHF radios and you'll be Heiress and I'll be Cabin Girl and we'll call each other all the time.* Cabin Girl was all that was left of Christine, so Jo took it, though no one else knew why.

She put Kay Stanley, the old caretaker's daughter—Will Stanley himself had died in his bungalow on Bear Island just two winters ago—in charge of day-to-day operations, calling in the right people to check the septic system, overhaul the old Wendaban boats, install the solar panels, deliver the propane that still fueled the interior of the lodge because Carl Verdyne had liked the feel of it. Kay moved soundlessly the way heavy people do, her short arms swinging, her eyes disappearing into her muscular cheeks when she smiled.

It was Kay who hired Luke Croy, a handyman on the lake, to replace the rotten boards on the wraparound porch. He arrived one morning in a blue steel open boat that held clean pine lumber, backlit by the sun that was just edging over the pointed tops of the fir trees so she couldn't make out his face. When she could—Kay introduced them down at the dock—she could tell he was getting to be an old lake man even in his thirties, where all the colors of flashy city places settle over time and what's left are the browns that make a man indistinguishable from the wilderness. His long hair was pulled back neatly into a ponytail; his skin had a bright kind of windburn. He wore a loose cotton shirt and a leather carpenter's belt. She found his lack of conversation unsettling, so as he pried up the old boards with more care than she would have thought they deserved, Jo went back to sweeping the plank flooring of what was called the Grand Parlor at Wendaban. She kept an eye on him through the front windows as he measured and cut and sanded and hammered.

Over a week, Luke the silent handyman finished the porch repair and went to work on the roof over the kitchen, where water damage blackened the logs. At lunchtime, he disappeared up the lake in his blue steel boat for an hour or so—"Eating his lunch?" Kay shrugged when Jo asked if she knew what he was doing—and the rest of them planned the gala fundraiser for what Jo hoped would become the Wendaban Center for Environmental Studies. She and Kay and Benoit, the prickly cook from Québec that Kay had found, and Minette, a summer resident who was better connected on the lake than the hydro lines, were discussing whether it was more environmentally friendly to string Chinese lanterns or stake torchières, when the first call came over the VHF radio.

"Cabin Girl, Cabin Girl, Cabin Girl," the strange high voice leaped into the room from the small box Luke had installed on the mail table in the corner, "this is Black Heart. Over."

Jo didn't recognize the caller's handle, but as she loped over to the microphone, she could see Kay frowning. "Black Heart, this is Cabin Girl. Over."

"Cabin Girl"—it was a strained falsetto, not male, not female, filling every syllable with a kind of calculated insanity Jo had never known existed—"tell them what you did to Christine."

TELL *them what you did to Christine.*

She couldn't tell them: she didn't know. After sixteen years, she still didn't know. Jo left the others sitting there and walked stiffly up the creaking stairs to her room—her old room on the second floor of Wendaban, the one she had for thirteen summers, on the sunset side of the lodge, next to the back stairs, where the logs sloped and her friend Christine, the nurse's girl, would sneak in laughing in her long white batiste nightgown and crawl under the covers with her. At twelve they rubbed their feet together for warmth even in July because the Temagami nights were chilly. At thirteen they made tiny braids in each other's hair and applied lipstick to each other's lips and Jo told her how the Hackett boy had kissed her, which was okay, she guessed, if you like kissing a fish. *Someday I'll show you how it's done,* Christine sat back, erasing some of Jo's lipstick with her pinkie—*oh, not on me, silly,* she was quick to say, *on the mirror.* Christine's hair was white with moonlight as she flung herself back down on the mattress. *I know because I used to follow my brother around before he went to live mostly with our dad.* Then she folded her hands across her little breasts and smiled a smile that had nothing to do with Jo and her eyes only seemed to be looking up at the sloping logs but Jo knew she was looking right at whatever the knowledge was, which meant it was for real.

Tell them what you did to Christine.

Black Heart.

Someone named Black Heart knew how Jo ended up dressed only in a red shirt she had never in her life seen, floating unconscious in an old Wendaban skiff in the darkest part of the shallows, where the bay curved away from the lodge and the reeds were high, the night Christine died. Someone named Black Heart was saying it wasn't an accident.

For three days the only calls for Cabin Girl came from cottagers wondering whether Wendaban was open for dinner business. Otherwise, the VHF was a source of weather, messages relayed to youth camps from anxious parents wondering whether Johnny was managing without his teddy, and someone named Little Dorrit who sounded like she was a hundred giving a fruit and vegetable wish list to the long-suffering Irish Stu who went into town on a regular basis.

The fundraiser was a month away, and in addition to the indispensable Minette, and Walter, the Tums-chewing Toronto lawyer, the planning circle now included Cheryl, an event planner, and Guy, the University of Toronto professor working on putting together a consortium for the Wendaban Center. Providing them all with beds and food for as long as they needed reminded Jo of the old Wendaban, when a tough orange tabby patrolled for mice, and chess and bridge were played nightly by hurricane lamps in the Grand Parlor. Luke still stayed apart, stripping away the bad shingles over the kitchen—the day it rained hard he came inside and replaced a leaky seal around the toilet in #10—and when Jo climbed the ladder high enough to offer him a tumbler of lemonade, he shook his head, "Thanks, no," and turned back to his work. For some reason, Luke was one of her failures.

Jo heard the boat just as the motor sputtered to a stop and she set down the framed enlargement of the famous photo of Wendaban in 1904 that she and Kay were mounting over the stone fireplace. It was a black-and-white shot that found its way into any pictorial history of Lake Temagami: an Ojibway woman stood far back on the path leading up to the porch of the fine, solid lodge with its rough-hewn posts, set back in a stand of old growth pine in that decade before World War I. There was a grand stasis to the picture Jo always liked: everything was straight and plentiful, then, the jobs, the money, the pleasures, the people. She went to the double front doors and peered through the screen.

A man had tied up a runabout and was standing on the main dock, his hands in his pockets, slowly looking around. Jo held up a hand to Benoit, who was griping to her in two languages about these paltry inexcusable framboises, and asked Kay to take a look. The man was wearing a white polo shirt and nylon khakis, and in the sun that wasn't quite high enough yet, his skin was the olive gold that certain blonds have who get to spend a lot of time outdoors. When he moved over to the lamppost where the main dock abutted the rocky shore, she could tell it was the Hackett boy, some sixteen years after the experimental wet kisses in the same spot.

Tom Hackett.

Someone from those few summers before Christine died, when loon chicks slid on and off their mothers' backs and mayflies rose by the thousands over the lake like soft weightless gold shavings in the twilight and she wore her frilly halter top and one pair of shorts she didn't change for weeks because she was too busy chasing spotted toads into the woods until she either caught them or she didn't, her belly brown and showing in all the days of those early summers, when Carl Verdyne played the mandolin and guests leaned, listening, nearby. Tom Hackett. As she got to him he dropped his sunglasses and she thought it strange she should be so happy to see someone who only ever followed her around, someone she wouldn't let join her when she went out fishing because all he had to recommend him as far as she could tell was what her grandfather called the Hackett fortune even though he had great hands with a fishing pole because old Will Stanley had taught him, too, just like Jo, and even then he had a frank crinkly smile which to the twelve-year-old Jo was only disturbing. "I heard you were back," he said to her now, scratching the side of his nose as she held out her arms—amazed to find him standing on her dock—as if to say, *well here you are.*

"CABIN Girl, Cabin Girl, Cabin Girl"—Jo spun to face the radio—"this is Black Heart. Over." She didn't move. It was late afternoon and Luke had gone for the day and Minette was in town at a fish fry and Tom Hackett had ferried Benoit to the landing to pick up the Wendaban mail in one of the battered green group mailboxes. "Cabin Girl, Cabin Girl, Cabin Girl, this is Black Heart. Over." It was the same high sexless voice, a concentrated malevolence that sounded like no one she knew. No one she ever knew. Jo grabbed the mike just as Kay came out of the kitchen.

Her thumb was twitching as it held down the button. "Black Heart, this is Cabin Girl. Over." She let the button go.

"Cabin Girl"—the voice went higher, slower—"I know how you killed Christine."

Jo felt herself flayed open. She looked down to make sure, crossing her quaking arms over her torso just to hold everything in, not understanding why there was no blood or organs. Her first thought was to turn off the radio and give Black Heart no more access to her, but the radio was her sole connection with the rest of the lake, the only way she'd learn about fires or medical emergencies—the way the lake was hearing the harassment of her by someone calling himself Black Heart. Kay stood at her side as she held down the button on the mike. "Temcot, Temcot, Temcot," Jo raised the radio operator at the Headquarters for the Cottagers Association, "this is Cabin Girl. Over."

"Cabin Girl, this is Temcot. Over."

"Get me the police, Andy. I want to report a crime."

Millie T. called her, then, a middle-aged lady who told her to give the bastard hell.

Bar None called her wondering who Christine was.

Bevel Boy, who turned out to be Luke, saying he'd come back if she wanted.

My Blue Haven called offering legal advice.

Irish Stu, who wanted to know if she needed anything in town.

And Windjammer—Tom Hackett, who said he'd meet her on the dock of Wendaban for another shot at it—just to make her laugh.

But the Ontario Provincial Police who came in their blue and white patrol boat and took a few desultory notes told her what she already knew: there was no way to figure out who it was, not as long as Black Heart stayed on the VHF radio. He could be anyone anywhere—all he needed was an antenna—on one of the thousand islands of Lake Temagami, or within range on the mainland—or on a boat. She listened while the OPP advised her to get rid of the VHF radio and install a telephone with caller ID, not telling them it would be a betrayal of her grandfather, and she felt her eyelids droop in pain as it occurred to her that maybe her whole presence on the lake was now just a betrayal of another sort. When the cops asked about the Christine mentioned in the harassing calls, she told them the truth: Christine was her summertime best friend—the daughter of the nurse at Wendaban—who died in a fall one night the summer they were both thirteen, and she heard about the death the next morning. The lurid parts that only shimmered shapeless in her memory, all sixteen years that followed the event, she left out—left out because a speck of corrosion was beginning in the part of her brain where fear resides, and it was making her wonder whether the torment by Black Heart was, after all, correct.

Back inside the lodge Jo stood without moving in the Grand Parlor, her body just a broken mobile of dry bones, while Kay brought out dinner plates. The simple act of eating anything set before her seemed like the only joy left in the world. "Cabin Girl, Cabin Girl, Cabin Girl"—at the sound of the voice Jo let out a sob—"this is Black Heart. What happened to the red shirt you wore the night you killed her?"

SHE was undecided about the effects of suffering. Did it close over her like some kind of carapace and keep her safe from all sharpened speech and damaging looks? Or did it make her into a cluster of unprotected dendrons, a bouquet of stripped filaments completely incapable of blocking sensation? Benoit's incisors clicked when he spoke. Luke rubbed his left thumb and ring finger together before he ate. Kay had a smell of wet ashes when she passed. They were all becoming more formal with each other, which she realized is what happens when pain fills the spaces between people. Black Heart wanted her to suffer, wanted her to pay, that much she knew. *What happened to the red shirt you wore the night you killed her?* She didn't know. Didn't know what had happened to it. Didn't know why it was important. She remembered waking up in the skiff in the middle of the night—only the dock lights showed her she was back at Wendaban, only the dock lights located her somewhere in a world where she had always found comfort—thirteen and wet and bruised and naked in a large red shirt. *What happened to the red shirt you wore the night*—She had stumbled out of the boat someone had tied to the old crooked dock in the shallows near the back of the property—without Christine, who must have rowed them back, left Jo there, and gone up to bed. The shirt was mystifying, but she staggered noiselessly up the back stairs and fell into her own room. In the morning came the news, and in her grief over Christine—and her failure to confess to the events of the night before—Jo never wondered again about the shirt. But Black Heart had seen her in the red shirt. Or Black Heart had dressed her in the red shirt. She felt sick at the thought. *What happened to the red shirt*—The question was about a piece of clothing; there was no question at all about the killing. Had Black Heart seen it happen? Had she and Christine not been alone, after all?

Cheryl the event planner took charge of the RSVPs as they came in and kept insisting on floral arrangements, which Jo refused. Guy and Walter pushed for a short video presentation on Wendaban and Lake Temagami—"You've got to give people something for their money, Jo," they argued—and she agreed. A leaky shower pan in #16 led to water damage downstairs in #4, so for the week before the fundraiser, Luke appeared to be in at least three places at once, looking grim when he told her he couldn't get his hands on a new shower pan that would fit and he was damn well going to have to put in extra hours if she wanted all the repairs done in time. Jo paid her bills, handled the workers, and—when no one was around—ripped through old trunks and stashed boxes, looking for a red shirt.

Overnight the temperature dropped and Jo was up, cold, before daybreak. She went into the kitchen to start a pot of coffee. Outside the rain was soft and metallic on the pines and the bald rock. In it she heard the sound of everything she ever knew that flowed or healed, and without putting on a rain jacket, she took her coffee outside and walked the shore of Wendaban to the old crooked dock, where she sat. Rain added to the mug. Rain added to her face. Night was leaving, and a fine white Temagami mist was slung low, she could tell, over the water. A fish jumped. Jo cried for her grandfather, who had loved her—who sorrowed for her as much as for the dead Christine the morning he came into her room with the sloping logs and told her Christine had met with violence, which was just how he put it. Met with violence. Jo had no voice. He had gone on to say the girl was found dead on the rocks at the bottom of Stone Maiden Cliff. Her clothes were gone. They didn't know yet whether she had been—interfered with—he said, frowning, and she wasn't sure what he meant. But there were signs of a struggle at the top, and he was so grateful his Jo had been home asleep all night. Then, as he patted her shoulder in a gruff sort of way, she wondered, stricken, who did this to Christine?

Who did this?

And then she knew: she did.

And she started to scream.

She screamed because she had pushed her friend off Stone Maiden Cliff. She screamed because she could never tell anybody. She had been home asleep—just like her grandfather said—all night. All night. Every night. Home. Home asleep. The bruises were under the covers. The red shirt was on the floor. She could never look at any of it. She could never tell. *No one will know,* Christine had said, only she was wrong. Black Heart knew. All along.

Jo curled up tight on her side on the old crooked dock, fanning her fingers against the wood, like an underwater dying thing. A black dock spider eased a leg joint up between the boards. They weren't hand to leg, the two of them, but they were close enough. The rain was stopping. She heard a boat coming, making its slow small way to the main dock at Wendaban. Blue. Luke's boat. She curled up tighter, not letting herself feel relieved he was putting in more hours to get the job done. Without moving her head from the boards, she could see in the thin new daylight more world than she ever needed—a water skimmer rowing silently across the lake surface, a duck quacking softly along the near shore, the misty lower branches of the far pines. She heard him come over and stop just a few feet away. He set down his toolbox without making much noise.

"How long have you been here?"

Jo fanned her fingers. Her lips felt strange. Unfamiliar. "All my life." All he could do was grunt. She raised her face. "Why don't you like me?"

"Why does it matter?"

"Things matter."

"Do they?"

"Of course they do."

"Things like a red shirt?"

She jerked away from him. "What do you know about it?"

"I heard the call."

"I could use a friend."

"I give you good work for a fair price." He picked up the toolbox and started to walk away. "We don't have to like each other."

IN the late afternoon the day before the fundraiser, Kay set out some cold cuts and store-bought potato salad—Benoit refused to handle them—for the helpers to grab a quick bite while they worked. At the crowded dock, boats were tied up to other boats, bumping softly against each other in the light wind. Minette was out front directing her teenaged son's friends on just where to hang the banner saying WELCOME TO WENDABAN in Ojibway that Kay had got some Bear Island children to paint. Tom Hackett was tying up the VHF radio with calls placed by the radio operator at Temcot HQ to the Ministry of Natural Resources, trying to get it straight whether torchières were considered open fires during a fire ban. Jo stood so long waiting for an answer that Luke took the bed linens out of her arms and went upstairs to make up the bed in #12. Minette's boy was trying to drive a torchière into the thin Temagami soil, poking it around for a better grip, then started bellowing out "John Henry." Jo stepped outside as his friends joined in, and for a moment everything was robust with youth and goodness. *Hammer be the death of me, Lord, Lord, hammer be the death of me.* The strong boys, the imperturbable clouds, Minette's laughter as the wind took the banner off one of its nails and it rippled sideways in a half-fall.

One of the old Wendaban skiffs was floating unmoored out in the wide bay, the result of too many lines being tied and untied, she guessed. She called Tom outside, who saw it right away, and they got into his runabout. "Let's go get the stray," he said, while she pushed them out from the other boats, and he backed up. She felt like they were running away—doing something daring going off together—the clouds, the boys, the fallen banner, even the voices getting more robust, *And he laid down his hammer and he died, Lord, Lord*—for those moments as he stood at the wheel and headed slowly toward the skiff, she believed in their own youth and goodness, and with no thought of the past she turned his face toward her and kissed Tom the golden Hackett boy who had, she was pleased to see, the good sense to shift into neutral while she did.

She liked it that he said nothing afterward and as they approached the skiff she took a boat pole to pull it alongside so she could grab the bowline. At first she thought it was a paint rag in the old rowboat, but she couldn't figure it out since no one had been using it. The hulls of the two boats were jostling as Tom kept the runabout in neutral. "We can just tow it—" he called to her, but she cried out and scrambled over the gunwales and into the skiff. There, laid out on the middle seat, was a very old red shirt.

* * *

HER head was coming off from a headache no amount of aspirin could reach. She slept badly, twitching in and out of sleep, and cried at the thought that the fundraiser for the Wendaban Center for Environmental Studies was going to find her pale and baggy-eyed and bedeviled. Yesterday she had wanted to load the skiff with rocks until it sank, bearing the red shirt to the bottom. But she folded the shirt instead and locked it inside the small steel safe in her grandfather's closet—just so it wouldn't disappear again. As she handled it, her fingers felt detached from her body.

By the time the guests started to arrive, she had changed into a yellow summer shift and managed to smile and pull off the handshakes, thankful that Tom Hackett and Guy eased into the void she couldn't help creating. Someone handed her a drink that was even paler than her face and she stood as straight as she could and listened to Tom Hackett tell an important dean from the University of Western Ontario that he was prospecting for diamonds in the province. And she listened to Guy tell a woman from the Toronto *Globe and Mail* that two of Wendaban's outbuildings would be converted into labs. And she listened to Benoit tell everyone that the tiramisu, if he must say so himself, was particularly excellent. Somewhere out back Kay and Luke—who had buttoned his top button and added a string tie for the occasion—were quietly hosing down a kitchen table they had dragged outside when the champagne punch bowl shattered.

Jo got through the video presentation without watching any of it. At ten-thirty Minette invited anyone who wanted to do wishing boats to come down to the dock. A few who were staying the night went upstairs, but Jo watched several others follow Minette, their way lighted by the Chinese lanterns Cheryl had driven all the way to North Bay to find that afternoon when they got the word from the ministry that the fire ban made torchières out of the question. Minette had unscrewed the dock lights and one by one the shadowy guests set out on the lake a flotilla of lighted candles fixed on cardboard squares, launched with silent wishes. In the windless night they were tiny flames adrift until the cardboard soaked through and they sank.

Jo watched them go from inside the double screen doors, while Guy, Tom Hackett, and the others were left looking at the architect's plans for renovating the outbuildings. "Cabin Girl, Cabin Girl, Cabin Girl—" *No, not now,* Jo pressed herself into the logs of the front wall, *not here*—the same awful voice—but she didn't have to answer and none of the guests would know she was Cabin Girl—

"Jo"—Tom Hackett moved toward her—"do you want me to get it this time?"

She shook her head as people turned to look at her.

"Cabin Girl," Black Heart—who knew she was listening, knew he didn't have to raise her again, knew formalities meant nothing when the accusation was murder—went on in that high, malevolent voice to a room that was completely silent, "tell them what you did with her clothes after you killed Christine." Jo started up the stairs as she heard Tom explain to the others that Jo had been the victim of a wicked joke. She nearly laughed at how reduced it all sounded, then found herself listening almost like a normal person to the woman reporter coming toward her who was wondering what Jo wanted her to do with the laundry in the bathroom of room #12. Jo said she'd take care of it.

She walked through #12 to the bathroom, and swung open the door. Submerged in the tub half full of water was a white sleeveless top and green shorts. She stared at them for just a second before she shrieked, seeing Christine peel them off at the top of the diving cliff. Luke was first into the room. "What the hell—?"

Jo stumbled out of the bathroom. "It's a mouse."

"It's not a mouse."

"Leave me alone."

"What happened?" He looked into the bathroom.

She saw it all. "You were in here today."

"So?"

"You made up the bed."

"So?"

"Who are you?" she hissed.

"Why does it matter?"

She yelled at him to get out—get out for good—and it was Kay who put her to bed in her old childhood room down at the sunset side of the lodge where the logs sloped and girls cuddled safe under the covers for years and years until they were very old women together. She knew it was Kay who kept the others out—she heard her arguing out in the hall with Tom Hackett and Minette—and little by little as the lodge grew quiet, she didn't know who had decided to stay overnight with the crazy screaming murdering lodgekeeper and who had gone, instead, to the mainland on a wild night ride with Ellroy the tattooed cabby. She felt an isolation she could never repair as long as she stayed at Wendaban, but whether she died in her sleep or lived to leave the lake forever was a matter of complete indifference as she pulled the covers over her head and she dreamed once again of Christine.

IN the morning she rowed the old skiff the two miles to Stone Maiden Cliff, in a bay near the opening to the North Arm. Kay watched her go from the edge of the main dock. The sun was strong and the clouds were mountainous, cut sharply into the sky as the wind kicked up. At the base of the diving cliff she tied up to a stringy overhanging cedar and listened to the boat bang rhythmically against the small rocks as she started the steep climb. It was harder at thirty than it was at thirteen. Her feet slid back, her hands could hardly pull her up, she weighed more. She made it to the top of the twenty-foot cliff and rolled in the brown fallen pine needles, the way they always did, for flavor, Christine said.

It had been a quick, quiet row that night, sometime close to midnight when they were not supposed to be out. But it was July and they knew the lake well and they wanted to swim naked by starlight. They tied up out of the wind and scrambled to the top and lay there on their backs holding hands for the longest time. The moon was up, so the stars were fainter, but Christine pointed out Perseus. Then they stood up and stripped quickly, Christine peeling the white sleeveless top and green shorts, then kicking them behind her. At the edge they looked down at the cliff, the way it sloped in one place into a slanting shelf, the way a red pine sapling was growing bright and hopeless right out of the rock. They jumped together the first time, the way they always did, and crawled like naked dripping white monkeys back to the top. It was exhilarating, slamming into the water they could barely see in the black Temagami night. They clung to the sheer vertical face of the cliff as they treaded water, the little waves drawing them, pushing them, the rock so strangely warm still against their skin. They sputtered and groaned and laughed from the cold.

Then at the top Jo stood shivering and stamping her feet with a sudden chill, her arms tight across her chest. And in the next moment Christine changed their lives forever by stepping in close and putting her arms around Jo, who froze. Christine kissed her first just next to her mouth, then on her mouth, whispering, *No one will know.* And what happened next was a struggle that made her sick the minute it lasted—Christine saying her name over and over—Jo first trying to get out with a smile and ripping her brain apart to make sense of losing her friend forever while she had never held her closer—the soft kisses, a hand on her waist, the powerful foreignness of the flesh next to hers—and then she kicked—and then she pushed, oh yes, she pushed—and the scream was a gulp, but Jo was pulled over, too, aware all at once that she was stopped by the sapling and her head slammed into the rock, and the hands that slid down to her ankles dropped away and a terrible weight was gone for good.

Sixteen years later she lay crying quietly on her back at the top of Stone Maiden Cliff and thought about all the campers and canoe trippers and lovers who had been here diving since that night. She tried telling herself she had been thirteen and that tenderness is only something you can learn when you've been afoot in the world long enough to see how bleak all things are without it. Her name would cease to be a good name if she stayed in Temagami because Black Heart would see to it. Suffering, he was telling her, wasn't in recollection—it was in exile. Early that morning she had found her grandfather's old personnel files in a storeroom near the back of the lodge. The nurse, Aimée Delacroix, Wendaban employee for two years until her daughter died and she left Temagami, was divorced with one son—Jean-Luc Delacroix, four years older than Christine—"Bright young man, good with his hands," her grandfather had written in the margin. "Can we use him somehow?"

HERE *is how the story begins: night fishing with old Will Stanley some sixteen years ago. He begged the old man to take him out. Night fishing: flashlight when you need it, cigars for warmth and satisfaction, navigating by the moon, whizzing off the boat, even, now and then, a fish. They were anchored off the far side of Stone Maiden Cliff when the girls went over. The boy, who was in the bow of the boat, saw it happen. Will Stanley muttered* shit *a couple* *of times and quickly started the motor. He and the boy nearly fell out of the boat to get to the one lying white and broken in the shallows.* This one's dead, *Will Stanley said to the boy who was trying to keep the discovery, the sight of all that death and nakedness, down in his stomach.* Leave her. *A loon called somewhere close by, and the boy jumped.* Leave her?

She'll be found in the morning and you're not even supposed to be here and I'm an old Indian standing here with two naked white girls and I only have just so much explanation in me, boy. *Will Stanley scrambled up the side of the cliff to the sapling on the shelf, where the other girl was knocked out, and managed to hand her down to the boy, who didn't know where to grab her. She was banged up and knocked out but he grabbed her around the ribs since it made some sense and yielded him a quick feel that was goddamn the least she owed him after what he had just seen—*

WILL *Stanley dressed her in his red shirt and set her carefully in the Wendaban skiff. Then he pulled the dead girl up farther on the rocks out of a kind of decency, the boy thought, and said,* I'll row this one back and leave her out of sight. You give me half an hour and come after me, and I'll get you home as soon as I can. *The boy watched him row away toward Wendaban, bare-chested, an old man with just so much explanation in him, and he grew darker and more indistinct as he went. When he was out of sight, the boy sat near the dead girl until he couldn't take it any longer and climbed shivering to the top of the cliff to collect the clothing. It wasn't until later that he could see—with no more explanation in him than the old man—there was no easy way to return the clothing of the dead.*

It has taken two days since he set the ax next to the furnace to feel satisfied with the letter he wrote confessing to the events of four years ago, and the contents of the other envelope, a deed addressed to Cabin Girl. It is 2 A.M. *and sleeping upstairs is a woman named Diane he found and married just after he drove Jo Verdyne forever from the lake and then never answered any of her calls. Overhead is a single light, seventy-five watts, enough to work afterward with the razor.* A good light is everything, *Will Stanley used to say without much more in the way of explanation. But to Will Stanley, everything was everything.* A good net is everything, boy, *he'd say. And other times,* A good meal is everything. *But surely a good ax is something, Will Stanley? And a good razor?*

No one answers.

If he had a wishing boat, he would light the candle and launch it from the main dock of Wendaban, many hours away from this house in Nashville that has no meaning for him, and wish that he had never bought the Wendaban property through a holding company when Jo Verdyne put it up for sale and then never brought the wrecking ball in by barge. Much of the lodge had to be dismantled—dismembered, someone called it that day, and that seemed closer to the truth—and the very deep wrongness of it all didn't strike him until sometime after the rubble had been cleared away. He stood bewildered that he didn't feel more pleasure in getting what he had worked toward for months. And when the drilling yielded nothing, after all—not so much as a speck of kimberlite—he thought for the first time in his life that maybe he was a fool.

No, not a fool, exactly, because he had always been a clever man. No one, for instance, the night of the fundraiser at Wendaban, had seen him slipping his hand under the table where the VHF radio stood and detaching the Walkman he had Velcroed in place. By then Jo was shrieking in the upstairs bathroom and everyone was rushing over to the stairs. Black Heart's last message to Cabin Girl had been prerecorded and was just about as fine an alibi as a man could want.

He picks up the Sears Craftsman ax that someone named Jimmy sold him and starts up the basement steps. It is time to gather in those parts of him that will suffer when the letter is found. If he had a dog, he would have to gather it in for it would be the dog part of him that would remember forever what he had done. Now he will gather in the wife part of him that will only feel shame, but the blunt end of the ax is a good gatherer. And afterward the razor will draw a quick hard line below his chin and say there will be no more lies or false smiles from everything above this line. Do good for the people, when you grow to a man, you hear? *Will Stanley told him softly from the darkened stern of the boat as they fished quietly off the far side of Stone Maiden Cliff.* I will, I promise, *the boy said, but he stopped baiting his hook as the wind edged them closer to the front of the diving cliff and he looked up and saw something remarkable. Two naked girls kissing. He knew them. Their heads and arms and hips moved in the starlight that excluded him for all time.* You got the money, Tom, boy, but you also got a good heart. And a good heart is everything—

ONE OF US

Tom Savage

"AREN'T you ready *yet*?!" she cried as she burst into the bedroom. "We're supposed to be there at seven, and it's already six-thirty. I swear, you've been lying there for *hours*! What have you been doing all this time?"

"Thinking. I'm not really looking forward to this."

She rolled her eyes and emitted a long, pained sigh.

"Of course not," she muttered, dropping onto the stool before the vanity table and inspecting her face in the mirror. "I suspect you'll be very uncomfortable, which is exactly what you deserve."

"You're still mad at me, aren't you?"

She swiveled on the stool to look at her husband, who had not risen from the bed.

"You're *so* quick, Robert!" she hissed. "Nothing gets by you! Now, get up and get dressed, for heaven's sake. I've even laid out your dinner clothes on the chair over there. I swear! Lying there, stark naked. It's positively indecent!"

"You used to think it was sexy."

She picked up the lip gloss from the table and began expertly painting her already perfect lips.

"That," she sighed, "was before all *this*."

"Oh, boy. Here we go again."

She glanced at his reflection in the mirror. He was sprawled on his back, one arm flung over his face as if to shield his eyes. Poor dear, she thought. He always does that when he can't confront something, just like a little boy. Well, too bad!

"Look," she said in that kindergarten teacher tone of voice that had always infuriated him, "I think I'm being very good about this. I should *kill* Valerie! Most women would, but not I. Oh, no, my dear, not I! I'm going to her house for dinner, of all things. Now, if that isn't civilized, I don't know what is. It's *more* than civilized. It's positively Noël Coward!"

"We don't have to go, you know."

She picked up her silver-plated hairbrush, contemplated throwing it at him, and thought better of it. Instead, she ran it through her sparkling gold pageboy.

"Oh, you'd love that, wouldn't you, Mr. Casper Milquetoast!" she said. "Forty-six years old, and you're still afraid of embarrassing scenes. Well, I'm not. In fact, I'm rather looking forward to it."

She was playing with him now, just to see how he'd respond. She was not disappointed.

"What do you have in mind? What are you planning?"

"Oh, nothing," she sang, applying eyeliner to her already painted lids. She dropped the pencil and picked up the mascara. "After all, Valerie isn't aware that I know anything about the two of you."

A horrible thought occurred to her then. She whirled around to face him.

"*Is* she, Robert?" she demanded.

"No. I didn't tell her."

She turned back to the mirror.

"Well, then," she said, "I shall appear to be as I have always been. She's my best friend, after all. I shall be perfectly charming to her and that grotesque she calls a husband."

Oops, she thought, I've gone too far. Now he's angry. She cringed slightly, waiting to see if he would actually jump up from the bed and come over to confront her.

He didn't. "You leave Frank out of this. He has nothing to do with it."

She relaxed and raised a penciled brow.

"He has nothing to do with *her*, apparently," she observed. "That must be why she finds it necessary to seduce other people's husbands."

She inspected the staggering array of perfume bottles and atomizers spread out before her, wondering for the thousandth time why it was that men caught in this classic, disgusting situation never felt compelled to defend themselves or their paramours, but always stood by their male friends. Even—and this was the most bizarre aberration of men—when the male friend in question was the very one they were cuckolding. What *is* it about them, she asked herself, that makes them place such ridiculous emphasis on each other's virtues? Bonding, she supposed: that exclusive club to which every male on earth automatically belongs, of which every female on earth knows so little. Shrugging her shoulders in superior exasperation, she selected tonight's scent, Norell, and dabbed it behind her ears and on her wrists.

Of course, he *would* have a comment about that. "You just did that a little while ago. This place reeks of the stuff! Why are you putting on more perfume?"

She did not deign to answer. Women, she mused, have an exclusive club, too. *Ha!*

She heard a long, low hiss from the room behind her. For

a moment she thought it might be Robert's editorial comment on the subject of women's rituals. Then she heard the faint clanking and realized with satisfaction that it was only the radiator in the corner. The heat was on: good. The weather reports had predicted snow.

Smiling her most languorous, most irritating smile, she stood up and went over to the walk-in closet. She reached up to the top shelf and selected the right purse to go with her sequined dress. Then she dug swiftly into the bag, just to make sure. Yes, the little pearl-handled revolver was there. She checked the chamber: two bullets left. That would be sufficient. Snapping the bag shut, she stepped out into the room.

Her husband had not moved.

"Oh, *do* get up, Robert!" she cried. Walking over to the chair in the corner, she scooped up his clothes and threw them at him. "I promise, no scenes."

He is so stupid, she thought. He always believes what I say. There'll be a scene, all right. Oh, *boy,* will there be a scene! I can't wait to see Valerie's face when she sees the gun. That will wipe away her self-satisfied smirk! That Valerie. Ever since we were girls, she's had this neurotic need to best me, to win at whatever game it is she's playing. A bigger debut, a bigger wedding, a richer husband. And now this. *My* husband. God, if it weren't so tacky, it would be funny. . . .

She took a long, deep breath, steadying herself. When she spoke again, she was once more in complete control. "You have exactly five minutes in which to get dressed. We are then leaving. I called the car service, and our usual driver, Nicholas, will be waiting outside. We will arrive at Valerie's at seven, in time for cocktails. We will be perfectly dressed and perfectly mannered. Valerie will not suspect that anything is wrong. *Do* you understand?"

Without waiting for a reply, she walked into the marbled

bathroom and shut the door. Turning on both faucets to cover her sounds, she reached into the medicine cabinet and selected a little bottle of pills. She'd already taken two in the last three hours. Oh, well, where was the harm? She placed two more in her mouth and washed them down. She gazed at her immaculate reflection in the bathroom mirror as the warm surge of beautiful energy flooded through her.

It had been three hours since he told her.

He hadn't beaten about the bush, either. He'd simply told her, without preamble and without apology. Of course, there had been other women in the past, years ago, and she'd known about them. Brief, unimportant flings with a client and one of his secretaries and some actress or other. Nothing really threatening. She had looked the other way, accepted the humiliation in acquiescent silence.

Then, three hours ago, he'd come home early from his brokerage firm, fixed himself a drink, taken a quick shower and returned to the bedroom, at which time he'd simply announced to her that he and Valerie were in love. That they'd been carrying on in secret for the better part of four years. That he wanted a divorce. . . .

At first she'd merely stared at him, incredulous, trying to take it in. Then she'd burst into laughter. After that brief fit of hysteria, she'd—well, she couldn't remember it all now, but she'd taken charge of the situation in a remarkably short period of time. Then, as ever, she'd immediately begun to plan her defense strategy.

It was amazing, really, how capable she could be when the chips were down. She'd always been dependent on others for her safety, for her happiness; first her mother and father, then Robert. Always rich, always indulged and protected. She'd never in her life been alone, and she'd often wondered what she would do, how she would behave, if she were ever faced with the prospect of loneliness.

She'd staved it off thus far in the only way she knew: she

had been a perfect wife. She had made this house their home, fed him and tended to his needs, entertained countless clients and associates. Parties, weekends, committees, charity functions. Always beautiful, always dutiful, always available to him.

She'd borne him a son, but the baby had not survived. It was the only real blot on the otherwise pristine landscape of their marriage. That ordeal had brought the two of them closer together, or so she'd believed. He'd stayed by her in the hospital and all through the long months in the clinic afterward, whispering soothing encouragements. It had been his finest hour, as far as she was concerned. Now, all these years later, she still felt the gratitude. It wasn't until after that, after she was finally home and everyone was saying how much better she looked, that the business with the other women had begun.

They'd seen it all, she supposed, the two of them. They'd been through happiness and tragedy and success and all the rest of it. Twenty years. Twenty years, and never once the threat of being on her own.

Until now.

The bathroom mirror reflected her grim determination. Desperate times, she thought: desperate measures. The little gun she'd bought two years ago. Ironic, she thought now. She'd bought the gun after Valerie had been mugged, in case of robbers or rapists on the mean city streets or here in her home. If it hadn't been for Valerie, she wouldn't even own the damn thing!

Valerie. Her closest, oldest, most trusted friend. Her only friend, really. She'd known Valerie for most of her life, ever since that first day of junior high school. The two of them had gossiped and dreamed and plotted the courses of their lives. My God, she realized now, the ironies! It was I, so happy in my own marriage, who had introduced Valerie to Frank! I have always loved her, always been there for her.

And now . . .

The scenario was clear in her mind. She would walk into Valerie's house and smile and kiss her cheek. Then she would calmly pull the gun from her purse. Aim it at Valerie, right there in front of everybody. Then, when her erstwhile best friend screamed or laughed or whatever, she'd—

She'd what? Pull the trigger? Shoot Valerie? *Kill* her?

She shut her eyes tightly, trying to imagine the moment. Valerie, eyes wide with shock, with the sudden, surprising pain, sinking slowly to the floor, her pale hand reaching up toward the little spot of blood on her breast. Frank, his bored, patrician features for once animated, his slack, girlish lips moving in speechless disbelief. The Hansons, the ugly congressman and his uglier wife—they were going to be there, weren't they? Probably: Frank and Valerie were always sucking up to people they imagined to be powerful.

Mrs. Hanson would faint, of course. And then there would be the awful, unnatural silence, as they took the gun from her hand and she sank into a chair. She would stare down at the intricate blue and red pattern of Valerie's Oriental carpet, not daring to look up to meet everyone's anguished, accusing gaze. Then rough hands would lift her up, and there would be cold steel on her wrists, and a long ride in the backseat of an unfamiliar car. Someone—a woman, presumably—would lead her down a long white corridor to a barred, impersonal room, to sit again for hours on a cold, hard bench in her sequins and fur, surrounded by such women as she had only seen in films and on television. And all the while Robert would be—

Would be where? What would he be doing? What would he be thinking? She couldn't form a clear picture of that in her mind because . . . because . . .

Because it wasn't going to happen.

At that moment, as she stood there in the bathroom, she was possessed of a sudden inspiration. The obvious solution to her dilemma took her completely by surprise. Her lacquered nails gripped the cool porcelain edge of the sink to keep her from losing her balance, so great was her relief.

Robert can stop me, she thought.

He can, if he wants to. If he loves me. I'll take out the gun and aim it at Valerie, but I won't fire. Not yet. I'll give him the option. If he reaches out and takes the gun away from me, that will be the end of it. I'll scream and cry and be hysterical, and he'll never do this again. Not *ever.* He'll realize how much I love him.

And I do love him, she thought. Even now, after this. Oh, God, I love him so much. . . .

The faint, faraway sound reached her through the jumble of her thoughts. She paused, inclining her head toward the connecting door. It was difficult to make out the sound over the rushing of the water in the sink. At first she didn't recognize what it was: it had been so long. Then, when she placed it, a warm, breathless tingle of hope suffused her.

Well, for heaven's sake, she thought. He's *whistling!* He hasn't done that since—what is that tune? Of course: "Dancing in the Dark." Our song. They played it at our wedding. . . .

In her mind's eye, she saw him getting up from the bed and slowly, perhaps reluctantly, stepping into his clothes. Shorts, trousers, shirt. Fumbling with studs and cufflinks. Inhaling deeply for the cummerbund. Moving to the mirror to knot the tie. Running his long, gentle fingers through his full, wavy brown hair. Finally, a splash of Grey Flannel from the bottle he would find among her bottles on the vanity table. She had always loved watching him get dressed.

Damn Valerie! Damn that woman to hell!

The tears in her eyes surprised her. She stared in horror at her face in the mirror. Oh, no, she thought. I mustn't lose it now. I have to be completely in control. I will go through with this, and I will look sensational doing it. Otherwise, the gesture is meaningless. I'm not going to lose him—not to her, at any rate. I'll kill her first. I'll kill *him* first!

She froze. Now, why would such a thought occur to me, she wondered, at this of all times? What a horrible thing to be thinking about. Valerie, yes: I can aim a gun at her, even fire it. But him? Robert? My *husband*? I've got to pull myself together. . . .

She reached for a tissue and dabbed at her eyes. Thank God for waterproof makeup, she thought. She placed the pill bottle in her bag and turned off the faucets. Then she took another deep breath and smiled.

Everything's going to be all right, she told herself. He'll be there. He'll stop me. But if he doesn't stop me, I'll kill her. I swear to God I will.

She listened. The whistling had stopped now. She lifted her chin, picked up her bag, and walked out into the bedroom.

"You're ready at last," she said, smiling. "Good. Fix your tie, Robert, you look like the hired help. There. Now, which coat should I wear? The mink or the chinchilla?"

"What does it matter? You'll look gorgeous in either of them."

That pleased her. "Do you really think so? What a lovely thing to say. You can be a darling. When you're not being a bastard, that is. The chinchilla, I think. White fur and silver sequins. Yes. . . ."

She entered the closet and took the coat from its hanger. The warm, soft fur enveloped her, caressing her naked arms, giving her strength. She could do this now. She was dressed for it. She found Robert's warmest coat and rummaged on the lower shelf for his scarf and gloves.

"You'd better wear these tonight," she told him, dropping them on the chair next to the bed. "It's freezing outside. I don't want you catching a cold."

She allowed him time to put on the coat, returning to the vanity table for one more dab of Norell, one more quick check in the glass. Yes, she thought, perfect. Then she switched off the bedroom light and headed for the stairs.

"Of course," she said over her shoulder as she descended, "I could shoot Valerie with the gun in my purse."

"Don't be ridiculous. You haven't got a gun."

She laughed. "Of course not, darling. But I might just make a scene."

"You said you wouldn't." She noted the warning tone.

"I'm a woman, darling," she replied. "We're allowed to change our minds."

When she reached the bottom of the stairs, she turned and went into the living room. She crossed over to the bar, selected two tiny crystal glasses, and filled them with his favorite sherry.

"Before we go," she said, "a toast. Do you realize that next month is our twentieth anniversary?"

"Of course."

"Well, think about it," she drawled, and raised her glass. "Happier days, Robert."

"Yes. Happier days."

She drained her glass, licked her lips, and looked out through the big, velvet-curtained front windows. It was already dark outside, dark and cold. In the light from the street lamp in front of their townhouse, the first white flakes drifted softly down onto the bare black branches of the trees in the little park directly across the street.

" *'The birds have eaten the breadcrumbs,'* " she whispered, remembering the fairy tale her mother had always read to her when she was little. " *'We are lost in this wood.'* "

With a rueful smile, she placed the two glasses on the coffee table for the housekeeper to find in the morning.

"Neat, as always." His wry tone was unmistakable.

"Yes," she said lightly, ignoring the tone. "I'm a good

wife. I really am. I'm more than you deserve."

"You try anything tonight and I'll stop you."

She stared. "Will you? Will you really?" She said it as softly, as hopefully, as she could. This was no time for him to suspect sarcasm.

"Yes, I will. I won't let you hurt Valerie, and I won't let you disgrace yourself."

She pulled on her kid gloves, picked up her heavy bag, and swept out of the room. Crossing the foyer, she hammered the last nail into place. "I won't disgrace myself, but I *might* hurt Valerie."

"You will not. I'll stop you."

She threw open the front door and turned.

"One of us will have the upper hand," she said. "But *only* one of us."

Then she smiled. It's going to be all right, she thought. I know it is. I won't have to go through with it. I won't have to shoot Valerie. I can see it in his eyes, I could hear it in his whistling. When I feel his hand on mine, lowering the gun, I won't fire. He'll stop me. He will he will he *will*. . . .

She turned and looked down into the street.

"We're in luck, darling," she cried, ignoring the fresh tears that formed in the corners of her eyes and seemed to crystallize immediately in the brisk winter air. "There's the car. We'll be right on time. Now, smile and take my arm. That's right. We're the beautiful people, Robert. The perfect couple. Come, my cavalier, escort me to our carriage."

The back door of the limousine stood open, and the chauffeur waited beside it, smiling at her as she arrived at the bottom of the steps.

"Good evening, ma'am," he said, reaching out to take her extended arm and help her into the car. His gaze moved past her, up to the doorway of the house behind her, then back. "Won't your husband be joining us this evening?"

She stared at the driver as the frigid wind blew snowflakes in her hot, flushed face, shocking her senses.

"My—my husband?" she whispered. She turned to look at the empty space beside her. "Robert . . . ?"

It all came rushing back to her at that moment, and she swayed and nearly fell. The voice. *Bang!* The whistling. *Bang!* The dinner jacket laid out with such care, then tossed so carelessly at her husband on the bed. *Bang!* His winter coat, scarf, and gloves. *Bang!* Two sherry glasses on the coffee table, only one of them empty. The pearl-handled revolver, four shots fired, two bullets left. . . .

"Robert," she whispered again.

The driver was holding her elbow firmly now, squeezing it. "My name is Nicholas, ma'am. Are you all right?"

Then she drew herself up. She turned to the young man and smiled, the gracious smile born of a gracious life.

"I'm quite all right, Nicholas," she said, eyes clear, voice steady, "but my husband is not with me. He's—lying down. There's just one of us tonight."

He nodded and handed her into the limousine, and the door beside her slammed shut with a loud, final resonance. Nicholas got in front, and the car glided smoothly forward. She relaxed back in the seat, holding the purse with its heavy contents close against her, revising her scenario. Valerie. . . .

Two bullets left. . . .

She began to laugh softly to herself, as softly as birds steal breadcrumbs from a forest path, obscuring the way home.

A Trail of Mirrors

Tracy Knight

"**Certainty** is the mind's salve, quelling life's pervasive anxiety," Dr. Maxwell Deguise wrote in his bestselling book *Embrace Stress Like a Lover.* "Regrettably, it is also altogether illusory."

When the graves came into view, Dr. Maxwell Deguise hoisted a trembling index finger. "There are crystalline moments when one must boldly act in order to successfully revise one's life story . . ." he croaked, quoting from his *Paths to Editing Your Life*, ". . . and one must always—*always*!—design and pursue goals that forcefully embody the central theme of one's existential *magnum opus*."

It was astounding enough to hear an elderly psychologist with failing mental faculties quoting himself so precisely, especially since I'd come to suspect that recently, he might have begun having difficulty remembering to consistently don his underwear *before* his pants. What made this moment even eerier was that, as he quoted those lines, we—seventy-eight-year-old Dr. Maxwell Deguise and I, Dr. Elliot Albert, his colleague, biographer, and trustworthy caretaker of ten years—were lying on our bellies in the moist grass outside the Konner County Veterinary Clinic, noses pressed against the grimy basement window as we peered at rows of at least twenty tiny graves uniformly spaced across the sodden floor.

Other than an indolent midnight breeze, only a chorus of crickets and frogs kept us company. The mercury vapor pole light outside the clinic rendered Max's face and bald pate a chalky purple. I marveled at how his appearance had changed during the decade I'd known him. Once he'd looked like a leviathan among his fellow men, standing straight and tall. Now, he resembled nothing more than a melting statue of a gnome.

I sniffed the night air, and I swore I smelled madness coming off him in sour, sultry layers.

I turned toward him and whispered, "I'm not sure it's a good idea for us to be here."

He *harumphed* like he was going to choke up something thick and bold, then raised his eyebrows, twin tangled nests that flitted stiffly in the dim light. "Elliot, with the data before our eyes, there can be no question about the direction I must travel." Then he began quoting himself again, this time from his bestseller *Suturing Life's Open Wounds:* " 'Our perception is all. It, more than biology or instrumental conditioning or cognitive schema, determines our behavior. We must ensure, however, that the map we draw of life as we live it is not mistaken for the territory itself.' You see? With these data, I know my territory, Elliot. It's as clear as a sunrise. Now it's just a matter of dispatching justice in a decisive, final fashion. It's time, my friend, to write the end of this particular story."

It was at that very moment I knew for certain that my world-renowned mentor was intent on murdering a veterinarian.

How to explain a psychological transformation such as

the one I witnessed in Dr. Maxwell Deguise, a metamorphosis from kindly, brilliant psychologist to tongue-lolling assassin?

His transmutation, I was certain, began only ten hours earlier . . .

"I WAS seventeen years old. My initial meeting with Dr. Maxwell Deguise after a sold-out lecture at Coe College evermore molded my future. Perhaps noticing the openness and empathy I'd brought to our encounter, he soon exposed his soul to me as perhaps he had to no one before. He described the tragic loss of his wife to cancer only three months before, as well as the deaths of their four beloved cats over a two-year period, the last of which had succumbed to diabetes a mere week before I introduced myself to him.

"He was lost, alone in the world. He needed me.

"Though at the time I didn't know it, Dr. Deguise was to become my mentor, and I his surrogate son. He graciously paid for my doctoral education and then took me under his wing for my post-doc internship, eventually making me a full partner, intending to pass along his wisdom and, eventually, his practice . . ."

"So? What do you think of it?" I asked, resting the typed draft of *A Trail of Mirrors* in my lap. "It's just a section of my Introduction. I figured since I'm nearing the end of the manuscript, I'd give the opening a try."

Max was leaning back in his chair, gazing at the ceiling as though life's secrets were darting about in the corners of the room. "Why, I think that's fine, Elliot, just fine," he said in his calm, even voice, scratching his bald head as though he were subjugating a rash.

I smiled and sat a little taller in my chair. "That's great to hear. I've never written a book before, much less a biography. Do you think it's okay that I bring myself into the story and mention that personal stuff? After all, this is *your* story."

He sat bolt upright and pointed his rheumy eyes my direction. "Aha, you *are* part of my story, a central part, my boy. And I think the more that personal facets of my life are revealed, the more readers will understand my career and the fortunate path it's taken."

I cleared my throat and pressed a finger against my lips, uncertain whether or not this was the appropriate moment to bring up the Candy Lorber case.

After a few seconds of reflection, I resolved to forge ahead.

His eyes had become momentarily unfocused, so I tapped my foot sharply against the floor to secure his attention before proceeding.

"Max, I'm sorry but . . . well, we need to have a section about Candy Lorber in the manuscript. It can be brief."

His eyes widened. "For heaven's sake, why?"

I shrugged. "Omitting it would rob readers of an important, instructive drama in your career. Anyway, most of them probably read about the case in the *National Enquirer* or the *Star*."

"But that was thirteen years ago." His face rumpled like a washcloth.

"Doesn't matter," I said. "People already know about it and I'm sure that if we don't address it, the readers—not to mention the critics—will only focus upon what's *missing* in your story, not what's there."

He grunted, then jiggled his hand as if preparing to shoo an oncoming gnat. "You know, Elliot, I believe it was Jung who once said that many people come to therapy not to eliminate their neurosis, but to *perfect* it. Such was the case of Candy Lorber."

I pulled my legal pad to the top of the stack and prepared to take notes.

He paused briefly, then said, "I'm convinced that far from

coming to me for assistance in casting out her personal demons, she ultimately came to therapy in order to make a horrendous personal statement against all therapy, all therapists. She was the most sadly hateful and pathological human being I've ever encountered. Beyond that, I'm saying nothing. If that doesn't satisfy the readers and critics, well, to Hades with them."

I raised my hand. "Hold on, just a second. Let me look through my other notes."

I flipped through several sheets and began reading.

CANDY Lorber was forty-seven years old, twice divorced, 350 pounds, and seemed to carry the full weight of the world on her bowed shoulders. Her graying, stringy hair hung down, partially obscuring her face. She wept throughout the first hour of her therapy with Dr. Deguise, and was so distraught that he remained with her, though her fifty-minute session was clearly over.

"I don't want to live," she wailed, eyes streaming tears. "Don't you understand?"

"I don't believe you," Dr. Deguise replied, his voice as flat as the prairie.

She reached into her purse and pulled out a straight razor, flicked it open.

Then, with Dr. Deguise watching impassively, Candy Lorber carefully drew the razor across one wrist, then the other.

She dropped the razor as blood began slowly dripping onto her shoes and pooling on the carpet.

Dr. Deguise said nothing. Not a word.

Facial features stretched like a balloon ready to burst, she said, "I just want to walk out of here. There's a blizzard outside. I just want to walk and bleed until I'm no more. Until I die. Unless you can help me."

"Can you find your way out?" Dr. Deguise said. Then he got up and left the room.

Just like that.

Candy Lorber remained seated for a few harrowing moments. Then, overtaken by despair and abandonment, she walked out of the office.

She trudged through a blinding snowstorm, came upon a nearby community college, pulled out a pistol she'd hidden in her purse that night, and shot three students and four security guards before police gunned her down.

She lived for three days before dying . . .

MAX interrupted, "Can't you examine your notes later? Ask me something else. Is that all you're wanting to talk about? That unfortunate Lorber woman?"

"No, one other thing," I said, laying the stack of notes and typewritten pages at my feet, then grabbing a nearby file. "I had a client yesterday I wanted to ask you about. Not for the book; just a brief consultation, if you don't mind."

He brightened. Nothing innervated him more than a challenge to unravel a clinical mystery.

I opened the file folder and said, "I have a new client who's a veterinarian, fifty-three years old, married. Over the past several years he's developed the most unfortunate and severe compulsion I've encountered since joining the practice." I paused, then continued slowly enough for him to construct the images in his mind. "He tortures animals—cats, specifically—that are left in his care, and then buries them in tiny graves in his clinic's basement. He tells the owners that they died unexpectedly. He can't stop himself, as hard as he tries. He's lost count of how many cats he's tortured to death. Until psychotherapy can help him, what can I do, ethically? I can't just sit back and listen anymore."

"Who is this vet?"

"Dr. Randall Jones."

Abrupt tears shimmered in his eyes. "Elliot, he was *my* vet. He's the one who—"

I clapped my hand over my mouth. "Oh, my God. He took care of your cats?"

Leaning his forehead against his hand, he said, "So that's why they all died. All of them. Excuse me a moment, son."

He pulled a handkerchief from his front pocket and wiped each eye in hasty, flicking succession.

I reached over and patted his hand. "I'm sorry, Max. I'm sorry to hit you with this. But really, I'm stumped. What can I do?"

"Call the authorities," he said with a flap of his hand.

I shook my head. "I can't. Violation of confidentiality. He hasn't threatened himself or others."

He sighed. "Then persuade him to turn himself in."

I held out my hands, palms up, highlighting my helplessness. "He won't do it, Max, not in a million years. He'd be throwing away his career."

He went silent for what must have been two minutes. Then, slowly and deliberately, he began to nod. "A conclusion has taken form in my brain," he said. "Come back to me at the end of the day. I'll give you your answer."

Dr. Maxwell Deguise was universally esteemed for his unique and insightful interventions for any type of human psychological problem, being able to transfigure his insights into effective clinical action.

Perhaps this is why, in a 1999 survey of psychologists, he was voted one of the ten most influential psychologists in the world.

Ranking highest among the adjectives that could be used to describe his therapeutic approach is "astonishing."

But to listen to him, the formula was a simple one: "First, throw a monkey wrench into the pathology machine in whatever way you can; then, present a door to beneficial resolution. People will always walk through that door."

HE bounded into my office a little before 5 P.M., exuding a level of energy I hadn't witnessed since meeting him. A smile spread across his face as thin and flat as a steak knife. His sideburns angled backward like gills.

"I have reached my conclusion," he said. "Elliot, you know me as an innovator. Well, this time I'm going to surprise even you."

I set aside the manuscript and leaned toward him. "You sure seem elated."

"I am, my son." He sat down and reclined, maintaining his smile as he let his eyelids go to half-mast. "Certainty does that. Elliot, you know the one frustration that goes with being a psychologist?"

"Well, I'd say—"

"It's that so often, in the drama of life, we therapists, in essence, do nothing. Nothing. I've personally beheld every manner of human pain and foible and, typically, my clinical instincts have allowed me to help the clients examine their life-maps, chart a new course, and blaze a fresh trail with my support."

"True. That's a direct quote from *Secrets of a Clinical Master*, isn't it?"

"Indeed. But don't you see, Elliot? That restrictive viewpoint shackles us from what might be more effective facilitation of healing. There have been so many cases in which I've wished, fantasized that I could really *do* something, play a more active role in my clients' lives. Hear me out: Haven't you ever worked with an abused wife and wished you could sneak into the house one night and bludgeon her bastard husband into a tattered pile of flesh? Haven't you worked with a child who's been psychologically beaten down to the point of emptiness by uncaring, neglectful parents who think of no one but themselves? And haven't you wanted to take out a contract on the monsters and simply take the child home and raise him yourself? Haven't you ever seen a client who's so forlorn and lost in life that you've wanted to put your arm around her shoulders and take a nice long walk in the woods, just to comfort her, instead of just saying, 'You seem to be feeling pretty hopeless today'?"

"Well, I guess we all have those fantasies. It's part of the profession. But how does that relate to the case I presented?"

He clenched his fists in front of him and gritted his teeth so forcibly I heard them creak. Then he said, "We're talking about defenseless animals here, Elliot. Cats . . ." He paused. His head dropped and he wiped his eyes free of unexpected teardrops. "*My* cats."

"I still don't understand. You're not making sense—"

"That's all you need to understand, Elliot, because I won't have you involved. I probably shouldn't have said a word to you about this. Remember, Elliot: Your only job is to remain the supportive therapist for Dr. Jones. Just know, in your heart, that after tonight your client's difficulties shall disappear completely. I am so certain of what I must do."

"But . . ."

He clapped his hands once, rose, and left the room moving lightly, like a dancing ghost.

I picked up my pen and began to write.

YEARS of constant contact with another human being induces what might as well be termed ESP. Having witnessed and heard the twists and turns of their reasonings, the modes by which they fashion their perceptions of and approaches to life, soon their thinking becomes second nature to us, whether or not we realize it.

Although I knew that my ethical obligation was to prevent Dr. Deguise from doing something foolish and dangerous, not to mention to warn his intended victim, what can I say? Sometimes one finds one's most meaningful life paths amid unexpected territory and I knew my destiny was to be with Dr. Maxwell Deguise.

I needed to be there.

I WAITED until well after sundown and drove to a country road that ran parallel to the vet clinic's road, parked, then crept through an adjacent cornfield to the outer perimeter of the clinic property. Even with only the illuminating bruise of the single pole light outside the clinic, I could make out the crouching figure of Dr. Maxwell Deguise amid a cluster of bushes.

Parked in the lot out front was a muddied Ford pickup truck displaying the license plate ANML DR.

So the vet was there, and already, Max was present and ready for action, whatever action it was he had ultimately designed.

Bent over like a damaged marionette, he skulked across the yard, over to a window from which golden light shone. I ran, tiptoes barely skimming the earth, timing my arrival so I'd intersect Max's trajectory.

He heard me coming, turning until I saw that he was holding both a flashlight and a pistol in his gloved hands. His eyes widened and he quickly pushed the pistol into his suit coat pocket.

"Elliot?" he said as I approached. "What in the devil are you doing here?"

Panting, I answered, "I came . . . because I needed to. . . . You've always been there for me. . . . I want to be here for you."

He scowled and shook his head. "If you must. But no matter what you see, please let this night run its course—"

Hearing no disagreement from me, he gestured for me to follow him to the basement window.

We lay on our stomachs and then, our heads only inches apart, we peered through the window and saw the rows of tiny graves, swellings of piled dirt, each no larger than a watermelon.

"I'm going to do it," he muttered, and then lay there mutely, his flashlight beam playing back and forth across the graves like a honeyed pendulum.

Minutes later, we stood up and moved to yet another window, where a light had switched on.

Simultaneously, we crouched down when Dr. Jones walked into the room. Dressed in blue jeans painted with some manner of dung, and wearing a T-shirt from the University of Missouri, he carried in his hand something I thought, at first, was a cattle prod. It was a long, thin rod and out of its end protruded a slim four-inch needle. The device contained a long, thin transparent tube filled with violet fluid.

"What's that thing?" I asked.

"I'm not sure," Max replied, "but I think it's what vets use in order to inject caged animals with the euthanizing solution without their having to get close. A coward's tool, if you ask me."

Sure enough, that was true, since the next thing we saw was Dr. Jones setting aside the rod-like syringe, then wheeling two large cages into the room. One contained a mother dog and several puppies who lay suckling. The other cage was crammed full of cats of all shapes, ages, and sizes, perpetually moving like a writhing rug.

"I don't get it," I said. "If he tortures the animals, why would he euthanize them? How can we be sure?"

"Oh, we can be sure," Max said. "Remember what we just saw? A graveyard in the basement. He's up to no good. I'm certain of it. And I'm here to put an abiding stop to his quiet evil. Forever. Come with me."

I followed him to an entrance. Befitting a rural practice, the door was unlocked.

Max placed his gloved hand on the pistol in his pocket and patted it.

Sweat had appeared on my forehead and began trickling down into my eyes.

As he opened the door, I laid my hand on his shoulder. "Steady, Max. Please. Think. Don't do this."

He shook his head. "This time, I'm not sitting back and just letting the story unfold before my eyes. I'm taking action. I'll end this suffering in its dark tracks."

I made sure the door shut softly behind us, then trailed Max into an empty exam room. The vet was just around the corner, whistling to himself.

I made a vain attempt to grab Max's arm but he shrugged me off with amazing ease.

And then, suddenly, we were face to face with Dr. Jones.

He was six feet tall, thin as a summer cornstalk, and had salt-and-pepper hair, cut curiously like Moe Howard's.

Amazingly, when he saw we had slipped into his death chamber, he smiled.

"Hey, how ya doin', Max?" Dr. Jones said, letting the death rod hang at his side. "Nice evening, isn't it?"

Max grinned and I heard his teeth chattering. "We are fine, Dr. Jones, but I presume that the animals to whom you are charged to heal are *not* so fine. In fact, I daresay that the animals in those cages are doomed."

He nodded and smiled wistfully. "You're right. When I see these strays show up at the pound, it reminds me of how irresponsible most people are. Truth be told, I have more respect for these creatures than I do for the people who brought them in."

Max brandished his pistol. "Enough of this. Take us into your basement of death."

Dr. Jones initially smiled, but then seemed to notice the

murderous look in Max's eyes. "What is this about?"

"It's about delivering a bit of justice to this world. It's about avenging helpless animals who are being tortured by a subtly insane sadist."

Dr. Jones cocked his head like a hound. "Are you one of those animal liberation people? I mean, if you are, as far as I'm concerned, you can take these strays, let them loose, do whatever you'd like. I get no pleasure out of euthanizing them."

Max aimed his pistol straight at Dr. Jones's head. "You heard me. Take us to the basement."

"Why? There's nothing in there."

Max chuckled. "I beg to differ. Tonight, my colleague and I came and had a look. There's much to see down there, testament to the suffering you've caused to those who are powerless to defend themselves."

The blood left Dr. Jones's face, rendering it the color of ash.

Still gripping the euthanizing rod, he turned and headed toward a door, opened it, and flicked on the basement light, then began slowly walking down the steps.

We followed.

When he had reached the bottom of the stairs, Dr. Jones said, "My God! What is this?"

He went up to one of the numerous dirt mounds that we'd seen through the window and kicked it. A small, dark mote of dust floated into the air, then eddied into nothingness.

"I have no idea what these are," Dr. Jones said. "No idea at all."

"I'll tell you what they are," said Max. "They are the graves of animals who were loved by their human companions. Tell me, Dr. Jones, where is my Phil? Where is my Suki? Where are the small creatures who cherished me without hesitation, who told me I'm alive by their very presence? Are they here?"

Dr. Jones dropped the rod to the floor. "What the hell . . ."

Hatred seemed to trill from Max's mouth when he said, "I've never even heard of such a level of vicious abuse in my fifty-odd years of practice."

Dr. Jones laughed quietly. "Abuse? Max, you sound crazy. Are you serious?"

Max raised the pistol and fired toward the ceiling. The explosive sound caused all three of us to jump.

"What do you do to the poor little souls?" Max demanded. "Do you skin them, experiment on them, bury them alive—?"

"I *what*? Why, I've never—"

"Shut up! I won't hear any more from the likes of you. I entrusted my loved ones with you and you killed them! You took away the last joys in my life."

Suddenly, I stepped in front of Max. He wasn't used to my being assertive with him, and thus paused long enough for me to easily grab the pistol from his hand.

"Elliot," Max said, "what are you doing? I told you, back at the office, that this was *my* task. I didn't want you here."

"I couldn't have missed this, Max. You see, I set this up. All of it. I set *you* up."

"What are you saying, my boy?"

"I'm not your boy!" I shouted as I felt my facial features stretching into something approaching derangement. Then, seeing Dr. Jones beginning to back away, toward the stairs, I aimed the gun at him. "Stay put, you! I'm not done with either of you. I haven't even started."

Max spoke again, and this time his voice trembled. "What is this all about?"

"It's about using your own skills against you, Max, using your own certainty to control you, to right a wrong. Can't you see it? Or is the perception I created for you imposing itself without resistance? Dr. Jones doesn't torture or kill animals. I'm sure he's a very nice vet. Over the years, you've spoken so warmly about him, how he took care of your cats. He's never consulted with me at all, Max, never even set foot in our office. After my plan formed, I sneaked out here with a shovel last night, sneaked into the basement and created these little mounds of dirt. They aren't graves at all. But you see, perception is all, just like you've always said."

"You orchestrated this?"

"Every bit of it. I threw a monkey wrench into *your* pathology by bringing up Candy Lorber—thus introducing insecurity and self-doubt into you—and then I presented a door to resolution by telling you Dr. Jones was a cat torturer. Under the circumstances I created, you had no choice but to take action."

"Why? After all I've done—?"

"Shut up! Do you want to know what you've done? You've all but adopted *the son of Candy Lorber.* That's right. That was *my* mother you abandoned to die, the woman you couldn't take time to comfort, the lady who had to shoot up a college campus just to tell the world she hurt."

He was stunned by my revelation. "She was your mother? My God, she never would tell me the name of her son."

My voice trembled as much from grief as rage. "I was in college when she died, the very college where she lost her life. My life was adrift until that night. But once I knew what you'd done to Mom, I had a goal in my life. What is it you wrote? 'One must always—*always!*—establish and pursue goals that forcefully embody the theme of one's existential *magnum opus.*' I established and pursued one central goal: revenge. After changing my name, I sought you out, begged for your help, and thanks to you, I earned my doctorate in psychology and joined your practice. And you know what's kept me going all this time? Well, I'll tell you.

It was the knowledge that this moment would come. It was just a matter of fashioning your perceptions for you. Drawing your life map. Perception is everything, Max.

"So you see how perfect it is?" I continued. "I'll shoot Dr. Jones here. Then I'll inject you with the euthanizing fluid. It'll look like you killed Dr. Jones and he managed to valiantly fight back. The police will find two dead bodies. Case closed. And of course, then I inherit your practice."

"Oh, my boy," he said, pity informing his voice. "You were right in quoting me about certainty. It is the grand salve and also the greatest illusion."

"Exactly. Ironic that it turned out to be your downfall."

He shook his head and smiled sadly. "No, my son, it was *your* downfall."

He took two steps toward me, arms outstretched like he was going to hug me.

I aimed at his chest and pulled the trigger.

Click.

"You see, Elliot," Max said, "I had only one bullet in the gun and, as you saw, I fired it into the ceiling. It was a blank, to boot. Just for show."

"But—"

"No, Elliot, now *I* talk. You underestimated my clinical and personal acumen, it seems. I've seen your deterioration these past months. I've seen you trying to manipulate me, so much so that I decided to feign a bit of encroaching Alzheimer's. That way, if you were intent on nefarious deeds, you'd feel freer to show your true colors. And you did, in spades. The fact is, as soon as you told me Dr. Jones had consulted with you, I simply called him up and explained my suspicions about you. He volunteered that he'd never consulted with you, and he was kind enough to play along tonight. You see, I knew you'd want to be here when I came although, I admit, I didn't know you wanted to kill me. I just assumed you wanted to put me in an embarrassing trap, then take over the practice. You disappoint me, my son."

Dr. Jones reached down and picked up the euthanizing rod.

Instinctively, I prodded the pistol in his direction before it occurred to me that other than throwing it at him, the gun was useless.

"Drop it," said Dr. Jones, and I did.

Max said, "Sit down, Elliot."

I lowered myself to the sodden floor and crossed my legs Indian-style.

Dr. Jones leaned forward and pressed the euthanizing rod's needle against my sternum.

"I am truly sorry for you," Max said. "For the life map you created back when you were in college was utterly false. Tell me, Elliot, what made you think that I abandoned your mother, that I didn't care what happened to her? Did you read it in a tabloid?"

I lifted my eyes to his. "No! That's what Mom told me. I saw her in the hospital before she died. I was with her . . ."

Max shook his head. "As I said, I'm truly sorry. Your mother, Elliot, was a master manipulator, much more adept at it than you are. And it seems her last act in life was to manipulate *you*."

"Bullshit," I said, then spat at him.

He calmly removed a handkerchief and wiped the spittle from his pants. "If you'd just told me the truth when we first met, told me she was your mother, I could have helped you.

"Elliot, your mother was filled with hatred. Hatred for the world, hatred for the therapists who hadn't helped her, hatred for her family. And hatred for the son she bore out of wedlock, the son she never wanted, the son she wanted to kill because she perceived him as having ruined her life by his very birth. Hatred for *you,* Elliot. What she threatened that night was to kill you. When I tried to reason with her, she cut her wrists, then attacked me and ran from the office. I called the police but they didn't find her until they'd received word that she was rampaging on the campus, where she'd gone to find and kill you."

"You're lying," was all I could manage to say, but even then I felt my world crumbling about my shoulders.

Patting me on the shoulder, Max said, "I'm sure you believe I'm lying. Certainty is a curse, is it not? Elliot, that night I called the police because I was concerned about her . . . and about you, though I didn't even know your name. I've never spoken or written about it because I wished her family no more pain. But you could have read the police report, Elliot: I told them what happened that night. You could have attended the inquest. You could have read the interviews with me in the newspaper accounts. You could have talked with me. I could have helped you."

I felt like I was melting. "I didn't think I needed to know any more. I'd already talked to Mom. I *knew* who was responsible."

"I know, my boy, I know," said Dr. Deguise, "and it seems that you have two choices here. You've already attempted murder, technically speaking. And if you attempt to attack us, I suppose Dr. Jones can inject you with the euthanizing fluid. The gun has your fingerprints on it. The police will find one body, the body of a misguided soul in this basement who tried to kill an innocent veterinarian and a world-famous psychologist."

"Do I have any other choices?" I asked, feeling as though I were shrinking into fetus-hood with each passing second.

"Of course you do. In life, there are *always* other choices."

And then Dr. Maxwell Deguise interlocked his fingers and recited it like a liturgy: " 'One must always—*always!*—establish and pursue goals that forcefully embody the theme of one's existential *magnum opus*.'

"What is your story to be, Dr. Elliot Albert?" he asked me.

WHEN I began writing Dr. Deguise's biography, how was I to know that *A Trail of Mirrors* was ultimately to be *my* story?

I only became truly conscious last week. Apparently I lapsed into a catatonic state that night, under the weight of the knowledge Dr. Deguise had shared about my mother. Until I woke up, I sat here in the psychiatric hospital, being fed by aides, and led from bed to dining room and back again.

I have replayed our visit to the Konner County Veterinary Clinic a thousand times, and written more pages about my mother than I can imagine. But it doesn't help.

Perceptions die hard, if they die at all.

The story my mother told me that emotion-laden night in the hospital room has so embedded itself into me that now, one hundred twenty days after my involuntary admission to the psychiatric unit, it remains as crisp and vivid as if it had happened to me. As though I had been there.

Could my mother have hated me so profoundly and never expressed it directly to me? Could she have wanted me dead?

Or had Max all along planned to scuttle me out of the practice, to use my youth and enthusiasm until it threatened him and then to dispense of me like trash through his masterful manipulations?

A terrifying thing in this life, I have concluded, is uncertainty.

It's nearly as terrifying as certainty.

I received a letter this morning. Its postmark suggested to me that it was mailed by Max. It read:

Dear Max,

If you don't see fit to take responsibility for your son, I'll take drastic action. Mark my words. You can't hurt me anymore.

Candy

A tiny typewritten note was stapled to the letter:

Our own lives have become clear, have they not? We must talk soon, Elliot.

Love,
Dad

How do I go about revising my life story?
How can I ever know if it's finally true?
I wonder where they keep the razors here.

ALONG FOR THE RIDE

Aileen Schumacher

"YOU working mighty close to the edge, babe. In case you ain't noticed, it's a hell of a ways down."

Lee ignored Jack-off-Jake and kept pounding nails. She didn't need pointers from anyone, hadn't needed any for a long time now.

Silence never fazed Jake. "You got some dynamite curves, Lee-baby, but if you take a dive, ain't none of them curves big enough to hitch you up to any scaffolding on the way down."

Fat Frank stepped off the construction elevator at the right moment to hear the jive, had to throw in some of his own. "If you're gonna fall down this elevator shaft, Lee, you holler. I'll run throw myself on top of this contraption, cuz honey, you can fall on top of old Frank anytime."

Luke was watching a concrete pour fifty feet away, had to yell to be heard. "You telling us you can actually run, Frank? If you somehow manage to get your fat body on top of that elevator, let me know. I'll heave a bag of cement over, just so you can practice having something land on top of you."

Lee could take care of herself. Still, it was nice to hear Luke's words.

Young, black, female, working high-rise construction, the concept of a male-dominated industry held no meaning for Lee. Her entire existence was defined by men—past, present, and future. Lee had never experienced, didn't know, and didn't expect anything different.

"You're not just pretty, Lee, you're smart," Mo used to tell her. "Don't ever forget that. You're gonna do something special someday."

Mo was right about that.

Sixteen-year-old Mo lied about his age to save Lee from going into foster care when their crack-whore mother finally had the decency to die. They had four good years together, carving out a life for themselves in a Miami neighborhood where cops never came alone.

Mo didn't hold with drugs, gangs, or slacking on the part of his twelve-year-old sister. Lee made good grades, kept house, and babysat whenever she got the chance. There was no slacking on Mo's part, either. Most of those four years, he worked three jobs at a time.

Mo wasn't around a lot, but Lee knew she could depend on him. Mo always kept his promises, and he told Lee that they would buy a car when she turned sixteen. She thought the day would never come, and she was right—it never did.

Three weeks before Lee's sixteenth birthday, a car hit Mo while he was crossing the street, coming off the late shift, working hospital security. The driver was drunk—he never saw Mo and Mo never saw him, so that part was a stand-off. But the driver had thousands of pounds of Jaguar wrapped around him; Mo only had his uniform. Mo died at the scene.

Twenty-four-year-old Brett Rubin, heir apparent to Rubin Construction Company, went to court a month later.

He didn't have anything to say. His lawyer talked for fourteen minutes, then Brett Rubin walked away a free man.

Lee knew exactly how long the lawyer talked because she timed it. Mo got buried in the past, then Brett Rubin defined the present.

Lee couldn't tell anyone about how long Rubin's lawyer spoke and what happened, because she wasn't supposed to be there. Forty-eight hours after Mo's death, Lee listened to the social worker tell her how great foster care could be for someone in her situation. She didn't say anything, just nodded then walked through the kitchen on the way to her room to pack and grabbed the soup can where Mo kept their cash. In the bedroom, Lee dumped everything out of her backpack, stuffed in the cash, some clothes, then climbed out the back window.

They'd lived on the fourth floor, so the trip out the bedroom window was a good start on Lee's new career. She was going to work high-rise construction.

It was hard in the beginning. But even with minimum age requirements, unions, the requests for references, there was always someone willing to pay cash under the table for cheap labor—especially if it was good cheap labor.

Lee was a competent carpenter by the time she turned seventeen. Now, three years later, she could do finish custom work as good as most, but here she nailed together wood forms for concrete pours. Working on a Rubin Construction high-rise apartment building, Lee was right where she wanted to be. She could do this work in her sleep, but she considered this particular job to be the pinnacle of her career.

Tomorrow, construction started on the final phase, the fourteenth floor. Tomorrow was the future, and Luke was Lee's man for that.

Lee was tied to Mo by birth and to Brett Rubin by fate, but she selected Luke. Lots of guys worked concrete pours, but Luke was experienced, and he wasn't young. Luke had a long gray ponytail and just the hint of a limp. Lee heard he'd seen "hard action" in Nam, but Luke never said anything about it.

Lee could understand that. She figured she'd seen hard action practically every single day of her life.

Luke was a good choice. His eyes, banked with the dim but unmistakable glow of suppressed desire, tracked Lee from the beginning. She could feel it with her finely honed survival instincts, just like she'd learned to feel the beginnings of a drug deal going down.

Lee liked the fact that Luke wasn't crude and he didn't push it. He even acted as if he wanted to get to know her a little before throwing down.

"Lanky Lee," he named her at lunch break the very first day. "How come you ain't got one of those fancy names, you know, like all the other sisters? I never met a black woman named Lee. How 'bout you guys? Don't sound natural, does it?" Then the others started in, trying to top each other.

Lee ate her sandwich, kept to herself. The conversation was good-natured—still, there were things about names that Lee would never tell anyone.

Lee's brother was named Moses.

Lee didn't remember hearing anyone call him Moses, not until that one day in court, and Moses wasn't near as bad as Ma'DeLisha.

Ma'DeLisha, shit.

Their crackhead mother must have been trying for some stupid foreign sound, or else she was too coked up to spell Madonna. The woman probably never sobered up long enough to realize that it came out "Mad-a-Leesha" whenever any well-intentioned person tried to sound it out.

Lee defined her own name the first time she was old enough to fill out a form on her own.

Even if Luke didn't know the whole story, he liked Lee's

name just fine. He liked to say it as he kissed her when they got drinks after work.

Lee knew exactly what Luke wanted, but Lee wanted something in return. Mutual needs should be made clear, even if not spoken out loud too quickly.

"Luke, would you do me a favor sometime?" Lee decided it was okay to ask the first time he took her home, when he halfway knew, and she knew for sure, that she wouldn't be spending the night.

"What kind of favor?" he asked, feathering kisses down her neck as he unbuttoned her shirt.

"Make something disappear for me."

That got his attention. Luke lifted his head, distracted from liberating Lee's breasts. "You mean make someone disappear?" Luke's eyes narrowed. He might think with his dick like the rest of them, but he wasn't stupid.

"Of course not, you silly man."

Luke sat up all the way now, ignoring Lee's gaping shirt. "Don't talk to me like that, Lee. It doesn't even sound like you. Tell me what you want—tell me right out."

Lee lay on her back, looking straight up at him, making her eyes as wide as possible. "Be cool. I'm talking 'bout a little thing." She showed him with her hands. "It happens all the time. Someone throws something in a concrete pour, and it's gone for-ev-er." She strung out the last word.

He wasn't convinced. "Looks like the size of a gun, what you're showing me."

Lee put her arms around his neck. "I wouldn't never ask you to do nothing like that."

"A knife then?"

Now it was time to be insulted. Lee sat up, pulled her shirt together. Hell, she clamped it together, like maybe it would never come open again.

"Don't be mad," Luke told her.

" 'Course I'm mad. I ask one little favor. What you

think—I'm humping some gang-banger, asking you to lose a weapon so my homeboy don't do no time?" Lee used to talk another way. Now she talked like this.

Luke closed his eyes a moment, as though she'd unearthed some unpleasant memory.

"This thing you're talking about, is it gonna have blood on it?"

"No." Lee looked straight at him, making the one word short, clipped. It hung in the air between them.

"Let me think on it," Luke said after a while. It was good he didn't ask any more questions, because Lee had no more to tell him. "We still on for drinks after work, Friday?" he asked.

"I'll think on it while you thinking on the other."

For better or for worse, the cards were on the table now. Lee had planned to play this hand for years; she could wait to see if Luke was in or out. Turned out, Lee didn't have to wait much longer before she discovered something that tipped the tables in her favor.

The next day at the end of lunch break, a lead-footed mason tripped over Luke's lunch box, sending everything tumbling out. Lee helped gather up the stuff without thinking, not listening to Luke tell her he didn't need any help.

There was a small black plastic vial spilled out with the sandwich wrappings and orange peels. Kind of like slow motion, maybe like it was meant to happen that way, the top came off and two capsules rolled out.

Lee didn't need to complete any high school health class to recognize the AIDS drug AZT. She had her hand over the pills practically before they'd seen the light of day. She picked them up, put them back in the vial, screwed the top down tight.

Everyone else gone, Luke still squatted there on his heels, looking at her. "Guess that rips it, huh, Lanky Lee?"

"Not for me, Slick."

He stared at her. "You're crazy, girl."

"I don't much count on being around in ten years, know what I mean?"

Luke looked at Lee another long moment, considering. "Guess I'll have to take your word for it."

"You do that, Slick." And so the deal was sealed, then and there, without any more discussion, even before the third floor was started. Then Lee could turn her attention to other things.

Security at a construction site was always relative. The goal was to pay the least money possible to prevent pilfering and theft. Security was also supposed to keep kids from screwing around after hours and falling off something, allowing some fancy attorney to claim big bucks for negligence.

But anyway you looked at it, guys working security at construction sites weren't exactly the same ones you'd hire at a bank.

Job safety was a different issue, but still, the bottom line was limiting liability, because liability always translated into big dollars lost. A violation of OSHA regulations could mean hefty penalties. Unlike site security, job safety didn't depend on how many people were hired to walk around. Job safety was threefold: required procedures, proper equipment, and redundant systems.

The construction elevator was an example of a redundant system. It had two mechanisms to prevent it from falling. After all, a construction elevator carried human cargo, which society sometimes deemed to be more precious than supplies and equipment hoisted by a flat-bed lift.

Even it if hadn't been against OSHA regulations to ride a flat-bed lift, Lee would have loved construction elevators for themselves. A construction elevator was even better than those fancy glass-enclosed ones inside ritzy hotel lobbies. On a construction elevator, one could not only see out, one could feel the air whistle past.

A construction elevator somewhat resembled the scaffolding to which it was attached. Its mechanical system was exposed, not hidden by an acoustical ceiling piping out elevator music. One could watch the cable wind and unwind around the reel, the reel held in place by one elegant, slender metallic pin.

The backup system consisted of four connectors, one at each corner of the square floor piece. These were secured to the scaffolding before anyone stepped on or off the elevator. These were heavy-duty connectors that could keep the elevator in place all by themselves, independent of any cable connection system.

Lee had studied construction elevators from the very first time she ever walked onto a high-rise site. She was particularly fascinated by the pin, that one, single bit of essential metal. Thin, cylindrical, and less than a foot in length, it called to her. The little part of the pin that protruded from its setting practically sang out to her.

The pin was held in place by two things, the fitting and the load resulting from the weight of the elevator. Lee had thought about both. She'd also thought about site security and the gala event scheduled to celebrate the fact that the top floor, the fourteenth one, was now under construction.

On a site this size, there were lots of potential hiding places, and Lee knew most of them. She left her lunch box in one. She bought a sandwich for lunch that day—it wasn't possible to eat black tights, a black T-shirt, a fine-gauge drill, some industrial lubricant, and a roll of the thinnest, strongest transparent fishing line that Lee could find.

Lee lagged behind when everyone else knocked off work and hid herself. She waited for night to fall, then put on the black clothes. Maybe this was a redundant safety system itself considering the color of her skin.

Heights held no fear for Lee. She shimmied up the scaffolding by the elevator and went to work on the pin.

She drilled a hole through the end, the end that protruded out of the fitting, the end that had called out to her for so long. Then Lee tied the fishing line through the hole. Next, she worked some lubricant in and around as much as she could. The trickiest part was unwinding the thin filament of fishing line now attached to the pin, making sure it wasn't caught up on anything anywhere before she hid the spool.

Lee put everything else back in her lunch box and took it with her when she slipped away. The security crew didn't make a single round the whole time Lee was busy at work—maybe there was something really good on TV. Lee thought about checking that out when she got home, but she forgot and went to bed.

There was a festive air everywhere on site the next day, not that the construction workers would be a part of any celebration. Lee kept a close eye on the proceedings while she made up work for herself near the elevator and the roll of fishing line.

Finally, the man who mattered arrived.

Brett Rubin, his father, their attorney, the mayor, some sleek dark-haired woman, and two reporters rode up together to the fourteenth floor. Speeches were made, applause followed, champagne flowed. For the most part though, the construction crew just kept on working.

When the celebration ended, Artie ran the elevator, taking guests down. That was too bad; Lee genuinely liked Artie. Lee bent down, picked up the spool of fishing line from behind a box of nails.

Brett Rubin, his girlfriend, and the attorney stepped onto the elevator together. Lee didn't think anyone was watching her, but it wouldn't matter now. Holding the spool over her head, the line between the pin and her hands was almost level. Lee pulled as hard as she could.

The pin slid out smooth, fast. It hit a *few* places and

clanked some as Lee pulled it to her, but no one noticed. Everyone watched the guests of honor, still glad-handing each other before leaving the party.

Lee cut the line and stuffed the spool in her jeans, allowing herself the luxury of briefly fondling the pin she held in her hands. She was already walking away when the corner connectors were disengaged.

She'd worried about that.

If the connectors came off one at a time, it would become apparent that the elevator was no longer secured by the cable and pin. But people were eager to help, so the four safety devices were disengaged pretty much at the same time.

Lee reached Luke just before the construction elevator fell fourteen floors. She handed him the pin in one fluid gesture. Just as smoothly, Luke dropped it into wet concrete pouring out from a mixer, and the pin became part of a bearing wall in a Rubin Construction high-rise apartment building.

Lee gaped, open-mouthed, just like everyone else, when people started screaming.

"You said it wouldn't have blood on it." Luke spoke directly into Lee's ear, over the din of death. He wiped his hands as though he'd touched something dirty, a gesture not seen often on a construction site.

"Did you look at it?" she asked him before she walked away. "Wasn't no blood on it no how."

Three days later, cops, OSHA inspectors, and the elevator manufacturer were still trying to sort it all out. Lee met Luke for drinks after work.

"I guess you got him," Luke said, looking at his beer.

"Got who?" Lee asked.

"After all that went down, I did some thinking. Then I did some studying up on you. I guess you got Brett Rubin Jr. good, and then some."

Things didn't surprise Lee very often, but this did.

"Rubin Jr.?" she asked. "He was just along for the ride. It was the attorney I wanted."

Luke looked up from his beer then. "I don't think we should see each other anymore," he said. He stood up, walked away.

Lee shrugged. "Have a nice rest of your life," she called after him.

It shouldn't be so difficult to find something to put into those AZT capsules Luke kept so secret. It wasn't as though people on construction sites carried locking lunch boxes.

And the higher and mightier they came, the harder they fell.

Red Meat

Elaine Viets

Ashley had a body to die for, and I should know. I'm on death row because of her.

You want to know the funny thing?

My wife bought me Ashley. For a birthday present.

I was turning sixty that July, and I could feel the cold wind at my neck. I wasn't bad-looking for my age. I still had all my hair. But that semipermanent twenty pounds of lard around my gut had turned into thirty. I had chicken skin on the insides of my elbows, like an old geezer. And women didn't give me appraising looks anymore.

Not that I need to look at other women. My Francie had kept her figure just fine. She was ten years younger than me, and worked out with a personal trainer. Recently, people had started asking if Francie was my daughter. I'd laughed it off, but it bothered me. I told Francie maybe she should dye her hair gray so she'd look her age. She said, "Maybe you should lose thirty pounds, Jake, so you'd look your age."

I'd thought about going to the gym. We had a good one, right here on Sunnysea Beach, Florida, owned by a former pro linebacker. I'd see Jamal Wellington out running on the sand. You know those fake-heroic chests guys strap on so they look like gladiators? Jamal had a real chest like that, and arms and legs to match.

Francie and I had a beachfront condo about a mile from Jamal's Jym, but beach life makes you lazy. I never got around to walking down there. I'd think about joining the gym, but I'd always lie back down until the fitness fit passed. Instead, I'd pop another brew and watch another movie. I had a state-of-the-art entertainment system with five clickers (Francie put the clickers in a basket so I wouldn't leave them lying around).

Now that I was retired, I had time to catch up on my movies. I'd been comparing the classic Bond films starring Sean Connery to the later ones with Roger Moore. In my opinion, Connery was the one true Bond. Moore looked like a Sears shirt model.

When Francie came home from work that night, I said, "You can't trust movie critics. This so-called critic says *For Your Eyes Only* is a superior piece of escapism."

"I don't know what you need to escape," snapped Francie, slamming her briefcase down on the kitchen table.

I could tell Francie was peeved, so I put down my beer and took her to the Beachside Bar for dinner. I thought she'd be happy she didn't have to cook. Instead she glared at me when I mopped up my steak gravy with my butter bread. She got testy when I downed my third martini. By the time I ordered key lime pie with extra whipped cream, Francie was steaming. She didn't say anything, but the air around her got dense and crackly, like she was generating her own personal thunderstorm.

Francie's bad mood was gone by my sixtieth birthday, two days later. She smiled and slipped on her silky leopard-print robe I like so much.

"Happy Birthday, Tiger," she said, handing me a ribbon-wrapped box. "I got you a twenty-three-year-old blonde for your birthday."

"I like my fifty-year-old brunette," I said, patting her rump.

I opened the present. Inside was a gift card. It said I should meet my personal trainer, Ashley, at Jamal's Jym at 2 P.M. today for my first workout.

"Ashley? What kind of name is that?" I snorted. "She probably looks like a Russian Olympic gymnast. I bet she shaves more than I do." Then I shut up. I realized I was grumping like a sixty-year-old.

"Wait and see," said Francie, smiling.

I walked down to the gym that broiling July afternoon, feeling sorry for myself. I felt like I was walking barefoot across a hot stove. Sweat ran off me like rainforest waterfalls. I couldn't believe my own wife bought me a personal trainer to make me sweat more. I passed the WaterEdge condo building, its units hidden behind hurricane shutters. Those people had the sense to leave south Florida in July. I was stuck here with a bearded woman trainer.

At Jamal's Jym, I presented my gift card to a young guy named Barry. He wore only black gym shorts and running shoes. I wished he would put on more clothes. The guy's bare stomach was so flat you could bounce quarters on it. His muscles rippled when he typed in my name in the computer.

"Your wife got you Ashley," Barry said, with a knowing smile. "Welcome to the club." I didn't know if Barry was talking about the gym, or some other club. I didn't care, either. A blonde walked out of the Staff Only door, and I couldn't stop staring at her.

She looked like a cross between Wonder Woman and the captain of the girls' volleyball team. She was tanned to a golden brown and wearing a black spandex sports bra and short-shorts that revealed eye-popping development, front and back.

She had muscles, but she wasn't gnarly and knotted, like those women in the bodybuilding magazines. Ashley was sculpted like a statue. Her breasts were high and round and real. Her eyes were blue-green, like the ocean on a summer day. Her long golden hair rippled in sunlit waves.

"I'm Ashley," she said.

"Jake," I said, which was all I could manage with my stomach sucked in.

Ashley had me work out with what she called light weights. After that, I had to do two hundred push-ups, then run on the sand for two miles.

I went home so exhausted, I fell into bed and slept until the next morning. I missed dinner, but I didn't mind. I dreamed of Ashley, looking like a blonde goddess in black spandex.

I met with Ashley three times a week. Sometimes I slogged through the sand. Other times, I lifted weights. Always, she barked orders: "Slow down! Watch your form! Point those feet straight ahead. No penguinning!"

I was lying on a slant board while a beautiful blonde yelled at me.

I loved it.

I also loved that all the other guys stared when Ashley and I ran on the sand together. I was the envy of every man on the beach. Even the lifeguards looked at me with new respect.

"How'd you get so lucky to get Ashley?" asked Nick, the bartender at the Beachside Bar.

"My wife bought her for me," I said.

"Yeah, right, and my wife bought me Britney Spears," he said.

Nick didn't believe me. I could scarcely believe it, either.

Ashley had definite ideas about fitness. She wanted me to ditch my Diet Coke for bottled water. "Too many chemicals, dude," she said.

So I laid off the Diet Coke, and started drinking eight bottles of water a day, the way Ashley wanted. I wouldn't tell anyone, but I liked the taste better.

After six weeks, the chicken skin on my arms began to disappear. After eight weeks, my gut began to deflate. Women were giving me the eye again. My Francie started calling me "stud muffin." I hadn't looked this good in twenty years.

"I'm making progress, Ashley," I said. "But I can't seem to lose more weight."

"What are you eating, dude?" she said.

"Not much. That's what is so strange. I skip breakfast and lunch, then eat a big dinner."

She shook her head. "Bad idea. Your body can't run efficiently on no fuel. You're not eating enough."

"That's not what my wife says."

"You need to eat every three to five hours. But you need to eat right," Ashley said, firmly. Everything about her was firm.

She put me on a protein diet. I should have been happy living on mostly meat, but this wasn't what I called meat. Ashley wanted me to eat white meat of chicken and turkey, water-packed tuna, and broiled fish. I could have an egg-white omelet, but no butter or cheese. The only bread was whole wheat, and none of that after three in the afternoon. I could have a baked potato at lunch if I ate the skin, green vegetables like broccoli, and when I was feeling wild, graham crackers. That was it except for cranberry juice and two cups of coffee a day.

"Where's the steak?" I said. "Where's the hamburger?"

"Red meat's bad for you," said Ashley, looking commanding but adorable, like a dominatrix in a porno movie.

"Ashley," I said, "you are what you eat. I am two hundred pounds of red meat. I am a red-blooded male. I need my red meat."

"Mark my words, dude, red meat will kill you," Ashley said. She was right.

But I loved my porterhouses, filet mignons, even flank steaks. Red meat. Bloody meat, oozing deliciously on my plate.

I ate broiled chicken breast, though it tasted like warm Kleenex. I had whole wheat buns, though they were dry as old attic insulation. And egg-white omelets, though they tasted like nothing at all. I drank bottled water until I felt like one long stretch of plumbing. I sweated at Jamal's Jym, with Ashley barking orders, for two months on this dull diet.

I didn't lose an ounce.

"Hmm," said Ashley. "I know this diet can be slow to kick in, but you must be doing something wrong."

She gave me a little notebook and said, "Write down everything you eat each day."

The notebook was her first gift to me. "My diet diary," I joked.

It's amazing how your sins add up. I saw my life as one unending stretch of virtuous eating. I forgot about the jar of cashews I ate at four o'clock, the candy bar I sneaked at six, the occasional steak to break the monotony. I didn't think a little sour cream and butter on a dry baked potato was a big deal. I sure didn't think a couple of drinks were a problem.

But Ashley did. Lord, the lecture that woman gave me when she saw my diet diary.

"Listen, dude," she said. "I thought you were serious about this bodybuilding."

"I am," I said, mesmerized by her pectoral development. She'd built an amazing body.

"Then you've got to get serious about your food," she said, showing me those fat-free buns as she bent over to pick up a pencil. That improved my heart rate, let me tell you.

Ashley graded my diet diary like a kindergarten teacher. The turkey, fish, and egg-white omelets got smiley faces. The red meat got a frownie face. The martinis got "THIS IS TOO MUCH ALCOHOL!!!"

"Ashley, this is like being in prison," I said, because back then I didn't know anything about prison. "Even the doctors say a glass of wine is good for your heart."

"You can have one—only one—glass of wine with dinner," she said, sternly.

I showed Francie the Ashley-corrected diet diary. I thought she would make sarcastic remarks about the smiley faces, but Francie only patted my newly bulging biceps and said, "Ashley has done wonders, Tiger. Listen to her."

I smiled. Those thirty-two smile muscles were the only ones that didn't hurt.

That was something I didn't talk about. I hurt. All over. All the time. I looked better than I had in years, but those toned muscles let me know how they felt about getting back in shape. My shoulders hurt. My torso ached. My legs hurt.

When I say my legs hurt, I mean my calves, thighs, ankles, even my feet were sore. Each part hurt in a different way. My stretched calves were a dull ache. My sore feet were a sharp pain. My glutes shrieked when I sat down.

I was sixty years old, for god's sake. This was too much.

I told Ashley about the constant pain, but she only said, "No whining, dude."

Francie didn't take me seriously, either. "If that's all you have to complain about, you're doing pretty darn good," she said.

I admit all the compliments made me feel better. Take the night we were having an early dinner with four friends (I had to see Ashley at seven the next morning). They showered me with "you-look-terrifics," and "you've-been-working-outs." When I told everyone that Francie had bought me Ashley for my birthday, they could hardly believe it. The guys, Harry and George, winked and nudged each other.

Kaye said, "How do you feel about him working out with a twenty-three-year-old blonde, Francie?"

"Every woman should have an Ashley," she said. "For years, I've been telling him that he eats the wrong food, but would he listen to me? Oh, no, I was just a wife. I was just a nag.

"But when Ashley says he needs to eat more vegetables, it's bring on the broccoli, boys. When Ashley says he's eating too much red meat, he switches to fish and chicken. When Ashley says he drinks too much, he cuts back to one glass of wine a day.

"Could I get him to do that? Not me. I'm only a wife. But Ashley can. That's why every woman should have an Ashley. I wish I'd had her twenty years ago."

Everyone laughed, but I thought I heard a nasty edge. My delight in Ashley diminished just a bit.

I began noticing little things. Like how many times I saw Ashley running on the sand with paunchy guys between forty and sixty. Guys who looked ready to drop from exhaustion. I wanted to talk to them, but Ashley made sure they kept moving. She'd wave at me and never stop. The paunchy guys trotted along beside her.

So I asked her outright: "Those other guys you run with, did their wives buy you as a gift, too?"

Ashley said, "No talking, dude. It breaks your concentration."

Six months into the workout, the pain stopped. That's when I made my final, fatal mistake. I said, "Ashley, it doesn't hurt so much anymore."

I wanted to celebrate. But Ashley said, "Then we need to step up the workouts, dude. We can't have you enjoying yourself. No pain, no gain."

When she said those four stupid words, that was the first time I wanted to strangle her.

Then Ashley brought out the blue bands.

They did not look like much: four feet of rubber tubing with triangular handles on the ends. Such simple things, but so many instruments of torture are simple. A simple electric drill in a kneecap can cause excruciating pain. A simple tire iron can break every bone in your body.

Ashley's exercise bands tripled my misery. She made me wrap them around a palm tree and pull them, while I held my hands and feet at impossible angles. We'd—no, I'd—work out in humiliating poses while fat red tourists, buttered with coconut oil, stood around and laughed.

"Come on, dude, work harder," Ashley would command. "Pull! Pull! Pull!"

I would pull until my arms quivered and my neck ached, but it was never enough for her. "Come on, you're not crippled," she would scream, entertaining the slug-butt tourists.

I smiled through my pain, but that night I went out and had a Diet Coca-Cola. Then I wrote it defiantly in my diet diary. It was my way of getting even. Diet Coke upset Ashley more than beer. She said beer at least had some natural ingredients. "Diet soda is nothing but chemicals, dude."

I felt ashamed when I drank my Diet Coke. I used to down martinis and single malt scotch. Now I was chugging Diet Cokes—and worse, feeling guilty. All because of Ashley.

I couldn't even get any satisfaction in my rebellion. Ashley only said, "You've come a long way, dude. Who'd have thought an old boozer like you would be sneaking sodas and feeling guilty about it?"

Then she laughed. The cords in her short, powerful neck stood out, ugly as tree roots. I was so mad, I wanted to kill her.

That night, I dreamed I strangled Ashley with one of her own exercise bands. I knew it was time to stop.

Next day at the gym I asked, "Did my wife buy you for one year?"

"A year? No, your wife got the deluxe package, dude. This is a life sentence." She smiled, but her mouth was harder than Arnold Schwarzenegger's abs.

"Life?" I said. I felt the prison doors closing on me. I would never know another pain-free day. I would never eat another steak without feeling guilty. I wouldn't even drink another sinless soda.

"Look, Ashley," I said. "This has been fun, but it's time to stop. It's been a year. Refund Francie her money and I'll go quietly. I'm sick of all this good health."

"Can't, dude," she said. "No refunds. Francie knew that when she paid up-front."

"Well, I'm sorry she'll lose her money," I said. "But I quit."

It felt good when I said that. I wanted my old life back, and if my old body came back with it, so be it. Maybe I didn't used to look good, but I felt good.

I saw myself ordering one of Nick's straight-up martinis with an oily slick of vermouth and a sliver of lemon peel. Then I'd have a long wet lunch of red wine and rare steak. Red meat for a red-blooded male.

"Quit?" said Ashley, and her lip curled. Even her blonde hair curled in contempt.

"What will you tell everyone? That you're not man enough to keep me? The whole beach knows we work out. Stop now, and I'll tell everyone you weren't tough enough to work out with a *girl*."

I remembered all those lifeguards and beach bums grinning as I made my proud progress on the sand, Ashley at my side. I remembered Nick the bartender's envy. I saw my friends at dinner, nudging each other. I'd never be able to explain how tired I felt. I'd be a laughingstock.

I'd been given a blonde for my birthday and I was too tired to enjoy her.

"I don't care!" I said.

Jamal came over then. I guess we'd been talking louder than I thought.

"Anything wrong?" he said, looming over me like a mountain.

I shook my head. I was too tired to do anything else. I hurt in places I didn't know I had.

I showed up as usual for my next session. I was tied to Ashley until death parted us. For the first time, I actually looked forward to keeling over on the sand. Eternal rest took on new meaning.

Now that I couldn't escape her, everything Ashley did irritated me. I hated that she called me "dude." I couldn't stand those silly smiley faces in my diet diary. Not that I saw many. I was not only drinking Diet Cokes, I was piling mayonnaise on my grilled chicken—at six fat grams a spoonful. Yet now I didn't gain weight.

"Can't you just lie like everyone else?" Ashley said, as she read my acts of dietary defiance. We were working out on the empty, sun-bleached beach.

"Who's everyone else?" I said, furious at all the frownie faces.

"The other guys whose wives bought me. I'm a paid nag, dude. It's my job to buff up the old boys, tell them to eat their vegetables and drink less. Wives pay me well so they don't have to say those things."

"You mean my wife . . . My wife knew that you . . ." I could hardly breathe, I was so angry. Ashley ignored my anger, just as she ignored my pain. She kept hitting me with her taunts. Each one was another slam to my tortured body.

"They all do. Every woman in Sunnysea would love to have me, but not the way you would. They know old guys are suckers for sweet young things." She laughed, a cruel, cutting laugh.

"That's what I am—one of your suckers?" I'd never felt

more humiliated. Ashley didn't notice that, either. She handed me the hated exercise bands.

"Hey, don't bust a gasket, dude," she said, still laughing. "It's not your fault you can't get it up, old man. Energywise, I mean. Let's work on your upper body strength."

"It's fine," I said, wrapping the blue band around her neck and squeezing as hard as I could. I kept my elbows at a perfect ninety-degree angle. I kept my knees slightly bent to support my lower back. I kept my feet straight out, not splayed to either side, so Ashley couldn't say "no penguinning."

Ashley couldn't say anything. She was gagging, gasping, and clawing at her neck. She was strong, but I was stronger. I had another eighty pounds of solid muscle. She'd worked hard to build my arms. I pulled the band tighter. Her struggles grew more frantic. Her legs kicked futilely. I kept pulling, all the pain and rage I'd endured strangling my reason.

Ashley stopped struggling.

She was dead.

Slowly, I became aware of my surroundings again. I'd strangled a woman to death on Sunnysea Beach at two in the afternoon. I was fifty feet from a lifeguard cabana. But the guard, whose head was as thick as his neck, was staring at three squealing kids hitting one another with boogie boards. He didn't notice us.

The storm-shuttered windows of the WaterEdge condo were blind, too.

Even the tourists weren't out on the boardwalk in this heat.

If I'd lost my temper in the high season of December, some cop would be reading me my rights. But this was July. In Florida, on a summer weekday, the beaches could be as empty as a gym rat's head.

No one saw me. I was lucky. Better yet, I got out of half my class.

But how long would my luck last? I couldn't leave her

there. Everyone at Jamal's Jym knew I worked out with Ashley at this time.

My condo was a mile away. No way could I carry her body there. How was I going to get Ashley off the beach?

Don't panic, I told myself. Think.

I unwound the blue band from around Ashley's throat and shoved it in my pocket. Her face looked awfully red. I put my sweat towel down on the sand, then put Ashley on top of it, lying on her stomach. I turned her head so her long hair covered most of her face. I put my water bottle near her head, to further block the view of her face. If you didn't look too close, she seemed to be napping on the beach.

No one noticed me doing this. More luck. I ran all the way home and got my car. A 1997 Lincoln has lots of room.

I found a meter, another lucky break, and parked a block from where Ashley was on the sand. I only had a quarter, which buys fifteen minutes in Sunnysea.

Now came the hard part, getting Ashley off the beach and into the car. I knelt down on the sand, and shook Ashley gently, pretending that I was waking her from a sound sleep. Then I talked to her, as if she could hear me. I wanted it to look like she was my daughter or my girlfriend, and she was a little sun-sick or tipsy.

I rolled her over on her back, then sat her up. She leaned against me. Her right arm flopped back down and nearly dented my quads. Her face looked swollen and awful, but her hair was hanging down, covering it. I got behind her, put my arms under her pits, and pulled her into a standing position.

I now knew what a real deadweight lift was. What did Ashley weigh? One hundred twenty pounds max? She felt like two hundred. I got her up and leaned her against me. She was oddly rubbery, but more cooperative than usual.

I draped her right arm over my shoulder and put my arm around her waist. She leaned against me like a drunk. That was good. I had a little spiel ready. "Out cold," I planned to say, with an indulgent smile. "Too many piña coladas."

I didn't see a soul when I carried Ashley to the car. It was my lucky day. I didn't even mind the ten-dollar parking ticket on my windshield. It was a small price to pay.

I opened the back door, and Ashley fell into the seat. She hit her head with a nasty THWAK! She didn't feel a thing, but I was hurting. She'd strained my already sore muscles. Soon those muscles would never hurt again.

But now I had to get rid of Ashley's body. I wasn't going to risk the ocean—it's too shallow here, unless you get about three miles out into the Gulf Stream. The canals were too risky for the same reason. But if I drove west, I'd be in the Everglades. The "river of grass," they call it. It was full of alligators. Perfect. I wondered if the gators would find Ashley as tough as I did. I smiled at the thought.

I was on Highway 27, which ran along the edge of the Everglades, in about an hour. I turned down a gravel road, bumping past a dusty-looking ranch and then a palm tree farm. The road petered out in the sawgrass, mud, and murky water that mark the start of the Everglades. They don't call it sawgrass for nothing. That stuff can literally slice your arm off.

I wrestled Ashley out of the car. I was sweating like a hog. I dragged her into the water, ignoring the mosquito stings and the sawgrass slashes on my arms and legs. The water was shallow and tea-colored. I didn't want to think about what was in there.

I looked for some big rocks to sink the body. But when I got back with my first rock, Ashley was gone. A few seconds later I heard a loud plop! It was an alligator, sliding into the water. My own stomach plopped a bit at the thought, but I knew Ashley was gone for good. I wouldn't have to worry about anyone finding the body.

I was home long before Francie got off work. She found

me on the couch watching *You Only Live Twice*, sipping single malt, and eating salted cashews.

"Jake!" she said, surprised. "What would Ashley say?"

"Not a damn thing," I said cheerfully. "She's taking a long rest. So am I."

The scotch made my tongue slip. Francie didn't seem to know what my remark meant, but I'd have to be more careful. I'd have to make sure to go to Jamal's Jym at my regular time Thursday.

I didn't get a chance. Two police detectives, one fat and one skinny, were on my doorstep the next day. They told me Ashley's body was found in the Everglades by a fisherman. Jamal said I was her last appointment, and she never came back. No one had seen her alive since two o'clock yesterday.

I wondered why that alligator had not taken care of my problem, but I didn't say anything. I was cool. I told the cops that Ashley and I worked out as usual. The last I saw, Ashley was running south on the sand to Jamal's. I was headed north, toward my home. I may have sweated a little when I said this, but it was July, wasn't it? The detectives finally left. They seemed satisfied with my answers.

They were back the next day. The fat one asked me to describe my last afternoon with Ashley again. I said we'd worked out on the beach, then I ran home and she ran off the other way.

"You ran home?" the fat cop said.

"All the way," I said, smugly.

"Then why did your car get a parking ticket on the beach about the time that Ashley disappeared?" the skinny one said.

"Uh," I said, and shut up until my lawyer showed up. The cops got a warrant and impounded my car. I wasn't worried. I'd taken it to a carwash.

But the police found three of Ashley's long blonde hairs

in the back seat and her sandy footprint on the inside door. I'd tipped the carwash guy ten bucks, too. Good help is hard to find in Florida.

There was no point in claiming we'd had a little afternoon delight back there because the police found traces of some nasty substances on the seat. The body sort of lets go, you know. No, I guess you wouldn't. You've never killed anyone.

The cops also found plenty of motive. Jamal testified that I'd had a "bitter quarrel"—his words—with Ashley at the gym and tried to get out of the contract.

My wife told the court about my strange behavior on the last day Ashley was seen. I couldn't believe my Francie would do that.

The jury, which was mostly men, couldn't understand how I could kill that gorgeous blonde. They didn't understand she was killing me.

So here I am on death row in Florida. Today is my last day on earth. The chaplain asked if I was sorry.

I am.

I am very sorry I didn't come up with a better body disposal plan. You can't depend on alligators. They don't really like humans, and only eat them if they're desperate or disturbed. It's crocodiles who find us tasty. I learned that in the prison library. I had a lot of time to read while my appeals were being denied.

The warden served up the final irony.

"You can have anything you want for your last meal, Jake," he said. "Even steak."

I couldn't stop laughing when he said that. I remembered what Ashley had said: "Mark my words, dude, red meat will kill you."

That's all we are. Red meat.

And Ashley's one hundred twenty pounds of red meat killed me.

THE MAIDS

G. Miki Hayden

WHEN some of the cows dropped dead in their pasture, Little Marie merely laughed.

"Oh, that's terrible," I said, not understanding. "Those poor things—and now the children might not have milk for their breakfast."

Little Marie gave me quite a wicked look. "And why should the Benoit offspring have milk every day? Do my own children have such luxuries? No. They are whipped and made to fetch and carry for the master, with only what we ourselves grow for their food. If the Benoit children, like the cattle, drop dead, I will not care. And you should not either, Luisah. You have the pink stripes on your body from the mistress's whippings."

Little Marie and I spoke in the language we had taken with us from our home in West Africa. In the house, we were supposed to speak only French, so I glanced around nervously and hurried away, digesting the ideas she had given to me.

To wish the children of this house to die was wrong, was

it not? I was a Catholic and must not think such things. Yet my back and my soul bore the marks of our mistress's malevolence. And I had many troubles in my life, the source of which were solely she and the master, who intended only, always, their own wealth and comfort.

Had I asked to be stolen away from my parents and brought to Haiti, or Sante Domingue, as this was called—the island of Hispaniola—when I was six? Had I asked to be put to work as a house slave from that age until now, so far eighteen years? Had I asked to be married to the slave Michel Benoit, a cruel man, and one of those who helped to oversee the field slaves? Or to have my two children torn from me and sold to a neighboring plantation? No. All this was at the wish of those who owned me. And Little Marie, a fierce adherent of the Vodou priest Ras Berbera, did not entirely shock me with her imaginings.

I brought the morning milk pail to the kitchen. And let that be the last of it for them to drink. I had many questions to ask Little Marie about what she had said. Yet so much work to do, as well. I must scrub the kitchen floor each day before breakfast and help the cook. Once the family was up, I must serve the food, and then begin to make a fire outside for a boiling vat. I must then strip the bedding and place the linen in the tub where I wash each sheet clean every other day. I then heat the iron on the stove and take the wrinkles from the cloth—so that when it goes back on their sweet-smelling beds, the feel and the appearance are just so, to Madame's satisfaction.

This is the start to my day that ends near midnight, when my husband, should he choose, takes the opportunity to abuse me. After which, I may have some six hours—the only ones in the day—to myself, and those spent in the dead sleep of exhaustion.

Angelina stepped up behind me and pulled my cap, setting my restless hair askew. I whirled and smiled. Might I slap her? Only if I desired to be hung from the tree behind the kitchen door, where I have seen others like me hung—black girls who misbehaved and were disrespectful.

"You are up so early, Miss Angelina," I said in French to the twelve-year-old. "Have you had sufficient rest?"

"I am riding to Cap François today, with Mama to buy many exquisite new frocks. A boat has come in from France with the latest fashions." She looked quite pleased at the prospect of making herself pretty.

For sure, she had the basic good looks to be a beauty, with flaming red hair—but sometimes the fiery temper to match. Her parents worried that the girl might not attract a husband because of her lack of amiability. I heard them discuss this. I listen to everything freely in the house, since I am a part of the furniture and nothing to notice.

"You shall be lovely," I declared. But somehow I thought of what Little Marie had said about the children dropping dead, and the idea failed to pain me. "In to breakfast with you, then."

After their meal, the mistress told me I would come to town today with her and her daughters—Angelina and Angelina's eight-year-old sister, Brigitte. If I behaved well, I might be given the job of personal maid to Mademoiselle Angelina, since her own black maid had died of a yellow fever the previous week. I curtsied in gratitude, although I was not sure I was exactly grateful. The new position meant I would dress the girl throughout the day and bathe her, in addition to the regular duties of my own. Such was the life here.

I rode on the outside of the carriage with the driver, Andre, a man who had come as a youth from his home in the Congo. We passed the place where the cows had died. A similar plague had broken out across many of the plantations, the master had told his wife at breakfast today. Madame did not pay particular attention, as she never cared to listen about business. The cows were being burned as we went by, so as not to infect the other livestock.

Death has a certain sense of comfort here, because those who die need not labor any longer. Since my two children were taken from me, I have learned to abort the *pauvres*—the poor little ones—before they are born. We maids have discussed this. We don't want our children to suffer our own fate. So perhaps *this* dying is good, too, for the animals. I do not know. Maybe the Fathers could tell us in church on Sunday, although I do not understand them or the language that they mostly speak.

On top of the coach, I broiled in the fierce sun of Haiti and was jounced mercilessly along the stony road. I thought further on the idea that the Benoit children might soon expire and was not perturbed. My own youngest had died soon after being sold to the master at a nearby plantation. Beaten to death. This was not unusual and no one thought of the matter again, save for me.

I went in with the ladies and helped Angelina and Brigitte try on new clothes. Angelina kicked me once in her displeasure at my clumsy buttoning of her dress. When they were done with me, I went out to wait, before going to the next shop. Finally, after all the dresses and some cloth were purchased and stowed in the coach, they entered the hotel for their lunch. Of course I had forgotten to bring either food or water for myself, but I stood on the square in the area where the slaves loitered in wait for their masters. We must stand somewhere, after all, must we not? Not being invisible.

In a few minutes, Andre, the driver, came across the open park from the carriage. "Come sit on the step of the coach," he urged. "You will find a little shade."

I accepted, and while I sat there, fanning myself with my hand, he brought a sweet yam grown in his own garden to share with me and, after, carried, in his own cup, water from the fountain for me to drink—not once but twice.

No man had ever shown me such kind regard. In fact, no other human had.

A little while later, I thought the mistress and her daughters might be coming back and I stood. Now I was on a level with Andre, where we could speak.

I broached the subject of my earlier talk with Little Marie. "Many of the plantations have dead cows and sheep," I said. "At some of them, the families, too, are dead. Do you think we black slaves can die from this awful disease, as well?"

"No," Andre answered me at once. "This is not an illness for the blacks to suffer. Just the whites and their animals. The disease is of greed and greed is not catching, the Vodou priests say. You must come and hear them."

Indeed, I was a Catholic and I feared the Vodou for more than one reason. "What do your priests tell you?" I asked, in curiosity.

"Not only the priests but the Maroon chief François Mackandal has talked to us. He was once owned by the Juin family, but set himself free. He says that we may rid ourselves of the plantation owners forever." A spark of excitement brought Andre's face to a life he had not shown before. "Mackandal said that in the homeland of the French, the peasants talk about revolt as well."

"Ah," I exclaimed. I had heard the Benoits speak of farmer uprisings in their native land, yet not with approval. But perhaps such a thing was now permissible. The Maroons, of course, I knew about—disobedient slaves who had run off to the hills. Had they a chief?

"The priest says the God of the French must be cruel, because they act cruelly in obedience to him, but our loa, the spirits we serve, are full of love only. Those of us who worship before the altars in the Vodou temple are loving to all who wish us well. The French do not, so we need not tolerate them any longer, but may seek out vengeance." Andre smiled, empty spaces showing where teeth were gone, either through beatings or simply because our teeth fell out from lack of nourishment.

I smiled, too.

"The houngans—our priests—and the mambos—our priestesses—say the bullets of the French will turn to water. They cannot touch us. Our God will protect us and theirs will fail."

I had a great deal to think about on the ride home, past fields of cane and sugar-cane presses, past cotton fields and land where the indigo grew. This island produced bountiful riches. The master praised it often for its cocoa and rum and molasses—none of which I knew by taste. What if those who worked the land were to own it? What if I had a fancy silk frock—ruffled on the bottom to keep off the mosquitoes? Perhaps Andre, who would work his own property, would buy me frocks and never hit me with his fists.

With our wheels rumbling deeper into the countryside, the stench of death grew. Fallen sheep lay scattered like logs in the neighboring pasture. Mistress must be frightened by the sight, revolted by the smell. In the distance, I observed flames and dense, black smoke. When we came nearer, I saw a plantation house on fire. The fine home was quickly consumed as we drove by, with slaves outside laughing, and no owner sending for water to fight the blaze. Where were the master and the mistress and their children? Dead of the plague?

I jolted awake the instant we reached the Benoit wrought-iron gate, and, soon, Andre fetched me down, daring to risk a moment's delay in opening the coach door to our mistress and the children.

* * *

I KNEW what all the slaves were told. Rules had been passed by our masters for us to live by and those rules said that no slaves might congregate during the day or night. We must not sing, except in the fields. And no drums were to be heard anywhere in Haiti. These things were expressly forbidden to us.

What I knew from listening to the master's conversation with his friends was that other rules had been passed in the colony as well—the Code Noir, which said we must be fed a certain amount of food every day and given two hours after lunch to rest. We must have Sunday off to say our prayers. But the owners laughed and continued on, as they chose. Yet the rule on the black slaves against our meeting together was strictly enforced. And that meant we were not to gather for Vodou ceremony.

I am a Catholic, as I have said, and always attended services with the family. As a Catholic, I know right from wrong and I have been told that the practice of Vodou is a grave wrong. But add to that, since it is not allowed, I am afraid to go because of the punishments. After I smooth the clothes with my hot iron, sometimes it is used to sear the skin of a slave who has misbehaved. Other times, a very bad slave will have honey poured on him and be staked to the ground, where he is eaten by insects. Other times . . . oh many evil things are done. Perhaps the Vodou priest is right. Perhaps their God, Jesus, is no good, since the acts of the whites are so very wicked.

Early the next morning, Little Marie invited me in quiet whispers in our tongue to come to the Vodou ceremony that same night.

I wondered what had inspired her to ask me that. "Has someone told you anything about me?" I inquired. I was jealous. Perhaps she and Andre were close and they had talked. Perhaps they were lovers. I must shake the dresses he would buy me from my mind.

The blankness in her eyes seemed to tell my answer. "We must know those we can count on," she said. "Not cook. She is old and unreliable." Little Marie darted her head around, watching to see if anyone spied. "Midnight," she murmured. "Toward the swamp. Past the stables."

This was out of the question. A Vodou ceremony was no place for a baptized Catholic. I practically shivered I was so afraid to think of it—although Andre would be there and many others. Could they crucify or hang us all? But they might. The idea was not entirely inconceivable.

Thus, when I found my weary self at something like midnight on the path to the swamp, I knew that I must turn back. I was a Catholic, which was enough, although many who were Catholic for Sunday were Vodou, too. But the Vodou slaves were those who had come here grown, who were already Vodou from their homeland. I had come here too young to know the ways of the loa—the spirits—or to worship them.

When I arrived at their meeting place, the bonfire was a small one and not a sound could be heard. The field slaves danced—and Little Marie and Andre—the only ones from those who worked in the house. The dancing was silent, since we were forbidden to sing or to drum.

Some on their knees or on the ground jerked in their bodies. I resolved not to do that because my dress must remain very clean. The difference between a house slave and a field slave is our clothing. Our garments are not rags like theirs. We must not offend the eyes of the family.

Andre, who saw me after a time, smiled. He came to meet me and pulled me into his circle. Was I now Vodou? The Catholic Fathers would say that this was wrong.

I did not feel wrong, however, only pleased, as the mistress is pleased when she goes to a ball at Cap François. I had never had such a time before.

* * *

AFTER dancing and listening to the soft worship and the talk of the priest, I understood. The cattle had not been infected with a disease. They had been poisoned. The Maroon chief François Mackandal had given the slaves a deadly plant to scatter where the cattle grazed. At many of the big homes across the whole island, this poison was put even in the family's food. So, no wonder we blacks could not catch this illness which was for the whites only. And this, Andre had known. I was surprised.

Creeping back to the frond-thatched hut I shared with Michel, surnamed Benoit to mark him as their property, I wondered in regard to the rightness or wrongness of killing the whites. The Fathers might say that this went against the wishes of their Jesus, but the Vodou priest said the black people's God would strongly approve.

I always tried to act to please this powerful Jesus, who would be kind when I finally arrived in his heaven—but now I was not sure. If Jesus belonged to the white people only and the loa, like the Twins and Yemaya, to the slaves, perhaps I was more meant to serve the gods of the blacks. I did not know and could ask no one here. I might ask the Fathers if their God could love me as black as I was, but I already realized that the answer must be no. The French did not love me, so how could their God? Still, I had been a Catholic since I was six, eating the holy sacrament each week, and was thus claimed.

I could not have entered my hut more quietly. If Michel had been sleeping properly as he ought to have been, I would not have awakened him. But no, he had been lying in wait for me, which, tonight, only meant that he pushed me out of the bed onto the floor. I was used to sleeping on the floor when he preferred me to. I should not have gotten into his bed, though, because then he sat up, reached to me, and grabbed his hand into my hair, tearing at it. He shook me that way until my brain felt rattled and my neck nearly broken. Then he let go with another strong push. Although tears came to my eyes, this was not so bad as sometimes. I was not punched.

Without a word, Michel fell to sleep and I moved further away so that he could not reach me. I waited for my head to settle down before I, too, slept, my bruised body uncomforted by the packed dirt.

Over the next two weeks, I attended the Vodou several times more. Less frightened than I had been, I was, nonetheless, afraid. If we were caught . . . But at the Vodou, no one treated me badly. I was accepted as one of them. We danced, and no matter how tired I was from my work, I felt strengthened by what we did there.

I saw the future and pictured going on this way, until I perhaps died of the fever or of a beating from Michel. I had no idea that anything would change. How could it? What would change? More cows had died, and several of the horses, but new ones would be bought. We would go on as always. I would become a little more tired each year and my face and body more scarred and ugly. That was all.

"You must be the one to do it for us all," whispered Little Marie to me one morning. She pressed a small, closed wooden box into my hand and gestured for me to hide it in my apron. I placed it there, while she nodded approvingly. "Don't touch what's in there with your fingers," she warned. "It will kill you dead."

Naturally, my eyes went wide with great amazement. This was the poison fungus they talked about and I must hold it? I could not be calm.

Little Marie clenched her jaw grimly and went and looked into the other rooms to be sure no one was hiding there. Of course, we spoke the language of our own tribe, the Bagandas. But still. "You are the only one beside cook who handles the food directly and cook is not on our side. We cannot trust her."

We heard the rustling of a silk dress on the way down the hall, so we parted, and I was left only half comprehending what I must do. They trusted me—that was all I understood. I was trusted and cook was not. I was Vodou like them, even though a Catholic. But, of course, as a Catholic, I must not poison the family because Thou Shalt Not Kill. This was correct, was it not?

I felt fairly sure that I must not poison the Benoits, that Jesus, whom I was sworn to as a servant, and baptized in his name with the holy water, would not want me to. I must think of a way to say no to the Vodou slaves.

In the meantime, the wooden box seemed on fire against my body. Every step I took, it clacked and bounced. Would the poison come out of the box and attack me? It hit against the stove and made a noise. I jumped. I even broke a dish that day and cook tattled to the mistress, who slapped me hard across the face. "You stupid black girl. Why must I deal with these stupid blacks in this Godforsaken country?" Madame said.

Oh, if she would find the wooden box, I would be buried alive. I felt ill all day and went straight to bed that night, hiding the wooden box behind the cabin door, which Michel left open to get a little air. But I should not have stayed home that night for Michel abused me and then hit me many times for his extra pleasure. But he is neither Christian nor Vodou and only does the bidding of Pierre Benoit.

In the morning, Little Marie could only glare at me meaningfully. Again, the box was in my smock because I had no place else to hide anything that I might own. Luckily, the single possession to my name was an old wooden comb, and that I carried in my pocket always, though many teeth were missing from it and it did not comb my hair at all well.

That night I went to the Vodou ceremony. Where else was I to go that offered the company of friends, and solace? François Mackandal, the Maroon chief, was present and came to me personally during the dancing to whisper hot words into my ear. He called me a good girl, a smart girl, one who would help the blacks of this island claim our own—before the white men killed us off altogether, as they had the Indians who had lived here before. Where were those Indians? Dead slaves on the trash pile of the whites. I was a good girl, a smart girl. Only one answer remained for our kind.

Andre walked me quietly across the fields. "I'm afraid of the punishments," I whispered to him. "The whites will punish me with a great deal of pain."

"They will be dead," Andre assured me. "Too dead to punish. And we will all run off. We will be Maroons."

"I can't run off alone." I hesitated.

"We will *all* run off," Andre said, pulling me by the arm closer to him as we passed under the shadow of the stables. "You and I will run off together."

The horses inside snickered and we hurried on.

The next day, I got what little milk the milkers handed me and stopped before I reached the kitchen door. Carefully, I opened the wooden box with the hem of my apron. Inside was a gray powder. Would this make the milk look spoiled? I shook some in and the powder settled on the top, like dirt. I closed the box and placed it back in my apron. This was no good. The milk would not work. I could not get all of the poison in.

By the time I got the milk onto the pantry shelf, it looked the same as everyday cow's milk, white and foamy. But I had not placed enough poison in it, so the drink would probably only make the family sick. That was possibly better, since, as a Catholic, I was not actually supposed to kill. I would tell François Mackandal that the failure had not been my fault and Andre and I could still go to the Maroons.

Master came down early and I served him his coffee with plenty of the milk. "The coffee is too white, girl," he said. "It will not be hot."

"I'm sorry, sir. Will you drink that? I will run fetch you another cup." I went and stood in the pantry and stared into the milk, then I went back out to the dining room. "The coffee is boiling, sir. I will bring it in an instant."

The master's hand was on his chest and an odd look marched across his face. "Are you unwell, sir? Shall I go get Madame?"

He shook his head and I dared to stand in place and watch him, feigning concern. In a moment, he slumped to one side and collapsed on the floor. The poison must be very strong or the master must be very weak.

I did not feel at all bad, but I ran for Blanche, the mistress's personal maid. "Hurry upstairs and tell Mistress that the master is ill. She must come at once."

I passed the master on my way back into the kitchen. He did not twitch.

In the pantry once more, I stared at the milk, which looked quite ordinary still, though the froth was gone. I listened to cook in the kitchen banging her pans and waited for whatever was to happen next. I had not meant to kill him, possibly. That much powder had been very little. I would make my apology to Jesus later in a prayer and to the Twins and to the Dead, which I supposed now included Pierre Benoit.

Too nervous to stand still another minute, I went out the pantry door to the yard. I barely knew what I was doing. My only thought was to stay away from the master for a minute or two until the mistress was over her initial shock. But I might have been sorry for leaving the safety of the house because, unfortunately, Michel was out there.

"I have been banging on the door, you lazy black girl. Didn't you hear me? Go and tell the master I am here, as he called." Michel reached to give me a smack across my face, but I jumped out of the way in time.

"Oh, Michel, something terrible. The master is ill. He has the white plague."

Michel shook his head. "No, it isn't possible."

I wrung my hands. "Yes, it is true." I could barely keep a nervous smile off my face. But I thought with some sense of accomplishment that I had for once spoiled Michel's assurance of mind. He must worry about his own position on the plantation now, must he not? "Poor Michel," I added. "I hope this will mean nothing too bad for you."

I could not tell what was going on in that odd brain of his, since he had a way of keeping his thoughts to himself while acting superior, but I supposed he would be very glum.

"Don't talk so stupid, girl, or I'll give you a beating." He pretended he would advance on me, though I knew he would not. If the mistress saw him, she would chide him for wasting his time.

"Poor Michel," I repeated. "I feel sorry for you. But in any case, I will bring you a small cup of milk."

I ran into the pantry and poured my husband half a cup of the liquid, rushing out again, lest he go before he'd had his refreshment. If Jesus meant for him to die, Michel would be there and drink the milk and the poison would be sufficient to bring him low. And maybe he would only become very, very ill.

Michel wrapped his giant black knuckles around the delicate porcelain and I recalled that very fist cracking into my face and breaking the bone beneath my eye. I ran my fingers over the spot on my cheek, but quickly took my hand away and smiled encouragingly. He drank. I really hadn't served him much. I took the cup back and brought it into the kitchen. There, I set it into the trash, under a heap of eggshells and coffee grinds, so no one would drink from it accidentally. Cook was in the middle of preparing the meal.

I had not dressed Angelina yet this morning. She must be livid. I went back out to the yard.

"Oh, poor Michel," I cried out at once. He was on the ground, gasping. He had not died straightaway like the master. I supposed he was stronger. He might even live. "Are you not well?"

The day had been a brilliant one, but now some clouds covered up the sun. That would be a relief from the intense heat, making our trip to the Maroons in the hills that much easier.

Michel no longer seemed to be breathing and I reached over and pinched the flesh of his arm very hard. I wanted to see if he was dead or alive and that was one way to tell. Since he didn't move, I assumed the worst and dragged him into the outdoor larder, where the less perishable staples are kept. I saw no sense in leaving his dead body lying out for anyone to see.

"I'm sorry, Jesus," I said out loud. "But, Michel, you were not a very good man. Did you think nothing would ever come of your badness? That you would never be punished?"

I went into the house and the dining room, where a crowd was gathered around the mistress and around the master's body. "How terrible," I said, nearly wailing. "The plague has struck." Then the idea occurred to me, finally, that Jesus himself had used me as the instrument of his revenge. Was not their God a wrathful God? Oh yes. This was a very sensible and logical thought.

"Poor Mistress," I consoled her quietly, as I was suddenly tired and yearned to lie down. The killing of men, though it might not take physical strength, is an effort to exhaust one.

Mistress's eyes met my own and for once her face was fragile, as bone China is fragile.

I shooed the other slaves away from her presence and

helped the mistress to a chair. "I will get you a coffee," I suggested. "The day will be a long one for you." Not actually, it wouldn't, however, and wasn't the right thing for her troubles to be over, too? Could a woman like her live without her husband? But in any case, I wasn't truly concerned with her best interests, simply eager to fulfill what had been asked of me by the Maroon chief and by God.

The milk was not running at all low and the liquid still appeared very ordinary. I gave Mistress the sugar to her coffee, as she preferred. I could have sworn for one moment when I handed her the cup that she almost said 'Thank you.' But she did not, and of course, I bobbed my head anyway.

She sent one of the men slaves for the surgeon, although the fact that the master was dead should have been quite obvious to her. "The plague, Mistress," I explained. "He has expired of the plague." I put on a sad face, since that was what one usually did.

I didn't like to watch her die, so I went back into the pantry and poured three goblets of the milk, one for each of the children—the two girls and the boy. I set them all on a tray and brought the tray out with me. As I passed the dining table, I saw a vomit coming out of the mistress's mouth. The poison in the milk had not lost its power, although it had already killed two men. Upstairs, I first brought the Benoit son, Henri, his milk. "Here, young sir. We are late with the breakfast. Have this to tide you over, until we serve."

I did the same for the two girls, but Angelina was in a rage. "I've not had my bath, you lazy, lazy girl." She hit me on the shoulder with the back of her hairbrush, then hit me again. I barely felt the blows because my mind did not think of them, spinning as it was with so much else.

"I am wrong, Mademoiselle, and I pray to Jesus Christ to forgive me."

With that, she was appeased and turned and drank down her milk.

So it was that I obeyed the summons given to me by God or the devil, I really don't know.

Downstairs, the house slaves milled about in some confusion with the mistress, too, dead on the carpet. Little Marie came over and hugged me. I didn't recall having been hugged ever before. "I will go and get the others," she said.

When she left the room, I went upstairs again to be sure the children were all dead. Like the cows in the field, they had each breathed their last. How quickly the Vodou poison worked.

Angelina lay sprawled across the floor in her nightdress, her plump white limbs quite akimbo, her soft, blazing-red hair shining in the sun. I took the silver comb from Angelina's dressing table top. In its place, I put my old wooden comb, a sign that I did not care to steal.

Andre was in the house when I went down and we nodded to one another as an acknowledgment that our work was complete. The field slaves would burn the Benoit house to cinders and the bodies of the family with it—along with the dead overseer, Michel. Andre and I headed toward the hills to claim and work our parcel of land.

And several decades later, I did not forbid my then-grown sons to go to Cap François along with the priest Boukman to overcome the still-ruling whites. A few years after that, Haiti became the country of the loa, with the Indians dead, the Spanish departed, the French overthrown, and only we blacks and some few mulattos left to harvest the island's rich and hard-won soil.

Guardian Angel

Elaine Togneri

I LIKE to think my friend Jenny knows an angel watches over her now . . . now that it's too late. The angel's marble eyes stare at traffic on the busy county road, not the verdant spring brush or weathered Jersey scrub pines surrounding the cemetery. With wings partially unfurled, ever ready, the angel safeguards her—a guardian angel, the kind she always wished for—the kind she never had.

Pulling purple foil off the hyacinth I purchased at a Cranbury Road farm stand a few miles away, I caught a breath of sweetness, then knelt at the side of Jenny's grave. I couldn't bring myself to lean on her, though I'd had no qualms about the assorted other souls I'd walked on to reach her. I told myself I didn't want to crush the sparse newly sprung grass attempting to cover her portion of dirt. I hoped it fared better than the flowers I had planted over the last four weeks—two sets of imported tulips that wilted to the ground overnight, carnations that died within a week, the gladiolas . . . I stabbed the ground with my trowel and dug around their dried brown leaves. They crackled and crumbled in my hand as I grasped them, but the plant pulled up easily enough, and I set it to the side. A few more shovelfuls and the hole was big enough for my new offering. I depotted the hyacinth. Its vibrant purple reminded me of the silk dress Jenny had worn to my daughter's wedding. How alive she'd been then, full of joy for her goddaughter, Sandra, and the husband she'd chosen. The image of Jenny twirling on the dance floor, long dark hair swinging, full skirt shimmering with each movement, haunted me.

I blinked back tears and placed the plant in the hole. Jenny had had a good life, I told myself, then recognized it for what it was—a platitude to comfort those left behind. Most of her life had been rotten. Overcontrolling parents. An abusive ex-husband. Painful memories she couldn't even talk about. Only the last several years had been good.

Not that mine was much better. I'd lost my husband when my daughter was only ten. I hadn't been to his grave since she moved away. Was it five years already? We used to make an annual pilgrimage on his birthday to bring flowers and clean off the stone. But now, I'd even given up wondering why he died or what would have happened if he'd lived.

And here I was back in a graveyard. I patted the dirt smooth around the flower and whispered, "Take care of this one, Jen. Rest in peace." I splashed a bottleful of water around the base, then stood. The petals drooped noticeably. I sighed and closed my eyes. I knew what I had to do.

I WENT directly to Mel's.

"Whose boat?" I asked him as I stepped on the brass rail to take a seat at the bar. Two spaces of the parking lot had been given over to a Grady White pleasure boat with a prominent homemade FOR SALE sign.

His mouth opened, then he froze for a moment. "Um, ah

. . . well . . . let me get you a beer." He strode over to the tap, selected a tall glass from the freezer, and studied the amber liquid foaming down its tilted side.

Red heat seared my face in spite of the air-conditioning. "That's not . . . ?"

Mel nodded as he set a coaster on the polished bar, then placed my glass exactly center. He couldn't meet my gaze, and rightly so.

"And you're letting him sell it here?" I let the heat flush through my whole body. I didn't reach for the glass. "I thought you were Jenny's friend."

"Come on now, Barb. . . ." Mel inched the beer closer. "It's not like he pushed her or anything. It was an accident."

"If Greg Stevens wants to have an accident on his boat, then he should be the dead one." I jumped off the stool. "Not Jenny."

"Maybe if life was fair," he whispered. "But it sure hasn't been for me." He shot a piercing look at me. "Not for any of us."

I thought about his youngest, sick with leukemia, and pinched the bridge of my nose. "Yeah, you're right, Mel." I straddled the stool, raised my glass, and gulped a mouthful of foam before I hit the cool brew. After a swallow and a shrug, I added, "I just want to know what happened. Maybe . . . make some sense of it all."

"I can't make sense of anything." His eyes glittered with tears. "Not one damn thing!" Mel turned abruptly and grabbed the remote. He cleared his throat several times as he stared at the TV screen.

One elbow balanced on the bar's edge, I leaned my chin on my hand and watched with him. Swatches of color and unintelligible bits of noise flashed past—lives never completed. I took a slug of beer to clear my own throat.

Mel stopped clicking when he hit the golf channel, vistas

of green as far as the camera could see and the soothing tones of a whispering announcer.

I zoned out everything else until I finished my beer. After a trip to the ladies room, I found another draft waiting. "Thanks," I said, sliding back onto the stool.

"Least I can do." Mel dabbed a cloth at a drop on the counter. "Some bartender I turned out to be. Geez! I'm supposed to cheer people up." He shook his head and straightened my coaster. "I'm sorry. I know you must be hurting."

"I just want to know how it happened." And understand why. But was that possible?

"They were here that afternoon." He polished as he spoke, shining the laminated counter as if rubbing would improve its finish. "Drinking heavy." He stopped and stared straight into my eyes. "You want to blame somebody. I'm your man. So lost in my own sorrows, I sold them a case without a thought for what could happen."

"You didn't put them on the boat, send them out to sea." I picked up my glass, and another drop of condensation hit the bar.

"No, I didn't. Didn't make them drink it either." He rubbed at the drop. "But I had my part in it, didn't I? Didn't we all?"

Not me, I thought, draining my glass.

Mel worked on another section of the bar, drawing circles with the rag.

Experience told me he was finished talking. I tossed a couple of bucks on the counter and left him to his ritual.

Two beers and here I was out in the parking lot, drunk enough to sneak aboard *The Scavenger.* With sweaty hands, I grabbed hold of the ladder and boosted myself to the first step. Well, I had a right, and one not gained solely from the bottle. Jenny was my friend and more—my confidant, a coconspirator in the endless battle to win at life, and maybe, one of the few who could understand my pain. The last step of the ladder creaked as I bounded onto the deck, blinking against the brilliance of the sun.

It shone too brightly in a world without Jenny.

The boat's scuffed wood trim and reeking mildewed carpet spoke of years of heavy use. I held my breath as I descended into the cabin. A built-in table and cushioned benches provided seating in the open area. A tiny bathroom lay forward and sleeping quarters aft. According to the newspaper report, Greg and the others didn't hear a sound as Jenny fell to her death. Too drunk to watch where she stepped.

Not the Jenny I knew.

Covered with sweat and lungs complaining, I burst out of the cabin.

A man's head and wide shoulders appeared above the railing. "Can I help you?" he asked. He swung his legs on deck.

"That depends," I said, lifting one hand to shade my eyes. "Are you Greg?"

He smiled. "Yup, the boat's mine. Needs a little work, but—"

"I don't care crap about the boat."

His smile faded. "And you are?" He stepped toward me.

"I'm Barbara, as in Jenny's best friend Barbara." I held my place.

Greg turned sideways and sighed. "Oh, yeah, I remember Jenny told me you were away. At your daughter's or something, right?"

"What happened?" I turned to face him. "What did you do to Jenny?"

"Huh? I don't know what you're thinking, lady. It's what she did to me."

"That's a laugh. She's the one who's dead."

"On my boat . . . I used to love the ocean." He gripped the rail. "I was out on her every chance I could get. Not anymore." He wrenched his hands to his sides. "That's why I'm selling her. I've been a fisherman all my life. Now, I can't even look at the sea."

"I repeat, it's Jenny who's dead."

He leaned into my face. "And you'd rather it was me. Well, let me tell you, lady. So would I." He twisted away and stomped toward the ladder.

"Wait!" I yelled and dodged after him. "Wait."

Greg paused at the bottom of the ladder and squinted up at me. "Why?"

"Jenny was my friend. I've got to know."

He shrugged. "Seems to me you've already made up your mind."

I swallowed hard. I wouldn't say please. "You owe me that much." I scuttled down the ladder as he considered my statement. He'd have to refuse me face to face. I stood between him and the entrance to Mel's. "What happened to Jenny?"

"You don't want to hear this." He shook his head and sighed, then met my unwavering gaze. "I think . . . she jumped."

"You're a liar. Jenny wouldn't." No way. My brain said get out of there, but my feet wouldn't respond.

"I don't know what else to think." He looked off into the distance. "We sailed out to watch the stars and started drinking boilermakers. We were making toasts with each round, giggling and joking. Just having a grand old time.

"Jenny insisted we had to find the big dipper. We all staggered on deck. By that time, we couldn't tell one constellation from another. I started making jokes about dippers. Me and Bill got thirsty from laughing so much and went down for another drink." Greg shook his head. "Like we hadn't had enough already. Susie had to go to the john. Jenny stayed topside. I never saw her again."

"Then how can you say she jumped?"

"Look, the front of the boat has rails. Back here the sides are as high as your knees. You don't just fall over them."

"Then somebody must have pushed her."

"You're crazy, lady. As crazy as your friend. She as good as told me she was going to jump."

"When? Why? Sounds like more lies."

"Believe what you want, but at the bar, she told me drowning was a good way to die. It couldn't hurt half as much as living. If I'd known she was serious, I'd have run away in one hot minute."

I couldn't listen any longer. I forced my feet to respond and sprinted to my car. Inside, with a shaky hand, I turned the key. I floored the gas and zoomed out of the parking lot. The radio blared Weather Report's "Birdland," and with each note my mind replayed the words, "Jenny jumped." I snapped off the sound. Greg was wrong. He had to be!

Then why did one part ring true? Jenny had told me once about a rip tide that pulled her out to sea. Far from shore, battered and exhausted, she gave up and let the waves take her. She closed her eyes and waited for death, but instead, thudded up on shore far from her blanket. "I guess it wasn't my time," she said, "but that's the way to die, being rocked to sleep by Mother Nature." She'd laughed.

If she had fallen in, half-drunk, could she have closed her eyes and waited?

Blinking away tears, I slammed on my brakes too late, swerved, and rammed the back of a van.

THE road service towed my car to a body shop. With the bumper crunched in toward the tire, I couldn't drive it, but the garage assured me it wouldn't be a big job. I figured it wasn't half as big as the one I was tackling.

A tall, thin mechanic with half-moons of grease under his fingernails gave me a ride home and left me with instructions to call my insurance agent. I promised I would, much as I didn't look forward to the hassle. Insurance companies brought up bad memories.

My husband's suicide.

Them dragging their feet with the payment. Me falling behind on the mortgage. Sandra and I almost out on the street. Bad as my marriage had been, I was used to it. I knew what to expect—late nights, alcoholic fights, and a next-day apology when he swore it would never happen again. Financial hell wasn't much better. A nameless, faceless bank stealing my home. How could I fight back?

That's when my friendship with Jenny blossomed. She stepped in with advice, even recommended a lawyer. One letter from the uptown lawyer, and the insurance company paid up. I owed her a lot. Thinking about her good deeds and caring nature eased the tension between my shoulder blades, and I relaxed with a deep breath.

Fifteen minutes later, no-car-phobia kicked in. My mind kept presenting all these places I needed to go—if I only had transportation. The trouble was, I did—Jenny's car, a cute little red sports car, she'd left me. It sat in the garage with a couple of boxes of pictures and mementos on the back seat ever since the registration was transferred to me. Jenny's cousin had taken many things, but was selling the rest and had boxed what Jenny wanted me to have. I hadn't gathered the gumption to go through it yet.

I didn't have to actually look at the pictures to use the car. I could just move the boxes off the back seat onto the garage floor. They would get lost in the collection of newspapers, boxes, and exercise equipment that littered my garage. Maybe I'd never have to deal with them. I was sure I'd forget all about them once I arrived at the mall. Shopping, every woman's opiate, would take care of that.

* * *

THE car's tires looked dangerously low, so I made my first stop a service station with an air pump. When the bell stopped ringing on the last tire, I remembered the donut. It had to need air. I popped open the trunk and tossed aside a worn navy windbreaker, an old clothesline, and a small black leather case that felt heavy. A softball, bat, and glove were stuffed into one corner, a plastic garbage bag, probably keeping an emergency blanket clean, in another. As I filled the shameful excuse for a tire foisted on the American public by some cost-savings mogul at the auto companies, I stared at the leather case, wondering what it contained. If it was anything valuable, I should call Jenny's cousin and let her know.

The donut didn't look much better after I filled it, but that's how they were. I wrapped the hose around the air pump's lever. Before slamming the trunk, I grabbed the case. I tossed it on the passenger seat, then started the car. Soon, I found an opening and pulled into the traffic building on Route 18. Of course, the light at Tices Lane turned red. As I waited, I unzipped the case and flipped open the top.

A gun! My foot slipped from the brake. I jammed it back on, and the car jerked abruptly. What was Jenny doing with a gun? A horn blared behind me, and when I glanced up, I saw the light had changed. I passed Tices Lane and took the next turn, driving on automatic pilot until I found myself back at my house. After turning off the car, I pressed myself against the seat back, held my hands over my eyes, and let my mind whirl, trying to assimilate the gun into what I knew of Jenny.

I stumbled into the house, pushed aside a pile of strewn mail, and gingerly placed the case on the kitchen table. It might be loaded. I didn't even know how to check. I flipped open the case again. The gun had a chrome finish with a fake pearl handle. On the side, the manufacturer had etched in two halves of a snake with the letters "BOA" in between. Below that, it read "CAL .25 Auto Pat. Pend."

I wondered if Jenny had registered it. Should I call the police to check? And if she hadn't? What about her cousin? She might know something. How would I start the conversation? I had to think.

Wait a minute, it might not even be Jenny's gun. That made the most sense. She was holding it for a male friend. But who? And how did I get it back to him? I sure didn't want to keep it. I grabbed the case and started toward the car. Bad idea. There was no way I could drive knowing the gun was rolling around the trunk. I returned to the kitchen, extracted the gun, careful not to touch the trigger, and turned the case inside out. No license. No bullets. That proved my theory. If it was hers, she'd have both. Relieved, I slipped the gun back in the case and stuck it in the rear of the pantry behind some vegetarian beans I'd bought with healthy thoughts in mind, but never eaten.

I headed out to the mall again and ended up at the library, standing in line at the reference desk, prepared with a most outrageous lie. The librarian had sympathetic eyes, obviously corrected by contacts from the way she held them so wide open.

"I need to find some books on guns," I started.

Her eyes opened even wider.

I shrugged my shoulders. "This guy I just started dating . . ."

She nodded, her eyes sympathetic once more, perhaps a casualty of the dating game herself. "Let's try *The Shooter's Bible* to start with," she said and hustled me off.

By the time I left the library, I knew the gun's make, model, and date of origin. It used a magazine that held seven shots. The magazine would release with a button, so I could see if it was loaded. And as far as the librarian was concerned, she'd helped the cause of true love.

But none of this information told me who owned the gun. I popped open the trunk in the parking lot. Maybe the license had fallen out. The windbreaker had a huge pocket in front. I fished out a ski hat, gloves, and . . . a magazine chock-full of bullets. Oh, Jenny! I slammed the trunk.

After opening the car door, I sank into the driver's seat, fighting nausea. I had never realized the depth of Jenny's fear. No wonder she wanted a guardian angel. She needed protection in case her brutal ex-husband showed up. She hadn't told me much about her life with him. Just that running away from home was the smartest thing she'd ever done. Yet, she must have been prepared for a battle royal if she was carrying a gun. I swallowed a mouthful of bile. For all of my professed friendship and loyalty, I hadn't even suspected.

I cleared my throat, trying to quash the vile taste of partially digested beer. Jenny had been fearful of reprisal from her ex, and now, she was dead.

Maybe Greg or Bill knew him . . . maybe, one of them, or even both. That would make sense. They covered for each other. They pushed her off the boat because she'd left the guy, wounding his ego. I knew all the classic signs, having been there myself and having escaped by a tiny piece of luck—my husband had ultimately chosen to turn his violence against himself.

I ran back into the library and looked in the phone book, waving my helpmate back to her reference desk. A petite woman named Susie had also been on the boat that night. If she'd heard something or knew something . . . I owed it to Jenny to find out. I found her address quickly, an apartment complex nearby. Stopping by a liquor store on the way would guarantee me a greeting as an old friend, even though the only thing we had in common was Mel's.

I WAS right about the invitation, only Susie had started without me. I gritted my teeth. There wasn't enough liquor in the world to alleviate guilt. She needed to confess, and I would listen until she did.

"Which one pushed her?" I asked, watching carefully in case I needed to dodge a spill, as she poured the last of her bottle of wine into my cup.

"What you talking about, girl?" She hiccuped and erupted into peals of laughter.

"Jenny. I'm talking about Jenny. And I'm going to keep talking about Jenny, until you tell me."

"You gonna open that?" She pointed to the bottle of cheap Merlot I'd set on a cork coaster so I wouldn't chip the glass in her coffee table. Although she had a set of wine-glasses on display in a china cabinet, we drank from nine-ounce plastic cups.

"As soon as I get an answer," I said. "Remember that night on the boat with Jenny?"

"Yeah, now, that girl could drink. Didn't like none of that beer either." Susie gulped a mouthful of wine. "No, classy stuff. Like what you brought. Had to have a cork for her."

Some of that was true anyway. Jenny liked good wine. "So she was drinking wine?"

"Yeah, the guys told her switch to beer. They were so drunk! You know how drunk they were?" She leaned close to me and stabbed me with a long purple fingernail.

I tried not to flinch. "No. How drunk were they?"

"Theys was so drunk; they couldn't even pull the cork." She giggled. "Bill was gonna push it in, but she didn't want no cork in her wine. No way." The fingernail stabbed me again.

I rose, gripping the Merlot. "I'll just open this. Go on."

" 'Bout time." She drained her cup and pushed herself to her feet with the other hand, then followed me into the kitchen. "Anyways, the guys went down for another beer.

Me, I needed to freshen up and all. You know how that sea air just melts your makeup."

I nodded, twisting the corkscrew.

"Jenny had that bottle between her legs, yanking on that cork for all she was worth. Told me she was used to showing guys up." Susie's burp turned into a sob. "That, um, yeah, that . . ." She whimpered, "I never saw her after that."

The cork popped and wine splashed, burgundy spots pooling in the stainless steel sink. I just stood there. Susie, drunk as a skunk and telling the same tale as Greg. Was it true? I refilled her cup and set the bottle down.

A few more sips, and she started bawling in earnest. No amount of coaxing would turn off the tears. Fearful of my own, I gave her a dishtowel and headed for home. It'd been a long day.

After I arrived, I carried the boxes from the garage into my living room, without a care for the dust or grime they'd leave on my light blue carpet. I settled into my high-backed reading chair and snapped on the pole lamp. My stomach rumbled. Hours had passed since supper was due. In spite of that, I grabbed a handful of photos from one of the boxes. Some things were more important.

An hour later, I gave in and made a plate of cheese, wheat crackers, and a sliced apple that had softened over the last week. The boxes held mostly pictures. Pictures of Jenny and her friends, their kids, their dogs. Just pictures. Some loose, some in envelopes, some in albums. Some faces I recognized, other I didn't. On the bottom of the first box, I found a long, flat, sealed envelope. Was opening it an invasion of privacy? Do the dead even have privacy? These things were mine now, right?

I tore the sealed edge and extracted the contents, a photo—a professional one of Jenny in all her dark-haired glory, eyes challenging the camera. I flung it onto the pile and dashed to the bathroom for a tissue. In the mirror, my eyes lacked her daring; they flooded with tears. Three tissues later, I carried the box into the living room.

I sorted through the mementos next—a cookie jar shaped like a Victorian House, a large black velvet jewel case, a couple of books. The books were hardcovers, autographed by their authors—all of them women—a couple feminist tomes and several mysteries. I opened one. The bookplate declared, "This book belongs to Jenny Solgani." Underneath, a crowd of flowers alternated hues of pink. I closed my eyes for a second, remembering her love of fresh bouquets. Then, I closed the book and set it on the carpet.

I opened the jewel case. On a raised flap, a string of pearls hung, the outline of luminescent lips, shining like Jenny's one conceit—her perfect teeth. I clasped the pearls around my neck. More tears flooded my eyes, and the box careened off my lap and bounced hard on one of the books, falling open and scattering its insides.

Another envelope—a small one. Having won the battle once, I didn't fight it again. I ripped open the flap. More photographs, black-and-white ones from a self-developing camera. The first showed a strange close-up of a man sleeping. He lay on a carpet, instead of a bed. The background was dark, and I studied the picture closely before I could figure out what bothered me about it. He lay in what I assumed was a shadow.

Blood! It was a pool of blood!

On the back, Jenny had written a date and a name that I didn't recognize.

Five photos later, I found someone I did. The man hung from a tree in a heavily wooded area, his tongue lolling from his mouth, his pants shaded with offal.

My husband.

How could she have gotten photos like this? From the police? But they wouldn't let a civilian . . .

I dropped them and covered my eyes with my hands.

Jenny? My friend Jenny? Bits of conversations skipped through my mind. "We all need a guardian angel to look out for us." "He wasn't the greatest husband, Barb," Jenny insisted. "Admit it." "Look how well you're provided for now." "I'm here for you whenever you need me."

I uncovered my eyes and stared at the lamp. This was reality, this electricity, shooting into this bulb, glaring on these snapshots. I hugged myself with trembling hands, then grasped the arms of the chair and raised myself unsteadily. I retraced my steps to the car and lifted the trunk—suddenly that ski hat I'd found earlier had turned into a ski mask, the clothesline, a rope. Jenny never played softball. The ball and glove were props. And the bat was a lethal weapon in the right hands.

Her hands . . .

I shuddered. I should call the police, give them the photos. I started back toward the house, impelled with an urgency I couldn't understand, my feet flying beneath me. I stopped dead at the doorway.

How could I turn in my best friend? My own guardian angel. She was right. My life had improved one hundred percent after my husband died. How could it matter now what she'd done? They were all gone. All dead and buried. How could I sully her reputation with her friends or in my daughter's eyes? Without giving Jenny the chance to defend herself?

After banging the door closed behind me, I dashed to the bedroom and lunged onto the bed. The tears came with racking sobs. It was all too much. I couldn't absorb anymore, and I felt guilty for my part in it. The Jenny I knew had disappeared. Had I ever really known her?

MEL'S was crowded now, mostly guys with protruding bellies, staring at the TV. Mel's wife asked me what I wanted to drink, a false smile pasted on her face under worried eyes. More bad news about the daughter?

I needed hard stuff to deal with my own troubles. Vodka. She dealt me a coaster and dipped a glass into the sink of ice. As she poured orange juice into the vodka, the ice crackled. I stared at the TV like everyone else in the bar.

"Come to interrogate me some more?" a familiar voice asked.

Greg.

I barely looked at him. "No." Mel's wife handed me my drink, and I clutched it like a lifeline.

"So what'd you find out?" He pressed a green bottle to his lips and took a swig. "Was I right?"

"I didn't find anything," I said. My eyes felt dead. "Nothing."

"Here's your chance to ply me with liquor." He placed his empty bottle on the bar and pushed it away from him to show he was ready for another.

I laughed, a short bark that barely passed muster. "Let me guess, Susie?"

He smiled. "It was worth a try. A guy gets mighty thirsty on dry land."

"I don't have the energy to trade barbs." I sipped at my drink. Couldn't he tell I wanted to be alone? But then, why had I come to Mel's? Seeking some semblance of community? I needed voices, clinking glasses, even the bing of the basketball machine. I turned to him, touched his wrist to get his attention away from the door. "What do you do when you discover something about a friend that you never wanted to find out?"

He sighed. "Damned if I know." Another beer arrived and he snatched it up like a shipwrecked sailor offered a glass of fresh water. I watched his Adam's apple bob up and down with each gulp. Finally, he took a break. "I'm sure it's nothing," he said. "But I wanted to tell you . . . that night was a haze. I could almost think . . . Bill . . . was gone for a moment. But it's impossible." In the dark, his eyes gleamed. "I just don't know. I guess we're both in the same boat. Pardon the pun."

I nodded, unable to speak. Accident, suicide, murder? Murderer. Jenny, anyway. I should drop it. Even if Bill . . . and Greg's not sure. Jenny's crimes would come out in any investigation. I couldn't do that to my friend.

The door opened and I checked out the newcomers in the mirror. Susie and Bill. Oh no. I took a gulp of my drink. Get out of here now, I told myself. But not a muscle moved. Instead, I followed their reflections as they passed the bar. Susie walked stiffly. Either she hadn't had enough to drink yet, or too much. I couldn't decide which. Bill led her toward a booth. A lock of hair swung away from her face, and I saw a dark spot high on the cheekbone. Makeup covering a bruise! Her awkwardness caused by a beating, not liquor. Memories of how to walk while minimizing pain caused me to straighten my own shoulders. I downed the rest of the screwdriver.

Suddenly, I knew. Jenny was on the boat that night for Bill. She must have feigned an attraction to Greg to get close. Bill was the one who was supposed to wind up drowned. She'd called it a good way to die and, in the struggle, had been the one to fall overboard.

Greg finished his beer and put his empty bottle on the bar. He stuffed one hand in his pocket and came up with his keys. "Gotta go," he said, his eyes focused on Bill and Susie. With a quick glance, I saw her flinch at Bill's touch. Greg mumbled something and headed out the door.

I should go too. I turned back to the TV, but a piece of me kept staring at Bill's reflection. I didn't feel hate or revenge. Just a calm certainty, filled with daring.

I had finally made sense of it all. Why Jenny sent me on this adventure through her life. No marble guardian angel for her. She wanted a real one, watching, waiting, ever ready, just like her. I kept my stony eyes fixed on Bill.

The Cranbury Road farm stand carried lily of the valley. Jenny would love to have those dainty, fragrant flowers planted on her grave. I wouldn't need the rope, bat, or gun she'd left for me. Only a plan. Lily of the valley had a wondrous side benefit—every part of it was poisonous.

The Day of the 31st

Henry Slesar

Austin Howard's birthday was a month away, but his wife still hadn't decided on his gift. He would be thirty-seven. Not exactly a milestone, but Delores wanted the gift to be special.

"It's the same old problem," she told her sister Libby on the phone. "He's the Man Who Has *Everything*."

Libby frowned. She was anxious to get to work. Colonial Trust was expecting bank examiners, and they were notoriously punctual. What if they arrived and the manager wasn't there?

"Get him a gizmo," she said. "How about a handheld computer? Or a laptop?"

"A laptop! Libby, you're a genius! Oh-oh, here's the man himself." She hung up as Austin came down the stairs, trying to button his jacket and juggle an attaché case at the same time. Paul Manners, his lawyer and closest friend, was already in the driveway. A car horn beeped twice.

Despite his haste, Austin stopped and caught his breath

at the sight of his wife. She had grown more beautiful in the three years of their marriage.

"You're sure about no food?" she said. "Not even a yogurt?"

"It's a breakfast meeting," Austin said.

"Morning, Mr. Howard." It was Hattie, their maid, all dressed up in her new seal coat.

"Where you off to, Hattie?"

"It's Thursday, Mr. Howard. My sister is coming in from White Plains. We got a lot of chit-chatting to do."

Outside, the horn beeped again. "Hattie, do me a favor. Tell Mr. Manners to keep his hands off that horn."

Hattie turned to his wife and said: "Mrs. Howard, I put the laundry that didn't get finished on top of the ironing board. And that food delivery's ten o'clock."

Hattie opened the door and Paul Manners was on the doorstep, an expression of disapproval on his lined but handsome face.

"Now I know why Austin's late every morning. He can't tear himself away from you."

"You got that right," Austin grinned.

Five minutes later, heading for the city with his friend at the wheel, Austin said, "How much luck can one guy have, Paul?"

"Don't ask me. Not much luck in my corner."

Paul and his wife were estranged. He worked six days a week, and suffered from indigestion.

"I get scared sometimes," Austin said. "Too many good things in my life, the gods get jealous."

Back home, Delores was stretched out on the sofa, flipping through a magazine. When the back doorbell rang. Willy Lauber, the delivery boy, was outside, the morning sun burnishing his blond hair. He was a handsome kid, but there was a vacancy in his sea blue eyes.

"Hi, Mrs. Howard." He hauled in the four boxes of food she had ordered for their dinner party.

"Hattie said you were going to deliver around ten. It's not even nine."

Willy stared at the kitchen tiles. "I thought I'd come early because of . . . well, you know." She looked at him blankly. He said: "You want me to put the milk and stuff away for you?"

"No, just leave them on the table."

Still not meeting her eyes, Willy said: "It was really something, driving over here . . . knowing I was going to see you."

Delores wasn't sure she heard him right.

"I kept thinking how it was going to be. When I rang the bell and you saw me. I wondered if you'd act just like always, or you'd be . . . different."

He put his hand on her arm.

"Willy, don't do that."

"Nobody's home, right? You said you'd be alone." His grip tightened, and he pulled her toward him. He was boyishly slim, but his hands were strong.

"Stop this, Willy," she said. "Let me go."

"We don't have much time." Now he was trying to kiss her, and Delores felt the first tremor of panic.

"What's the matter with you? Are you crazy?"

"Don't tease, Mrs. Howard, they'll expect me back at the store . . . Where do you want to? You want to go upstairs, to your bedroom?"

He kissed her fiercely. She struck his face, hard, and Willy looked surprised.

"Let go of me! I'll scream—I'll scream loud enough to wake up the whole neighborhood! Someone will call the police!"

In alarm, Willy clamped a hand over her mouth. "You stop playing games, Mrs. Howard! You stop that now!"

But the panic had become hysteria. She hit his cheek with her fist. He seized both arms and yanked them behind her back, pushing her against the table. She saw the kitchen knife out of the corner of her eye and snatched it up. Willy saw it at the same moment, and tried to wrest it from her. In the struggle the point of the blade entered her lower back, and she shrieked in terror. Willy looked startled. He could think of only one solution. He used the knife again, and then there was a blessed silence.

THE police were still there when Austin arrived home. Paul had dropped him off at the top of the hill; Austin enjoyed the quarter-mile walk to his front door.

But where was Delores? She always spotted him trudging down the dirt road, stood in the doorway with a mocking smile at his "exercise" routine. But the door was closed, and the windows of the house brightly lit, brighter than usual. And then an even more puzzling fact: Libby was there. She ran out to greet him. She wanted to talk to him before the police did.

They didn't let Austin see her body. They didn't ask him any questions about his whereabouts.

"You see, we know what happened," a burly officer said gently. "This kid could have drawn us a picture, the way he left things. Food all over the place. Didn't go back to the grocery, just took off."

"Who? Who?" Austin said hoarsely.

"Kid named Willy Lauber," the man said. "Delivery boy. He told a friend of his what he did. Says it wasn't his fault."

Libby, her face streaked with tears, stuffed a handkerchief into her mouth.

A uniformed cop came in and said something in a low voice to the plainclothes officer. Austin's hearing had suddenly become acute. He heard every word. They had found

Willy Lauber. He was in the police vehicle outside in the driveway.

Austin said: "I've got to get some air."

He was outside before Libby realized what he was doing. She saw him approach the prowl car, saw him fling open the door and drag out a startled, terrified boy with golden hair.

IT was two months before Austin saw Willy again. The bruise on his neck hadn't quite faded, the remnant of Austin's thwarted attempt to strangle him.

Willy wore a suit this time. His hair was carefully brushed. Beside him, David Lenrow, his defense attorney, looked scruffy and nervous. Lenrow hadn't seen the inside of a courtroom in years. He was the bottom of the barrel, but who else would want the hopeless task of defending Willy Lauber?

Claymore, the prosecuting attorney, called only one witness, the police officer who had arrested Willy. His name was Briggs.

"I arrested him at his house, or rather his uncle's house. He was sleeping."

"Sleeping. In the middle of the day."

"I had to shake him awake. There was blood all over his clothes. Then he apologized for what he did."

"What do you mean, 'apologized'?"

"He said, 'I'm sorry. I didn't mean to do that.' "

"Did you ask him what 'that' was?"

"Yes, sir, he admitted killing Mrs. Howard."

David Lenrow had a witness, too.

"We would like to call William Lauber to the stand."

The buzz was louder than a beehive. It had been assumed that the defendant would not testify.

"Why?" Austin whispered.

Paul shrugged. "Probably to show that he's dim-witted.

Get the jury ready for an insanity plea, or incompetence."

Willy took the oath. He smiled slightly when he put his hand on the Bible. He seemed to enjoy the spotlight. Paul's theory was that he saw the trial as a movie or TV show. Now he was playing a starring role, and loving it.

Lenrow asked his name, his age, his occupation. Willy gave him straightforward answers. Then Lenrow asked:

"How well did you know Mrs. Howard, Willy?"

"I went to her place about once a week."

"Did you like Mrs. Howard?"

"Sure, I liked her. She was pretty, but not much of a tipper."

"Did she like you, too, Willy?"

Claymore snapped out an objection, and the Judge denied it.

"Lots of women do," Willy said. "Some even want to get friendly with me. But most of them, well, they're not much to look at."

"If you liked Mrs. Howard, why did you hurt her?"

"It was just something that happened! She picked up this knife, and I got scared, and I tried to take it away from her. And then she got stabbed in the back, and I stabbed her again, this time in front. I guess I was afraid she would tell somebody . . ."

"But you still contend that it wasn't your fault?"

"No! It was her fault!"

"How could it have been her fault, Willy?"

"Because she acted the way she did," Willy Lauber said. "Like she didn't want me to be friendly, even though she was the one who asked me there." He gave the judge a look of triumph. "That's the truth, Judge. She asked me to come there, to be friendly with her!"

* * *

THE jury deliberated less than two hours.

There was barely a rustle in the courtroom when the foreman, a used car dealer named Houseman, read the Guilty verdict. No one had expected to hear anything else. But the foreman remained standing, hesitant.

"Your Honor, if you don't mind, the jury would like to make a recommendation."

The judge frowned. "Are you talking about the sentencing? That's a separate aspect of the trial. But go ahead, say what you have to say."

The foreman cleared his throat. "Well, sir, we're all sure the defendant committed this crime. But it seemed to us that he didn't really know what he was doing."

Austin would have stood up and said something, but Libby's hand fell on his arm.

"What we mean is, Mr. Lauber doesn't seem too smart to us, that his intelligence is pretty low, and maybe that ought to be taken into consideration when . . . you know."

The judge said, "We appreciate your thoughts, Mr. Houseman, but they're inappropriate at this time. It's the responsibility of the bench to make that judgment. Sentence will be passed at ten A.M. tomorrow."

He rapped his gavel once, stood up, and there was an "all rise" from the bailiff. The day was over.

There was silence in the car as Paul Manners drove Austin and Libby back home. Austin stared out the window, seeing nothing beyond it, his thoughts almost audible. Libby said:

"Please don't worry, Austin. I'm sure it's going to be all right."

"Is it? You heard what the foreman said. They're already looking for excuses for that murdering boy! Maybe they even believed what he said, that Delores wanted him to—"

He stopped, choking on the words.

Paul said: "Nobody believed him, Austin. Put that thought out of your head."

Libby stroked his hand. "Besides, it doesn't matter what they do to Willy now. If they don't execute him, they'll put him away for life . . ."

"It's not good enough! Delores is dead. Willy has to die, too. It has to come out even."

At ten the next morning, the judge asked Willy to rise. He stood up, only mildly concerned about what the judge had to say.

"William Lauber, a jury of your peers has found you guilty of the crime of murder in the first degree. It's now my duty to pass sentence upon you as required by the laws of this state . . . Yesterday, the court heard a heartfelt plea from the jurors to consider leniency in your case because of diminished capacity . . ."

In the silence of the room, they could hear Austin's sharp intake of breath.

"However," the judge continued, "the crime you committed was so heinous, so brutal, so unforgivable, I cannot in all conscience allow it to receive anything but the most serious punishment. For this reason, I sentence you to be put to death by lethal injection, this sentence to be carried out on October 31st of this year . . ."

The first thing Austin did when he arrived home was find a wall calendar. Then he marked off the date.

October 31st.

AUSTIN Howard didn't take much with him when he left the stone house on Willow Drive for a single room at the Hotel Holland. Two changes of clothing, a few toilet articles, and the calendar.

On the evening of the 7th, he was in a Scotch-induced sleep when the telephone rang. He had a visitor. "Who?" he said thickly. But the doorbell was already ringing.

It was Libby. He admitted her reluctantly, and she said:

"Well, well. Will the real Austin Howard stand up and shave?"

"How did you find me here?"

"If you must know, Paul told me . . . God, you look awful! You know how awful you look?"

"Paul promised me—"

"You look as if you belong in this room! That's how awful!" She threw her purse on the sofa and sat down.

"What did you expect me to do?" Austin said. "Stay in that house? Wake up every night thinking Delores was still lying beside me . . ."

"You could have found a better room than this!"

"This isn't a hotel room, Libby. It's a waiting room."

He looked at the wall calendar, and Libby followed his gaze.

"Oh, Austin," Libby said sadly. "You poor dope. Is that what your whole life has come down to? Staring at the calendar and waiting for them to inject that dim-witted boy . . ."

Someone was knocking at the door.

"It's Paul," Libby said. "He brought me here. But I asked if I could see you alone first."

Libby admitted him. From the moment he saw his pained face, Austin knew something was wrong.

"I couldn't tell him," Libby said. "I just couldn't, Paul."

The lawyer looked at the calendar on the wall.

"Austin, there isn't going to be any 31st."

"What are you talking about? There's always a Thirty-First!"

"I mean there isn't going to be any execution. David Lenrow's appeal was granted by the appellate court. They had Willy Lauber examined by psychiatrists. They agreed about 'diminished capacity.'"

Libby clutched Austin's arm.

"They've reduced Willy's sentence to life imprisonment.

He's already been removed to the Highland State Penitentiary."

The silence that fell on the room seemed endless. Austin, deadly calm, turned to Libby.

"Would you mind leaving us alone?"

She hesitated, but then picked up her purse and went out.

"I know this is hurting you, Austin. But life behind bars is a terrible punishment, too. For a boy like Willy, maybe worse than death."

"He'll be a model prisoner. He'll be up for parole, and he'll smile for the Board, and they'll see that he's just a nice all-American boy, and deserves another chance . . ."

Austin put down the glass.

"He's not going to get another chance. I'll make sure he doesn't. You'll have to help me make sure."

"How can I do that?"

"I'm going to kill him, Paul. I have to kill that animal or stop living myself. And whether you help me or not, that's what I'll do."

"The man's in prison! You can't get near him!"

"It'll probably cost money, but that doesn't matter. I've got a profitable business, don't I? I'll spend all the money I have to, as long as I can reach an arm into that penitentiary . . ."

"That's crazy, Austin! You wouldn't know how where to begin such a thing. You haven't had any contact with—people like that!"

"But you have, haven't you? You were in criminal practice, once. You know people. You could help me if you wanted to."

"But I don't want to!" Paul said. "It can't be done. And even if it could, I won't stand by and watch you murder someone—even at long distance!"

"Just tell me one thing." Austin went to the window.

The city view was bleak, a panorama of rooftops. "Tell me whose life you want to save, Paul. Willy Lauber's, or mine."

THE Steamer Bar was in a dreary neighborhood two blocks from the waterfront. It was early in the day. The bartender displayed no curiosity when Austin asked for the "billiard room."

The small Brunswick pool table looked like it hadn't seen any action in years. There was another table in the room, and Paul was sitting at it with a heavyset man who had shaved carelessly that morning.

"Austin, like you to meet Joe Lotts."

The stranger smiled pleasantly.

"Let's just get down to business," Paul said briskly. "Austin, Mr. Lotts was a client of mine, about four years ago. Mr. Lotts is in the transportation business."

"Long-distance hauling," Lotts said.

"Mr. Lotts has a brother, Leonard."

"A good guy," Lotts said.

"Unfortunately, the brothers got into a little trouble, involving a hijacking accusation. I got Joe off, but Leonard wasn't that lucky. He's serving a ten-year sentence." He paused. "At Highland State Penitentiary."

"Leonard's a good guy," Lotts repeated. "He made a lot of friends in the joint. In fact, he's a trusty."

"It's true. He's a trusted inmate, and even though he's made some mistakes in his life, he doesn't like cold-blooded killers, especially when they kill women . . . He could easily learn to hate Willy Lauber as much as you do."

Joe Lotts looked worried. "We ain't talking about 'favors,' you know?"

"We've agreed on a price," Paul said. "Twenty thousand dollars, with a bonus of five more if the . . . assignment is completed before the end of the month. Is that all right with you, Austin?"

"I want it in plain English." Austin put his palms flat on the table. "Will your brother kill Willy Lauber?"

Lotts looked surprised. "That's what we're talking about, right? Yeah, Leonard will whack him. That's what you want, right?"

"It's what I want."

"Leonard will handle it. Leonard's a good guy."

PAUL walked Austin back to the hotel. At the entrance, he said something about returning to his office. Austin didn't stop him. He went into the lobby, and saw Libby sitting in a plush chair. He looked at her guiltily, as if she could read his mind and know what he was planning to do to Delores's killer.

"I have to talk to you," she said. "About money."

"That's funny," Austin answered. "I was going to call you about the same subject. Do you know what I have in my checking account?"

"Don't you ever look at your bank statements?"

He shrugged. "I'm going to need some cash soon."

Upstairs, in his room, Libby said: "It's not your personal checking account I'm concerned about. It's your business account."

"Paul has been taking care of that since—" he stopped. "Paul said he would handle the business finances until I was feeling better. I expect that to be very soon."

Unconsciously, he looked at the wall calendar.

Libby was glad not to meet his eyes. She said: "There are payments I can't account for, Austin. Two payments that don't have any matching expenses, at least not in writing."

"I don't understand."

"Two company checks were drawn a week apart. Both

were for cash. Forty thousand and sixty thousand, respectively. Did you authorize their withdrawal?"

"No. I haven't thought about money for months."

"They were endorsed by Paul. The money went into his pocket, Austin. I know he's your best friend, I know how much you think of him. But I can't help suspecting that Paul Manners is stealing from you."

AUSTIN was in no mood to be the victim of another crime. When he arrived at the attorney's office, he dropped the canceled checks on his desk, and asked for an explanation.

He felt a perverse satisfaction in seeing Paul lose his tan.

"Did you think I stole this money from you, Austin?"

"If you did, I'd understand why. That ex-wife of yours is trying to bleed you to death, isn't she?"

"It's true. Fleur won't be satisfied until I'm sleeping in a doorway someplace." He sighed deeply. "All right. I'll tell you the truth, as much as I can afford to tell you . . . I took the money, Austin. I used it on your behalf."

"On my behalf?" Austin bristled.

"I had to buy something. From David Lenrow. From the prosecution."

"Buy what?"

"A piece of evidence. A small piece. It wouldn't have saved his client, Lenrow was smart enough to realize that. But it might have slowed things down, give the jurors something to disagree about . . . I knew how anxious you were to have a swift trial, to see Willy punished."

Austin's thoughts were frozen for a moment. Then he said:

"And what was this small piece of evidence?"

"I'm sorry, Austin. I can't tell you that. It might cost me a client—or worse, a friend. But I just can't tell you."

* * *

THE yard was crowded. So was the prison, for that matter, housing a population of two thousand when it was planned for less than one.

Leonard Lotts had no complaints about the overcrowding, not today. It was going to work in his favor. The guards would be blindsided by the density of cons shifting about the courtyard, moving restlessly, aimlessly within the confines of the walls.

From two-thirty on, he never took his eyes off Willy Lauber.

The kid was an enigma. He never lost his dreamy smile. His vacant blue eyes looked out on his dreary surroundings without interest.

It was two minutes to three. His pals, Phil and Matty, were off by themselves, their eyes on Willy's blond head, too. They looked at Leonard for the signal.

Leonard nodded. The three inmates moved into the thick of the crowd where Willy was standing, looking up at the leaden skies. Phil brushed by Willy, hard enough to make the kid indignant. Before he could voice a protest, Marty came from another direction, hit him hard with his shoulder, making Willy stagger.

"Hey!" Willy said. "What's the big idea?"

Now it was Leonard's turn. He raced into the group, pulling the knife out of his shirt as he did, driving the blade deep into Willy's chest. A burst of derisive laughter from some card players nearby covered up the sound of Willy's gasp. There were so many cons pressing around him that it took him a full five seconds to fall to the ground.

PAUL telephoned Austin in his bad-news voice.

"It happened," he said. "But maybe not the way you wanted."

"What do you mean?"

"They got to Willy in the prison yard. He was stabbed in the chest. But apparently the blade was deflected by his rib cage. Willy's in the hospital, but—he's alive."

IT could have been the same seedy bar where Austin and Paul had met Joe Lotts the first time. But Tucker's Tavern was on the other side of town, and Joe Lotts wasn't nearly as cocky as he had been on their initial encounter.

"Look, stuff happens," he said, looking back and forth at their solemn faces. "I know guys who took four, five bullets and lived to brag about it . . ."

"You were paid twenty thousand dollars," Paul said stiffly. "But you didn't make good on the deal."

"We didn't make no guarantees. You want your money back, forget it!"

"It's not the money," Austin said. "All I want is Willy Lauber's obituary. And I'm willing to pay if you still think you can make that happen."

Lotts's round face brightened. "Hey, that's just what I was thinking! Nobody pinned the job on Leonard. The kid himself said he didn't know who knifed him! And he won't be in that hospital forever . . ."

"Another ten thousand dollars," Austin said. "Twenty, if he can get it done before the 31st."

"Hey!" Lotts chuckled. "For another $20,000, Leonard will walk right into that ward and finish the job!"

Paul walked Austin back to his hotel room. He looked at the suitcase on the bed and asked:

"Were you leaving?"

"I was," Austin said bitterly. "I was going back home, put the house up for sale. I thought I could go back to some kind of normal life."

They had a drink. They had two. When Austin poured

his third, Paul tried to distract him by turning on the television. He regretted it the moment the Six O'Clock News began, and the newscaster's first words were: "Willy Lauber."

"What? What?" Austin shouted at the screen.

". . . the convicted murderer of Delores Howard escaped from the ambulance transferring him to a city hospital where he had been expected to receive emergency surgery . . ."

"Escaped!" Austin cried. "Did you hear that?"

"They got careless," Paul said. "They must have thought he was too weak—" He gripped Austin's shoulder. "There's no reason to worry," he said confidently. "They'll catch up to him."

"But Willy's a lucky boy, remember? He gets away with murder."

"They'll get him, probably in a matter of hours. The kid is wounded, he took a knife in the chest! How far can he get?"

"And what if they don't? What if Willy hops a boat for South America, or sneaks across the border to Mexico, finds some obliging spinster only too happy to shelter a handsome young boy?"

"Forget it! Willy's not smart enough to do any of those things. Look what he did after—after what happened at your house. He went home! He went home to sleep!"

"Yes," Austin said. "And I haven't slept since . . ."

HE felt a strong desire to see Libby again. He called her at home.

The restaurant was called Cielo's. Libby was already at a table when Austin arrived, with a bottle of Chianti in front of her. It was half empty.

"I didn't know you could drink so much."

"I learned how in these past two years," Libby said. "First

my divorce, then Delores, now you. Reason enough, right?"

"I'm no reason," he said.

"But you are." She filled his glass and then her own again. "Don't you remember?" She smiled briefly. "We weren't just acquaintances when I introduced you to my sister. For a while I though we were heading someplace. Obviously, I was wrong."

"We didn't date that often, Libby. Three or four times—"

"And then along came Del." The smile reappeared. "I'm sure you realize it wasn't a new situation. All through school, every boy I met faded out of my life after meeting Del."

"Did you resent her?"

"How could I? Del was a natural force. Like thunderstorms. Besides, it was my litmus test for boyfriends. If they chased after Del, I lost interest in them."

"That was wise of you."

"Not always. There was the occasional exception." She looked at her glass. It was empty. She filled it again.

"Easy," Austin said.

"I can't take it easy. I can't say what I'm going to say without—what do they call it?—bottled courage?"

"What do you mean?"

"I've debated myself about this, Austin. Not just since Del died, but long before that. Whether or not you should know the truth. Whether ignorance was bliss for you. And most recently—whether I should follow the old advice about—never speaking ill of the dead . . ."

Austin stiffened.

"What is it? Something about Delores?"

"I'm sure she loved you. I'm just not sure how she defined 'love.' She was unfaithful, Austin. No, you didn't have a rival. There was no 'other man.'

"There were many."

* * *

AUSTIN wanted to deny it. He wanted to tell Libby she was lying, that her lifelong rivalry with her sister was behind this terrible slander . . .

But he looked into her tear-filled eyes and knew it was the truth. Del, his Del, had been leading a secret life . . .

"Tell me how you knew," he said.

"Because she told me about it," Libby said. "Del always told me about the men in her life, ever since we were teenagers. It was important to her, to prove how desirable she was . . ."

"My God, Libby . . ."

"I thought it would be over when you married her. Remember those copper bracelets people wore because they believed it would cure arthritis? I thought that ring on her finger was going to be a cure, too."

"But it wasn't."

"It seemed to be, that first year. Then one day . . ." She put down her glass. "She told me about this Congressman she met, when she was working in that bookshop. She giggled like a schoolgirl. I tried to talk her out of meeting him, and she accused me of jealousy."

"Don't finish that glass, Libby. You're going to be sick."

"There were half a dozen men after that one. She changed them frequently, like bed linen. I thought of telling you, but I just couldn't do it . . ."

A terrible idea stabbed into his brain. "Libby—you're not suggesting that—Willy—"

"No!" she said vehemently. "All her men were 'important.' That was part of her game. They had to have 'substance.' And they had to be married . . . That was part of her satisfaction."

She went pale suddenly.

"You know, I think you're right. I'm going to be sick."

Austin took her home. She wouldn't allow him to stay; she preferred to be sick in solitude.

Austin returned to the hotel, trying not to think about what he had been told.

Joe Lotts was in the lobby.

Austin barely recognized him in the surroundings. But it was Joe, all right. Not looking apologetic.

"What do you want?" Austin said harshly.

"Maybe we better talk private."

He brought Joe into his room, fully expecting him to ask for the money he hadn't earned. But Joe surprised him.

"I know where the kid is, Mr. Howard."

"Are you serious?"

"I could hardly believe my luck. I mean, first my bad luck, this zitface breaking out of that hospital. Then my good luck . . ."

"Tell me where he is! And how you know!"

"There's a pal of mine, lives on East Avenue. Some kids in his neighborhood, like a gang, they prowl around the section where they're tearing down buildings. For a housing project, you know? They spotted this blond guy sleeping in one of the condemned buildings. They rolled him, thinking he was a drunk. Only he didn't have no money."

"What happened to him? Where is he now?"

"My friend goes to have a look for himself. My friend recognizes the prison outfit. He put two and two together."

"Where is he?" Austin said. "Where's Willy Lauber?"

"My friend, he's sort of got this guy in what you call custody. Sometimes there's a reward for turning in escaped cons."

"He won't call the police, will he?"

"Not if he gets a better offer."

"I'll pay him," Austin said. "I'll pay you both five thousand if you take me to him! Will you do that?"

Joe Lotts gave him a toothy smile. "Sure, Mr. Howard. Glad to help."

Austin said: "Are you carrying a gun, Joe?"

"Who, me? Why?"

"If you are, I'll pay you another five thousand for it."

Joe looked delighted; it was his lucky day, all right. He put his right foot on a chair and rolled up his pants leg. There was a small automatic pistol strapped to his calf. He undid the straps and handed it over.

"It's loaded and ready to party," he said.

Austin looked at the weapon as if it was a sacred relic.

HE took a taxi, and had himself dropped off three blocks from the demolition site.

There was no one in sight when he crossed the rubble-strewn streets. He could see the building Lotts had described. He identified the faded letters on the old brick. Hacker's Tobacco. He was grimly amused.

There wasn't a front door, just as Joe had said, but two boards had been nailed across the entrance. They were hanging loose. He pushed them aside and went up the stairs. They creaked loudly.

The sound must have alerted Willy. He looked up from a crude palette of flattened packing cases and filthy rags.

A faint smile appeared as Willy realized it wasn't the police. It was a civilian, maybe another squatter like himself. It was only when Austin came within ten feet of him that Willy put a name to the face.

"Mr. Howard," he whispered.

The boy had a starved look. His housewife-admirers wouldn't have thought him handsome now. Through his open shirt, Austin could see the layers of bandage across his chest, tattered and dirty. If Joe Lotts's automatic didn't kill him, sepsis would probably do the job.

"How'd you find me, Mr. Howard?" he said. "Are you going to call the police?"

"I am the police," Austin said. "I'm also the judge, the jury, and the guy who was going to give you that lethal injection. Do you understand?"

"I don't understand nothing," Willy said. "Things just happen to me, Mr. Howard. Like your wife, you know? I didn't want to hurt her, I swear I didn't . . . Half of it was an accident. The other half . . . I don't know. I just don't know."

Austin took out the gun.

"Look at me, Willy."

Willy looked, and asked: "You going to shoot me, Mr. Howard?"

"The word is execute. You know you deserve to die. My wife didn't, but you killed her anyway."

"She drove me crazy, Mr. Howard! It was her own fault."

"Did your mother ever teach you to pray? Now's a good time."

He lifted the gun and aimed it at Willy's forehead.

"She never should have done it!" the boy cried. "If she didn't want me to be friendly, she never should have sent me that note!"

The muzzle of the automatic shifted an inch.

"What 'note'? What are you talking about?"

"He should have told them about it! Mr. Lenrow! I asked him to show them the note Mrs. Howard wrote, but he said it wouldn't do any good!"

"My wife never wrote to you, Willy, that's just a lie!"

"But she did, she did! She slipped it into the basket I carry the milk in! I got all excited when I read it, when she told me she'd be expecting me, when she said she couldn't wait—"

Austin almost fired the gun then, his anger concentrated in his trigger finger.

"You ask Mr. Lenrow," Willy said, tears on his gaunt cheeks. "Mr. Lenrow has the note. I swear he does!"

Austin was frozen in space and time, and he wondered—did David Lenrow have such a note? Or—had he sold it?

EVER since his divorce, Paul Manners worked late, killing the lonely hours with torts and affidavits. Austin knew he would find him at his office, even at ten minutes past eight.

"Where the hell have you been?" Paul looked at Austin's soiled suit, the plaster dust coating his shoes.

Austin didn't bother to reply. He said: "Tell me about the note, Paul."

"What note?"

"The one Del sent Willy Lauber. The note you bought from the defense, with a hundred thousand dollars of my money."

Paul's lips tightened. "Is that what Dave Lenrow told you?"

"It was Willy who told me. Willy Lauber."

"Then they've caught him? He's back in prison?"

"Yes," Austin said. "Willy's in the hospital. They say he would have died if he didn't get treated. Funny, isn't it? I start out to kill him and end up saving his life."

"But how—?"

"I found Willy and turned him in. But not before he told me about Del's note."

"Exactly what did he tell you?"

"He said Del invited him to a rendezvous that morning . . . I told him he was a rotten liar, and he said Lenrow had the note that proved it. He didn't understand why it wasn't used at his trial. But we do, don't we?"

The lines in Paul's face deepened.

"I had to buy it, Austin. For your sake. The shock of Delores's death half-killed you. If you knew about that note, if you had sat in that courtroom and heard it read aloud . . . I thought that might finish you off."

Austin sat down.

"Libby told me the truth. About Del, about this madness inside her . . . And I didn't know! Can you believe that, Paul? That she was cheating on me, big time, with so many men—"

"You don't know how bad it was, and I doubt Libby knows either. If you ask me, Libby was always jealous of her sister—"

"All I'm asking you for is that note! I paid for it—I've got the right to know what it says!"

"The note's gone, Austin, I destroyed it. And I didn't try to memorize it. I knew it was best forgotten."

Austin was fighting tears. Paul's next words were gentle.

"You've got to forget it, too. You've got to put Del and Willy and this whole terrible year behind you . . ."

DAVE Lenrow was at his desk at eight the next morning. Just as Paul Manners worked late, Lenrow began his day early, a habit he had picked up from a diligent father.

"I told you there was nothing I could tell you, Mr. Howard—"

"But I have something to tell you. Do you know about the Complaint Review Board in this state? Do you know you could lose your license because of what you did? Suppressing evidence?"

"What is it you want from me? This note you're talking about, it's in your lawyer's possession—"

"I can't believe you didn't make a copy."

A few minutes later, it was in his hand.

Austin read:

Come early! About nine o'clock! Austin has a meeting so he'll be out of the house no later than eight-thirty. We'll have the whole house to ourselves, but the bedroom will be enough . . . I can hardly wait . . .

Willy was looking better against the clean sheets of his hospital bed, but his eyes were still apprehensive when Austin appeared.

Austin showed him the Xeroxed note.

"Was this it, Willy? Is this what you found in that empty milk basket?"

Willy studied it for a long moment, and said: "Yes . . . this is the note she wrote me. Only . . ."

"Only what?"

A blush added some color to his white face. "I didn't tell you the truth, Mr. Howard, the whole truth I mean. I didn't find the note in my basket, like I said. He gave it to me."

"He?"

"I guess he didn't want anyone to know, how Mrs. Howard liked me. That's why I made up the story, about her putting the note in the milk basket. But he gave it to me. In person."

THE real estate lady had just left when Libby appeared at the front door.

"I just heard—about Willy being caught again. They said you were responsible."

"It was nothing heroic. Willy was no threat to anybody. And as it turned out, I was no threat to Willy."

"I can't tell you how glad I am!"

She embraced him. Then she moved away suddenly and said:

"You went there to kill him, didn't you?"

"You're a mind-reader, Libby."

"The gun's still in your pocket. I could feel it."

Austin patted the bulge of the automatic, and shrugged.

"I have to go. I've got an appointment."

"Will you have dinner with me tonight?"

"All right," Austin said. "I'll meet you Cielo's at what? Seven-thirty?"

There was no one at the secretarial desk when Austin walked into Paul Manners's office. Paul was sorting through a stack of files, looking annoyed.

"Simone off today?" Austin asked.

"The old bursitis dodge," Paul grunted. He pushed the files aside and sat down. "You look better than you did last night."

"I don't feel any better," Austin said. "Not after seeing Willy in the hospital."

"You're getting awfully chummy with Del's killer," Paul said dryly. "First you save his life, then you bring him flowers."

"The visit was worthwhile. I got the whole truth out of him, about the note Delores wrote."

"Austin, stop chewing on this bone! I told you last night—put it all behind you, get a life—a new life."

"Willy said someone gave him that note. Handed it to him personally."

"You can't believe a dimwit like Willy Lauber!"

"The note was a lie, Paul. Libby was right. Del would never seduce a lowlife like Willy. She was after big game. Hot-shot executives, men with money, big jobs—wives."

"You know what I think about Libby's opinions."

"And now I know why she never liked you. Because you were supposed to be my best friend. And you were having an affair with my wife."

"My God, Austin, you can't really believe that!"

"You gave Willy the note. The note that had once been written to you. Only you told Willy it was addressed to him . . ."

"No! I swear I never did such a thing—"

"You wanted to punish her, for dropping you, the minute your divorce came through . . . Del didn't get any kicks out of affairs with divorced men. They were too easy . . ."

Austin took the gun out of his pocket.

"I'd like you to get down on your knees, Paul."

"For God's sake, put that thing away!"

"On your knees, in front of me." He pointed the gun. "Or else I'll ruin that nice leather chair of yours. Go on!"

The lawyer came around the desk and dropped to his knees. When Austin put the cold muzzle of the gun against his forehead, he began to sob.

"I didn't mean it to work out the way it did! So help me God, I didn't! I was angry with Del! I wanted to play a joke on her! That was all! Please, Austin, please!"

Austin didn't appear to be listening. He was looking at Paul's desk calendar.

"Do you know what day it is, Paul? It's the 31st."

He squeezed the trigger. The click made Paul cry out.

Austin said: "I emptied the magazine after I saw Willy. I didn't think I needed bullets anymore." He put the gun back in his pocket and went to meet Libby at the restaurant. For the first time in months, he was hungry.

Another Night to Remember

William E. Chambers

My car was parked half a block away from the pub I own in Greenpoint, Brooklyn, a "Mixed-Use" Neighborhood of old apartment buildings, private homes, small shops, and some heavy industry. All the surrounding businesses, except mine, closed early because it was Christmas Eve, and the shadowy street *seemed* deserted. But just as I stuck my key in the Oldsmobile's door, a voice from behind said, "Don't move. I'm holding a gun."

"I'm not moving," I assured the voice in as nonchalant a tone as I could muster. "What do you want?"

"Your money."

"I've got about three hundred bucks"—I felt something hard touch the back of my leather jacket—"in my pocket."

The voice patted me down from behind, found I was clean, and said, "Unlock the car. Front and back doors."

I opened the front door, reached over the seat, and pulled up the button that locked the rear door of my aging Delta 88. The voice said, "Get in."

My unwanted companion climbed into the back seat

while I slid behind the wheel. When both doors were locked, he explained, "We're gonna drive to a place with no phones. Then you're gonna get out and walk while I ride away in this heap with your money."

The face in the rearview mirror was pale, early thirties, and somewhat familiar looking. The fact that he didn't mind my seeing his features bothered me. He asked if I knew the West Street piers, and when I told him I did, he named a certain one and ordered me to take him to it. My mind spun like tires on ice as I began driving. I prayed a police car would pass by so I could plow this hunk of steel into it. None did. I thought of doing the same thing to any car at all but felt it was too risky. While he might hesitate to shoot me if cops were involved, I wasn't sure civilians would be a deterrent.

He might even kill them.

West Street was poorly lit and empty of cars and people. When I turned down the block leading to the pier, he said, "So far, so good, Callahan. You can stop at the edge of the dock."

The beauty of Manhattan's luminous skyline on the other side of the East River did nothing for my frayed nerves. Wood planking creaked beneath my tires and abandoned warehouses formed dark shapes along the Brooklyn shoreline to my right and left. Wind buffeted my car. Aside from the two of us, the area was devoid of life. A condition I expected myself to be in if I didn't do something quick. So I stomped the gas pedal and dived down, wedging my body between the seat and the dashboard.

A roar rocked the car. I saw sparks above my head and an acrid smell filled the air. The windshield webbed while my front tires bounced over the lip of the pier. Another shot rang out and the windshield disintegrated as the car flipped over. The man behind me hit the roof with his head and shoulders, dropping his weapon as the Olds slapped water.

Then he thrashed about, screaming wildly in fear of the river that rushed in through the shot-out windshield below me. Knowing there was no bucking this icy torrent, I held my breath and waited. I was pounded repeatedly by a world that was cold and black and wet. When the force suddenly stopped, I heard the plunk of an escaping bubble and felt the car float downward.

Clawing blindly, I found the steering wheel and pulled myself toward the missing windshield. I tasted salt water and crude oil as I shoved my torso through the gap and kicked my feet against the fender of the descending car to begin my desperate upward swim. The blazing red and green Christmas lighting that adorned the Empire State Building's peak welcomed me to the surface from all the way across the river. I sucked in freezing air and paddled to a slimy piling. Somehow I managed to shin up that greasy pole and scramble onto the dock.

I knew civilization wasn't far off but it seemed beyond my reach as I trudged forward on quivering legs. It was only three blocks but the walk seemed to take forever because I had to stop several times to ease my burning lungs. Finally, I saw the kielbasa-laden window of a Polish delicatessen whose dim lights indicated the store was about to close. I staggered through the front door and said, "I need your phone . . ."

The slender, blond-haired lady who was emptying the cash register muttered something I didn't understand then switched to English addressing me with the Polish word for mister that sounded like, "Pon! What has happened to you?"

"Please . . ." My teeth were clicking. "Accident . . . almost drowned. Need a phone . . ."

She led me through long red curtains to a back room where an elderly gentleman with a white mustache eyeballed me curiously. The woman punctuated staccato sentences in Polish with agitated gestures. When she dropped her hands and inhaled deeply, he motioned me to a phone on the wall. I dialed a police captain named Crowley. Luckily, he was still in his office. I asked him to come and get me and told him I'd explain why later.

The Polish couple demanded I dry off and change clothes, and insisted I drink something hot. I thanked them for their kindness and promised I'd bring the clothes back freshly laundered. Then, while my hosts resumed closing, I sat at the kitchen table in their rear-store apartment, sipping a cup of tea and mulling over the events that led to this situation.

THERE are some exes in my life. I'm an ex-husband to a woman named Amanda and I'm an ex-lieutenant, having retired from New York's Finest after being shot, an experience that left me with an aversion to guns. What I am now is the owner and proprietor of Callahan's Pub, an Irish-styled establishment in the largest Polish enclave on America's East Coast. Now, like all good publicans, I follow the tavern keeper's holiday custom of spreading Yuletide cheer in the bars and restaurants of my colleagues in the food and beverage business. I accomplish this by having a drink or two with each of the owners in their establishments and they reciprocate by visiting me in mine. I kicked off this season of good tidings by making my first stop at an out-of-the-way place called Connors' Corner near the East River in Long Island City.

Barry Connors usually made his daily bread through the lunch and early evening trade springing from the factories and warehouses surrounding his saloon. So I was surprised when arriving there rather late one evening to see yuppies, hard rockers, punk rockers, and some people who looked like they were off their rockers milling about the bar and occupying all the tables along the wall. Two family tragedies within a year, coupled with my efforts to keep a heavily mortgaged business afloat, kept me from socializing, so I didn't keep up with the changes here. A young lady bartender with long brown hair and what seemed to be two rockets stuffed into her sweater approached me, smiled and said, "Hi."

"I will be," I told her, "if I drink too much."

Her smile flashed brighter and was highlighted by a full, throaty laugh. Then she asked, "Now, what can I do to get you started drinking?"

"Scotch on the rocks is a good way to go."

"You've got it."

"Is Barry around?"

She shook her head and set up my drink. "Hasn't been in yet."

I thanked her, sipped some scotch, and studied the crowd from a professional standpoint, what you might call an owner's point of view. It wasn't long before I spotted some strange goings-on. I noticed a tall, thin gentleman of olive complexion prancing in and out of the kitchen, which was located in a room to the side at the end of the bar. He brought out dishes of chips and pretzels, which the lady bartender distributed. He also made very frequent trips to the men's room, which was next to the ladies' room across the floor from the kitchen.

During the course of an hour, I saw three new customers enter the bar. Within minutes of each arrival, Olive Skin would saunter into the gentlemen's lavatory, stay briefly, then return to the kitchen. The recently arrived patron would soon make for the john himself. When he returned, Olive Skin would go back in.

I slowly nursed another two drinks and noticed the same thing happen when two young females walked in. While they sipped their drinks at the bar, Olive Skin returned to the men's room. When he came back, a young man sitting alone at a table went to the john then came back and sat down. Minutes later, the young ladies at the bar waved to the loner and acted as if they were surprised to see him. He seemed just as astonished at their presence and motioned them to join him at the table. Meanwhile, Olive Skin went back to the can. So I got up, walked over to the pay phone located in the alcove between the bar's double-door entrance, and dialed Barry Connors's home number. When he didn't answer, I returned to the bar, paid for my drinks and left.

I PHONED Barry several times over the next few days and caught him at home the night before Christmas Eve. When he answered my ring, I said, "Barry, I've got to talk to you about something very important. Are you free right now?"

"Sure, Marty. Come on over."

BARRY lived in a converted loft above a furniture storage warehouse in an industrial section of Astoria, Queens. Pressing the intercom, I exchanged greetings with him before he buzzed me into the hall. Then I climbed a long flight of wooden steps and found him waiting in his opened doorway. When we shook hands, I could see by his red-veined complexion that he was oversampling his most toxic in-house products. He had a bar in his apartment that was almost as long as the commercial one he made his living from. Thumbing me toward it, he said, "Come in. Let me fix you a drink."

"Sure."

"What'll ya have?"

"Beer's fine."

I straddled a stool and made room on the bar by shoving some racing forms aside. Barry ambled behind and opened a frosted brown bottle from the refrigeration unit below, then handed it to me. He poured himself a double sour mash and raised a toast to the season. I clinked my bottle to his tumbler and said, "Merry Christmas."

"And a Happy New Year to you, Martin, my boy. Glad you're out and about after all the family troubles."

"Life must go on." I sipped my beer and he downed his Jack Daniel's.

"Very true. God's will."

"I stopped by your place a couple of nights ago, Barry. Joint was jumping."

"Trade's picked up a lot since I hired Cynthia."

"Is that the lady with the long brown hair?"

Barry refilled his glass. "That's Cynthia."

"Who's the tall skinny guy with the olive complexion?"

"You must mean Faro. He's her boyfriend. Why?"

"I hate to be the bearer of bad tidings, Barry, but he's dealing drugs."

The glass in Barry's hand never made it to his lips. "What?"

"Cocaine, probably."

"Cocaine!"

"You should pop in on your help when they don't expect it, pal. Hell, you taught that rule to me."

Barry lowered his glass, compressed his lips into a tight line, and ran a set of pudgy fingers through his thinning white hair. "Marty, are you sure of this?"

"Before I bought the pub, I was a detective and I haven't forgotten my training. You never lose your experience, you know."

"Guess you're right about that," Barry nodded and knocked back the drink.

"Faro's action's slick enough to fool the untrained eye, but when something's shady, *I* spot it."

After I explained Faro's routine, he said, "No wonder business has been so good lately."

"Barry, a little over a year ago drug dealers killed my nephew with their crap although"—I swallowed hard and forced myself to tell the truth—"nobody forced him to indulge. Still, I hate these drug-dealing slime-bags. Look, I can help you with this. Remember Captain Crowley?"

Creases formed on Barry's forehead. "That detective friend of yours?"

"More like a close acquaintance. When I was on the job, I helped him crack an insurance fraud case that spanned his precinct in Queens and mine in Manhattan South. So he feels he owes me. I could have him stake your place out and bust this operation."

"The scandal would ruin my business." Barry sighed and shook his head. "Who else knows about this, Marty?"

"Nobody."

"Not even your girlfriend?"

"No. Tammy's in Florida. Visiting her aunt. Comes home tomorrow night. I'm picking her up at LaGuardia. Nine P.M. flight."

"Look, don't tell her—or anyone. I'll take care of this myself."

"Are you sure—"

"I'm sure." Barry blinked thoughtfully. "Just leave it to me."

"Okay. But if you need help, call. You showed me the ropes when I opened my business and I don't forget favors."

"You don't have to tell me that, Marty." Barry reached out and shook my hand. "I know what a memory you have."

THE sound of Captain Crowley's voice out front snapped me out of my reverie. When he walked into the kitchen, I greeted him wearing a sweatsuit, wool robe, and fur-lined slippers. He looked me up and down, then said, "Where's the brandy and cigars?"

"Forgive me if I don't see the humor in that, Captain," I answered, biting back a chuckle in spite of my condition. "I'll explain everything while you drive me home."

I told Captain Crowley about Tammy's incoming flight, so he radioed for a patrol car to meet her at the airport, then drove away from the curb saying, "Okay, let's hear it."

TAMMY walked into my apartment mortified at having been picked up by two uniformed police officers at LaGuardia. She thought it was my idea of a stupid joke. But when I told her about my chariot drop into the brine, her wide brown eyes stared at me without blinking. Captain Crowley settled his long lean frame onto my sofa and stared at me as well. His gaze seemed to say, "Are you going to tell her the rest of it?"

I nodded to him and I told her my thoughts.

I BUZZED Barry Connors and announced my unexpected visit over his intercom. I explained I had placed an order for bar goods with my Queens supplier and thought I'd stop by since I was in the neighborhood anyway. When I walked through his door, he pumped my right hand and said, "I'm glad you're all right, Marty."

The tabloids picked up the story of my ordeal from Captain Crowley. I spoke to a couple of reporters as well. Now the word on the street was that nobody carjacks Marty Callahan and gets away with it. I reinforced that idea by saying to Barry, "That lowlife, whoever he is, won't rob anymore."

Barry waved me toward the bar. "Some way to die."

"Better him than me."

"You're a hard man, Callahan," Barry laughed. "I read that he had no identification on him. That right?"

"Yeah."

"Beer?"

"I think a scotch will do me tonight."

"Scotch for you. Jack Daniels for me." Barry poured the drinks, handed me a tumbler, and touched his to mine. "Wish you told me you were stopping by tonight."

I emptied the glass, then asked, "Why?"

"Would've thrown a party to celebrate the fact that you're alive." He grinned. "Guess we'll have to party alone."

"Wish my nephew Rodney could be here to party with us."

"Ah, yes. Your nephew was a good kid. Smart kid. I mean, became a Wall Street Broker, no less." Barry shook his head sadly. "God rest him."

"*And* one of your best customers when he wasn't mastering the financial world, if I remember right."

"True. We talked a lot. He thought the world of you, Marty. He said he'd always owe you for helping put him through school."

"My brother-in-law David died of a massive heart attack when Rod was a baby. Dave owned a flower shop that was just getting off the ground on borrowed money. Left nothing but bills behind. So, I had to help. Rod and my sister Loretta were the only relatives I had left. When she lost Rod, Loretta fell into a depression and never really recovered."

"Seems I remember you taking her to therapy."

"Yeah. It seemed to work—for a while. Then one night, she swallowed a bottle of pills . . ."

"Sadly, I remember. Didn't know her well. But your nephew always ran errands for me until he went off to college." Barry laughed. "I kept him employed as a kid just like you asked me to."

"That's right. I introduced him to you and he liked you and trusted you and it was probably your coke that blew out the blood vessels in his head."

My host continued pouring a new round but his bushy white eyebrows knitted together. "What are you saying?"

"*You're* running drugs." I thrust my forefinger so close to his face I damn near poked his eye. "And you put a hit on me."

"That car dive"—Barry rolled his eyes—"must have rattled your brain."

"Why'd you go into the drug business? Are you addicted?"

"Addicted!" Barry spat the answer out. "Sure!"

"Gambling debts, then? Are you in over your head?" I gestured toward the racing forms. "Sure looks like it."

"Why . . . after all I've done for you!" Barry's rising voice was filled with indignation. "Get the hell out of here! Go or I'll call the cops!"

"No need. You'll be seeing plenty of cops in the future."

"And what is that supposed to mean?"

"I'm going to ask my NYPD colleague Captain Crowley to send you some business. Nothing official. Just some off-duty officers who like to drink and hang around and watch things."

"You mean you haven't asked him already?"

"No. Because I wasn't sure about your complicity before."

"But you're sure now?"

"Dead certain."

"And why's that?"

"That gunman who took me for a ride looked familiar. And the reason he looked familiar has been haunting me until just now when you poured my drink. It just dawned on me that he was one of the yuppies I had seen in your bar."

"Nonsense!"

"Captain Crowley won't think it's nonsense. His watchdogs will either put you in jail or—"

Barry leaned forward, his right hand disappearing under the bar. "Or what?"

"Or you'll clean up your act and I'll have the satisfaction of knowing I ruined your dirty little business."

"All right. If you must know, it was *my* cocaine that did your nephew in, Marty." Barry's hand came up clutching a snub nosed. 38. "Seems his blood pressure couldn't handle it. But like you said yourself, nobody forced him to take it. He even brought me Wall Street trade."

"If I had known, Barry, I would have straightened him out and my sister would be alive today."

"No way would you've straightened him out. Success made your nephew cocky. But I'm going to straighten you out."

"By shooting me with that revolver?"

"Why not? Must protect my enterprise, Marty. This area's deserted at night. My friends will make you disappear later. And who'll be the wiser?"

"The police. I'm wired."

"Wired?" The color drained between the whiskey lines in his face. "I don't believe it."

"Look!" I yanked up my shirt and showed him the bug taped to my side. "The truth about your half-assed hit man *really* dawned on me right after I went for that nerve-racking ride. I thought about how that gunman frisked me for a weapon, and called me by name. Then I remembered seeing him in your bar. After that, I knew you set me up for a carjacking gone awry. Cops would be chasing teenage stickup artists and never connect to the drug trade. Very neat."

We were both startled by the crash of the vestibule door downstairs. When the intercom buzzed as well, Barry closed his eyes and sighed. The sight of my forty-eight-year-old sister laid out in her casket just months ago flashed through my mind. Something twisted in my stomach as I said,

"Your ship is sinking, pal. What was the first *Titanic* movie? *A Night to Remember*? Well, this is another night to remember."

That remark wrenched Barry. His eyes snapped open and a shiver ran through him. I seized his gun hand, and as I bent it away from me, one of my fingers slipped through the trigger guard. The roar plugged my eardrums and the flash stung my eyes. Barry fell from my grasp. I squinted several times, swallowed hard, and shook my head. Once I refocused, I saw him lying, blood spattered, behind the bar. Footsteps pounded up the stairs and two uniformed cops, guns drawn, burst in. Captain Crowley was right behind them. He looked about, then said, "What happened?"

"Barry panicked. Started waving the gun. So I tried to grab it. Next thing I knew, he was dead on the floor."

Crowley shot me an odd look, then shrugged. "One less case for our overburdened legal system."

The police raided Connors' Corner that very night and found quite a stash of narcotics hidden around the premises. Faro was wedging packets of cocaine between the toilet tank and the wall in the men's room when Crowley nailed him. Obviously the customers would close the stall door, remove the product, and replace it with cash. But Cynthia had nothing on her person and she denied everything, saying the goods must belong to Barry. The captain later persuaded Cynthia that she could do time anyway, then convinced the District Attorney to grant her immunity if she flipped. So she turned "State's Evidence" against the love of her life. Faro's going to do some heavy time according to Captain Crowley's prediction. It also came out in court that Barry, my friend of many years, succumbed to his gambling addiction and owed his existence to bookies and loan sharks, one of whom had taken me for a ride. Barry chose to redress his problems by selling cocaine. Tammy feels justice was satisfied somewhat but that it's grossly unfair for Cynthia to walk away free. I agreed, saying, "Sometimes people just get away with murder in this city."

The Trouble with Harry

Stefanie Matteson

"WOULD you mind picking up your feet, please?" Barbara asked.

Harry didn't hear her. He had turned the TV volume on high so he could hear it over the sound of the vacuum cleaner, pressing the volume control on the remote repeatedly in irritation at being disturbed.

Barbara wondered just when she was supposed to vacuum. He sat in front of the TV a good eighteen hours a day. And the volume was loud even when the vacuum cleaner wasn't running. Though he never would have admitted it, insisting that the problem was due to the fact that everyone around him mumbled, Harry was a little deaf.

But even with perfect hearing, there was no need to have the sound on at all, much less at top volume. He always watched the same shows. High-speed car chases and natural disasters were his favorites, along with real-life emergency and police dramas. Sirens and gunshots, along with some commentary—always at the same hyperexcited pitch—were all the volume delivered.

Barbara despised the constant blaring. The noise was wearing her nerves to a frazzle. And there was nowhere to get away from it; the house was too small. Even earplugs didn't work. For that matter, the constant blaring had become such a part of her life that it droned away in her head even when she wasn't in the house.

If she had to be married to a couch potato, why couldn't she at least have been married to someone who was addicted to golf tournaments, with the quiet, civilized voices of their commentators? But then, there was a lot to regret about being married to Harry.

It was a high-speed chase he was watching now—an aerial view of a motorcycle speeding down a palm-lined California freeway, police cruiser in hot pursuit. "The speed of the motorcycle is now in excess of one hundred and twenty miles per hour," said the commentator. The motorcycle zoomed past the traffic as if it were standing still.

Barbara waited until the motorcycle hit the bus at the intersection. She had seen the clip so many times that she knew what was going to happen. Then she restated her question: "Would you mind picking up your feet, please?" she shouted. She was standing at the side of his recliner with the nozzle poised in her hand.

Harry shot her an irritated glance, punched up the volume a couple of more notches—*Didn't she know she was disturbing him?* was his unspoken comment—and then reluctantly obliged her by lifting his slipper-clad feet while simultaneously reaching into the bowl on his lap for another handful of popcorn.

Bits of popcorn tumbled to the floor, and Barbara vacuumed them up. "If you put a squash in a chair, you'd get more life out of it than you do out of Harry," her sister had said just last week. Her sister had never understood why Barbara stayed with him. Nor, much of the time, did she. It was fall, and her sister had been reminded of the huge orange squashes that are displayed at farm stands, which Harry, in the orange T-shirt he had been wearing that day, did closely resemble.

That was the trouble with Harry. He never moved. The upholstery on the arms of his recliner was worn away, the stuffing coming away in little bits, and it was only a year and a half old.

She had hoped it wouldn't be like this. Counted on it, in fact. "We'll get a motor home when you retire," he had said. (He had retired two years before she.) "Travel the country. See the national parks. Go to Alaska."

She'd always wanted to see Alaska. It was only this prospect that had gotten her through the last couple of years as an ER nurse, the years that Harry had been at home and underfoot. But all she had seen was her own backyard on the fringes of the New York suburbs.

They had bought the motor home all right. With funds from her 401k. Far be it for Harry to dip into *his* retirement fund. It was secondhand, but it still had enough bells and whistles to thrill Barbara: a TV over the dresser, snugly fitting natural wood cabinets, a refrigerator, stove, and microwave—even air-conditioning and its own burglar alarm! Small but perfect, like a ship's cabin. All they needed, really. She often ate her dinner out there in the evenings with her toy poodle, Daisy, then stayed on to watch the news. She'd made curtains and throw pillows to coordinate with the floral bedspread and fastened down her knickknacks with poster adhesive, to prevent them from breaking on the road. She'd even picked up a coordinating china pattern on sale—a service for four, which was more than enough for the two of them. After forty years of keeping house, she loved the sweet compactness of it—not a square inch wasted, everything fitting together as neatly as the pieces of a jigsaw puzzle.

But they had never gone anywhere in it. In fact, she

didn't think Harry had ever set foot in it, apart from the day they'd looked at it in the dealer's lot.

It just sat there in the driveway, arousing a welter of confused feelings in Barbara's breast every time she set eyes on it, which was about twenty times a day, since she could see it from her kitchen sink. There was the urge to hit the open highway, despair that it would never happen, and hope that one day Harry would decide he was finally going to start enjoying life. As she was always pointing out to him, it wasn't as if he'd been doled out an unlimited supply: there was only so much of it left.

And that was dwindling away, moment by moment, day by day, Barbara thought as she stood at the sink after finishing with the vacuuming, drinking a glass of water, and looking out at the vehicle that was to have been the agent of her liberation.

IT was while she was standing there that she heard it: a squeal of brakes, a sickening thud. Daisy! Her heart leaped into her throat. But the little dog was curled up on her bed in the corner. Which meant that the car had hit a deer. It happened several times a year, and it was the only thing Barbara knew of that would arouse Harry from his vegetative state. He hated the deer that had overrun this corner of suburbia. Hated the way they ate the shrubbery, hated the way they crapped all over the yard, hated the way they stood in the driveway when you pulled in, refusing to get out of the way. "Deer with attitude," he called them. It was typical that the only emotion Harry seemed to feel was hate. He maintained an extensive list of categorical hates, to which he referred with tiresome regularity. Shellfish, children, piano music, New York City, green leafy vegetables. At the top of the list were incompetents, which in Harry's eyes was a category to which most of the world belonged. Next was deer. Barbara, on the other hand, loved them: their lustrous brown eyes, their graceful leaps, their attitude of quiet repose.

"The kings of Europe spent huge amounts of money to create deer parks on the grounds of their castles, and here we have a deer park right in our own backyard!" she would point out to him when they argued about it, which was often. "But that was for the purpose of killing them," Harry would reply. He had done some deer hunting in his younger days and liked to think of himself as a big-game hunter.

After calling the police, Barbara headed out to assure the driver that an officer was on the way. Harry's chair was empty, she noticed as she passed through the living room. He must already have gone out. It looked oddly vacant without Harry in it. Many nights he even slept there; she would awake in the morning to find the TV still on. At least she could look forward to him being in a good mood, she thought. Nothing made his day like a dead deer, especially one that had met its end right in front of the house.

Warren Miller was just pulling up in the police cruiser as she reached the road. The dead deer—a good-sized doe—lay in front of their privet hedge, its entrails scattered over the pavement. The car must have broad-sided it. The driver had pulled over on the opposite shoulder; the left fender of his car was crumpled.

Harry stood at the side of the car in his slippers, probably reassuring the driver that his wife had called the police and that an officer would be there shortly.

The police were good about coming out right away. Getting the road crew out right away to clear the carcass too, before it started to putrefy. Residents didn't like dead deer decaying in front of their houses. The dogs were also apt to get to them. Barbara would never forget the day Daisy had come home proudly clutching a foreleg in her teeth.

"Another dead deer. You must be happy, Harry," Warren

said, after he had finished writing up his report. "And a doe besides," he added, sharing in Harry's pleasure that one less doe meant one less opportunity for the despised animals to reproduce. "How many are we up to so far this year?"

Harry kept a running tally of the town's deer fatalities, along with their locations. He gleaned the information from a combination of anecdotal accounts, empirical observation, and the "Police Beat" column in the local newspaper. In the event of any confusion, he checked directly with the police department.

Which meant that Warren Miller was well acquainted with Harry's peculiar obsession.

"This makes a hundred and fifty-two. Twenty-nine on Prospect Street alone," he replied. His indignation at the fact that the deer population was greatest in his own neighborhood was tempered by the fact that this meant that the most deer fatalities took place there. "Thirty-four more than last year," he added.

Warren nodded. "At this rate, the lime pit's going to be full before the year's out; we're probably going to have to dig another one." He was referring to the pit behind the public works garage where the municipal road crew dumped the deer carcasses.

Warren had dismissed the driver of the car and was now adding a few notations to the accident report. Finishing, he closed the cover of his book and nodded at the motor home that sat in the driveway behind the small white Cape Cod–style home. "When are you planning on heading out in that thing?" he asked.

He raised this subject every time they saw him, which was several times a year. His interest was prompted by a personal dream of taking a summer off with his family to tour the country in a motor home.

"In the spring," Harry replied definitively. "Now that Barbara's retired, there's nothing to hold us back. But we're going to wait until the weather's better. We want to head up to Alaska—that's always been Barbara's dream: to see Denali National Park."

"Like to see that myself," Warren said as he got back into the cruiser. "That, and a whole lot else." He started the engine. "You take care now," he said, and drove off.

Nothing to hold us back, thought Barbara, except a remote control.

THE irony was that it was the death of the doe that finally blasted Harry out of his chair. The sight of the mangled carcass had ignited a blood lust that he claimed could be quenched only by hunting. "I'm going to get my license this year and get myself a deer," he announced. Barbara paid no attention. She'd heard it all before. Plus the idea of her overweight, diabetic couch potato of a husband traipsing around in the woods was too preposterous to bear contemplation. But to her surprise, he actually did it: got the license, the grunt tubes and rattling devices, and the 30.06 with a fancy scope—the whole nine yards. And to her even greater surprise, he actually shot a deer—a trophy buck with a nineteen-inch rack—which was probably due more to the fact that deer were thicker than ants at a picnic than any hunting expertise on his part. But at nearly two hundred pounds, Harry's buck not only kept them in venison chops, it lifted Harry out of his depression. He now devoted the hours that he used to spend watching TV to reading hunting magazines; his intimacy with the remote control was replaced by that with his shotgun; and he spent hours planning his campaign for next hunting season. As far as Barbara was concerned, if it took the life of a single trophy buck to bring about this transformation, the sacrifice was well worth the price.

Meanwhile, the motor home still sat in the driveway. But

Barbara was hopeful that Harry's newfound success as a whitetail hunter would provide the psychological boost to finally realize their dream of seeing the United States. And at Christmas, wearing the new orange vest she'd ordered from a hunting catalog, he had stunned her by saying: "I think we should head out west right after Saint Patrick's Day. Start in the Southwest, then work our way up to Alaska. If we hit Alaska in late summer, we could be back down to Oregon for elk season. I'd like to do some elk hunting."

Barbara's jaw fell open. A plan at last! Then he kissed her under the mistletoe. That night, they made love for the first time in years.

In fact, she was delighted with the new Harry, even if his attire did make him look like a mercenary for a banana republic. The only aspect of their new life together that she found to complain about was, well . . . "Harry." That's what they called the deer hide that was the souvenir of the buck Harry had taken, along with the ten-point rack that now hung over the fireplace in the family room. The hide was huge: it must have been five feet long, including the legs. And it was smelly, the odor being a product of the tanning process that Harry had been assured would fade, but had yet to do so.

It was their little joke. They'd named the hide after the old Hitchcock movie in which "Harry" was the corpse that the characters couldn't find a place to dispose of. "Harry" had started out in the living room, but Barbara complained that it ruined her decorating scheme. Then they tried it in the family room, but it was too big to fit on the only wall that came close to accommodating it. It finally ended up in the rec room, but when they realized that the smell wasn't going to fade, they moved it out to the motor home.

It was now being used as a coverlet in the sleeping compartment over the cab, and if that meant the motor home smelled too much for Barbara to eat her dinners out there, that was fine. She was eating dinners with Harry now anyway.

"Where'd you put 'Harry' now?" was the running joke. And after all those dreary years, it was nice to have something to laugh about with her husband.

THE second honeymoon didn't last. By the end of January, Harry was back in his chair, his hand in its usual death grip around the neck of the remote. In fact, the remote had become more of an issue than ever. Harry had become forgetful and would leave it around the house. But would he admit to this? No. He would blame her, bellowing accusations from the depths of the recliner. Then the search would commence, and she would find the remote on the vanity next to the toilet seat or on the counter next to the refrigerator or buried in the seat of the chair. It didn't take a Sherlock to figure out where he had left it given the fact that he now moved for only three reasons: to eat, to use the bathroom, and to get his daily shot of insulin, for which he didn't even leave the chair, but merely adjusted his position. He'd even gotten lax about personal hygiene, neglecting to shower and shave. Any talk of a trip had been abandoned. She'd suggested that he see a counselor, but this only provoked his ire: the problem didn't lie with him, but with her. She was a controlling bitch; she was never satisfied; she only wanted to spend his hard-earned money; she only thought of herself. His list went on and on.

She tried not to take it personally. His complaints were the same about the rest of the world; nobody could do anything right. She ate in the motor home almost every night now, which no longer smelled since the hide had been banished to a box in the garage. Once her refuge, her house had become her prison, and it was only in the motor home that she felt at peace.

After delivering Harry's dinner on a tray, she would head out to the motor home, where she would spend the evening organizing her trip. She had bought a filebox, which she had fitted with hanging files for each of the states. Into these, she put maps, travel brochures, information on campsites, and articles on tourist destinations. She also spent time learning about how to set up the vehicle's various systems. Occasionally she even took it out for a test drive so she could practice backing up and making sharp turns. She wanted to be ready when the time arrived.

It was on an evening in early March that Harry finally pushed her over the edge. She had eaten her dinner in the motor home and was coming back for her dessert. She could hear him as she approached the house. "Come here, you stupid bitch!" he was shouting, a note of hysteria in his voice. He must have been calling for her ever since she'd left.

She presented herself at the side of his chair. He was watching a disaster documentary that he'd probably seen a dozen times already; it was about tornadoes. He was still wearing the bathrobe and slippers he'd been wearing the night before. "Where's my remote?" he growled, his voice hard with anger. His eyes didn't leave the screen, where two tornado chasers were speeding after a huge funnel.

"Did you look next to the seat cushion?" she asked.

"Why should I look in the cushion when I know you took it?"

Never mind that she rarely watched TV in the house and, if she did, watched it in the basement rec room. It was her fault. "Can you please get up?" she asked him calmly.

He rolled to one side, as if presenting a buttock for his shot, and she reached down into the chair. As she suspected, the remote was wedged between the cushion and the arm.

She pulled it out and handed it to him. "Here," she said.

He took it without a word of thanks.

Harry didn't know it yet, but he was about to experience his own private disaster.

SHE'D been thinking about it for a long time. Harry was a diabetic. A diabetic who didn't take care of himself. He snacked on sugary junk foods; he never exercised. As she saw it, he was a goner anyway. In fact, if it weren't for her, he probably wouldn't even be around. It was only because of her close monitoring that he'd maintained the delicate balance between too much blood glucose and too little that was required for control of his diabetes. She would only be hastening the inevitable. Probably save him a lot of pain and suffering into the bargain. And from her ER work, she knew exactly what to do. She even had access from the occasional shifts she still filled in on to the highly concentrated insulin used in diabetic emergencies. Such a drug was a lifesaver for patients whose blood sugar had soared out of control, but could cause the blood sugar of patients whose diabetes was under control to plummet, leading to coma and death. Her only concern was the autopsy: a sharp pathologist would be able to tell the death was due to an overdose. And although she'd read of murderers who had done so, she doubted she could pass it off as accidental. If nothing else, it was unlikely that an experienced ER nurse could claim ignorance of the symptoms of insulin shock. She would have to make Harry simply disappear, though how she was going to do this was still a mystery.

She was still pondering this question when she heard the familiar squeal of brakes. It was usually at this time that the deer collisions took place: twilight, when the drivers were returning home and the deer were out foraging. In her usual panic, she checked for Daisy, who was safely lapping up water from her bowl. Then came the sickening thud of metal colliding with flesh.

"Harry, I think it's a deer," she shouted into the living room.

When she received no response, she went out to the living room and announced: "A deer has been hit." It was a testimony to the depth of Harry's melancholy that he didn't even look up. He had long ago given up on his count of deer fatalities.

It was then that it dawned on her what to do with Harry's body.

SHE gave him the shot just before dinner a couple of weeks later, as she always did—in the butt. The thigh in the morning, the butt at night—alternating sides to keep the injection sites from becoming irritated. She went through the procedure exactly as usual: inserting the needle through the rubber lid, pushing the plunger down to force the air in, inverting the bottle to mix the contents, and finally filling the plunger with the proper dose. Then she wiped Harry's cheek with an alcohol swab, pinched the skin between her fingers, pushed in the needle, and depressed the plunger.

It took only a half an hour or so before the drug started to take effect. She was preparing dinner in the kitchen—corned beef and cabbage for Saint Patrick's Day—when she heard him call. It wasn't his usual demanding bellow, but a request; it might almost have been called polite. "Barbara, can you come here?"

Emerging from the kitchen, she stood at the door of the darkened room and looked inquiringly into his face, which was enlivened only by the reflected images that flickered across the surface of his glasses. "What is it?' she asked, paring knife still in hand.

"I don't feel so good," he said. "I think I need a sugar pill."

It was a fact of a diabetic's life that despite the most regular of routines, the blood glucose level is prone to unpredictable swings. As a result, an insulin dose that reduces the level to normal one day can reduce it too far the next, inducing the symptoms of hypoglycemia. Such symptoms can be relieved by a quick fix of a sweet snack or a glucose pill, which most diabetics have at the ready.

"I'll get your meter," Barbara replied. She noticed that behind the glasses and the stubble, he looked pale. Beads of sweat had broken out on his temples.

In a moment, she was back at his side with a blood glucose meter. After pricking his finger, she dabbed the blood sample on a test strip and inserted it into the device. According to the readout, Harry's blood glucose level stood at fifty-two, with fifty being the level for hypoglycemia. She took his pulse; it was already racing.

"Yes, it's low," she agreed. It was a good thing his attention was riveted to the arrest taking place on TV; he didn't see how low. "I'll get your pills."

She had planned for this eventuality too. Instead of his usual glucose pills, Barbara gave him inert placebos that researchers at the medical center were using in a double-blind study on the effect of a new medication.

After handing him three, she retreated into the kitchen. No sooner was she back at the sink than he called her again, this time for a blanket, which she brought him, tucking it neatly around him. She noticed that his skin had become cold and clammy.

A few moments later, he called again. He was saying her name, though his speech was so slurred she could barely make it out. When she entered, she found him with his head thrown back against the back of the recliner. He was sounding a low, steady moan.

"Are you okay?" she asked.

There was no reply.

As she stood there, his body stiffened; his arms were thrust straight out in front of him. Though his eyes were open, he didn't appear to be conscious. Then his entire body started to convulse. He was having a seizure.

It was only a matter of minutes before it was over.

HER most elaborate preparations had been for the disposal of the body. Inspired by the deer collision, her first thought had been to wrap it in the deer hide. But she quickly realized that wouldn't work. The hide simply wasn't big enough, trophy buck or no. Then she remembered another hide in the attic—a memento of a kill from Harry's younger days. This she sewed together with "Harry," punching the holes with an awl and stitching the edges together with leather shoelaces. She had spent a couple of weeks' worth of evenings on the queen-sized bed in the motor home engaged in this task while watching TV with Daisy. The result had been well worth her time: a sleeping bag–like deerskin pouch with an opening at one end. It was probably not unlike the sleeping gear that Indian squaws had once stitched for their braves.

Once she could no longer detect Harry's pulse, she retrieved the deerskin bag from the motor home and spread it out on the carpet next to the recliner, which she extended fully by pulling the lever on the side. With the chair extended, it was a simple matter to roll Harry's body over the arm. She was used to moving inert bodies around from the hospital. It landed on its side with a thud. After binding the arms and legs, she worked it head-first into the deerskin bag. Harry hadn't been a large man, and it fit perfectly, forming a neat package about five-and-a-half feet long. His feet stuck out a little, but she could fix that by bending his knees when she sewed up the end.

After half an hour, her handiwork was complete, and she stood back to admire it. As deer went, Harry was fatter than most, but she doubted this would arouse suspicion since many of the carcasses cleared from the roadsides had already begun to swell. All that was missing was the head, which looked down at her from over the mantel, though whether it was with reproach or approbation she wasn't sure.

The next step was loading the body onto the hand truck. She was a strong woman and almost as large as Harry himself, so it wasn't difficult. Finally she wheeled the hand truck out to the garage, which was attached to the house—all the better to shield her activities from nosy neighbors—and maneuvered the load into the trunk.

THE deer disposal pit was located in the woods at the rear of the public works garage. She had scoped it out one evening the week before. A gravel driveway led around the garage to the edge of the pit. If the best place to hide a body was a battlefield, as it was said, then the next best must be a charnel pit, especially when that pit was for deer and the body was covered with a deer hide. By now it was after ten and the site was deserted. Barbara backed the car up to the edge of the fence surrounding the pit and popped the trunk. Then she opened the gate, lifted Harry's body out—this took some effort—and rolled it over the edge. He didn't fall far: the pit was nearly full of deer carcasses. These would be covered over tomorrow with a six-inch layer of soil, which she had learned was done every Wednesday. It was a good thing, too: the smell was getting bad.

Concealed in the deer hide, Harry's body was indistinguishable from the other carcasses. But to make sure that no one would recognize it as such, she covered it with a layer of lime from the barrel at the edge of the pit and then sprinkled it with leaves and twigs to make it blend in with the carcasses cleared from the roadsides.

The deed was done.

SHE was packing up the last of her clothes two months later when she heard the familiar squeal of brakes, followed by the thunk of metal on flesh. This time there was also a crash: the driver must have lost control of the car. After calling the police, she went out to the road. The driver had hit the maple in front of the house across the street, but appeared to be okay. He was inspecting the damage to the front of his car. A dead doe lay on the roadside at the rear of the car; it must have been flung over the roof by the impact.

Warren Miller arrived a few minutes later, followed by a pickup from the public works department. While Warren wrote up the accident report, two members of the road crew hoisted the carcass into the back of the truck. The damage to the driver's vehicle wasn't great, and after a few minutes the scene of the accident was cleared up.

"How's Harry?" Warren asked once everyone was gone. "I expected to see him out here. Isn't he keeping his deer count anymore?"

"Nah," Barbara replied. "He couldn't keep up. The numbers were getting too great. Plus, the paper stopped reporting deer collisions in the 'Police Beat' column, and he wasn't about to start running out to count every carcass."

Warren shook his head in sympathy. "Yep, it's getting worse and worse. It's carnage on the roads. Especially out this way. We've had to open a second deer pit. The last one was filled up after only three months; we thought it was going to last a year."

"Oh really?" Barbara commented innocently. "When did that happen?"

"We covered the old pit just yesterday." He nodded in the direction of the departing pickup. "I expect this doe will be the first occupant of the new one. We're looking into hiring an outside contractor for disposal. There's just too many to keep up with."

Changing the subject, he nodded at the real estate company's SOLD sign on Barbara's lawn. "I see the house is sold. Are you and Harry finally going to take that trip out west that you've been talking about for so long?"

Barbara turned to look at the motor home in the driveway. "Yes, we are," she told him with a smile. "We had a house sale last weekend. Sold most of our belongings. The rest we're putting into a storage locker."

"Footloose and fancy free at last," said Warren.

"You bet," Barbara replied, her voice ringing with delight. "We're leaving on Tuesday. First we're going to Alaska. Then we'll meander south. We don't have any plans, other than to visit all the national parks. That's always been Harry's dream."

"Mine too," said Warren, his youthful countenance alight with enthusiasm. "But I don't think it's going to happen in my lifetime. Or at least not until the kids are grown. How long do you figure it's going to take you?"

"Oh, years!" exclaimed Barbara. "There are thirty-nine major national parks in the forty-eight contiguous states alone."

"Then you're not planning on coming back?"

Barbara shook her head. "Maybe for a visit."

"Do me a favor," Warren said.

"Of course," replied Barbara.

"Send me a postcard."

IT was three months later that Warren Miller got the postcard. It was a view of a snow-capped Mount McKinley at sunrise, with *Denali National Park* written diagonally across the photo in red script. On the back it read:

On the road, Aug. 4
Dear Warren,

It feels great to be on the road at last. We're at Denali National Park now and getting the hang of our rambling lifestyle more and more with each passing day. Our address now is Alaska, but after that who knows? The continent is our neighborhood now. We love our little house on wheels. We caught our first red salmon the other day: cooked it on the grill and shared it with a fellow we met in Washington State. We've been traveling with him for a while now and we get along very well. We don't have a single regret. We would do it again in a heartbeat.

Cordially, Harry and Barbara (Daisy too)

Any Old Mother

Charlotte Hinger

THIS would make the third mother she'd done. Dazzled by the beauty of this estate, Annie rang the doorbell. As she waited, she eyed the shiny brass knocker and the carefully trimmed shrubbery. The two-story brick house was enormous. It was centered on beautifully landscaped acreage framed by old oak trees. Her heartbeat accelerated with the approaching footsteps on the other side of the door.

She clutched her good leather purse to her side, knowing it was just the right touch. It was important not to look too poor, or too rich. Seconds away now. She had her speech down cold. Every word, every gesture worked out in advance.

It wasn't as though this was a cold call. She had spent two months collecting information. This mother was a widow, worth a small fortune, with a platoon of lawyers and accountants guarding the gates. Today was the downstairs maid's day off. Mrs. Elaine Simms would answer the door herself.

Like the other two mothers, Elaine Simms had given a

baby up for adoption. Looking back, Annie decided it was as though the first two women were for practice.

For the first mother it hadn't taken much. A little gold cross, some scruffy loafers, run-down heels. She would never forget the face of the good Christian woman when she answered the door.

"Mrs. Woodruff?" Annie had asked cautiously. Then, "Mother! You're my mother."

"Oh God, oh God, oh God," the woman cried out. "Oh please no." Furtively, she'd looked around. "My husband. Please. Please. He doesn't know."

"I've had a terrible life," Annie said. "You abandoned me to a cruel home. Terrible people."

"I didn't know," Mrs. Woodruff whimpered. "I swear to God I didn't know."

From there on, it had been easy. All she'd gotten was ten thousand dollars. But it was enough for Annie to realize the potential. Working in the state adoption agency gave her access to all the records. Once she found her mark, she did not have to fake any of the feelings. An adopted child herself, orphaned now, she had never really fit in.

"You're special," her parents had told her. "We chose you." Well, she had never thought *they* were very special. Not special at all. They were mediocre middle-class little worker ants and she knew in her soul she had been born to better. It was just a matter of finding them.

The second mother was solid, shrewd. Sized her up in about three minutes. *But she'd believed her*, Annie thought with a smile. *Oh yes, she'd believed her*. The big secret was worth twenty-five thousand to that one. But Annie had known better than to ever come back.

Annie's stomach tightened with anticipation. The dead bolt clicked. She had big plans for this mother. Her blood pounded in her ears. *She's old*, Annie reminded herself. *Going to die soon anyway*. What's life worth to an old bat like her?

Through her snooping around, she had learned this woman had an invalid daughter, on dialysis. Perhaps Elaine Simms's life was worth something to the daughter, she thought, with a grim smile. Invalids did best with a mother's care.

At last. The woman on the other side peered through a crack, then slid back the chain and opened the door.

Elaine Simms was a slim woman, patrician, with beautifully arranged white hair. She had perfect carriage and wore a brightly embroidered denim tunic over matching pants. On her wrists was an array of slender turquoise and silver bracelets.

"Elaine Simms?" Annie asked tentatively, lowering her voice to a whisper. "Mother?" But the well-rehearsed words stuck in her throat. Before she could get them out of her mouth, the woman's face drained of color. Simms gave a little gurgle and silently worked her mouth as she clutched her hand to her chest. She fell against the door jam, her head bent.

Terrified, that she was having a heart attack, Annie reached to steady her. This mother couldn't die now. It was too soon. It would ruin everything.

"Oh please," begged Annie. "Please, please be all right." Dazed, she tried to make sense of the woman's reaction. All she had done was say her name.

Then Mrs. Simms's head shot up and she clasped Annie's cheeks between her palms and smothered her face with little kisses. "Darling, darling girl," she murmured.

"Laurie," she called loudly. "Laurie. Annie's here. Your sister is here!"

Disoriented and light-headed, Annie took a series of deep breaths. From the hallway, she could see a flash of chrome; a chair rapidly propelled by strong efficient hands silently whooshed down the long oriental runner. She stared at the woman who wheeled into the doorway. Stared at her own features. The face before her was broad, beautiful, faintly

Slavic with high cheekbones and a distinctly cleft chin. Her eyes were blue. Even their honey blond hair was styled in the same tousled cut.

Annie's hand trembled as she touched her own face; to assure herself that her nose, eyes, and mouth were in the right place. She had an eerie sense they had been snatched from her body and pasted onto this Laurie, this stranger. Laurie Simms wore a long gathered white linen skirt, and a bright scoop-necked appliquéd top, extravagantly Southwestern, reeking of money. Exactly the in-your-face kind of outfit Annie would have chosen if she were an invalid.

Even in Annie's superior physical condition, the woman in the chair seemed to have the advantage. She sat beautifully erect, her eyes confident and judgmental. Annie winked back tears. You couldn't buy this kind of poise. *It comes from being sure of your place*, Annie thought bitterly.

"Annie," said the woman in the chair. "I've waited, waited for this moment."

"My darling baby," gushed Mrs. Simms. "My own darling little girl. You were twins, of course, identical twins."

Jesus, Annie thought. *What a gold mine*. Her mind whirled. Stocks and bonds and land and this house. This fabulous house. The potential was slowly dawning on her. Then she was jolted by another thought; this wasn't just any old mother. This was her real mother. She had actually found her real mother. Her very own sister. How had this happened?

"I don't understand," she said limply. "I just don't understand." Confused, she realized it was not total coincidence. After all, she had concentrated on mothers who had given birth the year she was born. In fact, even before she knew Elaine Simms was worth a fortune, Annie had focused on her because she had a daughter named Laurie. The Annie-Laurie bit had appealed to her sense of poetic justice.

"We've been looking for you for the last three years," said Laurie. "We hired a private detective."

"Why didn't he call us?" Mrs. Simms wailed. "I can't understand why he didn't let us know he had found you. We hunted everywhere."

"He didn't find me. I found you. I've been looking for you too. I was in a number of foster homes before I was adopted. So many it would have been hard to track me," Annie said carefully, knowing they would be put off by her raw rage that welled to the surface if she didn't keep strict control of her feelings.

"Oh my darling, we are all together again now. Reunited. And you are to start calling me Mother."

"And you can start calling me Sis," Laurie insisted with a charming smile.

"Are you sure?" Annie asked. Suspicious of her own good fortune, she looked into Laurie's eyes. Did this sister resent the intrusion? How would it set with her to be an invalid, then have a healthy identical twin walk in, bold as brass? *Not well*, Annie thought. *But that's tough sister. I'm here to stay.*

"Of course I want you to call me Sis," said Laurie. "Of course. How can you doubt it?" The tears in her eyes appeared to be genuine. They literally pulled her inside and led her to the kitchen, insisting she was one of the family, not parlor company.

Sitting at a huge oak island, Annie was astonished at the sheer size of the room. All the appliances were disguised by oak panels. A vast array of copper pans dangled on wrought-iron hooks. There was a glassed-in porch on the south side, containing a jungle of green plants.

I should have grown up right here, thought Annie. I should have gone to a finishing school. Learned to fence and play tennis. For an instant, she was swept by a wave of hatred for this sister who had had all the advantages.

"There are so many things I want to know about you. Where you live, what you do." Elaine Simms brimmed with tears as she settled beside Annie.

"Excuse me," Annie pleaded. "Bathroom, please?" She needed to escape. Think. She was terrified that she would say or do something that would screw her up later. She nearly ran down the hallway. Inside the ornate gold and rose powder room, she ran cold water over a washcloth and pressed it against the hot blood surging into her cheeks.

Then it dawned on her she could say anything, do anything, and they would believe her. If it didn't ring true, she could simply explain that she had been trying to impress them. She had wanted them to like her.

She pulled herself together and walked back into the kitchen. The two women were weeping and clutching each other's hands. Then moved to tears herself, she laughed and joined them.

She and Laurie couldn't keep their eyes off one another. They had an irresistible urge to play favorites. What's your favorite book? What's your favorite color? Your favorite movie? Annie realized everything she had learned about twins was true. Even raised apart in totally different backgrounds, they had developed nearly identical tastes.

They doted on her. Believed every word she said. She stuck as closely to the truth as possible, and when they asked her where she worked, she smiled tearfully and said, "For an adoption agency. That's where I got the idea that you just might be my mother. But I had no idea I was a twin. None."

And that's the God's truth, she thought, *or I would have been here a long time ago*.

"My sole reason for keeping such a painful job was to find you." She peeked at them from between her fingers splayed across her face. "I've been told I was vastly underemployed. Working far below my capacity. At a salary that's laughable to say the least." Then overcome, she whirled around and left the room.

When she returned, Laurie and Elaine's faces were alive with joy and the quiet resolution of persons who have come to a decision. "We have so much to make up to you," said Elaine. "So much we want you to know. Would it be possible for you to move in here? There simply aren't enough hours in the day for us to catch up!"

Annie trembled as she walked toward them. "This house? This wonderful house? I could live in this house? With you?"

"Oh, my darling child," Elaine said. "Of course. You're entitled."

You bet your butt I am, Annie thought. "There are a few arrangements I have to make."

"Do you have a boyfriend?"

"No. I've been told I have problems with relationships, because of what was missing in my early childhood." She said this with a brave little shudder and bright smile. She noticed a flash of guilty pain in Elaine Simms's eyes. "And I need to let them know at work. I won't bother with a full two weeks' notice."

Then seeing the frown on Elaine's face, as though she did not approve of a daughter who took her responsibilities lightly, she added, "There's been a few problems with my boss. He's a bit handsy."

It was the right thing to say. Elaine's face relaxed and Annie knew she should think Midwest from now on. Man's word was his bond and all that.

"Can we send someone to help you?" asked Elaine.

"No," Annie blurted. "I don't want you to see where I live." That was the absolute truth, and she was intrigued at how often now she was well served by the absolute truth.

Elaine's face softened with pity. "Oh, my own darling

little girl. I can't believe how we've wronged you. We're going to make it up to you."

ANNIE packed quickly. Looking around at the sheer squalor of her apartment, she couldn't wait to get out the door. Her pitiful pieces of furniture, her second-rate clothes belonged to another life. She didn't need them anymore. For anything.

Her new bedroom contained a splendid walnut four-poster bed with an antique lace spread and curtains to match. That night she sank into the feathery warmth of soft luxurious bedding, fit for a princess. But before she drifted off to sleep, her mind buzzed with questions. *Why had her mother kept Laurie and not her? Why had she been abandoned?*

The next morning she was slowly coming up from the deepest sleep she had ever known when there was a timid knock on the door.

"Come in," she called with a guilty glance at the clock. Ten in the morning. What must they think of her? The door opened and a maid came in bearing an enormous breakfast tray. Elaine followed her into the room.

"I can't imagine what came over me," Annie said. "Honestly. You must think I'm a terrible slugabed . . ."

"No, no, no," protested Elaine. She yanked up the raw silk shades and let in a blazing shaft of light. Her white hair gleamed like a halo against the window. "Darling girl. We want you to lie back. Enjoy! Let yourself be pampered. When was the last time you had breakfast in bed?"

The maid arranged the tray and began to prop up the vast array of feather pillows. She handed Annie the morning paper and a remote for the TV hidden in the wall opposite her.

"I am so very, very grateful," said Annie.

"We're the ones who should be thankful," Elaine said.

She handed Annie a clipboard. "I want you to sign this. I'm adding your name to my credit card at Neiman Marcus. You're to have a whole new wardrobe. There's a woman who will come here to fit you and show you fabrics, styles."

"No need for that," Annie protested as she signed the form. "I can go down to the store."

"Nonsense. You've never had the pleasure of someone working to satisfy you and you alone. You'll love it!"

That afternoon, Annie was overwhelmed by the array of expensive clothing.

"Don't even think about the price," Elaine said. "It's not even a consideration."

Oh, somebody pinch me, Annie thought. *This has got to be a dream*. She signed for a makeover from a well-known salon and a masseuse and approved of the fresh flowers to be delivered to her bedroom twice a week. She signed the forms adding her name to their health insurance and their car insurance.

"I'm going to get writer's cramp," Annie protested.

"You're part of this family now," Elaine said with amusement. "We want you to enjoy all the privileges. But when there's money involved, all the forms and legalities can be overwhelming."

When Elaine urged her to sell "or junk" her old car, Annie hoped she would volunteer to replace it with a racy little sports car.

"I don't want you driving," Elaine protested. "You're too precious to us. Our chauffeur will take you anywhere you want to go. I've spent so many years worrying about Laurie's health, I'm afraid you'll find me a bit of a prevention fanatic. Please! Wear your seat belt, take vitamins, and all that."

Although Elaine smiled to soften her words, Annie soon learned her every health habit was under constant scrutiny. She missed the freedom of driving her own car, and even more, the freedom to run around and do as she pleased. In her own velvet-gloved way, Elaine Simms exerted an iron control over the plethora of people required to run her household and this attitude was extended to her daughters.

After studying all the processes for Laurie's dialysis, Annie volunteered to stay with her and monitor the machine during the triweekly process. It gave her a chance to visit with Laurie. When she made the offer, Elaine was thrilled.

"It will be a big relief to me to know I can leave this house safely from time to time. Laurie's own sister will be here to cheer her. Even though there's always a nurse right in the next room, it will be a comfort to me."

Annie smiled gamely. She hated blood, urine—anything to do with medicine. She wasn't about to spend all of her days taking care of a sister with a bum kidney. They would have to go. *Both of them*, Annie thought grimly. But it would have to come after she was so entrenched she would be included in Elaine's will.

Just as she was giving the ways and means her full attention, Elaine floored her with another move. It was as disorienting as opening a door two weeks earlier and finding her real mother. Her mother came into her bedroom early that morning, trailed by a nurse carrying blood-typing tubes and all kinds of medical paraphernalia.

The nurse wound an elastic tube around her arm. "All you're going to feel is a little sting," she said.

"What's going on? What are you doing to me?"

Elaine positively glowed. "I have a wonderful surprise for you, darling. I'm going to adopt you. This shouldn't be necessary, but my lawyers insist that you have a complete medical workup. Given all the miracles people can work with plastic surgery nowadays, they want to be sure you're really Laurie's sister. They want blood typing, DNA testing. All that. We'll need your consent, of course, for all these proceedings." Elaine smiled as she handed Annie a clipboard containing stacks of papers requiring her signature. "I can't adopt you against your will."

"Why now?" asked Annie. "Why now when I'm an adult?" There was a hole inside her nothing could fill. It was too late. Nevertheless, she reached for the pen, zipped through the piles of required forms, then patted Elaine's hand to take the sting out of her words.

"Why now? There must be no question that you're my legal heir, the same as Laurie. Adoption is the best way to eliminate any complications."

Annie sank back into the bed, so ecstatic her toes curled. She beamed at the nurse. "Take plenty," she said as she watched the vial fill with her blood. There was no doubt in her mind that Laurie was her identical twin; and her own health was perfect. Just perfect. Now her biggest hurdle of all—one that had driven her crazy for the past two weeks had been cleared as easily as if someone had waved a magic wand. When Elaine died, she would inherit equally with Laurie. And then, she smiled. Then after a decent period, she would inherit her sister's share. Just like that.

SHE hated the dialysis machine but she didn't let a trace of that show. She now looked forward to the three-hour sessions three times a week with Laurie. At last, she was able to gain some information about her mother.

One day, she looked at Laurie and realized how much she liked her. For an instant she wished this sister were well. She would be the family she had never had. She wished Elaine were not so domineering. Wished Laurie were not so sick.

After she had checked all the monitors and tubes, she glanced at the array of medications the nurse had left out on Laurie's table. Lining them up, tidying the tray gave her a chance to read the labels.

She picked up a small bottle of morphine and turned to Laurie. "Are you in pain often?"

"No, I really do very well, but we don't like to take any chances. When it hits, it's terrible. We keep every thing I might need possibly on hand," she said with a weak smile. "As you can tell by the dates, I don't need any pain medication very often."

Just a bit too much morphine could fatally suppress respiration, Annie thought triumphantly. It was the perfect way. But first Elaine! She still had the problem with her mother. There was no real rush. The perfect way for her too would present itself.

Annie picked up a magazine and pretended to leaf through it. She and Laurie had quite a confidential relationship by now. Today, after her sister was relaxed, she would ask the heartbreaking questions that had always plagued her. She had a right to know. She waited until Laurie was drowsy and the sun was warming the cheery yellow room Elaine had furnished especially for this process.

"What can you tell me about our father?"

Laurie stiffened. "We will never know who our father was," she said softly. "Mother has never said."

"I just supposed hers was a young have-to marriage and that her husband, Howard Simms, was our father," Annie said truthfully.

"The man I grew up calling 'Daddy' was not our father."

Stunned, Annie sat silently for a moment before she asked the question that had plagued her all her life. The one asked by all adoptive children; "Legitimate or not," she said bitterly, "why didn't they keep me?"

Laurie was totally silent. Absolutely rigid.

Then Annie asked the question that had been tormenting her ever since she came to this house. She had not known before that she had a sister. "How could any woman, any mother, give away a twin?"

"There are some questions you must never ask," Laurie said softly. "Never."

"I've got to know."

"She didn't know we were twins."

"How could that be?"

"She's not our birth mother. I'm adopted. And you will be too, from what I hear."

"Oh my God," whispered Annie. "But the records show she gave up a baby for adoption—not that she was the one who adopted a child."

"She did give up a baby," Laurie said. "She became pregnant and her parents made her do it. They were very prominent socially and couldn't bear the stigma of an illegitimate grandchild. But Elaine nearly went crazy with grief. She married the man of their choice, nearly immediately afterwards. It was more a financial merger than a marriage. In hopes of saving her sanity, Howard Simms agreed to adopt a child at once. Her parents' lawyer put it all through at warp speed. A private arrangement, of course."

"No state agency would have been that careless," said Annie. "The lawyer didn't bother to find out too many details about the birth or he would have known we were twins."

"Big bucks for the lawyer and a one-shot deal," Laurie said.

"So the state records I saw just showed that she had given up a child. I didn't have access to ones showing that she also adopted another." Annie rose from the chair and stared out the window.

"So she's not our real mother then." *Just any old mother, after all*. It explained so many things, such as their Swedish blonde beauty that didn't seem to belong with the patrician hawk-faced woman. Most of all, it explained the slight antipathy she felt for Elaine Simms. If she had any qualms before about what she planned to do, they were now all swept away. "Not our real mother."

"No," Laurie said fiercely. "Put that thought out of your mind right now. I mean it, Annie, don't ever, ever let on that I've told you. She freaks out over this. As far as I'm concerned, she *is* my real mother."

When the dialysis session was over, Annie delayed asking the nurse to begin the elaborate dismantling and cleaning process. She needed the answers to several more questions.

"Why did she start looking for me just three years ago? Why would she start looking at all if she didn't know I existed?"

"My kidneys started to fail and we needed medical information," Laurie said. "It was a terrible time for us both. Just terrible. She had to tell me. It just killed Mother to admit she wasn't my biological parent." Her chin quivered. "I grew up thinking I was their little girl. I, we, sort of looked like Howard Simms. He couldn't have any children. And really, they didn't need any more. They had me."

Annie's stomach lurched. She should have been in on this fairy tale childhood.

"In fact, I had to beg Mother to let me out of her sight long enough to go to college. Vassar, you know."

Community college and night school for me, you know, thought Annie.

Two days later, Elaine came into the room during Laurie's dialysis treatment. She beamed as she announced to both of them, "Adoption proceedings are formally under way. My lawyers are satisfied that you are not a pretender. You will soon be a full heir in my estate. Now I have the satisfaction of knowing if anything happens to Laurie, our name and traditions will be passed on."

Tears of joy gushed from Annie's eyes. For an instant, she felt real warmth toward this woman. "Thank you," she said. "Oh thank you, Mother."

"There will be one more medical test. Since you're twins, I want to make sure you don't have Laurie's problem. And would you mind terribly, darling, taking the name of Annie Simms? While we're finalizing the paperwork, it would be a good time to make the legal name switch."

"I would be honored," said Annie. Nothing could please me more."

Hell, honey, you can call me Scarlett O'Hara, if it suits you, she thought. *Frankly my dear, I just don't give a damn*. After the paperwork was final, she would put her plans into motion. During the remainder of Laurie's dialysis, she spent the time daydreaming about a shiny black Mercedes and expensive trips. The money. The lovely, lovely money.

The next morning as Annie waited for the maid to bring her breakfast, she heard the nurse's voice in the halfway.

"This is the last round of tests?" asked Elaine.

Annie could not hear the reply, but in a moment, Elaine spoke again.

"Be careful what you leave lying out in Laurie's room. Annie has volunteered to sit with her during dialysis, and given her past, it's simply not a good idea to leave drugs lying around."

Annie shot up in bed, stunned that Elaine would put such a false wicked idea in someone's mind. She had never done drugs. Not ever. She liked being in control too well to risk the vulnerability. She didn't drink much either.

Steaming at Elaine's suspicion, she was barely civil to the nurse. She sullenly signed the papers, then thrust out her arm so she could draw blood. She tried to settle down. Elaine hadn't said she was a drug addict. She had just implied the possibility, given her past. Well, what in the hell did that woman know about her past? She had never shown any interest before.

"Are you awake?" Elaine called softly that night long after Laurie had gone to bed.

"Yes," said Annie, "come on in. Is it Laurie? Has something happened to Laurie?"

"No, darling. Nothing yet. But tomorrow is going to be a very big day for her. The biggest day in her whole life."

Annie looked curiously at Elaine, who was carrying a tray of medical paraphernalia.

"We need more blood," said Elaine. "The nurse called and said a lab technician dropped the sample she took this morning. I've been trained to do this, so there was need to have her come back tonight."

Christ, thought Annie. *Not again.*

"Just once more, darling." Elaine injected the needle into the big vein at the crook of her arm.

Annie was hit by warmth and a deep sense of peace. The room blurred as she stared at the needle. Blood was not flowing into it. Her mouth was dry. Elaine had injected her with something instead.

"Why? What?" she mumbled.

"Why? Oh you must know," said Elaine. "Surely you do? On your own, you would never have consented to donate a kidney to Laurie. Although you've signed consents to that effect."

Stunned, Annie remembered the array of documents. Papers she had barely glanced at. The myriad of blood tests.

"You'll never, never get away with this." The words were fuzzy, garbled, but Elaine understood them anyway.

"No? What could be more likely? A known drug addict. An overdose. And as often as I've warned the nurses to keep drugs locked up when you're around? I'm going to call 911 at once, of course. I'll ride with you in the ambulance. Pity they'll never be able to bring you out of the coma. They'll find an overdose of morphine. They'll see an arm with a few scars in the veins. And we will all decide together there is no point in wasting a good kidney."

Annie gasped, closed her eyes, tried to speak.

"A perfect, genetically matched kidney."

Guile Is Where It Goes

Dan Crawford

Waldo raised one long finger. "It is a world, Frederick, which is having no sensitivity whatever for justice."

Freddy slumped on the step at the back of the truck. "Yeah. It is."

Still with that long finger pointed at the sky, Waldo stretched long legs to march around the corner of the truck and back again. He passed Freddy once, and then swung back, pointing. "It is almost becoming enough, Frederick, to confirm one's depressing conclusion that the world was not, after all, prepared for the sake of men like you and I."

Now Freddy just nodded. Like most of Waldo's plans, it had been a work of art. That old plastic baby doll, the feathers, the pipe with the ice cubes and balloon—it had sounded so silly when Waldo talked about it (you never said anything to Waldo about this, though). But everything had gone just as Waldo predicted, even to the way they whistled as they drove away in the hijacked truck without anybody saying a word. And so now they owned a truck and everything in it.

Something to ride in, and something to sell to pay for the gas: Waldo had done it again.

Only when they came to look over the inside of the truck and see just what Waldo had done did the beauty of this work of art lose some of its luster.

The heavy cardboard cubes all held clear plastic bags of reddish brown liquid. According to the orders Waldo found on the clipboard, each package contained exactly one liter of cow's blood.

"But what is it for, Waldo?" Freddy had demanded.

Waldo simply threw the clipboard to the pavement. "It isn't going to be making much of a difference, Frederick."

Now Freddy set his back against the door of the cold truck and watched Waldo stalk back and forth, back and forth, around that corner of the truck and back again. This went on and on. Freddy was sure Waldo was capable of doing this until his shoes wore out, which would be expensive and was therefore to be discouraged.

So he sat forward. "Why don't we just walk away from it, Waldo?"

It stopped Waldo walking, at least. He fixed his eyes on Freddy's face, and his eyebrows met over them. "We have been four days planning this particular learning experience, Frederick. And now we have only"—he reached down and patted his pocket—"eleven dollars and ninety-eight cents left in the world. Do you know how far we can continue to keep traveling with eleven dollars and ninety-eight cents, Frederick?"

That index finger came up again; Freddy watched the tip of it. "How far, Waldo?"

"Not quite so far as a remote control could be changing a channel, Frederick." Waldo's mouth came out in a little pout. "No doubt this has been intended as a lesson to us, Frederick. We were taking for granted that we would succeed in selling anything we found on a truck."

He looked so unhappy. Freddy leaned forward. "But we could, Waldo! We could!" He sat back again as the finger pointed toward him. "Um, we could if our customers could just be vampires."

The glare turned on Freddy was dire indeed, but was replaced almost immediately by a frown of puzzlement. The long index finger waggled back and forth.

"Be silent a moment, Frederick," Waldo said, his voice quite different now. Freddy felt his shoulders rise with hope and just a hint of apprehension. He could see Waldo's genius working from here.

When Waldo spoke again, it was in a third voice, dreamy and distant, and Freddy knew the answer had been found. It came in the form of a question.

"Do we still have belonging to us, Frederick, those black suits in which we succeeded in fooling that little congregation in desirable old Abita Springs, Louisiana?"

Freddy nodded. "Oh, yes, Waldo. They do still smell just a little from when they threw us in the—"

Waldo raised his whole hand to cut off unnecessary reminiscences. "All the more to the better. Fetch them out, Frederick, while I am purchasing the essential necessities."

The necessities brought back by Waldo were a bucket of black paint and a box of bendy straws. The bucket of paint barely stretched to cover the whole truck; painting the truck stretched to cover the rest of the day. Then Freddy got behind the wheel and drove slowly as Waldo directed.

This had looked too nice a town by daylight to have a neighborhood like this. But the cars that went by the low black building seemed respectable enough. Guards stood at the door of the building, which a bright red sign declared to be GEKHENNA. So Waldo instructed Freddy to park the truck around the corner, well out of sight.

"Now what, Waldo?"

"Now we commence conveying to them our wares, of

course." Waldo stepped out of the truck and stepped around to stand under the only part of the truck not painted black, the letters that spelled the word DRINK.

"And Frederick," he said, pointing that index finger toward the letters, "we will concentrate on not letting ourselves lean against our transportation. I believe it has yet to finish its drying, and it is not good for business to stick to the walls."

They waited by the back doors of the truck. Freddy watched several people walk by wearing heavy black jackets, which must have been terribly hot. Others drove slowly past, studying the truck but making no remark. When Freddy eased up to the corner to peek, he found that people were stopping their cars in front of Gekhenna, giving the keys to a guard, and then strolling inside. And all of them did this without first spending any money at all at the nice black truck labeled DRINK.

He came back and asked, "Shouldn't we be shouting at them, or something, Waldo?"

"No, Frederick," Waldo told him, voice serene, "Merely continue to keep looking bored." He frowned at his shoulder. "I realize it isn't being an easy assignment, to be looking bored without leaning."

Freddy had no trouble looking bored, except when customers walked by. Two of them actually paused to look up at the word on the truck. The young man had close-cropped hair, long pointy eyebrows, and a short pointy beard. He wore an awful lot of earrings for each ear. How could he tell when he lost one? The woman wore a feathered headdress, and on her neck was a tattoo showing a girl with a horse's tail.

The young man sniffed. "Drinks? They sell drinks inside."

"Only having liquor in there," replied Waldo, looking at a streetlight, and not the young man at all.

The man puzzled this over. "Why? What've you got?"

"The usual." Waldo poked open the door and reached inside for a bag and a straw. The man stared at the bag.

"Is it good?" he asked, cautiously.

"Only getting the best here." Waldo hefted the bag. "Type O: the Universal Donor."

The man's mouth spread open; his eyes shifted a bit toward the woman. "How much is it?"

Waldo still wouldn't look at him. "The usual."

"Oh. Sure." The man reached to his back pocket and brought out a twenty-dollar bill. "That should cover it."

Freddy, at this point, would have snatched the lovely bill out of the lovely man's hand. Waldo had more control, and merely lowered his eyes a fraction to regard it. He sniffed. "You'll be wanting only the one, then?"

The woman pulled at the man's shirt. He produced another twenty. Waldo smiled, just a little, as he reached into the truck and brought forth a second bag and straw.

Freddy barely restrained himself until the two people were around the corner. "You did it, Waldo! You can sell anything!"

Waldo merely folded the money away. "Be so good as to be opening a few more boxes, Frederick. I'm feeling the luck roll in."

His feeling was accurate. Whether the first two told their friends inside Gekhenna about the Drinks Truck, or whether cell phones were involved, now nobody walked past without stopping. First by twos and by threes, and then by the dozens, they came up to buy cow's blood. All were darkly dressed, but very nearly undressed at the same time. Freddy saw a greater variety of tattoos than he'd seen since that ocean trip he and Waldo had accidentally taken, and he saw more colors of hair than he'd ever seen at all.

Some of their customers opened the bags and stuck in the straw to take a drink right there. (These were especially the ones who came in pairs.) Other ones said they weren't thirsty just now, or that they needed a glass, or that they preferred their blood warm. Waldo made no comment at all as he was required to move farther and farther into the truck to reach the stock; his apparent lack of interest was positively an insult to all of the interesting people who forced him to accept so very many twenty-dollar bills.

But at last the dozens gave way to trios and pairs again, and after a while, hardly any customers were stopping at the black vehicle. Only about half the bags had been sold, but neither Waldo nor Freddy was unhappy about this. Waldo patted the lump of money in his jacket pocket. "Perhaps closing for the night would be the wisest course now, Frederick. Tomorrow we might well—"

"Hello?"

A woman and three men had stepped up among the boxes of blood. She was a tall woman with immense dark eyes and long dark hair, at least on one side of her head. The ear Freddy could see was studded with little gold stars while chains and discs and other baubles swung below it. She was older than the other women who had stepped into the truck tonight, and she was very warmly clad, above the waist. The dark glasses stuck in her waistband were actually larger than whatever it was the waistband was holding up.

The men with her were dressed similarly, even to the stars in their ears. One carried a small hatchet instead of the glasses in his waistband, while another had a short whip. Freddy had seen other whips this evening, but he wasn't sure he liked it that this one wasn't at all glossy.

"Good evening," said the woman, gliding past the empty boxes. She stopped a few feet from Freddy, and tipped her head to one side, her eyes sliding all the way up to the left. Her face was very friendly, so friendly that Freddy took a step back. He couldn't have said why. All his life he'd considered having such a woman rest her head on his shoulder. Only maybe with not quite so much hardware.

"This is the only thing Gekhenna lacked," she said, her

voice warm and laudatory. "But aren't you afraid of health inspectors?"

Waldo shrugged. "We will be moving to convey our wares to the fortunate in some other location elsewhere tomorrow. Unless we are risking the danger that you will be doing some inspecting?"

She had the most beautiful laugh. "Only in the usual way, I think." Reaching behind her glasses, she drew out not one but four one-hundred-dollar bills.

Freddy stared; Waldo didn't even blink. He simply picked up the two nearest boxes and brought them forward. One of the men took them.

"Thank you so much," said the woman, sounding as if she brought every syllable from her innermost heart. "Perhaps we'll come find you at your new location tomorrow." She reached into the nearest box for a bag of blood as the four of them started for the door. Freddy was not too distracted by this new prospect to notice that she raised the bag to her lips and daintily bit through the corner of the thick plastic. He didn't especially want to watch this, and lowered his eyes again.

Therefore his gaze was elsewhere when the woman choked, spat, and snarled, "Fraud!"

The bag hit the floor, spreading its contents in an untidy fan-shaped puddle. Waldo opened his mouth to object to this, but that was when the woman turned, and the flames burst from her hands. "This comes from cattle!"

To Freddy's surprise, she was still smiling. Her smile was not in the least bit pleasant. "You dare!" Her flaming hands gestured the three men toward Waldo and Freddy.

"Tonight, my darlings," she announced, "we drink from the bottle!" Freddy could not help noticing how white her teeth looked. Or how very many of them there seemed to be.

Freddy saw six thick snakes slide from the bloodslick,

and after that things got a little mixed up. The truck seemed to be spinning, and people started to shout: this was absolutely going to hurt.

Waldo did not wait for his four customers to reach him. Snatching up a bag of blood, he strode forward and smacked the woman in the face with it. Then he ducked under a swinging hatchet. The man swinging this hatchet had to turn his back on Freddy, so Freddy threw a shoulder into it, blocking the man into his companions.

Freddy dove for the doors, and Waldo joined him a second later, clutching what was left of the torn black suit jacket. Thrusting this into Freddy's hands, he slammed the door shut and clanked the latch into place.

"Let us commence to motate, Frederick!" he shouted, heading up front. "Quickly! I'll be taking the wheel!"

Freddy looked at the truck. "But they're inside, Waldo; we'll be taking them along with us. Let's just run for it!"

"Run?" Waldo stared at him. "Running in this neighborhood? Carrying that amount of money?" He nodded toward the torn jacket. "We'd be more safer back in there with the vampires! Motate, Frederick: do not hesitate to motate!"

Waldo jumped into the seat, stuck the key in the ignition, and shoved his foot against the pedal. Freddy had just time to pull himself into the passenger's side before the truck screamed away from the curb.

In no time at all, they were on the highway and passing the outskirts of town. Shortly after that, the banging on the walls and doors behind them stopped. Freddy was inclined to think this was a good thing; perhaps it had gotten too cold for them all back there. But around that same time some very large, dark birds began to batter the windows with their wings. In his side mirror, Freddy saw empty boxes bouncing along the pavement behind them, and some very large dogs running among these, keeping up with the truck although it was moving far too fast for real dogs.

"This is not good," he told Waldo, as the birds began to thump on the windshield.

"The sound you are hearing, Frederick," Waldo said, as the truck began to bounce along the shoulder, "is not that of my feet dancing for joy."

They were not on the highway now, but Freddy couldn't exactly tell where they were. Black wings covered the windshield completely, but he could hear the screech of metal against his door, and wood splintering somewhere in front of him. Waldo's foot stayed right where it was on the pedal. "Keep holding on, Frederick!" he called. "Keep on holding!"

Freddy tried to do this, but when the truck turned over, it was difficult to know just where to hold on. He felt the roof once, and his door once, and then the truck came down hard on all four tires. He wondered why none of them popped.

"What . . . what now, Waldo?" gasped Freddy, shaking his hands and feet to make sure they were all still attached.

Waldo was only slightly breathless. "I have faith that when you were getting into the truck you were also locking your door, Frederick?"

Trying to keep his gaze away from the furry faces pressed against the glass, Freddy checked the door. He nodded.

"Then we shall be waiting." Waldo folded his arms. "And we will not be looking into their eyes."

"But look, Waldo!" Freddy replied, pointing to a growing crack in his window.

For his part, Waldo pointed at the windshield. "I am looking only in this eastwardly direction, Frederick."

There were fewer wings in front, but all Freddy could see was an old windmill, silhouetted against the rays of the rising sun. It was very picturesque, but Freddy couldn't understand why such a view was important. He turned to ask Waldo about it, and found that now the wings were gone completely from every window. He checked the mirror and saw that the dogs were gone as well.

Before Freddy could decide he was safe, however, something else thumped on the window. It was the fist of an irritated man, whose vocabulary was unequal to the task of pointing out all of the splintered fenceposts, dead chickens, and other debris spread across his property. All he could do was point and splutter. Freddy could barely make out one word, though whether that word was "Look" or something else he couldn't be sure.

Stepping outside, he found communication very difficult until he had the happy thought of resorting to a universal language. Each twenty-dollar bill made the man's complexion a bit lighter, and his voice a bit less shrill. Enough green bills made the shouting die into grumpy humphs. And soon Freddy was able to roll up Waldo's jacket and climb back into the truck.

"I am guessing that a request for breakfast here would bring us very little to eat," said Waldo.

Freddy nodded. "I guess."

"Then we will be trying to travel elsewhere."

To the surprise of both Waldo and Freddy, the truck actually did move, slowly, gently, when the gas pedal was pushed down. Easing around as many chickens as possible, they made it to the farm road and thence to the highway. The truck traveled gingerly for about four miles before finally deciding it had had a long night, and coming to gradual rest.

"We're out of gas," Freddy noted.

Waldo put the truck into Park. "As well to be leaving the vehicle now, Frederick. I would not like to be the one having to clean up."

Freddy thought about the boxes of blood and the rolling of the truck, and nodded. "We can be purchasing new transportation on reaching the next metropolitan area," Waldo went on. "How much has this experience profited us, Frederick?"

Freddy unrolled Waldo's jacket, and brought the change out of his own jacket as well, for better accuracy. He counted the money the farmer had not needed. He counted it twice to be sure. Then he took a breath, and spoke right out.

"It's . . . eleven dollars and ninety-seven cents, Waldo."

Waldo sat back against the seat and looked full in Freddy's face for a long moment. His lower lip slid a bit forward, and he raised his index finger.

"It is a world, Frederick, which is having an unjustified appreciation of its own sense of humor."

Freddy nodded again. "Yeah."

Doppelganger

Rhys Bowen

It was fate that brought Hofmeister and me together during the summer of '38. Fate, or in my case, luck. It was my final semester at the institute and funds were running low. My grandmother had died, her life savings already rendered worthless by inflation, and with her my only means of financial support.

Fortunately I only needed this semester to complete my diploma in engineering. I had just enough money to make it to July—with appropriate cost-cutting measures. No more eating in the mensa or restaurants, for one thing. No more drinking in the little weinstube around the corner and finally the realization that I would have to share a room in the student residence hall.

I had never shared a room before and the idea was repugnant to me. Having been raised an only child by my grandmother, I was unused to the company of other males. Their behavior at the institute always seemed to me a little too juvenile and boisterous after the isolation of my youth. I saw no need to participate in backslapping and horseplay.

In any case, I had grown to prefer my own company and a good book.

Thus I entered that room in the Studentenheim on the twenty ninth of April with much apprehension. What if he stank, or sang loudly in the bath, or smoked cigars or left wet towels and dirty garments strewn on the floor? What if he tried to sneak in women at all hours? So I was pleasantly surprised to find Hofmeister engaged in unpacking a modest suitcase and placing pairs of socks neatly in a top drawer.

"I've taken the bed by the window," he said, looking up as I came in. "Unless, of course, you'd prefer it?"

"No, take it by all means. I sleep better away from any form of light."

He came toward me, hand outstretched. "You must be Schwarzkopf. I'm Hofmeister."

We shook hands and clicked heels with the little bow that was customary even among fellow students. He didn't tell me his first name and I didn't suggest that he call me Jakob. I liked his air of aloofness and knew instantly that I should feel comfortable sharing a room with him.

It turned out that we had a lot in common. We were both final semester candidates for the diploma, specializing in the relatively new branch of aeronautical engineering. We were both somewhat quiet and withdrawn, orphans with no close family ties—he having been raised by an aunt who had died the previous year. And most remarkably, we looked alike too. The other residents started calling us the Twins. Since we were not very social and kept to ourselves, we gained the reputation of being snooty and standoffish. There were also hints that we were more than friends, for which there was no foundation, as neither Hofmeister nor I had inclinations in that direction.

We were both tall, slightly built, blond with angular features and the high cheekbones of the Slav. Perfect Aryan specimens, in fact. I often thanked my lucky stars that I had taken after my beautiful actress mother, rather than my dark and brooding playwright father. In fact, if she hadn't been stupid enough to marry him and thus give me a Jewish last name, then all would have been well. Especially since he had shot himself within a year of my birth. She, always fragile, had only outlived him by another two years and I had been raised as a good Lutheran, in the elegant town of Ludwigsburg by my maternal grandmother.

So I had passed through life pretty much unscathed and unaffected, avoiding the embarrassing street attacks, beard singeings, and rock throwings that befell more obviously identifiable Jews. I had come to believe I was immune when the director of studies summoned me to his office one day in May.

"You will take your final exams in July, Schwarzkopf. Is that correct?"

"Yes, Herr Direktor."

He sighed. "I am glad for you, for I have the unpleasant task of informing all my students of Jewish ancestry that they will not be welcomed back to the institute for the winter semester."

"Then I am indeed fortunate, Herr Direktor."

He looked at me for a long minute. "You are a gifted student, Schwarzkopf. You have maintained excellent grades throughout your time here. What will you do when you leave us?"

"I expect to be hired by one of the big aircraft companies. That is, after all, my sphere of expertise."

Another awkward pause.

"You haven't considered emigrating to, say, South America or the United States, where your qualifications would stand you in good stead?"

"I have no wish to emigrate, Herr Direktor. Any company in Germany would be foolish not to hire me when they see what I have to offer." I brushed a wayward lock of blond hair from my face. "Besides, in my case, I do not see that race will be a factor."

He sighed again. "I hope you are right. I wish you every success, Schwarzkopf."

When I recounted this conversation to Hofmeister, I was surprised with the vehemence with which he took the director's point of view. "I think you should seriously consider the Direktor's suggestion, Schwarzkopf—get out while there is still time, my dear fellow."

"But where would I go? I speak no Spanish and my English is also poor. Besides, I have no love for the American lifestyle. Too much noise and lack of moral fiber."

"It's a pity," Hofmeister said jokingly. "You'd have made an excellent Nazi."

"They invited me to join the Hitler Youth until they found out about my background, so fortunately I was spared countless singsongs and camping trips." I smiled. "What about you? I'm sure you'll make a wonderful Nazi yourself. Have they tried to recruit you?"

"Of course," he said. "Many times. But I'm not interested in politics. I just want to be left alone to conduct my research in peace. I'd like to be the first to develop a commercial jet engine."

"That would be a magnificent accomplishment," I said. "Jet propulsion also fascinates me. Wouldn't it be splendid if we were both hired by the same aircraft company and we could work on our research, side by side?"

"I've already applied to Dornier and Messerchmidt," Hofmeister said.

"So have I."

"Heard anything yet?"

I shook my head.

"Neither have I, but it's early days. They may want to wait for the results of our final exams." He got up and paced around the room. "I worry about your future, Schwarzkopf.

You're a good fellow, but being a good fellow won't count when the Nazis finally crack down. That piece of paper with your racial background—that is all that counts, I'm afraid."

"Surely not." I gave a half-embarrassed laugh. "My mother was a popular performer in her time and my father was not just any Jew. His plays are performed throughout the world."

As Hofmeister said nothing, I continued. "Besides, I'm hoping to make myself indispensable to a major aircraft company. They wouldn't be stupid enough to hand over one of their most gifted research engineers. Not with a war in Europe brewing."

"The Nazis have their spies everywhere, so I'm told," Hofmeister said in a low voice. "Trust no one, Jakob."

I was touched by his concern for my future, but I still felt no real alarm. I would emerge with one of the highest diplomas in Germany. My research had been on aspects of aviation that the Luftwaffe would need to maintain air superiority in the coming war. And I looked like a true Aryan.

The semester drew to a close. We sat our final exams, and when the results were published, Hofmeister and I were both at the head of our class—although I outscored him by a few points.

"Now those aircraft companies will come beating down our doors," I said. "I wonder who will hear first, you or I?"

He gave me a crooked smile. "I've already heard from Messerschmidt," he said and looked away. "They've offered me a post at their research facility in Dresden."

"Dresden? That's a long way from anywhere." We were both from the Swabian area of South Germany and Dresden counted as a foreign country in our eyes.

"But a good position, nonetheless. Much of their top-secret research is being done there."

"Then I hope they will hurry up with an offer for me too. I think I'll write to them with my results to give them a nudge—and maybe I should ask Herr Direktor to give me a letter of recommendation."

Hofmeister moved away and stared out of the window at the hills that ringed our city of Stuttgart. "You may not want to put him in an embarrassing position, Schwarzkopf. To recommend you would be to compromise himself."

"But I had the highest grade in the class."

"And you are, unfortunately, Jewish."

"Half-Jewish," I said. "With parents who were both public figures. Surely these things count?"

"I'll tell you what counts in the eyes of the Nazis," he said. "Aryan. Non-Aryan. That's all. If Jesus were to come back today, he would not be welcome in Germany."

His message was finally beginning to register. "You are saying that no aircraft company will want to hire me, because I am Jewish?"

He nodded. "I fear that may be the case. I hope I'm wrong. They may want to, but dare not. You have a fine brain, Schwarzkopf, and on top of that, you are a good fellow. Without the name and the identity papers, one would never know that you were Jewish."

"Then you really believe that I should get out of Germany?"

"I really do, and as soon as possible, if you take my advice, or it may be too late."

I took his words to heart and made inquiries at various embassies. I found that it wasn't going to be easy. No country was welcoming Jews with open arms, especially penniless Jews like myself. And war was looming. The price of transatlantic tickets had doubled and tripled for those with a Jewish last name. Nevertheless, I sent off letters to aircraft companies in Britain and the United States and waited hopefully for their replies.

The semester ended. Those students who had homes to

go to packed up their belongings and went home. Only Hofmeister and I had nowhere to go.

"I head for Dresden in a two weeks," he said. "I want to get myself settled into my room and learn a little about the town before I have to report to work." He put a hand on my shoulder. "I wish you were coming too. I'm sorry things couldn't be different."

"I wish so too. Think of me as I spend my summer laboring in some farmer's fields, trying to earn enough money to pay for my ticket to America."

Uncharacteristically, Hofmeister slapped me on the back. "I tell you what—I've just come up with a splendid idea. We have to be out of here by tomorrow and I have no plans until I go to Dresden. Why don't we take a final trip together to the Alps. We can hike and stay in hostels. It shouldn't cost much."

I smiled. "Why not? One last look at the good South German countryside before we face strange cities and new lives."

So we stored our trunks and took the train south to Munich and then the little post bus into the mountains. Then we set off with rucksacks and no planned route. It was glorious weather—warm but not too hot for walking. We went from village to village, over mountain passes and down again, crossing green alpine meadows full of flowers and cows and goats, eating picnic lunches by tumbling mountain streams and sleeping the night in a peasant's hay barn when there was no hostel nearby. We both became fit and brown.

On the last day we attempted our most ambitious stage. The trail led right over the Laufbacher Eck and down to Oberstdorf. It was a strenuous climb, but well worth it. As we stood, panting, on the high ledge, it was like being on top of the world. Snow-covered peaks glistened around us.

In the valley far below, a round blue lake reflected the sky. An eagle soared out below our feet.

Hofmeister spread out his arms. "This is the life, eh, Schwarzkopf. To hell with that nonsense down there."

The thought came to me in a blinding flash. I'm sure I had never considered it before, but maybe it had lain dormant for some time. I don't know. Anyway, I hardly had time to consider before I acted. I stepped up behind him and gave him a mighty push. He teetered for a moment, then waved his arms wildly, trying to regain his balance before plunging downward without a cry, his body bouncing from rock to rock like a rag doll until, at last, coming to rest at the foot of the cliff.

My heart was beating so fast that I found it hard to breathe. The world swam around me, so that I, too, was in danger of falling. I clung on to an outcropping of rock and stayed there with eyes closed until the vertigo passed. Then, with much difficulty, I climbed down to him. He was, of course, quite dead. Fighting back the nausea, I made myself go through his pockets and rucksack until I had replaced every piece of his identity with my own. Then I ran all the way down to the nearest hamlet to get help.

Everyone was very kind. They assisted me back to the nearest inn and gave me schnapps and warm blankets for shock. They wanted to know about poor Schwarzkopf's next of kin and were relieved to hear that there were none. I spent the night at the inn and then caught the train back to Stuttgart, where I retrieved Hofmeister's trunk from storage.

I was pleasantly surprised to find that he had just bought himself a new dark suit, also that he had a little money in his savings account. I used this, and the few days before I reported to Dresden, to visit his hometown of Ulm, where I acquainted myself with the facts of his childhood—the gymnasium from which he had matriculated, the apartment block where he had lived, the bakery on the corner. I found nobody who remembered him.

Thus reassured, I made my way to the city of Dresden and presented myself at the address where he had apparently already rented a room for himself. The landlady greeted me with deference and hoped that Herr Hofmeister would have an agreeable stay in her city. The room was spacious and well furnished and looked out over the old town. I decided immediately that I should enjoy living here. A letter had already come for me. The landlady pointed to it lying on my dresser.

It requested that Herr Hofmeister should report to the above address as soon as was convenient to meet with Herr Fischer and discuss his assignment. I put on the dark suit, which fitted me perfectly, and reported that very afternoon, anxious to be at work. The building was close to the city center, a faceless block of gray stone, among other similar buildings. There was no name plate on the outside, but I went up the steps and in through the front door. As I stood in the tiled central foyer, looking around at the various doors and staircases and wondering which to choose, a young woman came out and started in surprise at my standing there.

I gave her my name and asked to see Herr Fischer. She ran up the flight of stairs to my left then returned with a smile on her face. Herr Fischer welcomed me to Dresden. He would be delighted to see me, if I would just take a seat for a moment.

There were polished wood benches around the walls. I sat on one of these. After a couple of minutes the front door opened again and a man came in. He was shabbily dressed, mid-forties or maybe even older. He stood, looking around him, before taking a seat on a bench well away from me. He had removed his hat and clutched it in his hands, squeezing it out of shape as he played with it. Every time a door opened or footsteps were heard upstairs, he started nervously. At last he caught my eye.

"Who are you here to see?" he asked.

"Herr Fischer."

"You too." He dropped his eyes back to the battered hat in his hands. "I should never have waited. It was Hannah, you know. She was sick. And now it's too late, of course."

I wanted to ask him what he meant, and was phrasing the question in my head when footsteps came down the stairs. A young man this time, with close-cropped blond hair and wearing a black shirt and well-cut black trousers. "Herr Adler?"

The man sprang to his feet.

"This way. Room 224."

The older man shot me a despairing glance as he followed the black shirt up the stairs.

Now I was really confused. Why was this man so downcast at the thought of meeting with Herr Fischer? Perhaps, I decided, he was no good at his job and about to be fired. There was something disquieting about this place. It was gloomy and cold for a research facility, as faceless inside as it had been out. No pictures on the walls, except for the obligatory portrait of the Führer on one wall. No notice board, no buzz of conversation. Too quiet. I shifted uneasily on the hard bench. Would I enjoy working in these conditions? Or maybe this was just head office and the research facilities were somewhere else all together. Somewhere bright, out in the country. This thought cheered me. Then suddenly there was activity on the floor above. A door opening, running feet, a shout, and a single brief despairing cry. The young man in the black shirt came running down the stairs. As he passed me, he gave me a grin. It was not a friendly smile but a smile of triumph. I had seen it before when windows had been smashed and beards set on fire. A smile of cruelty.

Then a cold sweat crept over me as I realized where I was. This building had nothing to do with aircraft design. Of course the black shirt had looked strangely familiar. I was in Gestapo headquarters. Hofmeister had done his best to warn me. Their spies are everywhere, he had told me. I had scoffed at this idea, but he knew what he was talking about. He had been one of them. He had been planted at the institute and now he was to be their plant at the aircraft engineering facility.

My mouth had gone dry. I couldn't swallow. Even if Hofmeister had never met Herr Fischer before, it was only a matter of time before I ran into someone he knew, and then it would be all over. I couldn't imagine what they would do to someone who dared to impersonate a Gestapo spy. I looked around desperately, just as the man had done, and actually got to my feet. There was nobody down here. I could make a run for it. By the time they came looking for me, I could be across a border . . . That's when it hit me—I had nowhere to run.

The female receptionist appeared at the top of the stairs. "You can come up now, Herr Hofmeister," she said brightly. "Herr Fischer is ready to receive you."

BLOODY VICTIMS

Mat Coward

"THAT'S her!" Mrs. Rayner's stick slipped from her hands and rattled on the floor. "That's the little madam who had my bag!"

"Right you are, love." PC Blick gave the van driver a little wink, and the driver drove on.

"That's *her*," said Mrs. Rayner. She leaned over the back of Blick's seat and prodded a finger between his shoulders. "Aren't you going to stop?"

Blick helped her back to her seat, picked up her walking stick along the way. "Yeah, don't you worry, love. We'll send a patrol car after her. We'll have the little madam." One of the old men sitting at the back didn't bother to stifle a snorted laugh. Blick shot him a warning look.

"Yes, well, you mind you do," said Mrs. Rayner. "Because that is *her,* I'm telling you."

Blick yawned, settled himself back in his seat at the front. This was Mrs. Rayner's sixth trip on the Victim Bus. It was the ninth time she had identified the teenager who had mugged her outside the Oak Lane Post Office just after

Christmas. Blick had taken the first three identifications seriously. He wasn't going to make that mistake again. He knew why the poor old girl kept signing up for the tour: it was a day out. Nothing old folk like better than being driven around in a minibus all afternoon, even if it was only on a trip around the borough's most notorious Youth Assembly Points.

He hadn't thought it would be like this. He'd thought it was the big, bright idea that would free him from a uniform tunic that never quite fitted around the waist, and uniform trousers that were always two inches too long at the ankle. He'd thought this was his ticket into plainclothes. He'd told his inspector: "Robbers get arrogant, they get cocky, they think they're safe once they've got away with it, they don't think we're going to keep coming after them. So, a week, two weeks, after the offense we drive the victims around in a minibus, take 'em round all the usual gathering places, get them to ID their attackers. We've got a car following up, as soon as the vic spots a suspect, the car pulls up, does the arrest. We'll clean up. Can't lose."

One arrest in seven months. And he was too young to be charged.

"Where to next, chief?"

"Go up by the car park," Blick told the civilian driver. "We'll have some refreshments."

The driver chuckled. "Only reason they come, that is. Free tea and biccies."

"Piss off," said Blick.

"Language!" said a ninety-year-old Jamaican woman, who'd had her mobile phone snatched by four twelve-year-olds at the taxi rank outside the bus station.

"Piss off," said Blick. Silently.

* * *

THE driver was an irritating berk, to put it bluntly. Bad breath, a sarcastic nature, and a lousy driver.

"You ever think you're in the wrong job?" the irritating berk asked Blick, as they leaned against the side of the bus drinking tepid tea from paper cups.

"What are you on about?"

"Well, you're supposed to be a copper, yeah? You do all that training, you wear a fancy uniform—even if it was made for a slightly smaller man—you swear an oath to uphold the Queen's peace. Yeah? Twelve years in the job, and here you are, a bloody social worker, spending every Wednesday afternoon taking half a dozen old buzzards on a mystery tour round the shopping centers of suburban London."

"They're not *all* old." It wasn't a complete rebuttal, he knew that, but it was how policemen went about things: find the first mistake, and chip away at it.

"They're all blind, though," said the driver, chucking the dregs of his tea over the tarmac and tossing the cup in the general direction of a litter bin. "Or might as well be. They never bloody see anything, do they?"

"Pick that up," said Blick, pointing at the cup, "or I'll nick you for littering." He finished his own tea, crumpled up his cup, and pressed it into the irritating berk's hand.

The driver subvocalized energetically as he carried the two paper cups over to the litter bin. Just before he got there, Blick shouted his name.

The timing's the last thing to go, thought Blick, as the irritating berk, distracted for a vital second, walked straight into the litter bin, and then doubled over clutching his groin. It was bad enough being a laughingstock back at the station, without the bloody civilian staff joining in.

True, though; one arrest in seven months. No convictions. It had got to the stage now that he didn't fear management declaring the project a failure, closing it down—he longed for it.

PC Blick dragged himself back onto the Victim Bus, and announced that they would be moving off in five minutes. There were a few clucks and groans from the older passengers. *Driver's right,* he thought. *They are only here for the free biscuits.*

The one who wasn't old was a fat, shy girl of seventeen who'd been cornered by a gang of girls in an alley a couple of weeks earlier, on her way home from the cinema. They'd made her take her contact lenses out, and the smallest of the girls had then crushed them underfoot. Della's replacement lenses hadn't arrived yet, which made her presence on the Victim Bus a little academic.

"How you doing, Della?" Blick sat down next to her and treated her to what he hoped was an avuncular smile.

"Okay, Mr. Blick."

She didn't seem too scared by the smile, so he gave her another one. "I expect this seems like a waste of time to you, yeah?"

"No, not at all, Mr. Blick," said Della, her voice and face earnest. "You got to have a go, haven't you? You can't just let them get away with it."

He wished he could pat her on the knee without it seeming like he was . . . well, patting her on the knee. "You're a good citizen, Della," he said. "I'm glad you—"

"Little bastard!"

Blick looked up in time to see Mr. Holt, a retired local government officer, and Victim Bus first-timer, leap out of his seat, run down the bus, jump out of the door, and rush across the road. He was almost run over by two cars and one van, and actually collided with a courier on a racing bike. Mr. Holt picked himself up, gave the prone bicycle a kick, gained the far pavement, and threw himself at a short, thin youth with blue hair.

"Oh my God," said Della, squinting out of the window. "What's happening?"

"It's all right," said PC Blick. "It's just one of the victims murdering a child."

"I DON'T suppose there's any chance whatsoever that the boy Mr. Holt attacked is actually the boy that attacked Mr. Holt?"

The inspector had a private office, but when he needed to bawl out a junior officer, he preferred to do it in the open-plan area. It was little touches like that which convinced Blick, on his darker days, that he would never be management himself. It would just never have occurred to him to do that. He didn't have the imagination. Or the inner rage.

"No connection has so far come to light, sir, no. Not at this time."

"He wasn't armed?"

"He had an umbrella, sir."

"What?"

"Mr. Holt struck Dean Stubbs with a telescopic umbrella which—"

"Not Holt, the *boy.* Was the *boy* armed?"

"No, sir. Regrettably not."

The inspector, an ovoid man with an absurd amount of hair on top of his head but none at all at the sides, crossed his arms and hissed. "Not even a penknife?"

"No, sir."

"Was he carrying drugs?"

If he had been, it'd have been in the initial report, wouldn't it? "No, sir. Not so much as an ancient roach."

"And he has no record?"

"Not known to police, sir, no."

"God Almighty, Blick."

"Yes, sir."

The inspector kicked a swivel chair and hissed some more. The swivel chair was empty, but only—Blick suspected—by chance. "He's conscious, at least? The boy?"

"He has a broken finger—classic defense wound—but other than that he seems to be sound. They're keeping him in overnight just to be sure."

"Right. Well, your precious bloody Victim Bus is off the road until further notice—that goes without saying, I trust."

"Absolutely, sir."

"Meanwhile, you'd better sit in on the interview with Holt. Seeing as how he's one of your precious bloody victims."

"THE problem we've got here, Mr. Holt—"

"The problem you've got," said Mr. Holt, "is that you're in here harassing me, the bloody *victim*, when you should be sorting out chummy. The bloody *criminal.*"

"The problem is," Blick continued, not bothering to argue with the prisoner, and definitely not bothering to seek support from, or even to glance at, the ostentatiously bored woman who sat by his side, representing CID, "that the description you gave us of your mugger at the time was—and I'm quoting from your original statement here—a tall, well-built, white male, aged early twenties, with dark hair, pockmarked skin, and a goatee beard. Yes? Whereas, the lad you attacked by the car park earlier today is a short, thin fourteen-year-old with blue hair, no beard, and an enviably clear complexion. That, you see, is our problem."

Mr. Holt, a round man of high pink complexion, bald except for his ears, drummed his fingers on the table and made faces of incredulity at his lawyer. His lawyer—a young, solemn-faced Indian woman—tried to persuade her jaw muscles that she had not just seen the CID officer yawning. The ensuing struggle between reflex and professionalism caused her eyes to bulge and her nostrils to flare. Mr. Holt interpreted this as full-on support for his brave battle against police stupidity.

"He could have shaved it."

"Pardon?" said Blick.

"Could have shaved the beard. Dyed his hair. And I *said* he was white, didn't I?"

PC Blick sighed the sigh of a martyr. He rubbed his hands over his five o'clock shadow. "Mr. Holt," he said. "It's not the same bloke. Is it? I mean, come on—what's he done? Had surgery to reduce the length of his legs? Is he a basketball player who always dreamt of being a jockey, do you suppose?"

"Could have been crouching," said Holt.

"It-is-not-the-same-man," said Blick. "Be reasonable. This child is nothing like the young man who attacked you. You have beaten up, and seriously injured, an entirely innocent young boy."

"Innocent? I'll tell you what, Constable, I'd love to meet an innocent youth in this neighbourhood. Ha! Even *one.*"

"I'm sure your solicitor has explained to you the extremely serious nature of your situation. Now what I am going to ask you to do is to talk to her again, and to think hard, and to see if you can't come up with some way of explaining today's rather bizarre events to my satisfaction."

"Surely that is no great mystery, Constable?" said the lawyer, who had learned in the very earliest days of her legal career that talking is often an efficacious cure for yawning. "My client simply made a mistake of identification. We all make mistakes."

"That boy made one," said Holt, "when he decided it was all right to kick people in the crotch outside the snooker hall and run off with their wallets."

This time, Blick's sigh was unfeigned. "Mr. Holt—it was

a *different boy.* It was, in actual fact, a *very* different boy. Yes?"

The lawyer held up her hands, palms out. "Constable, I think I should like to consult with my client."

"Interview suspended because solicitor needs a pee," said PC Blick. Silently.

MOST people are not muggers. This piece of knowledge—as well as explaining why cops are often less cynical about human nature than their civilian neighbors—is crucial to the functioning of law enforcement.

There are three broad categories of crime. Crimes that almost everyone commits at least once (mostly motoring offenses and dope smoking); crimes that almost no one commits (such as terrorism or serial killing); and crimes that the same, small group of offenders commit over and over again—like indecent exposure or joyriding. Or mugging.

In an area the size of that policed by PC Blick and his colleagues, there was a core of between twenty and thirty young people, most of them drug abusers, which was responsible for almost all street robberies. This was one of the main theoretical planks of Operation Victim Bus: when Blick took his victims out on their tours, they weren't looking for a needle in a haystack. They were looking for a needle in a haberdasher's.

One look at Dean Stubbs in his hospital bed was enough to tell Blick that the boy wasn't a member of the local muggers corps. Of course, he could be a new face, but Blick didn't think so. Blick reckoned there was something else going on. Mr. Holt was lying—that was what was going on.

"I hope you've got the bastard pervert that did this," said the middle-aged blonde woman at Dean's bedside. "I hope you've got him safe behind bars, because if you haven't, my son'll have him. And that's not an idle threat, believe me. My son knows Tae Kwon Do."

"I know him, and all," said Blick, pulling up a chair. "Runs the Chinese chippy down by the leisure center?"

"Oh, that's right—have a laugh!"

"And you are . . . ?"

"I'm this poor little lad's Nan, that's who I am. This is my grandson's been beaten up like this. Have you seen his fingers? He'll never play the piano again."

Blick knew a feed line when he heard one. He ignored it. "Now then, Dean—are you feeling up to answering a question or three?"

"S'pose so." The kid in the bed was very small. His blue hair looked like a symptom.

Dean's Nan opened her mouth to speak, but Blick had been in the job long enough to know how to silence grandparents without leaving visible marks. He looked at her. She scowled, and became silent.

"The man who did this to you—did you get a good look at him?"

"S'pose so. It was a bit quick. I'm, like, walking along? And then suddenly he's like, wham! Bam! All over me."

"Did you recognize him?"

"Never seen him before."

"But you saw him well enough that you would have recognized him, if you had known him?"

"I'd have known him," said Dean. He added, in a smaller voice, "I'd know him again, an' all."

Kids are good liars, because that's all kids do. That's how they get through childhood. So Blick was only pretending to study Dean; really, he was studying Dean's Nan. As far as he could tell, she thought Dean was telling the truth. That didn't mean he was, of course. But it made it more likely.

Blick didn't think Dean was a mugger, and the nurse

he'd spoken to before he came in didn't think Dean was a heavy drug user. Dean definitely didn't look like Mr. Holt's mugger, according to Mr. Holt's own description.

Blick had entered the hospital expecting to discover some connection between Dean Stubbs and Mr. Holt, which would explain why Holt had singled him out for violence. He'd already checked the obvious ones—address, kinship, workplace, clubs, and so on—and none of those had produced anything. Holt had never reported any other crime—vandalism, say—which young Dean might have been involved in. Now Blick was starting to believe that maybe there wasn't a connection to be found.

He still thought Holt was lying, though. He just couldn't think what he was lying about.

BACK at the station, PC Blick went straight to the CID office, to speak to a DC called Jan. Before he could speak to her, she spoke to him.

"Blicky! The hero of the day!"

"Oh. You heard."

"I heard. I heard about your victims going around the place walloping teenagers. Excellent development! Before your next bus trip, can I give you a list?"

"Thanks, Jan. I knew I could count on your sympathetic support."

"Always, Blicky. Always."

She was his best friend in the job. They'd slept together once, a couple of summers ago, but somehow they'd survived even that.

"Jan, you were the officer dealing in the Holt mugging?"

"Yup—if you call taking a statement and filing it 'dealing.' "

"The assailant description—it wasn't anyone you recognized?"

She shook her head. She had nice hair, but at this stage of the shift it could do with a wash. "Nope. Definitely not one of our regulars. And it didn't produce a hit on the suspect index, either. Why—what are you thinking?"

"I don't know," said Blick, which was close to the truth. "And there haven't been any incident reports since, that matched that description?"

She reached out a finger and flicked his tie. He was glad there was no one else around, because flicking someone's tie like that—with just one finger—counts as foreplay in police circles. "You don't think the mugger exists, do you? Or at least, you don't think a mugger matching that description exists."

"I don't know," said Blick, which was slightly less true than it had been a few seconds earlier. "Was the victim drunk when officers arrived?"

"He'd been drinking, he wasn't drunk. He'd had a couple of pints at the snooker hall. But he hadn't been in a fight, if that's where you're going. No grazing to the knuckles, clothes weren't in disarray, no cuts or bruises. Well, except the bruises in his trousers."

"He did take a blow to the balls?"

"Duty surgeon said so."

Blick reset his tie. The superintendent was fussy about standards of appearance. Also, in case Jan wanted to flick it again. "Does that sound like a mugging to you?"

She thought about it. Her posture became a little defensive. She wasn't in a tie-flicking mood anymore. "There was nothing to suggest that this was a domestic."

"Okay, but—"

"What sort of man is going to report a domestic kick in the balls? And if he did—if he was a battered husband—why would he report it as a mugging? Doesn't make sense, Blicky. Think about it."

"Okay, but supposing he was cruising. Supposing he

came on to a woman, or a boy, thinking she or he was a prostitute. Picked the wrong person, got his nuts crushed as a lesson in manners."

"Well . . ."

"Makes more sense than a one-time-only mugger. A *successful* mugger, who retires immediately after his first performance?"

Jan swiveled her chair away from him. She had plenty of volume crime to keep her busy. She had no time for mysteries. "Well, Blicky, if you come up with anything, be sure to keep us informed."

"Oh, sure, I will," said PC Blick, which was entirely untrue.

"YOU'RE making a complete testicle of yourself, young man."

For a second, Mr. Holt's lawyer looked as if she might like to comment on this statement by her client, but a second later she looked as if she might prefer not to.

"Mr. Holt," said PC Blick, "this case will go to court. You can count on that. You beat up a child, put him in hospital, quite possibly destroyed any potential future he might or might not have had as a concert pianist."

For the first time in two interviews, the CID woman sitting next to Blick looked at him. She frowned. Could have been a smile, maybe, but Blick thought it was probably a frown. He continued.

"As I'm sure your solicitor will have explained to you, your best hope is to convince the judge that there were mitigating circumstances."

"Him being a mugging little bastard, for instance?" said Holt. "Would that do?"

"No one is ever going to believe that you mistook Dean for the man who attacked you. The court is going to believe that you attacked Dean Stubbs because you had some *reason* to attack him. Because he had done you some harm."

"He's a mugger," said Holt. "Is that harm enough?"

And that's when Blick got it.

"Mr. Holt. Could you please describe the man who mugged you?"

"Constable, my client has already—"

"I've told you what he looked like. I told you at the time."

"Yes, you did. And, of course, *I* told *you*, didn't I? In our first interview, earlier today. I refreshed your memory."

"My memory didn't need refreshing, young man. I know well enough what a mugger looks like, thank you very much."

"I'm sure you do, Mr. Holt. I'm sure you think you do."

Holt's face was pinker than ever. Pinker than Blick had ever seen it, anyway. "You, young man, are making a total testicle of yourself."

The lawyer threw her pen down on the table and said: "*Spectacle*! The word is *spectacle*."

Holt gave her a haughty look. "Perhaps it is where *you* come from," he said.

"THERE was no mugging, sir."

"Holt was never mugged?" said the inspector. "Then who kicked him in the balls?"

"He did it himself, I believe."

"Impossible. You can't kick yourself in the balls."

The inspector spoke with the certainty of one who had tried. Which caused Blick to lose his train of thought momentarily.

"I'm sure you're right, sir," he said at last, when he had cleared his mind of irrelevant speculations and unwanted images. "You can't do it to yourself deliberately. But you can do it accidentally—or at least, something that provokes similar bruising patterns. I'll bet teachers do it all the time, walking into child-size desks in classrooms."

"Your Mr. Holt isn't a teacher, is he?"

"No, sir, but he does play snooker. We'll never prove it, of course—"

"God, I hope not!" the inspector interrupted. "What sort of spectacle would that make in court?"

"—but I reckon if you were to compare Holt's inside leg measurement to that of a snooker table, you would—"

"Yes, all right, Blick." The inspector waved his fingers in front of his face. "So, he accidentally knackers himself. Why did he report a mugging that never took place?"

"So that he could get on the Victim Bus, sir."

"Not another of your bloody day-trippers, Blick? Looking for an afternoon on the town, courtesy of the taxpayer?"

"No sir. Looking for an excuse to attack a teenage boy."

"What? Why, for God's sake?"

"Because," said PC Blick, speaking slowly to let it sink in, "all teenage boys are muggers. Everyone knows that. That's what it says on the TV, isn't it? In the newspapers. It's common knowledge."

The inspector was so astonished by this that for a moment he forgot not to be intelligent. "And, of course," he said, "all muggers are big louts with pockmarked skin and goatee beards."

"Unless they're big scary blacks, sir, yes. Holt probably thought black would be too obvious."

"But Dean Stubbs isn't a big lout with pockmarked skin, is he?"

"No, sir. But he is just the right size for walloping about the face and body with a furled umbrella. Besides, one kid will do as well as another. They're all at it, after all—everyone knows that."

* * *

A COUPLE of days later, the inspector called Blick into his office and told him that the Victim Bus scheme was being permanently and irrevocably canceled.

"If you think that's best, sir," said Blick.

"I do," said the inspector.

"That is the best bloody news I have had in the last three hundred years. I am going to get so bloody drunk tonight they'll have to take me home in a bucket," said PC Blick. Silently.

Safety First

Marcia Talley

George stood on the steps of Lakeland Public Library—*his* library—and studied his reflection in the tall glass doors. Intelligent gray eyes set in a pleasantly round face, a full head of auburn hair, all his own, thank you very much. All in all, a cheerful sort of guy. Squinting at his reflection, he smoothed back an unruly lock with the palm of his hand, straightened his tie, and wondered, for the fourth morning in a row, why such a friendly-looking fellow deserved such punishment.

Years ago, sitting at a solitary cataloger's desk deep in the bowels of Lakeland Public, aspiring to be head of it one day, he wished he had known then what he knew now. Management would be simple, he told himself, if it weren't for all the people.

These doors, for example. He winced as the plain glass panels whooshed open automatically before him, followed by a blast of heat that ruffled his carefully styled hair. At their weekly staff meetings the circulation librarian, Jean McBride, had gone on and on about the old revolving doors.

"That's the second time this week a mother with a stroller's been caught in that door, not to mention the indignity of forcing our handicapped patrons to use the basement entrance!" Counterarguments about the architectural significance of the doors—made of brass, glass, and ornately carved wood, part of the original building when Andrew Carnegie dedicated it at the turn of the century—not to mention the added cost of heating the lobby, had fallen on deaf ears. When the readers' services librarian and the head of cataloging had stood in solidarity with their colleagues, George had capitulated. Now, fully ten percent of his fuel oil budget was going to heat four parallel parking spaces on Cuyahoga Street and keep the blasted forsythia bushes warm throughout the winter. He had the bills to prove it.

"Morning, Dr. Hopkins."

"Morning, Jean." It annoyed him that no matter how early he arrived at work, that damned woman was there ahead of him. Already his stomach was in knots thinking about the staff meeting he'd scheduled for later that morning. He prayed they wouldn't gang up on him again.

Jean had been a particular challenge. When he'd first taken the directorship, Jean had been manning the circulation desk wearing tennis shoes, slacks, dumpy sweaters, and once, to his horror, a Mickey Mouse T-shirt. At his first staff meeting, he'd impressed on her, indeed on all "front office" staff, the importance of their appearance. "If we don't look professional," he had admonished, "how can we expect our customers (never patrons!) to treat us as such?"

Today he smiled at Jean, who wore, he was pleased to note, a frilly white blouse under a chic, navy blue suit. He pictured navy hose ending in black, patent-leather t-strap shoes, but could only imagine this without leaning very obviously over the counter.

George punched the up button and waited, pacing, while the elevator made a slow, creaking ascent from the basement.

When the doors shuddered open, he climbed aboard and rode to the fifth floor, where his office was tucked into a corner with windows overlooking Lake Erie on two sides.

Lolly, his secretary, was already at her desk, head bent over her keyboard. When he pushed through the double doors, she popped up as if shot from a toaster. "Dr. Hopkins! Can I get you a cup of coffee?"

As he crossed the carpet to his office, Lolly orbited around her cubicle, keeping her body between her boss and whatever was displayed on her monitor screen. George's eyes narrowed. "Coffee will be fine, Miss Taylor." He took three steps toward his office, then suddenly turned, catching his secretary, already on her way to the coffee machine, off guard. "What's that on your monitor?"

Lolly smiled uncertainly. "Just a screen saver."

George squinted toward the monitor where manic dogs frolicked, gradually gobbling bits of the Word document Lolly had been working on. He scowled. "What's wrong with the one that came with the computer?" he demanded, thinking of the soothing, cloud-studded landscape that materialized on his screen whenever it had been idle for ten minutes.

Lolly's dark eyes bored into his, her lips forming a thin, hard line. She opened her mouth, then seemed to reconsider. "I'll change it back," she whispered.

George grunted. "What if a board member should come in and see that? Very unprofessional!" He unlocked the door to his office and slipped in, thinking this was not an auspicious start to the day.

For the next two hours, sipping the hot coffee Lolly periodically provided, hoping, vainly, to feel the revitalizing effects of caffeine surging through his system, George proofed the final draft of his annual report. On page twenty-seven, he added a paragraph that had just occurred to him about estate planning and the Friends of the Library Foundation. Then, exuding self-confidence after a short, but productively persuasive telephone conversation with an elderly, chronically ill donor, George gathered up the annual report, slid it into his secretary's in-box, and headed toward the conference room, smiling.

His confidence evaporated the minute he entered the room. Arranged in a horseshoe around the table was his staff, presided over like a malevolent Buddha by Claudia Fairfield, head of readers' services, narrow-eyed and unsmiling. Instantly, he regretted appointing Claudia head of the facilities management committee. Before he had time to pull up his chair, she thrust her triangular chin over the table and announced, "We have our report."

George swallowed, the coffee he'd recently consumed making an unwelcome comeback. On his left sat Jean McBride, hands folded on the table in front of her, quietly studying her painted thumbnails. On Jean's left was Belinda D'Arcy, the archivist, leafing through some papers and refusing to meet his eyes, still fuming, no doubt, over George's refusal to grant her request for leave without pay to take care of her mother. Next to Belinda sat Miles Nichols, the head cataloger who, with his floppy hair, flattish nose, and lipless mouth, reminded George of a lizard. Myles had an elderly mother, too. If George were to grant Belinda's request, soon Myles would be asking for leave, and the next thing he knew, the whole staff would be expecting George to bend over backward for them. There'd be no end to it. Time off to attend classes. Write a thesis. Get married. Go on vacations even.

George had done his homework on Belinda, at least. She'd threatened to quit, but George had been through her personnel folder and knew that the threat was an empty one. Just two years short of retirement, Belinda could hardly risk losing her pension.

As Claudia droned on about the annual picnic, vending machines in the staff area (including one that dispensed cappuccino), and electrical outlets in the ladies' rest rooms to accommodate their damn hair dryers, George zoned out. He found himself wondering about the package he was expecting from L.L. Bean and whether he'd have time to eat before his evening karate class.

"Overtime." The word sliced through his reverie like a knife. George had replaced his predecessor's rather lackadaisical approach to payroll with a computerized system, well aware that the institution of time cards would make him about as popular as mosquitoes at a nudist colony. But it had to be done. Now, it appeared, he was being punished for his pains. "Because of the Friends' meeting, I worked forty-nine hours last week," Jean was whining. "How does the library plan to pay me for it?"

Controlling his exasperation, George explained, for what seemed like the hundredth time, that overtime hours had to be approved in *advance*, and referred her to the new staff manual.

"Nobody told me I had to ask in advance," Jean complained.

"It's in the cover memo I sent out to all staff," George reminded her. He hastily finessed by referring Jean to the personnel office all the while knowing, with fear's cold fingers squeezing his gut, that before long he'd be summoned by the Brunehilde in charge of *that* office and forced to attend another session of "sensitivity training."

"And now," Claudia continued with relentless momentum, "we want to discuss some new concerns about library safety. As you know, Lakeland is an *elderly* library, and because of budgetary constraints, needed repairs have been shamefully neglected."

George knew all about budgetary restraints. He'd met with the Board of Governors just last week, and although he'd pleaded for more money, none had been forthcoming. Indeed, the bond issue in November had failed; the library would simply have to make do with funding at last year's level. George doubted he merited the confidence the Board had placed in him. With automatic cost-of-living salary increases and the price of magazines and newspapers spiraling out of control, George was at his wit's end. Even if he fired that good-for-nothing gaggle of Madonna wannabees who shelved the books with all the speed of molasses in January, he'd save only enough to buy a one-year subscription to *Science Citation Index*. It was discouraging.

"Nevertheless," Claudia forged on, "we must address some safety issues."

"Which are?" George inquired.

Claudia raised an index finger. "One. The dumb waiter. It doesn't work half the time. Yesterday I looked up the shaft to see what was holding it up and nearly got decapitated when it suddenly decided to come down."

George suppressed a smile. If *that* happened, Claudia's mouth would go on flapping a full ten minutes after her head had parted company with her body. He nodded sagely, his fingers tented over his lips.

"Two. The compact shelving. The hand cranks are stiff and difficult for our older staff to manage." Claudia braved a sideways glance at Belinda. "Nowadays, they're *electric*," she added, as if George had just emerged, dazed and blinking, from a time machine sent from the seventeenth century. "With automatic shutoff controls. I shudder to think what would happen if someone was reaching for the Bryant Papers when somebody else decided to check out the World War II correspondence."

Myles, who had until this point been mindlessly tracing the lifeline on his palm with a ballpoint pen, raised both hands in front of his face and brought them sharply together. "Splat!"

Belinda glared at him from across the table. "Not funny, Myles." Myles shrugged and returned to his doodling.

"Three." Claudia soldiered on, like a suffragette on a mission. "We've got to get rid of the halon."

"Why?" George inquired. "It's the most effective fire retardant ever invented. And since it's a gas, it doesn't ruin the manuscripts as water would."

"True," Claudia admitted, "But it does deplete the ozone layer."

"Like freon," Jean added.

All around the table, George's staff nodded sagely. Good God almighty! He was captaining a Greenpeace vessel. "But surely . . ." he began, until Claudia raised a caterpillar-like eyebrow.

"No choice, I'm afraid. Halon gas hasn't been manufactured since 1994, and in 2003 it will be banned altogether."

With fat, ringless fingers, she started a three-page Internet printout on a circuit around the table. When it reached George, everybody waited silently while he scanned the document. Indeed, halon was being phased out in favor of an alphabet of substances like FM200 and ETEC Agent A, but it was the price tag that caught his eye. If he handed over his entire salary for a year, it would just about cover the cost of a retrofit.

"Besides, it sucks all the oxygen out of the air," Jean commented. "What if there was a fire and Belinda was working in the vault when the halon went off?"

Myles threw his head back, eyelids fluttering grotesquely over the whites of his eyes and gurgled like a clogged drain.

"Nonsense!" George scoffed. "There are safeguards." Although he didn't have the vaguest idea what they might be. "Let me study the issue and get back to you. Anything else?" His question met a wall of silence. "Good. Back to work, then."

George stood, shook the kinks out of his calves, and concentrated on shoving papers back into his folder. When he glanced up again, everyone had gone except Belinda. "Dr. Hopkins?"

"Yes, Belinda?"

"I was wondering if you'd reconsider your decision about my request for leave without pay."

George stared. "I thought we'd settled that."

"Well, I consulted the city employees' manual, like you suggested just now, and it clearly states that leave without pay may be granted under certain circumstances." A button dangled from her cardigan by a thin thread and she twisted it round and round. "I met a clerk at the court house yesterday who's on three months' leave just to study for her bar exam!"

George tucked his folder under his arm. "If you had read those regulations carefully, Miss D'Arcy, you'd have seen that such leave is granted at supervisor discretion. If I let you go for so long a time, it's as good as announcing to the Board of Governors that I don't really *need* an archivist."

A tear slid down Belinda D'Arcy's cheek and made a dark splotch on her lime green blouse. "My mother has Alzheimer's, Dr. Hopkins."

"So you said." George leaned against the doorframe. "Look, I don't wish to appear uncompromising and hard-hearted, but I have a library to run, Miss D'Arcy. Surely there are, uh, arrangements you can make. Adult day care? Hospice? A nursing home? We certainly pay you enough."

Belinda turned and fled.

George stooped to pick up the button that had fallen from the archivist's sweater. "Wait! You've lost your button!" But the door to the corridor slammed, and Belinda was gone.

George spent the next week glued to the chair in front of his computer, plugging new figures into his Excel spreadsheet, moving them about from column to column like some elaborate chess game. If he put off the new photocopier acquisition until next year, he discovered, the dumb waiter could be fixed, but replacing the compact shelving and the halon system that protected the manuscript vault was simply out of the question, either now or in the foreseeable future.

Late one afternoon, with the cleaning staff busily emptying trash baskets nearby, George determined that the cranks on the compact shelving units did work a bit stiffly, but nothing that a little WD-40 couldn't fix. He worked the lubricant well into the crank mechanisms at the end of each row of shelves, then, beginning with the section where the atlases were kept, he knelt and began spraying WD-40 on the tracks that ran along the floor. He was so intent on his task that it took him a while to notice that the shelves were closing in on him. "Hey!" he shouted over the drone of the vacuum cleaner. "Someone's in here!" But the gap continued to narrow.

George scrambled to his feet and braced his arms, Sampson-like, against the shelves. "Hey!" he shouted again, feeling the flab on his upper arms quiver ineffectually beneath his sleeves. "Hey! Hey!"

It was an oversize *Atlas of the World: 1750, Volume IV* that saved him when he managed to wedge it into the narrowing gap between the shelves. Underarms ringed with sweat, he stepped over the blessed book and peeked out into the room. "Who's there?"

But he saw no one. Even the cleaning crew had vanished.

Later, relaxing at home with a cold glass of Chablis, his blood pressure and heart rate returned to normal, George almost succeeded in convincing himself that it was one of the cleaning crew who had moved the shelves but was simply too frightened to admit it. Yet a feeling of uneasiness hung about him like a cloud, and for the next couple of days, he rarely left his office.

Until Belinda D'Arcy called. "Please come down to the

manuscript vault, Dr. Hopkins. I have something to show you."

George laid aside his *Publishers Weekly* and sighed. It had been a fine, sunny day. He had eaten lunch at a picnic table in the park. Later, his mother had telephoned to say that she was *not* coming for Christmas this year. Yes, a near perfect day. The last thing in the world George wanted to do was spoil it by talking to Belinda D'Arcy. "Can't it wait until tomorrow?"

"No."

"What is it, then?"

"I'll have to show you."

George checked his watch. "Okay. If it's that important, I'll try to stop by on my way home."

In the next few minutes while George packed up his briefcase, locked his office door, and caught the elevator to the archives on Sublevel A, he wondered what was bothering the archivist this time. A dead rat, probably. Or a bit of condensation on the pipes. He found Belinda waiting for him in the spacious vault, standing behind one of two long, narrow study tables, her plain face unflatteringly sallow under the bright fluorescent lights. "What did you decide about the halon?" she asked.

"We'll need new cylinders, pipework, and nozzles," George explained. "I'm putting them into the five-year plan."

"But it's dangerous *now*," Belinda complained, moving between George and the door.

"Look," George snapped. "I've studied the installation carefully. I've read the manual. Even if halon should suddenly fill this room, it would last only ten seconds." He pointed to a gridded opening near the floor. "After that, those big exhaust fans kick in and suck it all out. Nobody's in danger."

"Really." It was a statement, not a question. "I've left a

report on the table," she said. "I suggest you read it."

Before he could reply, Belinda slipped out the door and slammed it shut behind her.

At first, George wasn't alarmed. It wasn't the first time Belinda had stormed out of a meeting; for someone in her sixties, she was surprisingly immature. The room was scrupulously neat so it didn't take him long to find the folder where she had left it for him, on the table farthest from the door. He skimmed over the report—something with an official-looking logo from a firm called Foggo, Inc.—but it didn't seem to contain anything he didn't already know. He put the report down and went to the door, but the damned woman had slammed it so hard that it was jammed. "Belinda?" Feeling foolish, he pounded against the door with his fist. "Belinda!"

Her voice was soft, and surprisingly close, just on the other side of the door. "I suggest you read the small print, Dr. Hopkins."

The woman had lost her marbles! George was caught up in some sort of macabre game, and if he wanted to get home tonight in time to feed the cat, the only thing he could do was play along. He grabbed the report and flipped through it again, noticing for the first time where someone—probably Belinda—had highlighted a footnote with yellow marker. *Caution. Do not place boxes, papers, or other objects on shelves or tables near the nozzles as they will be blown off by the extremely high velocities created by the gas shooting from the tanks. To minimize this potential hazard, install pegboard sheets at the ends of shelving units near the nozzles in order to allow penetration, but deflect the blast. Ceiling panels must be secured . . .*

George felt his face grow hot; blood pounded in his ears. He glanced quickly around the room. No pegboard sheets. Boxes all over the shelves. And how the hell was he supposed to know how the ceiling panels were secured.

"And by the way, *George,*" he heard Belinda say. "I think I smell smoke!"

George's stomach lurched. "Belinda! Open the door!"

"Fire, fire, fire!" she singsonged.

George knew the klaxon would be loud, but he was totally unprepared for the ear-splitting sound of the halon being discharged. It exploded from vents all around him, knocking the boxes off their shelves, sending their contents—manuscripts and letters and antique photographs—swirling about the room in a furious hurricane. Floor tiles erupted from their framework grid, narrowly missing his head as they shot toward the ceiling. All around him, the air shimmered as halon mixed with the oxygen in it.

Ten seconds? It seemed to George like ten years.

A tile flew up, striking a shelf, which tilted. A bronze bust of Commodore Oliver Hazard Perry teetered on the edge, then toppled, falling on an aquatint of the barge *Seneca Chief*, dated 1825, shattering the glass. A glistening shard spun through the air, sliced through his collar, and severed his jugular.

By the time the exhaust fans kicked in, George was already dead.

No Man's Land

Elizabeth Foxwell

In the gray queue of ambulances I slumped against the painted red cross on my own, smoking the latest in a series of gaspers. In the distance, the guns boomed their incessant thunder, yellow bursts flashing ominously along the darkening horizon. This French countryside should have been quaintly bucolic with green grass and woolly sheep instead of ripped asunder, the long rows of trenches and barbed wire plowed remorselessly into the earth. Around the cigarette, my chapped fingers shook.

"Ta ra, Knox." It was my rangy Australian bunkmate, calling from the depot door. "Long run?"

I coughed, watching the cigarette smoke snake upward like a ghost in the mist. "Heaps of casualties plus two cases of spotted fever—and that blasted marker for Hospital Number Eight's turnoff has gone missing again."

"Dinky die. Almost slid into a ditch with my lot. Sodding mud. If I was a rum driver like—"

Involuntarily our eyes traveled to the sagging ambulance at the end of the queue—all ugly twisted metal and smashed windscreen. Aussie's habitual scowl softened.

"Don't tear yourself up, Knox. She's gone and good luck to her." She jerked a grubby thumb at a handsome staff car and the two tall, uniformed Tommies polishing its bonnet. "And now the Pommie brass are nosin' around with their fool questions. Bugger it. Little Turnip's a better sight off." She scraped her boots on the step. "We saved you some cocoa and stale biscuits. A sweet offer and no mistake. Come out of this damp."

"In a moment."

"Some happy new year, eh. Nineteen bloody sixteen." She glared toward the thumping distance. "Bloody guns." With a snort, she dove inside, the warped door as usual failing to completely close.

I should heed her advice, choke down lukewarm cocoa and hard biscuits, talk to the other girls, snatch at sleep on the narrow camp bed in the guise of a normal human being. It was difficult to be normal after the daily scrubbing out of my bus with its blood and vomit from soldiers mangled by shrapnel; hard to blot out the sobs of pain, the stench of gangrene and decay. The fortunate ones died before the hospital door, escaping the ordeal of amputation or the hemorrhaging of lungs from gas or the prospect of an alien and uncomprehending home front.

Others died instantly, shot through the head by a sniper . . .

I inhaled the blessed, steadying smoke deeply. Such was the work expected of middle- and upper-class women, bred for perfect marriages, idyllic motherhood, and the laundering of the battlefield.

Through the cracked door, the murmur of voices rose and fell.

"Was her ambulance in good order?" An older male voice, gruff and official.

"Certainly. Part of our duties, maintenance. Most likely

she skidded in the snow. The ice can be fearful," said Finn, one of the other drivers.

"Could have been a tire," suggested another girl, Blake. "We puncture all the time. Did anyone look at the tires?"

"Of course, you twit," snapped Finn. "The left front is as flat as a board. But she smashed into the tree—she could have punctured before, during, after—it's anyone's guess."

"Perhaps," answered the gruff voice. "Or someone tampered with her brakes."

"Rubbish," returned our firm commandant. "Forgive me, General Ravenswood, but you wouldn't say such things if you were stationed here. This place is like Paddington Station. Who would have the opportunity?"

One of us, I thought. That's what was in the general's mind. One of us could mess about with Turnip's ambulance without challenge and spout something about assisting an exhausted friend. My resentment rose. In the grayest dawn and the blackest night, we drivers depended upon each other—was that trust to be destroyed by misdirected military inquiry?

"Another driver, Commandant," replied Finn, expressing my thoughts.

Aussie said a rude word.

"I have to agree with the sentiment of our Colonial cousin, if not her language," said the commandant. "My girls work hard, General, and don't merit idle accusations."

"No one is accusing anyone."

"Too right," said Aussie with scorn. "No sense to it. Can't see us fighting over Turnip's sparklers, or swish kit, or battalion of beaus—if they existed. The poor blighters are bleeding too much to paw us about."

"Not all of the men in France are wounded."

"We drive during the day," said Blake, "and are called out at night for the convoys. When we're not driving, we're usually asleep. Alone," she added with a gulp and probably a blush.

"The rules are quite clear about fraternization," noted the commandant, and I wondered if Blake was now the shade of a ripe tomato.

The general tried another tack. "May I ask where you all were when the incident occurred?"

"Oh, I see." Finn again, patrician and cool. "Gather the suspects into one room and someone will break down and confess?"

"I have to ask the question, Miss Finlay."

"If you must," said Finn. "Very well—we were on duty. At the time Turnip had gone west, I was driving a boy with pneumonia, two *poilus* with reeking cases of trenchfoot, and a Scottish sergeant with a terrific chest wound to Number Eleven. I'm sure they can vouch for me—if they were conscious, that is."

"I was transporting a doctor and a nurse," said Aussie. "From hospital to casualty clearing station and every aid station in between. Of course I could have gone walkabout between appointments, but the Doc would hardly wear it."

Blake was reported at No. 24—although longer than she should have been—and the other girls were either at the railway station or enroute to one of the other hospitals.

"And I was at the railway station as well. I hope those answers are sufficient, General?" said the commandant, satisfaction plain.

"For the moment, ma'am."

Another man—smooth, officious, somehow familiar—spoke up. "Was Miss Turnball troubled? Overwrought?"

"She wasn't unbalanced, if that's what you mean." Finn again, sounding more and more exasperated. "A little shallow, perhaps, a little silly, but not a lunatic."

"She did get all up in the air over that *Times* clipping," offered Blake.

"And came down again," Finn countered.

"Too right. You don't kill yourself over a society do," said Aussie. "So one of her mates got spliced to some posh fellow and is swanning about among the quality. A dead bore, if you ask me. Not worth a sausage."

"You never liked her," shot back Blake as if stung. "Said you'd wring her blood—blooming—neck."

"Because she nearly ran me and my lot off the road. Bloody stupid thing to do." I could practically see Aussie's shrug. "But it don't mean I was plotting to do her a bit of no good. Savin' that for the Huns and their ruddy guns."

"I think I feel sorry for the enemy," remarked the general.

"Ta, mate," said the gratified Aussie.

"Turnip could be thoughtless but she was as sane as any of us," asserted Finn. "Unless you believe, Captain, we all are on the verge of running off the rails?"

"It's a dangerous and difficult job—" started the captain.

"Perhaps we should be stowed away in a little ivory box in a high cupboard somewhere."

"Here, here," chimed in the irrepressible Aussie. "You tell 'im, Finn."

"We're not angels of mercy or delicate bits of porcelain. We have a job, Captain, the same as you. And we do it." Finn took a deep, aggravated breath. "Look, Turnip did not crash her bus due to a fit of the dismals. If she had cracked, she would have chosen something more dramatic."

"Such as—?"

"Wandering into the path of a convenient shell. Lord knows there are enough of them."

Finn was right. Athough dying behind the wheel would possess a certain glamour to the parents back home, it would be insufficient for Turnip. Turnball, I reminded myself. Her real name. In our world, nearly every new arrival was re-christened with a shorter—and not necessarily flattering—

form. We tended to forget the human being behind the amputated form . . .

I closed my eyes. She had only been nineteen and had lied about her age to the Red Cross to join up. "So handsome. So charming," she sighed about the officer she was secretly seeing under the nose of our hawklike commandant. Fresh from glittering balls and tennis parties and sophisticated nightclubs, she believed life could once again be gay. Only two years her senior, I knew otherwise.

"She was tired, poor cow," remarked Aussie. "Like all of us. And everyone knew she was a crook driver. She missed the turnoff and hit the tree. Dead easy. It's absurd that so many lives hang on a bit of ribbon."

"Ribbon?"

"Marks the turnoff. It's gone missing. Probably stuck in the mud like everything else."

"You said she nearly ran you off the road. How bad a driver was she?" asked the general.

"Don't you know? Christ." Aussie was contemptuous. "You should leave the chateau every so often."

The commandant rapped out a reproof—the man was a general, after all, and Aussie's behavior was unlikely to reap praise for either herself or the commandant.

"Let her continue," commanded General Ravenswood.

There was a distinctive snort—Aussie, uncowed. "Turnip cracked her bus up a fortnight ago and sent five of our boys to the graveyard before their time."

"Accident?"

So she had said. "It was an accident, Knox."

I held out a cup of Bovril, and she shook her head, lips compressing, almost turning green. "My tummy's giving me the gyp."

A common occurrence among us, given our strange hours

and even stranger meals. I ignored it, occupied with the more vital issue. "I don't understand. There was a full moon. The road was clear. I checked that ambulance myself, just as you asked. What happened?"

"It's not my fault." Her tone was petulant. "The road is pocked with shell holes."

"If you wore your glasses—"

"I don't need them, silly. They're just for reading." She shrugged, leaning closer to her mirror. "Anyway, it's perfectly all right. I told the commandant a shell hit near me and knocked my bus off the road." She giggled, fluffing out her curls. "She swallowed it, the stupid sow."

I felt sick, as if I had the gypy tummy.

"They were bashed up pretty badly. They would have bought it in hospital, I'm sure."

My lips felt numb. "What about that man who did survive? He had two legs before the accident."

"Well, naturally I'm very sorry for him and all that, but I can't concentrate with all that beastly screaming and moaning. Honestly, how am I supposed to drive in the pitch black with all that racket?"

"Shock is hardly their fault, Turnip."

"They ought to have more self-control. They're trained soldiers, aren't they?"

"Training means little if you've just seen your mate blown to bits." A thought struck me. "How fast were you traveling?"

Her eyes skittered from mine and she did not reply, absorbed in her reflection.

"Turnip. How fast?"

"I don't recall."

I turned on my heel, marched by the chattering mess room, and headed for the wrecked Vulcan that had been dragged back to camp. On a hunch, I felt under the driver's seat and produced a bottle. A slightly cracked, very empty bottle.

"Just to ward off the damp," said she, flushed, at my elbow.

"You were drunk."

"For heaven's sake, it's only red wine. The Frogs practically are weaned on the stuff."

"They don't drink and smash up their wounded." I jerked back, slamming the door.

"Are you going to the commandant?"

"I won't, if you move to day duty."

"Can't be done," she said airily. "Franklin's been shipped home and Hills is in hospital with a septic thumb. We're shorthanded."

"Then you come out with me on your time off. We'll drive the routes together."

"I'd like to see myself," she sniffed. "I have better things to do in my precious few hours off."

"Then I'll accompany you when *I'm* off."

"Oh, really. I'm not taking on a minder, for heaven's sake. Too, too humiliating."

"Turnip. . . . don't you realize what you've done?"

"How you do rattle on, Knox." She cocked her dusky head. "I believe you're jealous."

"Don't be absurd."

"It isn't. I see it all. I have a chap and you don't."

"A *married* chap."

"You would say that. You want to spoil my romance because you don't have one. Well, I won't let you. He loves me and I love him." Her voice dropped to a purr. "And we don't just have tea and sandwiches, don't you know."

"Go on and sleep with the entire Royal Flying Corps if you care to," I retorted. "What I care about are soldiers with mothers, sisters, and sweethearts who won't be going home to them."

She pouted. "You used to be such fun; now it's Granny Sobersides day in, day out."

"This isn't a game, Turnip. I will tell the commandant."

"Go ahead. Tattle your head off. See what good it does you." She plunged a hand into her kit bag, withdrawing a brightly colored scarf. "Do you think this suits me? I thought so in Camiers but now I'm not so certain. It might do for Mother; she's been agitating for a souvenir to show her club."

"Don't change the subject."

"Then spare me the sermon, Padre Knox, do." She clasped my arm, wheedling. "You're ever so much nicer than that. You're like a sister."

I exhaled. "What do you want?"

"I need your help again . . ."

"ACCIDENT?" Aussie was saying. "Sure, you could call it that if an accident can be caused by her own vanity. She was shortsighted and wouldn't wear her glasses. Just a matter of time before she killed herself, I reckon. At least she took no poor sod with her this time."

"Sir—" The commandant cleared her throat, sounding less assured than when I had confronted her. "Nothing to be done, Miss Knox," she had said. "We are short staffed and new drivers won't be arriving from England anytime soon."

"You could borrow some drivers from Calais. Move her to a desk job—hospital—canteen—anything but behind the wheel."

"Calais is handling heavier casualties than we are. And her aunt is a prominent patroness of the Red Cross. Funds could be cut; questions would be asked—"

"God forbid," I snarled.

"You don't understand the situation. At home there is a

vocal segment who question the wisdom and capability of female ambulance drivers. What do you suppose would happen if word got out about the wounded dying at the hands of Miss Turnball?"

I was very still. "Are you saying the Red Cross would shut us down?"

"Precisely."

"But you said yourself that we're overworked and there are no replacements. What are the wounded going to do—hail a cab?"

The commandant turned over her palms eloquently.

"We've done good work—Aussie was even decorated."

"No one said life was fair, Miss Knox."

Brilliant choice, I reflected. Expose Turnip, and we all were on the block. Keep mum, and the wounded were at risk. "No. I suppose not."

"Influence is the ranking officer here, I'm afraid."

"Yes, you're quite right, Commandant. Influence is the key."

"I'm as aware of Miss Turnball's connections as you are," said the general, all steel, echoing my thoughts. "But I should have been informed. Two accidents are significant. It would tend to confirm what Miss Finlay has denied—someone who was looking for a way to die."

"Look here, mate," interjected the unabashed Aussie, "If you really want to know about Turnip, you should talk to the driver outside. Turnip confided in her. Best in the unit. And before you ask the question, General, she was at Number Eight when Turnip bashed herself into potato and mash."

The voices murmured on. An officer emerged, straightening his service cap—a captain with a clipped mustache, clean chin, and shiny Sam Browne belt—the immaculate signs of a man well removed from the front line. I stiffened, dropping the smoldering stub of cigarette behind my back.

Smoking on duty was not the done thing, especially by a woman. He paused, staring at me.

"Why, Miss Knox. This is an unexpected pleasure." The plummy male voice—no wonder it had sounded familiar. My mind raced as he strolled over.

"Captain Blight—Brightman." I bit back the near slip of "Blighty" and ground the forbidden cigarette under my boot heel.

"I remember that Eton Garden Party. Can it be—five years ago? There were roses on your hat." He smirked. "I pinched one of them for my buttonhole, do you know. And you wore a particularly fetching yellow silk frock."

With my hair now hacked off to discourage nesting fleas and the stained khaki uniform hanging from my ill-nourished frame, I was a faint shadow of that fashionable and complacent figure. Still, his eyes wandered over the curves of my bosom and my tightly belted waist as they had not dared to linger at the garden party, with my vigilant brother in attendance.

"And here you are doing your bit. Splendid. Much more useful than Somerville."

I swallowed sarcasm. More useful than he. At Oxford, I'd been favored for a First in English, whereas Anthony Brightman would barely escape with a Second in History. The dim Blighty, however, was entitled to a degree, while I, a voteless woman, was not. My brother, responsible for Brightman's new and more fitting name, had scoffed at the irony, declaring, "All the boys will be left behind by your brains, Kath."

Far behind.

His voice dropped. "I was sorry about your brother."

"Thank you," I said woodenly.

"Did you know we were at Cambridge together? Yes, I suppose you must; Geoffrey said you were close."

Close. An inadequate word that did not encompass impromptu and hilarious jaunts on his motorcycle; the patient, good-natured instruction behind the wheel of Daddy's balky motorcar; the ready ear and equally sympathetic shoulder to cry on during schoolgirl crises. And I would never know if I had returned that boundless generosity even in part, or if he knew how much I had loved him.

The smooth voice went on, oozing like treacle. "A good soldier, Geoff, very gallant. I could scarcely believe when we were posted to the same unit and I became his CO. He was fortunate to see more action than I. Served his country bravely."

I remained silent, my opinion about military intelligence best kept to myself.

"Perhaps we can have tea together soon. There is a very jolly hotel in Hardelot-Plage."

"Yes, I know." No doubt planning for after tea, the cheeky bugger. "It's not possible. We're rather busy here, Captain."

"Such formality. There's no need. The wife's in London, you know," he said confidently, as if I had never spoken. "A Lady-in-Waiting at the Palace. Safely away. Unless you're thinking of your dragon the commandant. Strict segregation between the sexes and all that tosh." He stepped closer to me, his fingers wandering down my sleeve. "You're a woman of the world. Surely you know the old rules don't apply here, Miss Knox?"

The hand intruded on more than just my sleeve, and I met his gaze squarely. "Indeed I do, Captain Brightman. I think you knew Miss Turnball?"

His eyes shifted. "We were—acquainted. Nice little creature. No one seems to know the cause of the accident. No witnesses. Pity."

So that was why he had accompanied the general—to put on a properly sorrowful countenance and ensure his name was not linked to the dead girl. "You must be so distressed," I cooed. "She spoke of you so often." My eyes bored into his, and his shifted again.

"Er, quite. I—I believe she missed home a great deal."

"She did." We all did. But home was a fairy tale now, a place of magical hot baths and faraway comforts and impenetrable ignorance, where war was noble and tidy. Not betrayal, not horror, not hopeless yearning for an only brother rotting in the ground with his comrades.

I swayed. Captain Brightman grasped my arm, and my hand brushed against his breast pocket.

"Are you all right?

"Yes, thank you." I straightened and stepped back. "I missed dinner. A momentary weakness."

"You should eat. Shall we go and—"

"I cannot, Captain. Waiting for the call out." To the trains and their inevitable cargo.

"Yes. Yes of course. Well." He took my hand and kissed it. His lips were damp. "It's been a pleasure, Miss Knox. Katharine." He lingered over my name. "I look forward to seeing you again."

Not likely, I reflected. How quickly was Turnip replaced. I pulled my arm free. "Goodbye, Captain."

With a puzzled glance at me, he walked off, no doubt accustomed to women fawning over an officer's uniform. For them, I had only to look as far as the letters from old school friends who were busily awarding white feathers of cowardice to young men in civilian dress. Those fortunate ones, safely out of it. As Geoff might have been. I scrubbed my fingers against my sleeve.

Aussie's "Pommie brass" emerged from the depot, pulling on his gloves. My patience in the cold twilight rewarded, I tugged my uniform tunic into more regulation shape. "Excuse me, sir?"

His grizzled face drawn, he snapped, "Who are you?"

"Katharine Knox. One of the ambulance drivers, sir."

"Oh. Right." Then he stopped and examined me more intently. "Half a mo—not Sir Peter Knox's daughter?"

I nodded.

"Well, I'm blowed." He grasped my hand warmly. "How do you do. He and I served together. Boer War."

"Yes, I know."

"Splendid on horseback. He had great panache then."

"Yes, sir. My brother Geoff and I thrilled to his stories." Too much—the skirmish in France had seemed an easy passport to the adventure of the Transvaal. So Geoff had declared and I, as usual, had to follow where he led.

"And Peter was a remarkably fine shot."

"He still is."

"Oh, does he still hunt?"

"On occasion. He's an engineer, sir."

"Building things instead of demolishing them. Fitting."

"He speaks of you with great affection."

"Does he?" The general brightened. "Good man. Knew his duty. You're like him—straightforward, blue eyes, fair hair. Dashed good-looking, if I may. Yes. Doing your bit now, I daresay, just as Peter did."

"Yes, sir. I came out with Geoff, but he died at Ypres. Sniper."

His craggy face sagged—he who must have seen an endless roll of death, in both wars. "Sad business. Damn waste."

I warmed to his laconic but honest sorrow. "Thank you. General, about the girl—"

He shook his head. "Strange. Received a message to come here—from your commandant, I assumed, but she tells me I was unexpected."

"I thought some of your questions sounded odd."

"Heard that, did you? Would have looked into the Turnball matter anyway. Niece of an old school chum who is now a Member of Parliament—wants answers." He rubbed his chin. "That rather brash Australian has very definite ideas about the case—and my own shortcomings, I must say."

"Aussie's a good sort, sir, and brave as a lion. She—"

But he waved off my defense. "I saw the Military Medal pinned to her tunic. Unlike some of my counterparts, I don't punish candor or transfer a good man for a frivolous cause. Your Miss Blake, however, may be an entirely different kettle of fish. If that girl doesn't have something to hide, I don't know who does. I can't remember when I've seen such a shade of crimson."

"It's not for a nefarious reason, sir. Blake's worried that the commandant will find out about her young man at Etaples."

He gave me a shrewd look. "I thought you girls had no time for anything but driving."

"Some do manage. Miss Turnball, for one."

"Excellent. I've been hoping to run into someone like you, Miss Knox. A lass I can trust who knows the people." He lowered his voice confidentially. "Absent the company of your very decided commandant and equally decided friends."

"They are that, sir."

"Well, two ambulance accidents so closely together do raise uncomfortable questions. Only natural to feel beseiged and close ranks. You knew her well, I gather?"

"I did, sir." I hesitated delicately, like the properly bred young woman I was, and he prompted me.

"Distressin' for you, naturally. But if you know anything that can shed light on this incident, m'dear, you must tell me. Ease the family's grief."

"Yes, sir." I coughed, murmuring an apology for a throat taxed by cold, damp, and other unpleasantness while I weighed my words carefully. "Well, Turnip—Miss Turnball, sir—did talk to me. She was keeping company with Captain Brightman. I tried to warn her about regulations, but she was young and fancied herself in love."

"I see. And did he return her feelings?"

"She said so, General. But she did discover from the *Times* that he was married to an acquaintance of hers."

"Ah. So that was the way of it."

"Yes, sir. My brother was at school with Captain Brightman and served under him, so he couldn't pretend to me that he was unmarried."

"Risky. You could have told her."

"I did, sir. But it had no effect. She thought I was carping on her idol out of jealousy."

"Awkward business. His wife has deep pockets and pull at the Palace."

"So I gather, sir. And I have reason to believe Miss Turnball was in the family way." I had remembered the gypy tummy.

"Not a new tale. Poor child." He gave a gusty sigh. "Difficult to prove any of this, though."

"No, not especially. I expect if you search him and his belongings, you will find her letters. She was an indiscreet child, and Captain Brightman is, shall we say, sir, fond of trophies."

"Indeed. And if Miss Turnball was in the habit of writing letters to her uncle—" He fell silent and let the implication hang in the air between us.

"Yes, sir. Awkward indeed, for Captain Brightman."

The guns stopped, the abrupt silence equally deafening, and our heads turned as one.

"Ah. You will have to fill that ambulance soon, I regret to say."

"Yes, sir. I look forward to the day when I am out of work."

"As do I. Then perhaps your father and I can go bag some pheasants instead of more deadly game." He sighed. "My best to him."

"I'll tell him, sir, in my next letter." Softer than the harsher business of Geoff . . .

He saluted me, then marched to his aides milling by his car and barked a curt order. The commandant's whistle blew, the shrill summons to our convoy, and the girls rushed out of the depot to their ambulances. I cranked the engine, my coughing matching the engine's sputtering to life, the weather, tobacco, and the unaccustomed necessity of imitating the commandant on the telephone finally taking their toll on my throat.

I climbed creakily behind the wheel. In the swarm of people and vehicles, I saw Captain Brightman pushed into the staff car by the two very stern Tommies. The self-confident voice unleashed a string of protests as they rumbled away.

From my pocket I took out a fluttering of white ribbon, neatly snipped, and stared at it. The marker for the No. 8 turnoff. Because of the convenient "fainting spell," the other half now rested in Brightman's breast pocket, to be discovered by the ever-thorough military police.

Blighty was right. The rules were changed here—especially for Turnip, who saw no sin in betraying the men who had suffered so much and gave us their trust; and for Blighty, who had sent Geoff out on the perilous line while he, safely removed from the guns and the carnage, plotted his next sordid rendezvous. He deserved not to fall in battle, as more honorable men were doing, but hung by the neck until dead.

As the general had said, I knew my duty to my brother and my unit—and my Classics back at faraway Oxford. The Furies, pursuers of the murderer Orestes, were the daughters of Nox, or Night. Fitting my name, I had become a part of the black void all about me.

How simple it was to take a young girl's dreams of romance with an officer and twist them to one's own advantage. Listening to her confidences. Suggesting the route for a secret rendezvous at the jolly hotel in Hardelot-Plage. Making a few adjustments to her brakes.

Turnip was a casualty of war.

As were we all.

Repocketing the ribbon, I shoved the ambulance into gear and drove off into the dark.

The Lady from Yesterday

A Rory Calhoun Story

Jeremiah Healy

I WAS lying on a chaise lounge by the pool at the Lauderdale Tennis Club, eyes closed, every limb in deep relaxation. It was one of those bell-clear mornings in early February that make believers out of the snowbirds who experience them. For somebody like me, who'd been on the pro-tennis circuit until a chronic knee persuaded my thirty-something head to find it a more permanent home, the weather of South Florida was just the ticket, and the competitive level of the other members at the Club kept me sharp enough on the courts to still feel like a player.

"Rory," said Don Floyd's voice from standing height over my lounge, "this lady would like to speak with you."

Of course, I also had to earn a living.

Opening my eyes, I swung my legs over the edge of the chaise before standing myself. I'm nearly six-three, but I didn't tower over the woman next to Floyd. He wore an impish grin that, even at eighty-plus, would warn wives that they wouldn't want their husbands hanging out with him in bars. One look at his companion, and I could understand why Floyd was grinning.

She was a stunner, in heeled sandals that helped the elevation, though I'd still have bet on five-seven or -eight barefoot. The big hair in crow-wing black probably benefited from a bottle, with heavy pancake and warpaint on the facial features. Her breasts pushed the envelope of whatever pink material the long-sleeved, bare-shouldered top was spun from, and her waist seemed cinched by the belt holding up lime green Capri pants that rippled when the woman changed stance from hipshot-left to hipshot-right.

From behind sunglasses with reflector lenses the size of plums, she said, "Calhoun, you're gonna advertise yourself as a private eye, the least you could do is leave word with the gate guard."

The Club has a strict security policy: nobody gets past the sentry box unless a resident in one of the eight condo buildings leaves the visitor's name. "I didn't get a call telling me someone would be coming."

"Well," said Don Floyd, the grin widening, "I think I'll just leave you both to your business."

As he moved off, the woman looked around the pool area. I figured every male—and some females—would be focused on her, but she didn't appear to notice.

The woman said, "How's about we move out of the sun, okay?"

"Sure." I gestured to the part of the patio under the porch's orange-tiled roof.

She preceded me, her rolling gait in the heels reminding me of the expression "poetry in motion." But again, I didn't have the feeling my potential client was conscious of it. In fact, to the extent you can read somebody behind opaque shades, I'd have said she was distracted.

We were seated in the white resin chairs around the

small, matching table before the woman said, "Monica Lewin."

I was thinking that the name would have been a cross for her, what with the Clinton scandal. But as she extended her right hand to shake, I noticed each vein on the back stood away from the bones as the flesh sank between them, and I immediately upped her age from late twenties to high thirties.

"Rory Calhoun," I replied as we clasped briefly.

"And that's your real name?" Lewin withdrew her hand to hold the strap of a shoulder bag.

"My mother had a thing for the movie star, to the point of even marrying a guy with the same last name. When I came along, I'm afraid the first—"

"I don't need your life story."

That stopped me.

Lewin shook her head, took off the shades. Her eyes were darker than her pants but not by much. "Look, I'm sorry, I . . ." Now she sighed, and I got a whiff of bourbon strong enough that I'd have said I was holding a glass of the stuff under my nose, even though the clock on the wall over her hair read only ten thirty.

I said, "Want to tell me about it?"

Lewin's eyes now seemed more jaded than jade. "What, my problem, or the fact that I gargle with Wild Turkey?"

I started to like her. "I'm guessing they might be related."

A nod this time. "That they are." Now she resettled her butt on the resin chair, the pants squeaking a little. "Okay, the reason I asked about your name is I go professionally by 'Monica LaMonica.' "

"Professionally."

"I'm an exotic dancer. A 'gentlemen's club' called 'Cottontail's.' "

Driving north of downtown Lauderdale, I'd been by the place, though never in it. "Go on."

"You remember the headlines, last month?"

"Afraid I'm not much for newspapers."

A slightly disgusted look. "Another girl from Cottontail's was strangled on a cold night with her own scarf in the lot outside the club?"

The penny dropped. "I remember some TV news on it."

"All right." Lewin squared her shoulders now, as though about to deliver bad tidings. "Her name—stage name—was 'TNT,' which actually stood for her real initials, 'Tara Nancy Tate.' Only the animals at Cottontail's had a different nickname for her."

"Which was?"

" 'Two New Tits.' "

Cosmetic surgery wasn't exactly unusual in South Florida. "I'm not sure I see where we're going with—"

"Where we're going . . ." Lewin, realizing her voice was rising, glanced around at several people in tennis togs stopping to stare at her, then repeated more softly, "Where we're going with this is, the cops think I was the one who killed her."

"I didn't know."

"Yeah, well, that either makes you the best choice for me, or the worst." The jaded eyes again. "You're thinking I'm a flake, right?"

Maybe Lewin's clairvoyance came from a career looking out at men watching her. "Pretty close."

A grunt that wasn't quite a laugh, but seemed to change her mood. "An honest man. I don't run into many."

"Why do the police think you murdered Ms. Tate?"

"My, my. Polite, too, aren't we, doll?" Then she squared her shoulders again. "Christ, I'm slipping into role here. Okay, here's the story. Tara was a natural, but a little small up-north so she had a boob job." Lewin closed her eyes a moment. "You know what's involved?"

"Roughly."

"Yeah, well, 'roughly' is the right word. Couple of years ago a friend of mine wanted one, made me promise to 'be there for her.' " Lewin looked away, toward the pool where two girls maybe eight and ten were playing catch with a beach ball, laughing and squealing. "They painted her—naked—with this red stuff, maybe disinfectant or something. Then they . . . cut her, and pushed these implants—like yellow lily pads—through the slits. Only it was more shoving ten pounds into a five-pound bag, and I . . . I had to leave. Or throw up."

I didn't say anything.

After a moment, Lewin clucked her tongue. "But that's what Tara was willing to go through, to be a featured performer."

"Meaning a star?"

"Star?" Another almost-laugh. "Yeah, that's what she was, all right. Went around the country—well, the Southeast, anyway. Clubs all the way to Virginia, she said. But her husband was tied to here with a sick mother, so Tara did all the traveling on her own. Then she got tired of that, but not tired of the dancing. So she went up to Rocky, and said she wanted to—"

" 'Rocky'?"

"Manager of Cottontail's, and tough as they come. Well, once Rocky got a look at Tara's audition, that was it for me."

"I don't follow you."

The eyes went past jaded to just plain tired. "Tara replaced me as the lead act at Cottontail's."

"The reason the police suspect you?"

"That, and Tara—well, we had a little catfight that night before she got killed." Lewin used one hand to push the opposite sleeve of her top halfway up her forearm. "She gave me these scratches, and I guess when the cops checked under Tara's fingernails, they found enough of my skin for that DNA thing."

"You have an alibi for the time she was killed?"

"No, but near as I can figure, that's true for Tara's husband—or widower, now, I guess—and the Professor, too."

"The Professor."

Lewin mentioned the college. "He'd come to watch Tara, and I mean ogle her. The other animals, they'd hoot, or even heckle. But Jason—what he called himself, and talk about miracles, turns out that was his *real* name. Anyway, Jason would just sit there . . . I don't know, 'in awe,' maybe?" Now Lewin closed her eyes. "He'd even look at me that way, sometimes."

It was painful just to hear her say it. "I'm still not sure I see where I come in."

She opened the eyes, blazing now. "Look, Cottontail's isn't any palace like Solid Gold or Pure Platinum. It's a run-of-the-mill strip joint. But it's where I make my living. Or used to."

"This Rocky fired you?"

"Didn't have to. Publicity like we got from the killing? You think even the wives and girlfriends who don't wanna know what their guys are doing some nights would let them come to a place tied to a murder? So we've lost most of our regulars, and I'm dancing double shifts for nickels and dimes from tourists who won't pay the freight at one of the better places."

"Why not move on to another club, then?"

The fire in Lewin's eyes nearly went out. "My age? I'm gonna start auditioning again?" A wave that took in more than the pool area. "All the managers want is flawless. Tits, legs, ass. Without the surgery—'augmentation,' liposuction—that's just not realistic." Now she sighed again, the bourbon scent seeming sour now. "Besides, they'd see me as this Jonah from a club where another dancer got murdered. So I need to prove somebody else killed Tara."

"Which is why we're talking now?"

"Yeah. I want off the hook and back to normal."

I shifted in my chair, felt my arms wanting to cross. The universal body language for "no."

Lewin said, "You're not gonna help me, are you?"

"It's an open homicide. The police don't take kindly to—"

"I can pay."

"Wouldn't change their mind-set."

Lewin rolled her shoulders this time, her breasts roaming inside the pink top. "But if I laid you, that'd change *your* mind-set?"

I could feel a definite stirring below the drawstrings of my trunks. "Not that it isn't tempting, but I try not to mix business with pleasure."

"Or lechure?" The grunted, almost-laugh a third time. "To be honest, me neither. One rule I've always had. But try telling the animals that." Lewin shook her head—more her hair actually—and put the shades back on like they needed to be clamped in place. "At least you're honest about it. Not like the jerk managers who audition you and then say with a smarmy smile that you're not quite right for 'our image,' when what they're really trolling for is the kind of 'incentive' that 'sexual harassment' was supposed to stop. But that's another story." She stood abruptly. "Thanks for your time, anyway."

I rose, and we shook hands to say goodbye. "I'm sorry, Ms. Lewin."

"Yeah, well, I got to look on the bright side, you know?"

"Which is?"

"You're the first fucking guy in five years who's called me 'Ms. Lewin.' "

* * *

I HAD a tough match that afternoon at 5:00 P.M. against the number-three nineteen-year-old in Canada, who was staying at the Club. His game consisted of a big first serve—or "service," as Don Floyd and some of the other older members still call it—and booming topspin forehands. Nevertheless, I had the kid down 6-5 in the first set, when my own serve bailed. He went on to beat me in the tie-break, then cake-walked over everything I tried in the second set. Disgusted with myself after we finished, I spent half an hour in the hot tub, resolving to turn in early and *carpe diem* the next morning with an hour of serving practice on one of the back courts, maybe with Floyd watching to see if he could spot something mechanically wrong in what I was doing.

In fact, fourteen hours later I was at the outdoor tiki bar overlooking the pooi, about to order some wake-up coffee. Floyd, sitting on a stool with a newspaper in front of him, spotted me and beckoned.

Sliding onto the stool next to him, I followed his finger again, pointing now to a headline in the *Sun-Sentinel,* Lauderdale's major daily. It read, SECOND DANCER'S DEATH SOLVES FIRST, with a head-and-shoulders promo portrait of a smiling, younger Monica Lewin next to one of an even younger redhead captioned, *Tara Nancy Tate.*

Don Floyd said, "Wasn't this Lewin the lady from yesterday?"

Closing my eyes, I nodded.

DETECTIVE Kyle Cascadden looked across his desk at me and said with a deep-South accent, "Heard about you from Lourdes."

Lourdes Pintana was the sergeant in charge of the Fort Lauderdale Homicide Unit. Cascadden and I were sitting in the unit's large squadroom, the high ceilings not doing much to freshen the moldy air. He wore a short-sleeve dress shirt with a same-shade tie like a gangster from a thirties movie but for the badge on the right side of his belt near a big, holstered revolver. Cascadden's sandy hair, thinning and short on top, spilled in ragged curls over his collar in back.

Reclining in the swivel chair till it creaked, he said, "So Aun-*dray*, what does a tennis-bum private eye want from me?"

I assumed Cascadden meant "Andre Agassi," but I was in no position to take offense at the "bum" part. "Monica Lewin tried to retain me yesterday."

" 'Tried to,' huh? Good thing, otherwise her hanging herself last night would of meant you got fired."

Cascadden laughed, a grating, guttural sound, and I seriously thought about walking out right then. But that wouldn't have eased my conscience any. "Suicide for sure?"

"Plain *and* simple. Tied one end of her bathrobe sash to the kitchen doorknob—living room side—and tossed it over the top. Then got up on a stepladder—kitchen side, now—and tied the other end of the sash around her neck. One leg kick"—Cascadden sending his foot into the air behind his desk—"and old Monica 'exotic-danced' down the big runway in the sky."

Another laugh.

I said, "No evidence of anybody else being involved?"

"Just the manager from her strip club, finding the body." Cascadden darkened. "Why would you think there might be?"

"Seems kind of odd, the woman comes to see me for help midmorning, then kills herself by midnight."

He cocked his head. "How'd you know what time she got found?"

"Newspaper."

Cascadden hunched forward a little, and actually seemed concerned for a moment. "Look, Aun-dray, the city don't need this kind of publicity. Bad enough that first one, Tara, gets strangled. Twenty years ago, the college boys and girls on spring break wouldn't of given a flying fuck, but now that Lauderdale's all yuppie respectable, Chamber of Commerce just as soon see this case closed. Which Homicide says it is."

"Any other indications of suicide?"

A third laugh. "You could say that. Woman had enough tracks on her arms to start a railroad."

With Lewin's long-sleeved top, I hadn't seen any needle marks.

"Not to mention an empty bottle of Wild Turkey on the kitchen counter, reaching distance from where she lynched herself."

Which I couldn't argue against, either. "How about a note?"

"No." Cascadden leaned back again, the chair creaking the only sound in the room. "But then, not many leave one. Plus, you got to figure Monica's all fucked up in the boyfriend department, account of I never run across a stripper yet who wasn't."

"Lewin had a boyfriend?"

Kyle Cascadden clenched his jaw. "Time for you to go, Aun-*dray.* I got other cases to work."

"Especially since this one's 'closed,' right?"

"Out!"

COTTONTAIL'S fronted on a side street within sight of Route 1 North. Given the time of day, I wasn't surprised there were only a few cars in the parking lot to the side of the building, where Tara Tate had been strangled.

Leaving my Chrysler Sebring convertible—purchased

with my last tournament check—in as much shade as I could find, I walked up to the entrance, a white, fuzzy tail as big as a basketball over it. The tail appeared to be on a pendulum mount, so I imagined at night it would "twitch" over anybody going into the club.

The door opened to my tug on one of the handles, shaped like bunny ears. Inside, the canned music was loud, but the lighting low, and it took a minute for my eyes to adjust.

Except, that is, for seeing the very young woman on a slightly raised platform, half out of her minimal clothing and showing babyfat at most junctions, caught briefly in the light from the door's being open like a deer in high beams.

Out of the darkness, a female voice—raspy from cigarettes, booze, or both—yelled, "Shut the fucking door." Then, in a more coaxing tone, "Go ahead, Hon. Finish your routine."

Maybe I'd spoiled the mood, but I got the impression it was more the young woman's overall nervousness that made her seem shy, even scared, as she did a stiff bump/grind/strip that was all corners instead of curves. When the "song"—some techno, bass-dominated dirge—finally ended, the raspy voice said, "Okay, Hon. You start Friday. Be here by six, and stop at that store I told you about, pick up three outfits a size too small for you."

The young woman nodded, then crossed her hands over her breasts before she realized at least a couple of fingers were needed to pick up her clothes.

I now could make out the silhouette of a petite woman sitting at the bar, a plume of smoke also backlit to the point of inspiring romance. As I drew near her, I was aware of the younger one from the stage shuffling off into the shadows, clothes now clutched over her rump.

"Who the fuck are you?" from the barstool.

"My name's Rory Calhoun."

The kind of laugh that told me the petite woman was

old enough to recognize the actor. Up close, though, she surprised me. Her hair was conservatively permed, and her dress looked more Laura Ashley than Victoria's Secret.

"So, guy, what do you want?"

"I'd like to see the manager."

"You are."

Maybe she meant, "You do?" I said, "Rocky."

Extending the hand without the cigarette, the woman said, "That's me, Roxanne Devereaux, only I don't do boy-shows. And even if I did, you got the face, maybe, but that one arm is way-too-much bigger than the other for—"

"It's from tennis. Your serving side gets disproportionate."

"Tennis?" Devereaux stubbed out the cigarette. "The fuck *are* you doing here?"

After showing her my investigator's license, I told her.

"Oh, Jesus. Better come on back to the office."

We went past a couple of padlocked doors before reaching one that stood ajar. If there was anybody else in the place, I didn't see or hear them.

The office proved another surprise: sectional furniture with upholstery like oatmeal, oriental rug, cherry desk.

Devereaux said, "You expected a fucking dump, right?"

Another woman in the trade who could read my mind.

She waggled nicotine-stained fingers around the stale air. "Well, this is where I spend a lot of hours, so why shouldn't it be comfortable?" Devereaux motioned to one of the sectional pieces. "Sit, we'll talk."

After we both were settled, I said, "Why would Monica Lewin come to see me about Tara Tate's murder, then kill herself?"

"You're the detective, guy."

I tried a different approach. "I understand you found Ms. Lewin's body."

"Yeah." Subdued now. "Monica was supposed to dance a

shift last night. When she didn't show, I went apeshit, drove over to her place. "Jesus, I need a drink more than a smoke."

Devereaux opened the lower drawer of her desk, came out with a single-malt scotch and one tumbler. "Join me?"

"No, thanks."

She poured a generous couple of ounces into the glass, then downed it, shot-style. "Okay," in a raspier voice, "let's have your questions."

"Ms. Lewin told—"

"Look, let's drop the formality, huh? She was 'Monica,' I'm 'Rocky,' and that poor heifer you saw out front is gonna be whatever I can think of to call her, try to drum up a little business."

Since the young woman was already hired, I said, "She seemed kind of self-conscious."

"She seemed kind of awful, but losing Tara and even Monica inside thirty days is a little tough on the stable, you know?"

So much for "subdued," too, though Lewin had told me Rocky was "as tough as they come." I said, "You don't seem too emotionally involved."

"Emotionally . . . ?" I expected a raspy laugh, but Devereaux kept surprising me, coughing and swiping a hand across her eyes before reaching for a pack of cigarettes and what turned out to be a lighter in the form of—what else?—a rabbit bending over to touch its toes. "Look, that poor thing out there? She's two, maybe three months gone, and needs for the baby whatever money the animals out front will stuff wherever on her they can reach."

Devereaux used the same catchphrase Lewin had for Cottontail's customers. "I meant more about Monica."

"I know what you meant, guy. Monica, now, she had it, once." Devereaux took a deep drag, sent it out in another artsy plume. "When she first got started, Monica was just a kid—younger than the heifer, even. Had to lie about her age to get a job." Now the raspy laugh. "And Monica was stupid enough to last long enough to come full circle."

"Meaning, lying about her age?"

"You saw the girl. How old?"

"Thirty-seven, thirty-eight."

"Try forty-three. But Monica wouldn't go under the knife, so her ass was puckering from the cellulite, and without the suspension bridge she wore up top, those tits would sag low enough you wouldn't want her carrying your cafeteria tray."

Lovely image. "Rocky—"

"And the track marks on her arms? Jesus, why couldn't Monica shoot the shit between her toes like any normal person?"

I didn't have an answer for that one.

Devereaux took another long puff. "No, once you're over the hill, it shows. And not just in the goods. When Monica danced the last few years, it was only shake-and-jiggle, like she was floating on drugs, though she swore she wasn't, at least for the shows. But there was no choreography anymore, not even any . . . eroticism with the exoticism, if you get my drift."

I thought back to the jaded green eyes. "But I understand this Tara was different?"

"Tara? Oh, guy, you never saw *her*, now, did you?"

"No.

"Tara—'TNT' for short, which fit her like a glove. Original Sin with a cheerleader's face, and just the right amount of . . . surgical enhancement. Not those volleyballs some of the girls go for."

"So who'd kill her?"

Devereaux flicked some ashes. "I didn't know Monica so well, I'd have said she'd be the one."

"Because Tara had replaced her as the star act?"

"Yeah, but Monica was on the slide, and she knew it,

between the heckling getting worse and the tips getting smaller. So I never saw Monica as the killer, even if that idiot cop did."

No need to ask Devereaux who she meant. "Other candidates?"

"Tara's husband. He wasn't real happy about her dancing, period, and the time she spent on the road made it rough on both of them."

I had the husband's name from the *Sun-Sentinel* article, and remembered Lewin mentioning his mother. "On Barry Cardiff and . . . ?"

"And Tara. Who the hell we talking about here, guy?" Devereaux stubbed out the second cigarette. "She'd call me once in a while, from East Bugfuck, Alabama, or wherever, crying about how life traveling alone from club to club really sucked."

"Tara called you?"

"I gave the girl her first boost, back when I was house mom at one of the nicer joints in Lauderdale. Showed her how to do makeup, some of the moves—though, truth to tell, Tara was a natural in the dance department. And not just on a stage: She could fly across the room like a ballerina, or twist herself into a pretzel, give even guys with lousy eyesight the best beave in the Southeast."

"But when Tara came home, her husband Barry must have been happy?"

"Or relieved," said Devereaux. "Or even more suspicious, if he figured Tara earned her money other than from Polaroids."

"Polaroids?"

"The camera, guy. On the road, a lot of the girls will let any customer with ten bucks have his picture taken with her hanging out and hanging all over him. Something to show the boys back on the chicken ranch, you know?"

"So, by 'other than Polaroids,' you mean—"

"The dirty deed. But I've never tolerated any of that in Cottontail."

I nodded like I believed her.

Devereaux said, "I'll give Tara this, though. She had a brain, and she had a plan."

"A plan?"

"To retire. Or move on. Lots of the girls—Monica's a prime example—stay too long at the fair. But Tara, now, she had it worked out. So many shifts a week here, so many weeks a year, less operating expenses like costumes and capital improvements—"

"Capital . . . ?"

"The boob job, guy. Then, after so many years, out of *the* life and back to her real one."

"And Tara was well on her way with this plan?"

"So she said."

Felt like a dead end. "Monica mentioned somebody named Jason. A professor?"

A closed look now. "I don't like for anybody to be bothering my customers."

I named his college for her. "Would you rather have that stupid cop do it?"

A sigh as Devereaux snagged a third cigarette. "So talk to the Professor. I can't stop you."

"You have a last name for him?"

Another sigh, or maybe just the expulsion of smoke. "Nolan. But I don't know what he teaches."

"Monica have a boyfriend?"

"Not that I ever saw, though a lot of the girls play that hand close to the vest, least around the club."

"Anybody here close to Tara or Monica? Besides you, of course."

Devereaux stopped her cigarette on the way to her lips. "Lacey, maybe?"

"L—A—C . . ."

"E—Y. 'Missy Lacey,' though 'Lacey's' her real first name, just like Monica's was. Lacey Peevers, so you can see why we didn't go with the last one."

"This Lacey works here, too, then?"

"Couple nights a week. She's got a kid, but no man, so she does lap dancing, table dancing. Not in Tara's league, though, lookswise. Not even Monica's, till the last few years."

"Can I speak to Lacey?"

"Long as it's not on my time, okay?"

"Then I'll need a home address."

Sticking the cigarette in the corner of her mouth, Devereaux went to her Rolodex. "Only be careful of your dick, now. Lacey's kind of a barracuda."

"And here I was hoping for a blowfish."

Roxanne Devereaux first hacked, then sputtered a little on her smoke. "I'll say this for you, guy. . . . You're an optimist."

GIVEN the driving distance to the college, I called ahead. After being shunted around, a receptionist in the English Department finally told me that Professor (or "Doctor") Nolan was "working at home today." She wouldn't tell me where "home" was, but 411 got me Nolan's number, and the reverse telephone directory I keep in my car trunk came up with his address.

After going some miles west, I started to think college teaching must be paying better than when I attended, because Jason Nolan's place turned out to be hidden behind what seemed like nearly an acre of trees and shrubs. I pulled into the marl-graveled driveway and wound around two privacy curves before reaching a modest, gray-planked house that looked a hundred years old.

I left the Sebring as a man came around a corner from

the backyard. The first thing to strike me was that he had too much hair. Not just long, but like a mane rather than a 'do. The top also showed a darker brown than the surrounding fringe, and I was torn between a bad rug and a thick transplant. He was maybe five-ten and slim, with prominent cheekbones and a receding chin. Dressed in a denim shirt open at the neck, sleeves rolled up, and khaki hiking shorts over old running shoes, the man seemed wary.

"Can I help you?" in a modulated voice that implied he was sure he couldn't.

"Jason Nolan?"

"Yes?"

I introduced myself, flashing the ID. He insisted on reading the fine print. For an English professor, Nolan seemed to take a long time doing it.

"What's this about?"

"Tara Tate and Monica Lewin."

"Who?"

"Professor—or 'Doctor,' if it's more comfortable—I just spent an hour with Rocky at Cottontail's, so let's save both of us some time, all right?"

Nolan pursed his lips, then nodded once, resignedly. "Speaking of comfortable, perhaps in the back?"

"Lead the way."

If the front yard was a jungle, the back one rivaled Flamingo Botanical Gardens for flowers. I said as much.

"Thank you. It's my one vice." Then a sheepish grin, which I had the feeling he didn't use very often. "Very well, my only *other* vice."

Figuring this couldn't be easy for Nolan, I followed him to an arrangement of wrought-iron patio furniture. The cushions appeared bright and new, but like the house, the metal gave off an older look.

As we sat, I said, "Don't see chairs and tables like this much anymore."

"No. They came with the house. I bought it twenty years ago, when this was still 'the Land Beyond Lauderhill.' "

I knew just enough local geography to get the "middle-of-nowhere" aspect. "I don't suppose that kept the police from finding you?"

"Actually, they didn't."

Could even Kyle Cascadden miss somebody at Cottontail's as obvious as Nolan must have been? "How come?"

"I went to them, you see. Given my position at the college, thought it best to steal a march, so to speak."

"Beat them to the punch."

"Exactly. This was after Tara was killed—strangled. I thought the woman she was 'bumping'—forgive the pun—might have been her killer."

"Monica Lewin."

"Ah, no. Actually, a woman named . . ." Nolan blushed. "Missy Lacey."

I needed to get my signals straight. "Wait a minute. I thought Tara came back to Lauderdale—"

"And began dancing at the club, yes. But Monica was already . . . well, past her prime, so to speak. Therefore, I thought that Lacey was the more likely suspect, and I told this Neanderthal police detective as much."

"And Lacey was more likely because . . . ?"

"Well, Tara simply put her to shame. Tell me—Rory, if I may?"

"Fine, Jason."

That made him stop, but only for a moment. "Rory, are you a devotee?"

"Of strip joints?"

"Of exotic dancing?"

"Neither."

"Well, let me try to explain Tara's dancing, then. Man to man." Nolan clasped his hands in front of him, bizarrely like a minister about to preach a sermon. "One of the finest

British novelists once wrote, 'it was like meat and wine and the air one breathed and whatever else was essential to existence.' "

"W. Somerset Maugham."

Nolan perked up. "Name the book."

"*Of Human Bondage.*"

"Very good, Rory. But how . . . ?"

"I played pro tennis in a lot of countries where the used bookstores carried only the classics in English."

"I wish I'd had a student in the last ten years who'd know that Maugham quote without my teaching it." Then Nolan blinked. "But back to cases, eh? Tara was grace incarnate. Joyful as well. She really *wanted* the audience before her to have a good time, also to appreciate a certain . . . artistry about her work."

"Tara was top of the line."

"Tara was her *own* line. Young, unspoiled—oh, I know I'm laying it on a bit thick, but truly, she had no parallel in any other club I've ever visited."

"You've been in enough places like Cottontail's, your students never spotted you?"

A wise smile. "The beauty of South Florida, Rory. After the first few weeks of a semester, the only students in the exotic clubs are the ones visiting Lauderdale from afar."

I assumed he meant the residual spring-breakers. "Okay, Tara's the best. Lacey?"

"Ah, youth may not be everything, but sometimes it's enough. And she has the energy of a pony. 'Rookie fire,' I believe the baseball pundits call it."

"But not the . . . artistry."

A sad smile. "Please, Rory. Don't mock me for trying to help you, eh?"

Nolan had a point. "How about Monica?"

"Monica, Monica. I felt badly for her. I'd often stand a drink for her on nights when Tara wasn't performing."

"You mean Monica would come to your table."

"Yes. And we'd talk, but only a bit. I'm afraid Monica's natural endowment had fallen from between her ears to between her elbows. However, she was . . . 'poignant,' I'd put it. Like the last glass from yesterday's bottle of wine."

"You wouldn't be suggesting that she'd . . . breathed too long?"

"Why, Rory, what a nice turn of phrase," said Jason Nolan. "We may make a novelist of you yet."

"HEY, hey. If *you're* selling, I might actually buy something."

Jason Nolan proved right: Lacey Peevers had a certain energy about her. She was about five-six and a little to the stocky side of solid, with blonde hair, brown roots, and a flat tone that sounded Midwestern. Her "flatness," though, ended at the voicebox as her breasts jounced under the T-shirt and over the baggy shorts she wore answering the bell to her apartment.

"Ms. Peevers, I'd like to talk with you about Tara Tate and Monica Lewin."

The sunny expression faded, but only a little. "Oh, bummer. But, yeah, why not."

I followed her into a small living room strewn with toys. A toddler with sandy hair and his mother's features was sitting in the middle of them, chewing on a plastic duck.

"Hey, C.C., we got ourselves a visitor."

I looked down at the kid, who was smiling and giggling. "See See?"

"The initials. When I got pregnant, I wasn't absolutely sure whether the sperm who made the big swim was from this guy 'Chuck' or this other guy 'Craig.' Since I wanted to, like, keep my options open, I used both of their initials."

As I sifted through that, Peevers plopped herself into a worn but large couch. I took the chair opposite it.

"So," she said, "what can I do you for?"

"Let's start with who you think killed Tara Tate."

I wanted to hit Peevers with it, just like that, gauge any reaction. Instead of shock, though, there was only a frown and some nibbling on her lower lip. "Tara's husband. I'd say."

"Why?"

"Well, Barry'd always carry on about why she couldn't be around more, now that Tara wasn't on the road anymore."

"Around?"

"To help with his mom. She's kind of like this invalid. Not exactly a coma, though she slips in and out quite a bit, leastwise the times C.C. and I went over to baby-sit."

"To baby-sit Barry's mother."

"Uh-huh. That's why he got pissed at Tara. Barry couldn't see why his own wife couldn't help out."

I thought about it. "Why do you suppose Tara wasn't around?"

A naughty smile. "I think she was doing a little more than letting some customers bromsky her tits."

"Bromsky . . . ?"

"Her tits." Peevers lifted her forearm to her mouth and blew out a breath to make a farting sound last five seconds. Her son giggled some more. "Yeah, C.C., you know that noise, right? Dumpy dumpy."

The kid shrieked in joy now, his mom slaying him.

"So, Lacey, you think Tara was turning tricks?"

"Yeah. Oh, not hooking exactly. More like providing service to a small circle of friends. But she really was gorgeous and all, so she could, like, have her pick."

I decided to test Peevers. "Some of the people I've talked to think you might have killed Tara."

A hurt look, then the sunny expression again. "Well, I can see their point, I guess. You put Tara and me on stage together, I'd sure look like Miss Fifth Runner-up. But I learned from Tara, and I would've learned from Monica, too, she didn't go and hang herself."

"You think that's what happened?"

"Monica committing suicide?" A confused expression. "That's what the papers and all said."

Time to test Peevers a different way. "Would you be interested in making a little money beyond . . . a bromsky?"

Now a hard look, one I wouldn't have predicted Peevers had inside her. "Thanks anyway, but C.C. needs me more than I need that."

"Lacey, I appreciate your time."

A sadder look as Peevers rocked from the couch down onto her knees and pushed a different toy into her son's face. "Rory, you hadn't gone and brought money into it, you could have had a lot more than my time."

BARRY Cardiff's address also was an old house, but that's where the comparison to Jason Nolan's place ended. No jungle of shrubs out front, just some scrub pine and weeds. The clapboard exterior needed paint, and the left rear tire of the old Chevy in a tacked-on carport needed air.

I made my way up the overgrown path from the street, being careful not to cause any more damage to the crumbling front stoop. A knock on the front door brought a male's "Hold on a second" from somewhere inside.

When he appeared behind the wire mesh, I thought Barry Cardiff looked more like a bear than a man. He wasn't wearing a shirt above some tattered blue jeans, and his chest, arms, and shoulders were matted with hair. Maybe thirty, his face had the battered look of somebody who'd been to war and couldn't quite lose the memories of it.

Given his mother and his wife, maybe he'd been more victim than victor, too.

Cardiff said, "I don't know you."

I decided to vary the opening a little. "My name's Rory Calhoun. I'm a private investigator looking into the death of Monica Lewin."

"Monica? You mean the bitch that killed my wife."

That seemed to establish our ground rules. "Can I come in?"

A resigned shake of his head. "I suppose."

To the right of the door was a shabby living room that gave the impression of being less abused and more just unused. Cardiff didn't turn into it, continuing instead through the kitchen. A smell of something medicinal hit me as he entered a back bedroom.

Lying on some soiled sheets was a woman who could have been anywhere from sixty to seventy-five. She seemed shrunken, with noticeable black whiskers around the mouth, and hair half as thick as Cardiff's on her arms. Both eyes were closed, and her breathing was ragged, occasionally overpowering the hum of a small, oscillating fan standing on a night table inside the open window. Some videocassettes lay jumbled on the table's lower shelf, but I didn't see a VCR or even a television.

"My mama," said Cardiff.

"I'm sorry."

"*You're* sorry? She's been like this for near two-and-a-half years now. I took her to three doctors, and they sent her to three hospitals, and nobody can figure nothing about what to do for her except 'keep her comfortable as possible.' Only, Mama don't get better, and she don't die, neither."

I'd been in the room less than a minute, and already it felt oppressive. I wondered what I'd be capable of doing from desperation—or even just frustration—in Cardiff's shoes.

"Why do you think Monica Lewin strangled your wife?"

He looked ready to spit. "Jealousy. Tara was a beautiful girl, just beautiful. And Monica was drying up like Mama here, only Monica could see it every time she went by a mirror."

"Jealous enough to kill, though?"

Cardiff's eyes came up to me. More rolled up to me, really, as his head barely moved. "Tara and me got married before Mama here took sick. I was out of work, so Tara decided she'd make us some extra by dancing in a club. I didn't like it, and told her so, but somebody had to look after Mama, and that meant somebody else had to put food on our table. So Tara started her 'career.' "

Cardiff said the last term like it was a cussword.

I said, "And began traveling?"

Another spit look. "All the way to hell and back. Gone a month or more at a time, near killed the car with the miles she put on it. And put on her, too." Cardiff rolled his eyes up again. "Tara was fine the way she was, didn't need no . . . surgery. But she had it anyways, make her a 'better' dancer. Mister, I'll tell you it was like they disfigured her. The scars, the stretch marks, the way her skin . . . shined. Doctors couldn't help my mama, but they could hurt my Tara."

I fought the air in the room, the medicinal smell beginning to choke me, and I thought I could see why Cardiff's wife would want to travel as much as possible. "But then Tara came home, right?"

"Couldn't take the road no more. Too lonely, she said. Nobody to talk to who wasn't coming on to her. Nobody to joke with or hold her at night. Hell, that was my job, but she wouldn't let me do it." Cardiff looked to the bed. "I couldn't leave Mama, and Tara wouldn't stay here."

He was wandering, so I repeated my question.

Cardiff shook his head. "Yeah, Tara come home, all right, if you mean here to Lauderdale. But she'd still be out more'n half the nights. The best shifts are at night, she said. The biggest tippers. But I needed her here sometimes, too. For me and for Mama."

I decided to risk a fight. "There's some evidence your wife was prostituting herself."

Cardiff didn't jump up, he didn't even look up. He just reached a hairy hand over to the lower shelf of the night table and slid a videotape from the stack. "Found these yesterday when I was cleaning out Tara's closet. Don't matter, maybe, now she's dead. But it's the reason I can't even mourn her proper."

I took the cassette from him, the name "Frank" in curlicue handwriting on the label. "Mr. Cardiff, thank you. And I'm sorry."

This time he reached for his mother's forearm, squeezing it. And then Barry Cardiff began to cry.

THAT night, I ran "Tara Does Frank" through my own VCR. I didn't recognize the man. And while I'm no expert on production values, it seemed the camera stayed stationary, capturing the two of them but without "Frank"—if that was his real name—seeming aware he was starring in a low-budget epic. Of course, given how genuinely beautiful and sexually enthusiastic Tate appeared to be, Frank might just have been blinded by ecstasy.

I thought about going to Cottontail's, see if I could spot Frank in the crowd. Or even asking Roxanne Devereaux or Lacey Peevers to watch enough of the tape to identify him for me. Except that, for all I knew, Tara had filmed it on one of her road trips.

So I decided to sleep on it.

HOWEVER, the next morning I felt hollow inside, partly the result of talking with Barry Cardiff but mostly from watching the tape. Or more accurately, from realizing Tara Tate's probable purpose in making it and maybe others like it.

To clear my head, I picked up Don Floyd at his unit, and we walked to one of the back courts, a bucket of balls slung handles up over my shoulder the way Monica Lewin had carried her handbag the one and only time I'd met her.

Floyd said, "Rough night, Rory?"

"And a rough day before it, too."

He just nodded.

When we got to Court 19, Floyd took a seat under the awning on a little knoll so he could watch me practice. Over the years, I'd found that when my serve went down the toilet, the best cure was to break it down to its component parts, with another pro watching for telltale errors.

I started by folding a facecloth in fours, then setting it down inside the baseline about sixteen inches forward and between my lead left foot and my trailing right one. Then, holding the racquet in my right hand and a ball in my left, I practiced bouncing the ball and rocking my body until the rhythm felt right.

Only problem was, I couldn't get the case out of my mind.

Monica Lewin comes to see me. She's upset, but more angry than depressed over being a murder suspect. That night, though, she dies at the end of her bathrobe sash, Detective Kyle Cascadden is convinced—for political as well as police reasons—that it's suicide.

Floyd said, "Might want to try some tosses, now."

I tried to clear my mind, then rock in rhythm while tossing the ball from my left hand straight up, but not swinging at it, just seeing if it landed on the facecloth. One, two, three . . . all on the folded square.

Then, when I visit Roxanne "Rocky" Devereaux at her club, Cottontail's, I get a little better feel for the three people Lewin thought could have killed Tara Nancy Tate. The only problem is, each of them has a different idea on who murdered Tate. Professor Jason Nolan thinks it was dancer Lacey Peevers. Peevers thinks it was husband Barry Cardiff. Cardiff thinks it was my almost-client Monica. Which brings me back to where I started.

Floyd said, "Okay, now try to hit a first service, flat and down the middle."

I shook off the case facts, tried to put one eight inches inside the T of the box on the other side of the net. First two tries were long. Next two, into the net itself.

At least a couple of the people I speak with think Tara Tate might be moonlighting by turning tricks, though. Which makes sense, if the "retirement plan" she'd discussed with Rocky Devereaux was to come true. And if Tara wanted to speed up that plan, she might have used videos like the one of "Frank" as blackmail. The problem there would be who else fit into Tate's "small circle of friends," and how she'd been able to finesse past her husband the providing of—

Floyd said, "Rory, when I can't *ever* get the first one in, I generally try to focus on the second service."

I stopped with my racquet halfway through its arc, the ball just hitting the court. Or the facecloth, since there was no bounce. Then I stared up the knoll and under the awning.

"Rory, are you all right?"

It made sense, it was consistent. Only I had no proof.

Floyd stood. "Did you maybe pull something in your shoulder?"

Which didn't mean I couldn't run a bluff.

"Rory?"

"Sorry, Don, but I have to practice something other than my serve."

"And what would that be?"

"Somebody else's handwriting."

Don Floyd just scratched his head.

* * *

IT was a well-kept campus, if a little too new compared to the place I'd attended up north. The registrar's office told me where the class I wanted was being conducted and when it would end, so I just sat with my brown paper bag on a bench under a gnarly banyan tree that looked as though it was the only living thing to survive the bulldozer twenty years before.

Within half an hour, Professor Jason Nolan came out the front door of the classroom building, a couple of groupies coattailing him. Shifting a looseleaf notebook and text of some kind to his other arm, he noticed me, then turned to the students before all three nodded in a "see you next time" way.

Nolan walked toward my bench as warily as he had from behind his house the day before, the mane of hair standing up a little from his movement. "Rory, taking me up on that 'novelist' comment?"

"I know, Jason."

He faltered a little, then drew close but stayed standing over me. "Know what?"

"About you and Tara Nancy Tate."

"Of course you do. I told you all about—"

"Tate was an exotic dancer, but she was also a . . . service provider?"

Nolan frowned. "What Tara did on her own time could hardly—"

"I'm guessing that you and she started in around the time she started up, first at a club where Rocky Devereaux was the 'house mom.' Only Tara decided to go on the road, maybe to make more money, maybe just to get away from the conditions at her own home."

"I'm sure her mother-in-law's illness must have been a—"

"Only thing is, you'd gotten used to having her regularly, and then had to adjust to a more occasional, irregular schedule. But she was worth it, wasn't she?"

"I don't think I care to be insulted on my own—"

"However, when Tara got sick of the loneliness of being on the road, she came back. And you expected the schedule to revert to what it had been before. Only Tara had come close to achieving her 'retirement plan,' and she even figured out a way to . . . accelerate things."

When Nolan didn't reply to that, I brought the video cassette out of the bag. It was the one with "Frank" depicted in it, but I'd copied Tate's handwriting onto the new "Jason" label pasted over it.

I said, "Tara kept a copy."

Nolan saw the label and squeezed his eyes shut.

I waited. "So strangling her didn't solve anything."

His knees actually began to shake, and Nolan unsteadily moved to sit next to me on the bench, the looseleaf going to his lap, the text sliding to the grass. "You have . . . no idea what she was like."

I felt a lump inside my gut begin to dissolve. "Tell me."

Nolan took a sudden, gasping breath, but sounded all right when he began speaking again. "Because her husband was always home, tending to his mother, Tara usually came to my house. Its seclusion allowed us . . . freedom and privacy. I loved her, Rory. Plain and simple."

"Too much to stand losing her."

"She was standing in the parking lot outside Cottontail's that night, as though she'd been watching for me to arrive. When Tara told me about the . . . that tape—from one of our few 'motel trysts'—I couldn't believe it. That she'd blackmail . . . me." Nolan seemed to range inside himself, speaking next without any emotion. "The air that night was cold, even for January, so she wore a scarf, and I, gloves. It all happened so . . . quickly."

"And you got back in your car and left?"

"Yes. I went straight home, and stayed up till dawn, cleaning and vacuuming so there'd be no trace of Tara left. But by going to the police the next day and implicating Lacey, I was spared them searching my house, anyway."

"And you might have gotten away with it, except that"—I thought back to Don Floyd's comment at my practice session—"you realized you needed a second 'service provider.' "

Nolan squeezed his eyes shut again. "Yes. I broached it with Lacey one night over drinks. She was rather cool to the idea."

I remembered her reaction to my testing on the same point. "Which left Monica?"

"Yes. She—"

"Why not one of your students, though. You had—"

"Rory! That would be . . . incest. Academic incest, even without all the sexual harassment rules the college has now. The quickest way to lose all I'd worked for the last twenty years would have been to try something with a student."

Listening to Nolan's finely parsed ethical distinctions, I tried to keep a straight face.

Then he softened again. "And besides, there was something . . . better about having intimately one of the women I and hundreds of others saw publicly." Nolan looked me in the eye. "Rutting with the slut from the strip joint, you know?"

"Even the 'poignant' one."

"Quoted against myself. Or perhaps more in support of my confession, eh?" A sad smile, and he looked down at his textbook on the ground. "But when I went to Monica about it two nights ago, she was drunk, and that didn't make her any more . . . amenable to my proposed arrangement, so to speak. No, just the opposite. Monica swung an empty bottle of booze at my head, just missing, and as I pushed her off,

I came away with the sash to her robe. Then she strutted into the kitchen to call the police, accusing me over the shoulder of murdering Tara. Well, what could I do, Rory? I tied a quick slipknot in one end of the sash, and as Monica was setting down the bottle and lifting the wall phone from its cradle, I flipped the noose over her head and around her neck. But she struggled fiercely, and I didn't have the right leverage, so I tossed the free end of the sash over the top of the door and just pulled on it for all I was worth."

Nolan seemed to run out of steam. "When I knew she was dead . . . her eyes, even her tongue . . . I tied the end of the sash to the outside doorknob, and used a napkin to replace the telephone in its cradle and to move a stepstool to where a suicide might kick it over. I thought the empty bottle would lead the police in that direction, and it did."

When he didn't continue, I said, "Feel better now?"

"Strangely, yes. I remember us discussing Maugham before, but frankly the last two days from Monica—no. No, the last *thirty* from Tara—have been more . . . Dostoyevsky."

"Crime and Punishment?"

"Just so." Nolan took another of those gasping breaths. "Well, what's next?"

"What do you think? The police."

A nod and the sad smile. "I wonder, Rory, could I ask if you're a taxpayer?"

Now I did laugh. "A taxpayer?"

"Yes, because I have a favor to ask. And not an unreasonable one, I think." Nolan paused. "If you'd do me the courtesy of never telling anyone about what you've found out about—"

"Are you off your—"

"I'd like to spare our state's legal system some costs."

I looked at him. It bothered me that Nolan's point made

ninety percent sense. "What about Barry Cardiff and his mother?"

"Not your concern. It was Monica who approached you, correct?"

"And Tara Tate provided for her husband and—"

"Very well, then." Nolan blinked. "I'll change my will in the bargain. That house of mine and anything else I own can go to Cardiff to replace Tara's . . . income."

I weighed the deal. It was better than what'd be left after everybody's lawyers got into the act.

Which let me see a loophole. "What's to keep me from breaking my word after you're . . . afterwards?"

"I'll risk that, Rory." A pause. "I'm really rather short on options, aren't I?"

Leaving Professor Jason Nolan on the bench with his books, I promised myself to get up early the next few days and check the front page of the *Sun-Sentinel.*

About the Authors

BRENDAN DUBOIS is the award-winning author of short stories and novels. His short fiction has appeared in *Playboy, Ellery Queen's Mystery Magazine, Alfred Hitchcock's Mystery Magazine, Mary Higgins Clark Mystery Magazine,* and numerous anthologies. He has twice received the Shamus Award from Private Eye Writers of America for his short stories and has been nominated three times for an Edgar Allan Poe Award by the Mystery Writers of America. He lives in New Hampshire with his wife Mona. Visit his website at www.BrendanDuBois.com.

An old man slips two fingers in the coin-return pockets of a rack of pay phones: quick, practiced. Hurries on. A woman at the diner orders a cup of tea with a side of catsup—*nouvelle* tomato soup, what the hell. Invisible in plain sight, the make-doers live among us. **NOREEN AYRES** finds a story of a handful of such denizens in an affluent beach town, who for a moment guide effectively the hand of justice.

Author of three forensics-based mystery novels, Noreen edits technical documents at an environmental engineering company in Washington state. She holds an M.A. in English from Cal-State University at L.A. and has taught English, creative writing, and a number of subjects she knew by virtue of reading one chapter ahead of the students. Among her interests are ballroom dancing, competition handgun shooting, crafts, woodworking, and care of animals.

SHELLEY COSTA'S stories have appeared in *The Georgia Review, The North American Review, Crimewave,* and *Cleveland Magazine.* She graduated from Douglass College, studied acting and playwriting at HB Studio in Greenwich Village, and worked for two years in the trade division at Henry Holt and Company. Later, at Case Western Reserve University, she wrote a dissertation on suspense in classic American literature and earned a Ph.D. in English. These days she enjoys both Henry and P. D. James and works as an adjunct professor at the Cleveland Institute of Art, where she teaches courses in fiction writing and acting Shakespeare. Her home is Chagrin Falls, Ohio, and she vacations in the Canadian Northwoods, the setting of "Black Heart and Cabin Girl."

TOM SAVAGE is the author of four best-selling suspense novels: *Precipice, Valentine, The Inheritance,* and *Scavenger.* He also writes a detective series under the name "T. J. Phillips." *Valentine* was made into a Warner Bros. film. He is currently a director-at-large on the national board of Mystery Writers of America. Raised in St. Thomas, Virgin Islands, he now lives in New York City, where he works at Murder Ink, the world's oldest mystery bookstore. "One of Us" is his first published short story.

TRACY KNIGHT'S short fiction has appeared in numerous anthologies encompassing a variety of genres, including suspense, mystery, science fiction, and horror. His nonfiction, primarily focusing on psychological topics, has included a chapter in the Writer's Digest book *Writing Horror* and a column for *Mystery Scene* magazine. Recent novel releases have included a Western novel, *Beneath a Whiskey Sky* (Leisure Books), and a fantasy novel, *The Astonished Eye* (PS Publishing). Tracy, his wife Sharon, and three feline entities live in rural west-central Illinois, where he works as a clinical psychologist and university professor.

AILEEN SCHUMACHER is the author of the Tory Travers/David Alverez mystery series. Her second book in the series, *Framework for Death*, was nominated for the Anthony Award for Best Novel. The fourth book, the award-winning *Rosewood's Ashes*, was published in 2001. Her short fiction has appeared in *The Blue and the Gray Undercover* and *Murder, Mayhem, and Mistletoe*. She lives in Gainesville, Florida.

Publishers Weekly said **ELAINE VIETS'S** fourth novel, *Doc in the Box*, would give readers "perverse satisfaction." She has read all four of her mysteries for Americana audiobooks. Elaine takes her crime seriously. She is a graduate of the MedicoLegal Death Investigators Course at Saint Louis University. She is an at-large delegate to the national board of the Mystery Writers of America. Elaine was chair of the 2002 Edgar Best First Novel committee. She is also a national board member of Sisters in Crime. She lives in Hollywood, Florida, with her husband, Don Crinklaw, an author and actor.

A member and board member of Mystery Writers of America, **G. MIKI HAYDEN** has had a steady stream of short mystery fiction in print. Miki's novel, *Pacific Empire*, lauded by *The New York Times*, was well received by readers, as was her psychiatric mystery, *By Reason of Insanity*. Miki, the author of *Writing the Mystery: A Start-to-Finish Guide for Both Novice and Professional*, a

Writer's Digest Book Club selection, is the immediate past president of the Short Mystery Fiction Society, which presents the yearly Derringer Awards. Miki teaches, coaches, and book doctors from her home in Manhattan. Her e-mail address gmh2@rcn.com.

A member of the New York Chapter of Mystery Writers of America, **ELAINE TOGNERI** is also the founder and a past president of the Sisters in Crime—Central Jersey chapter. Her short fiction has appeared widely in the small press, including magazines: *Futures Mysterious Anthology, Mystery Time,* and *Whispering Willows Mystery Magazine.* A New Jersey native, Elaine graduated from Rutgers University and works as an information technology specialist.

HENRY SLESAR (1927–2002) was a mainstay of the fiction magazines of the late 1950s and early 1960s, the last big boom of the digests, which were just the pulps in more convenient size. He did it all and he did it well. In the course of his career he has won the Mystery Writers of America Edgar Allan Poe Award for a novel (1960), for a TV serial (1977), and an Emmy Award for a continuing daytime series (1974). He has written for many TV series such as *Alfred Hitchcock Presents* and *Twilight Zone,* as well as surviving many years as the writer-producer of a long-running soap opera, *The Edge of Night.*

WILLIAM E. (BILL) CHAMBERS served as Executive Vice President of the Mystery Writers of America and as New York Chapter President. His novels, *Death Toll* and *The Redemption Factor,* are available through Mystery Writers of America Presents at iUniverse.com. His short stories have appeared in *Ellery Queen's Mystery Magazine, Alfred Hitchcock's Mystery Magazine, Over My Dead Body, Mike Shayne's Mystery Magazine,* and anthologies in the United States and Britain. "An Ode to Freedom" was published in *Best Poems of the Millennium*, by the International Library of Poetry. Bill has acted in "Casino Beat," a vehicle being shopped to various television networks by Watersign Productions. Bill and his wife Marie once owned a bar restaurant named Chambers Pub in Greenpoint, Brooklyn.

STEFANIE MATTESON is the author of eight mysteries in a series published by Berkley Prime Crime. Her most recent mystery is *Murder Under the Palms*. Her other titles are *Murder Among the Angels, Murder on High, Murder at the Falls, Murder on the Silk Road, Murder on the Cliff, Murder at Tea Time*, and *Murder at the Spa*. All of her mysteries feature Charlotte Graham, a movie actress-turned-sleuth. Before turning to mysteries, Matteson was a newspaper reporter and editor. She lives in Mendham, New Jersey, with her two children.

CHARLOTTE HINGER, author of *Come Spring*, published by Simon and Schuster, won the Western Writers of America Medicine Pipe Bearer's Award and was a finalist for the Spur Award. Hinger has published a number of mystery short stories. "The Family Rose," which first appeared in *Ellery Queen's Mystery Magazine*, was later reprinted in two anthologies, *Murder on the Verandah* and *Murder to Music*. She was the editor of two comprehensive hardcover volumes of family/county histories. She has served on the board of the Kansas State Historical Society and is on the editorial board of *Heritage of the Great Plains*. Charlotte writes nonfiction about contemporary and historical issues in the rural West. She has completed the first book in a mystery series and is working on a historical novel. She lives in Hoxie, Kansas, where she and her husband own a livestock truck line.

DAN CRAWFORD, author of "And Guile Is Where It Goes," is familiar to readers of *Alfred Hitchcock's Mystery Magazine* as well as to those eight or nine people who bought one of his Rossacottan novels. At one time he thought to make his first million as a greeting card writer, but his line of humorous sympathy cards didn't take off. His career as a gag writer was shorter and even less profitable; he is now training for a position as Lottery Winner. He was once questioned by the FBI, but was found irrelevant. In his spare time he manages an annual book sale involving 200 volunteers and 100,000 books, primarily so he can mark up the prices on his own work.

RHYS BOWEN is British by birth but now lives in California. After college she worked in BBC drama in London and wrote several radio and TV plays. She was lured to Australia to work for Australian broadcasting, where she met her husband and moved with him to the San Francisco area. Under her married name she has written around 100 books, ranging from childrens books to sagas, before switching to her favorite reading material, mysteries. She is the author of six books in the Constable Evans series, set in North Wales, including *Evan Help Us,* nominated for a Barry Award for best mystery. *Murphy's Law* is the first book in her new historical mystery series set in New York 1901, featuring brash Irish immigrant Molly Murphy. It won the Agatha, Reader's Choice, and Herodotus Awards. Rhys has also written several short stories, among them "The Seal of the Confessional," which was nominated for both Anthony and Agatha Awards.

MAT COWARD is a British writer of crime, science fiction, horror, children's, and humorous fiction, whose stories have been broadcast on BBC Radio and published in numerous anthologies, magazines, and e-zines in the United Kingdom, United States, and Europe. According to Ian Rankin, "Mat Coward's stories resemble distilled novels." His first nondistilled novel—a whodunit called *Up and Down*—was published in the United States in 2000. His first collection of short crime stories, *Do the World a Favour and Other Stories,* was recently published by Five Star Press.

MARCIA TALLEY'S first Hannah Ives novel, *Sing It to Her Bones,* won the Malice Domestic Grant and was nominated for an Agatha Award as Best First Novel. *Unbreathed Memories,* the second in the series, won the *Romantic Times* Reviewers' Choice Award for Best Contemporary Mystery. Both were Featured Alternates of the Mystery Guild. Hannah's third adventure, *Occasion of Revenge,* is a *Romantic Times* Top Pick. Marcia is also the editor of a collaborative serial novel, *Naked Came the Phoenix,* where she joins twelve best-selling women authors to pen a tongue-in-cheek mystery about murder in a luxury health spa. Her short stories have appeared in magazines and collections including "With Love, Marjorie Ann" and "Too Many Cooks," which received Agatha Award nominations for Best Short Story. She lives in Annapolis, Maryland, with her husband Barry. When she isn't writing, she spends her time traveling or sailing.

ELIZABETH FOXWELL is a contributing editor to *Mystery Scene* magazine and a founding director of Malice Domestic Ltd. She has edited or coedited nine anthologies, including *More Murder They Wrote*; published five short stories; and writes frequently about mystery fiction. Her website can be found at www.elizabethfoxwell.com.

JEREMIAH HEALY was a professor at the New England School of Law when the release of his debut novel about private detective John Francis Cuddy, *Blunt Darts,* announced that there was a wise new kid on the block. Since then he has written more than a dozen novels featuring his melancholy PI. His books and stories since then have done nothing but enhance his reputation as an important and sage writer whose work has taken the private-eye form to an exciting new level. Winner of the Shamus Award in 1986 for *The Staked Goat,* he is one of those writers who packs the poise and depth of a good mainstream novel into an even better genre novel. His recent books include *Turnabout* and the latest Cuddy mystery, *Spiral.*